Thomas Campion

The Works of Dr. Thomas Campion

Thomas Campion

The Works of Dr. Thomas Campion

ISBN/EAN: 9783337424879

Printed in Europe, USA, Canada, Australia, Japan

Cover: Foto ©Andreas Hilbeck / pixelio.de

More available books at **www.hansebooks.com**

THE WORKS

OF

DR. THOMAS CAMPION

EDITED BY

A. H. BULLEN

LONDON
PRIVATELY PRINTED AT THE
CHISWICK PRESS
1889

CONTENTS.

	PAGE
INTRODUCTION	vii
A BOOK OF AIRS	1
TWO BOOKS OF AIRS	41
THE THIRD AND FOURTH BOOKS OF AIRS	85
SONGS OF MOURNING	133
MASQUE AT THE MARRIAGE OF THE LORD HAYES	145
A RELATION OF THE ENTERTAINMENT GIVEN BY THE LORD KNOWLES	173
THE LORDS' MASQUE	191
MASQUE AT THE MARRIAGE OF THE EARL OF SOMERSET	211
OBSERVATIONS IN THE ART OF ENGLISH POESY	225
EPIGRAMMATUM LIBRI II., ETC.	263
SCATTERED VERSES	396

INTRODUCTION.

DR. THOMAS CAMPION, whose works are now first collected, was held in high esteem by his contemporaries; but the materials for his memoir are very scanty. Dr. Jessopp, in the "Dictionary of National Biography," suggests that he was probably the second son of Thomas Campion of Witham, Essex, gent., by Anastace, daughter of John Spettey, of Chelmsford.[1] This suggestion cannot be accepted; for it appears from Chester's "London Marriage Licences" that Thomas Campion of Witham married Anastace Spettey in 1597,—when Dr. Campion was about thirty years of age. Sir Harris Nicolas, in his preface to Davison's "Poetical Rhapsody" (p. cxxi), pointed out that a Thomas Campion was admitted a member of Gray's Inn in 1586;[2] and conjectured that this was the poet, who is shown to have had some connection with the Inn from the fact that in 1594 he wrote a song, "Of Neptune's empire let us sing," &c., for the Gray's Inn Masque. Had Nicolas been acquainted with Campion's Latin epigrams, he might have greatly strengthened his case by adducing the following verses addressed, in 1595, to the members of Gray's Inn :—

[1] See the "Visitation of London" (Harleian Society, 1880, i. 134).
[2] See "Admittances to Gray's Inn," Harl. MS. 1912.

" *Ad Graios.*

Graii, sive magis juvat vetustum
Nomen Purpulii,[1] decus Britannum,
Sic Astraea gregem beare vestrum,
Sic Pallas velit, ut favere nugis
Disjuncti socii velitis ipsi,
Tetrae si neque sint, nec infacetae,
Sed quales merito exhibere plausu
Vosmet, ludere cum lubet, soletis " (p. 366).

The words " disjuncti socii " plainly show that
Campion had at one time belonged to the society
of Gray's Inn. But the legal profession (as we
learn from more than one of his Latin epigrams)
was not to his taste; and he does not appear to
have been called to the Bar. Applying himself to
medicine, he took his degree of M.D., and practised
as a physician. Dr. Jessopp supposes that his
degree was taken abroad; but we have clear
evidence to prove that he studied at Cambridge.
W[illiam] C[lerke] in " Polimanteia," 1595, noticing
various poets of the time, writes : " I know, Cambridge, howsoever now old, thou hast some young,
bid them be chaste, yet suffer them to be witty ; let
them be soundly learned, yet suffer them to be
gentlemanlike qualified." The marginal annota-
tion to this passage is " Sweet Master Campion."

---

[1] The name " Purpulii " has reference to the masque of
1594—" Gesta Graiorum ; or the History of the High and
Mighty Prince Henry, Prince of *Purpoole*," &c. Gray's
Inn was jocularly styled for the occasion " The State of
Purpoole."

But I can find no particulars about Campion's Cambridge career. He is not once mentioned in Messrs. Cooper's "Athenae Cantabrigienses."

The earliest notice of him as a poet is in the prologue to Peele's "Honour of the Garter," 1593. At that date he had published nothing; but some of his poems had been circulated, according to the custom of the time, among his friends. Peele addresses him as

> "thou
> That richly clothest conceit with well-made words."

The reference in "Polimanteia" is obviously to his English poems; and in Harl. MS. 6910, which is dated 1596, three of his songs are found. Probably much of his best work was written before the close of the sixteenth century.

The first of Campion's publications was a volume of Latin epigrams, entered in the Stationers' Register 2nd December, 1594 (Arber's "Transcript,"[1] ii. 666), and printed in the following year. So rare is the edition of 1595 that nobody at the present day appears to have seen it. There is no copy in the British Museum, the Bodleian, or the Cambridge University Library; and I know no private library in which it is found. But the collection, with large additions, was reprinted in

---

[1] "Richard ffeild Entred for his copie vnder the wardens hands in court/ a booke intituled TIIOMA CAMPIANE *Poema* . . . vj^d."

1619. The whole of the First Book of the epigrams in ed. 1619 seems to have been then issued for the first time. Cf. Epigr. 2, Lib. I., " Nuper cur natum libro praepono priori?" In the Second Book are contained the epigrams that belonged to the 1595 collection. The curious poem " Umbra" was written, in its present form, some time after the marriage (1613) of the Princess Elizabeth. We have no means of fixing the date of the elegies; but they seem to have been written in the glow of youth.

From the epigrams we learn something of the literary society in which Campion moved. Two epigrams (pp. 300, 332) are addressed to Charles Fitzgeffrey, the author of a spirited poem, " Sir Francis Drake, His Honorable Life's Commendation," &c., 1596. In 1601 Fitzgeffrey published a volume of Latin epigrams, "Affaniae," and addressed two of them to Campion. As " Affaniae" is a scarce little book, which few readers have seen, I will quote one of the epigrams :—

" *Ad Thomam Campianum.*
O cujus genio Romana elegia debet
   Quantum Nasoni debuit ante suo !
Ille, sed invitus, Latiis deduxit ab oris
   In Scythicos fines barbaricosque Getas.
Te duce caeruleos invisit prima Britannos
   Quamque potest urbem dicere jure suam.
(Magnus enim domitor late, dominator et orbis
   Viribus effractis, Cassivelane, tuis,

Julius Ausonium populum Latiosque penates
   Victor in hac olim jusserat urbe coli.)
Ergo relegatas Nasonis crimine Musas
   In patriam revocas restituisque suis."

Another friend of Campion was William Percy (a
son of Henry Percy, Earl of Northumberland), the
author of a collection of sonnets, "Caelia," 1595.
Percy was a member of Glocester Hall, now
Worcester College, Oxford; and to the same
society belonged Edward Mychelburne (or Michel-
bourne), who, with his brothers Laurence and
Thomas, was among Campion's most intimate
friends.   Wood calls Edward Mychelburne "a
most noted poet of his time;" but, with the
exception of two copies of commendatory verses
prefixed to Peter Bales' "Art of Brachygraphy,"
he published nothing.   Both Fitzgeffrey and
Campion thought very highly of his abilities, and
urged him to print a work which they had read
with admiration in MS.   Another member of the
Oxford circle was Barnabe Barnes, the lyric poet
and sonneteer.   For some unknown reason Campion quarrelled with Barnes, whom he assailed
with epigrams both Latin and English (see pp.
247, 251, 252, 268, 336).   Nashe, in "Have with
you to Saffron Walden," 1596, refers gleefully to
that "universal applauded Latin poem of Master
Campion's" in which Barnes is taunted with
cowardice (p. 336).   In or before 1606 a recon-
ciliation was patched up between Barnes and

Campion; for in that year Campion prefixed two copies of commendatory verses to Barnes' "Four Books of Offices." But the quarrel was subsequently renewed; and in 1619, when the book of Latin epigrams was republished, Campion not only retained the obnoxious epigram of 1595, but added another in ridicule of Barnes. One epigram (p. 339) is directed against Nicholas Breton. It is clever, but somewhat malicious:—

> "*In Bretonem.*
> Carmine defunctum, Breto, caute inducis Amorem ;
>   Nam numeris nunquam viveret ille tuis."

A couple of fine epigrams are addressed to Lord Bacon (pp. 303-4), whose "De Sapientia Veterum" is enthusiastically praised. To Bacon's learning, eloquence, and munificence Campion paid a worthy tribute :—

> "Quantus ades, seu te spinosa volumina juris,
>   Seu schola, seu dulcis Musa (Bacone) vocat!
> Quam super ingenti tua re Prudentia regnat,
>   Et tota aethereo nectare lingua madens !
> Quam bene cum tacita nectis gravitate lepores !
>   Quam semel admissis stat tuus almus amor !
> Haud stupet aggesti mens in fulgore metalli ;
>   Nunquam visa tibi est res peregrina dare."

Other epigrams show that Campion was jealous for the honour of his profession and viewed with contempt the pretensions of quacks.[1] From one

---

[1] Campion was a physician of note. He is mentioned in a copy of satirical verses, "Of London Physicians,"

epigram we learn that he was sparely built, and
that he envied men of a full habit of body (p. 321).

> " Crassis invideo tenuis nimis ipse, videtur
>   Satque mihi felix qui sat obesus erit.
> Nam vacat assidue mens illi, corpore gaudet,
>   Et risu curas tristitiamque fugat.
> Praecipuum venit haec etiam inter commoda, Luci,
>   Quod moriens minimo saepe labore perit."

I suspect that few will care to read all these
epigrams; but I have thought it best to give the
collection in full. Campion's Latinity is usually
easy and elegant. Some of the epigrams are thin
and wanting in point, but others have all the com-
pact neatness of Martial. In his handling of
hendecasyllables Campion seems to me to have
been very successful. Take, for instance, the
dedicatory verses to the brothers Mychelburne
(p. 314) :—

> " I nunc, quicquid habes ineptiarum
> Damnatum tenebris diu, libelle,
> In lucem sine candidam venire
> Excusoris ope eruditioris," &c.

The Sapphics, too, are gracefully turned. Meres,
in " Palladis Tamia," 1598, mentions Campion

privately printed (in 1879) from a MS. common-place book
of a Cambridge student, circa 1611 :—

> " How now Doctor Champion, musick's & poesies stout
>   Champion,
>   Will you nere leaue prating ? "

This is very mild satire. Many of his brother practitioners
are far more severely handled.

among the "English men, being Latin poets," who had "attained good report and honourable advancement in the Latin empire." It would be difficult to name any other English writer of that time whose Latin verse shows so much spirit and polish.

But it is not by his Latin verse that Campion will be remembered. In 1601 appeared the first collection of his beautiful English songs, "A Book of Airs." The music was written partly by Campion and partly by Philip Rosseter; but all the poetry, we may be sure, was Campion's. From the dedicatory epistle by Rosseter it appears that Campion's songs had been circulated in MS., "whereby they grew both public and, as coin cracked in exchange, corrupt"; further, that some impudent persons had claimed the credit both of the music and the poetry. The unsigned address To the Reader, which follows the dedicatory epistle, was clearly written by Campion. "The lyric poets among the Greeks and Latins," we are told, "were first inventors of airs, tying themselves strictly to the number and value of their syllables; of which sort you shall find here only one song, in Sapphic verse; the rest are after the fashion of the time, ear-pleasing rhymes without art." Let us be thankful that there was only one Sapphic, and that the rest of the songs were in "ear-pleasing rhymes." It would have been a sad loss to English poetry if Campion had abandoned rhyme and written his

songs in unrhymed metres formed on classical
models. In 1602, the year after the publication of
his " Book of Airs," he produced his " Observations
in the Art of English Poesy," in which he strove to
show that the "vulgar and unartificial custom of
rhyming" should be forthwith discontinued. The
specimens of unrhymed verse that he gives in his
" Observations "—iambic dimetres, trochaics,
Anacreontics, and the rest—have a certain interest
as metrical curiosities, and serve as a warning-piece
to wandering wits. There was a time when Spenser
busied himself with profitless metrical experiments
and sought the advice of such persons as Drant and
Gabriel Harvey; but both Spenser and Campion
soon saw the error of their ways. Rhyme found an
able champion in Samuel Daniel, who promptly
published his " Defence of Rhyme," 1602 (ed. 2,
1603), in answer to Campion's " Observations."
Daniel expressed his surprise that an attack on
rhyme should have been made by one "whose
commendable rhymes, albeit now himself an enemy
to rhyme, have given heretofore to the world the
best notice of his worth." He was careful to state,
with that courtesy which distinguished him, that
Campion was "a man of fair parts and good re-
putation." Ben Jonson wrote (as we learn from his
conversations with Drummond) a Discourse of Poesy
" both against Campion and Daniel "; but it was
never published.

" Ear-pleasing rhymes without art." Such is the

description that Campion gives of his songs. "Ear-pleasing" they undoubtedly are; there are no sweeter lyrics in English poetry than are to be found in Campion's song-books. But "without art" they assuredly are not, for they are frequently models of artistic perfection. It must be admitted that there is inequality in Campion's work; that some of the poems are carelessly worded, others diffuse. But when criticism has said its last word in the way of disparagement, what a wealth of golden poetry is left! Turn where we will, images of beauty meet our eyes. There is nothing antiquated about these old songs; they are as fresh as if they had been written yesterday. Campion was certainly not "born out of his due time"; he came at just the right moment. Lodge and Nicholas Breton were less fortunate; they could not emancipate themselves, once for all, from the lumbering versification on which their youth had been fostered. Campion's poetry is sometimes thin, commonplace if you will, but it is never rude or heavy. "In these English airs," he writes in the address To the Reader before "Two Books of Airs," "I have chiefly aimed to couple my words and notes lovingly together"; and he succeeded. His lyrics are always graceful and happy and unconstrained; never a jarring note; everywhere ease and simplicity. John Davies of Hereford (in the addresses To Worthy Persons appended to "The Scourge of Folly," 1610-11) praised him in most felicitous language:—

" Never did lyrics' more than happy strains,
Strained out of Art by Nature so with ease,
So purely hit the moods and various veins
Of Music and her hearers as do these."

The praise could hardly be bettered; for every reader must be struck by Campion's sureness of touch and by his variety. His devotional poetry is singularly excellent; but its worth has never been recognized. You may search your sacred anthologies and you will not meet a mention of Campion's name. But where will you find in these anthologies a poem that for spiritual fervour can compare with " Awake, awake! thou heavy sprite" (p. 59)? The achievements of our devotional poets are for the most part worthless, and our secular poets seem to lose their inspiration when they touch on sacred themes. All the more valuable, therefore, are these devotional poems of Campion. To fine religious exaltation he joined the true lyric faculty; and such a union is one of the rarest of literary phenomena. His sacred poems never offend against good taste. In richness of imagination the man who wrote " When thou must home to shades of underground," and " Hark, all you ladies that do sleep," was at least the equal of Crashawe; but he never failed to exhibit in his sacred poetry that sobriety of judgment in which Crashawe was so painfully deficient.[1]

[1] I may remark that there is no ground for supposing that Dr. Campion in any way shared the religious views of his namesake Edmund Campion the Jesuit.

In 1607 was published Campion's first masque, written for the marriage of Sir James Hay, and presented at Whitehall before the King on Twelfth-night, 1606-7. It is a pleasing and ingenious entertainment, the song of the Sylvans—" Now hath Flora robbed her bowers " (p. 154)—being in Campion's choicest style. The additional songs at the end (pp. 171-2) are not so successful ; but the Apology to the Reader, " Neither buskin now nor bays " (p. 170), is wholly delightful. In 1613 Campion prepared three masques : one, the Lords' Masque, for the marriage of the Princess Elizabeth, another for the Queen's entertainment at Cawsome [Caversham] House near Reading, and the third for the marriage of Robert Carr, Earl of Somerset. Chamberlain gives an indifferent account of the Lords' Masque in one of his letters : " Of the Lords' Masque I hear no great commendation, save only for riches, their devices being long and tedious, and more like a play than a masque " (Winwood's " Memorials," iii. 435). It is to be noticed that Chamberlain himself was not present; he wrote merely from hearsay. The star-dance, arranged by Inigo Jones, was surely most effective ; and the hearers must have been indeed insensate if they were not charmed by the beautiful song, " Advance your choral motions now " (p. 198). It is gratifying to find Campion at the close of the song commending Inigo Jones' skill and modestly putting himself in the background : " According to the

humour of this song, the stars moved in an exceeding strange and delightful manner, and I suppose
few have ever seen more neat artifice than Master
Inigo Jones shewed in contriving their motion,
who in all the rest of the workmanship which
belonged to the whole invention shewed extraordinary industry and skill, which if it be not as
lively exprest in writing as it appeared in view, rob
not him of his due, but lay the blame on my want
of right apprehending his instructions for the
adorning of his art." Campion's relations with
Inigo Jones were pleasanter than Ben Jonson's.
Of the masque in honour of the nuptials of the
Earl of Somerset and the infamous Lady Frances
Howard, presented at Whitehall on St. Stephen's
night, 1613, Chamberlain again speaks disparag-
ingly : " I hear little or no commendation of the
masque made by the Lords that night, either for
device or dancing, only it was rich and costly."
One thing is certain,—that it was infinitely too
good for the occasion. With what bitter mockery
the Fates answered the poet's prayer for the happiness of the bridegroom and the bride !—

> " All blessings which the Fates prophetic sung
> At Peleus' nuptials, and whatever tongue
> Can figure more, this night and aye betide
> The honoured bridegroom and the honoured bride."

It is to be regretted that Campion should have
come forward to bless so unhallowed a union.[1]

[1] " The Masque of Flowers," presented by the Gentlemen

The untimely death of Prince Henry, in November, 1612, was a heavy blow for the whole nation, and for men of letters in particular. There was no insincerity in the grief shown by the poets. Each felt that he had lost a friend and a protector; for this young Prince—he was but eighteen when he died —had shown himself a true patron of art and letters. To him Drayton had dedicated the "Polyolbion," and under his patronage Chapman had laboured at his translation of Homer. Campion, who no doubt had been personally acquainted with the Prince, was among those whose grief found utterance in verse. He issued in 1613 a small collection of songs entitled "Songs of Mourning," set to music by an eminent composer, John Coperario (whose real name was John Cooper). The songs are dedicated to the King, the Queen, Prince Charles, Princess Elizabeth, the Count Palatine (who had come to England to marry the Princess Elizabeth, and whose marriage had been postponed owing to the Prince's death), to Great Britain, and to the World. Good though they are, these songs do not rank with Campion's best work, for he was necessarily somewhat cramped by the nature of the subject. The elegy that precedes the songs bears eloquent testimony to the Prince's virtues and abilities.

of Gray's Inn on Twelfth-night, 1613-4, in honour of Somerset's marriage, has been hastily attributed to Campion; but I cannot discover that he had any hand in it. The poetry is of an inferior order.

Campion's second song-book, "Two Books of Airs," is undated; but it must have been issued after November, 1612 (probably in 1613), for in one of the songs there is a reference to the death of Prince Henry (p. 52). The first book consists of "Divine and Moral Songs," and is dedicated to the Earl of Cumberland, who appears from the dedicatory sonnet to have been a patron of Campion :—

"What patron could I choose, great Lord, but you ?
Grave words your ears may challenge as their own :
And every note of music is your due
Whose house the Muses' Palace I have known."

The second book, a collection of love-songs, "Light Conceits of Lovers," is dedicated to the Earl's eldest son, Lord Clifford. From the Address to the Reader we learn that Campion had many other songs in reserve ; "but of many songs," he writes, "which, partly at the request of friends, partly for my own recreation, were by me long since composed, I have now enfranchised a few."

In his latest collection, the "Third and Fourth Books of Airs," he enfranchised a few more. The third book was dedicated to Sir Thomas Monson, and the fourth book to his son, John Monson. In 1615 Sir Thomas Monson was examined in regard to the murder of Sir Thomas Overbury, and in October of that year a warrant was issued for his arrest. During his confinement in the Tower Campion was allowed to act as his medical atten-

dant (Hist. MS. Comm., Rep. vii., 671). It appears
that Campion himself was examined, on 26 October,
1615. He admitted that he had received £1400—
£1000 in gold and £400 in "white money"—from
Alderman Helwys (or Elwys) on behalf of Sir Gervase Helwys, for the use of Sir Thomas Monson, the
midsummer after Sir Gervase became Lieutenant of
the Tower; but he knew not for what consideration
the money was paid (Cal. State Papers, Dom., 1611-
19).[1] Suspicions attached to Sir Thomas Monson,
but no evidence of a definite character was forth-
coming. In October, 1616, he was released on
bail, and he was pardoned—not acquitted, but
pardoned—in February, 1617. Campion's undated song-book was published after Monson's
pardon had been granted, for in the dedicatory epistle he congratulated his patron upon the
fact that

> " those clouds that lately overcast
> Your fame and fortun are dispersed at last."

Prefixed to the fourth book is an Address to the
Reader in which Campion remarks, "Some words
are in these books which have been clothed in
music by others, and I am content they then served
their turn : yet give me now leave to make use of
mine own." I think there can be little doubt that
Campion did not reclaim all his poems, but that

---

[1] I have referred to the original document in the Record
Office, but it gives no additional particulars.

some are scattered up and down the song-books of
the time. In the autumn of 1617 the Earl of
Cumberland received the King, on his return
journey from Scotland, at Brougham Castle. Pre-
parations were made for a musical entertainment;
and the Earl wrote to his son Lord Clifford,
"Sonn, I have till now expected your lettres according to your promis at your departure : so did
George Minson [Mason] your directions touching
the musicke, whereupon he mought the better have
writt to Dr. Campion." The "Airs sung and
played at Brougham Castle" were published in
1618. Mason and Earsden were the composers
of the music; but I have little doubt that Campion
supplied the words. The charming song, "Robin
is a lovely lad" (printed in my "Lyrics from
Elizabethan Song-books"), is quite in Campion's
vein. In Robert Jones' collections we find some
songs that unquestionably belong to Campion and
were claimed by him; and I have a strong sus-
picion that Jones' "My love bound me with a kiss"
(also in the "Lyrics") is Campion's.[1] The subject
might be pursued further.

There is one work by Campion which I have
not reprinted,—"A New Way of making Four parts
in Counter-point, by a most familiar and infallible
Rule," &c., n.d. (1617 ?), 8vo. It is a strictly tech-
nical treatise, and its inclusion would considerably
increase the already large dimensions of the present

---

[1] See note, p. 318.

volume. For long it was considered a standard
work, and was frequently reprinted (from 1660 on-
wards) in Playford's "Introduction." I give here the
dedicatory epistle to Prince Charles :—

To the Flower of Princes, Charles, Prince of Great Britain.

The first inventor of music (most sacred Prince) was by
old records Apollo, a King, who, for the benefit which
mortals received from his so divine invention, was by them
made a God. David, a Prophet and a King, excelled all
men in the same excellent art. What then can more adorn
the greatness of a Prince, than the knowledge thereof? But
why should I, being by profession a physician, offer a work
of music to his Highness? Galen either first, or next the
first of physicians, became so expert a musician that he could
not contain himself, but needs he must apply all the propor-
tions of music to the uncertain motions of the pulse. Such
far-fetched doctrine dare not I attempt, contenting myself
only with a poor and easy invention ; yet new and certain ;
by which the skill of music shall be redeemed from much
darkness, wherein envious antiquity of purpose did involve it.
To your gracious hands most humbly I present it, which if
your clemency will vouchsafe favourably to behold, I have
then attained to the full estimate of all my labour. Be all
your days ever musical (most mighty Prince) and a sweet
harmony guide the events of all your royal actions. So
zealously wisheth

Your Highness'
most humble servant,
Tho : Campion.

In 1619 Campion republished, with large additions, his collection of Latin epigrams ; and on 1st

March, 1619-20, his burial was recorded in the register of St. Dunstan's in the West, Fleet Street.[1]

In the preface to " Lyrics from Elizabethan Song-Books," and again in the preface to " More Lyrics," I dwelt upon Campion's merits ; and I have nothing to retract from what I there said in his praise. The more we read his songs the more their charm will grow upon us. They tell of Love with all its sweets and sours ; of patience under suffering ; of faith in a benign Providence. So long as " elegancy, facility, and golden cadence of poesy " are admired, Campion's fame will be secure.

[1] " Thomas Campion doctor of Physicke was buried " is the entry in the register.

A Booke of Ayres, Set foorth to be song to the Lute, Orpherian, and Base Violl, by Philip Rosseter, Lutenist: And are to be solde at his house in Fleetstreete neere to the Gray-hound. At Lonond [sic]. Printed by Peter Short, by the assent of Thomas Morley, 1601. fol.

B

TO THE RIGHT VIRTUOUS AND WORTHY KNIGHT, SIR THOMAS MOUNSON.[1]

SIR,

THE general voice of your worthiness, and the many particular favours which I have heard Master CAMPION, with dutiful respect, often acknowledge himself to have received from you, have emboldened me to present this *Book of Airs* to your favourable judgement and gracious protection ; especially because the first rank of Songs are of his own composition, made at his vacant hours, and privately imparted to his friends : whereby they grew both public, and, as coin cracked in exchange, corrupted ; and some of them, both words and notes, unrespectively challenged [2] by others. In regard of which wrongs, though his self neglects these light fruits as superfluous blossoms' of his deeper studies, yet hath it pleased him, upon my entreaty, to grant me the impression of part of them : to which I have added an equal number of mine own. And this two-faced JANUS, thus in one body united, I humbly entreat you to entertain and defend : chiefly in respect of the affection which I suppose you bear him who, I am assured, doth, above all others, love and honour you.

And for my part I shall think myself happy if in any service I may deserve this favour.

Your Worship's humbly devoted,

PHILIP ROSSETER.

[1] For a notice of Sir Thomas Mounson (or Monson) see *Introduction*.

[2] Claimed.

TO THE READER.

WHAT epigrams are in poetry, the same are airs in music: then in their chief perfection when they are short and well seasoned. But to clog a light song with a long præludium, *is to corrupt the nature of it. Many rests in music were invented, either for necessity of the fugue, or granted as an harmonical licence in songs of many parts: but in airs I find no use they have, unless it be to make a vulgar and trivial modulation seem to the ignorant, strange; and to the judicial, tedious. A naked air without guide, or prop, or colour but his own, is easily censured[1] of every ear; and requires so much the more invention to make it please. And as* MARTIAL *speaks in defence of his short epigrams; so may I say in the apology of airs: that where there is a volume, there can be no imputation of shortness. The lyric poets among the Greeks and Latins were first inventors of airs, tying themselves strictly to the number and value of their syllables: of which sort, you shall find here, only one song[2] in Sapphic verse; the rest are after the fashion of the time, ear-pleasing rhymes, without art. The subject of them is, for the most part, amorous: and why not amorous songs, as well as amorous attires? Or why not new airs, as well as new fashions?*

For the note and tableture, if they satisfy the most, we have our desire; let expert masters please them-

---

[1] Judged.

[2] "Come, let us sound," &c., p. 23.

selves with better. And if any light error hath escaped us, the skilful may easily correct it, the unskilful will hardly perceive it. But there are some who, to appear the more deep and singular in their judgement, will admit no music but that which is long, intricate, bated with fugue, chained with syncopation, and where the nature of every word is precisely expressed in the note: like the old exploded action in comedies, when if they did pronounce Memini, *they would point to the hinder part of their heads; if* Video, *put their finger in their eye. But such childish observing of words is altogether ridiculous: and we ought to maintain, as well in notes as in action, a manly carriage; gracing no word, but that which is eminent and emphatical. Nevertheless, as in poesy we give the preemininence to the Heroical Poem; so in music, we yield the chief place to the grave and well invented Motet: but not to every harsh and dull confused Fantasy, where, in multitude of points, the harmony is quite drowned.*

Airs have both their art and pleasure: and I will conclude of them, as the poet did in his censure of CATULLUS *the Lyric, and* VIRGIL *the Heroic writer:*

Tantum magna suo debet Verona CATULLO,
Quantum parva suo Mantua VIRGILIO.

A TABLE OF HALF THE SONGS CONTAINED
IN THIS BOOK, BY T. C.

1. My sweetest Lesbia.
2. Though you are young.
3. I care not for these ladies.
4. Follow thy fair sun.
5. My love hath vowed.
6. When to her lute.
7. Turn back, you wanton flyer.
8. It fell on a summer's day.
9. The cypress curtain.
10. Follow your saint.
11. Fair, if you expect admiring.
12. Thou art not fair.
13. See where she flies.
14. Blame not my cheeks.
15. When the god of merry love.
16. Mistress, since you so much desire.
17. Your fair looks inflame.
18. The man of life upright.
19. Hark all you ladies.
20. When thou must home.
21. Come let us sound with melody.

MY [1] sweetest Lesbia, let us live and love ;
  And though the sager sort our deeds reprove,
Let us not weigh them : heaven's great lamps do dive
Into their west, and straight again revive :
But soon as once set is our little light,
Then must we sleep one ever-during night.

If all would lead their lives in love like me,
Then bloody swords and armour should not be ;
No drum nor trumpet peaceful sleeps should move,
Unless alarm came from the camp of love :
But fools do live, and waste their little light,
And seek with pain their ever-during night.

When timely death my life and fortune ends,
Let not my hearse be vext with mourning friends ;
But let all lovers, rich in triumph, come
And with sweet pastimes grace my happy tomb :
And, Lesbia, close up thou my little light,
And crown with love my ever-during night.

THOUGH [2] you are young, and I am old,
  Though your veins hot, and my blood cold,
Though youth is moist, and age is dry ;
Yet embers live, when flames do die.

[1] Suggested by (and partly translated from) Catullus'
    " Vivamus, mea Lesbia, atque amemus."
[2] This song is frequently found in seventeenth century MS.
commonplace-books.

The tender graft is easily broke,
But who shall shake the sturdy oak?
You are more fresh and fair than I ;
Yet stubs do live when flowers do die.

Thou, that thy youth doth vainly boast,
Know buds are soonest nipt with frost :
Think that thy fortune still doth cry,
"Thou fool ! to-morrow thou must die !"

I CARE not for these ladies,
   That must be wooed and prayed :
Give me kind Amarillis,
The wanton country maid.
Nature art disdaineth,
Her beauty is her own.
   Her when we court and kiss,
   She cries, " Forsooth, let go !"
   But when we come where comfort is,
   She never will say " No !"

If I love Amarillis,
She gives me fruit and flowers :
But if we love these ladies,
We must give golden showers.
Give them gold, that sell love,
Give me the nut-brown lass,

Who, when we court and kiss,
She cries, " Forsooth, let go !"
But when we come where comfort is,
She never will say " No !"

These ladies must have pillows,
And beds by strangers wrought ;
Give me a bower of willows,
Of moss and leaves unbought,
And fresh Amarillis,
With milk and honey fed ;
    Who, when we court and kiss,
    She cries " Forsooth, let go !"
    But when we come where comfort is,
    She never will say " No !"

FOLLOW thy fair sun, unhappy shadow !
    Though thou be black as night,
And she made all of light,
Yet follow thy fair sun, unhappy shadow !

Follow her whose light thy light depriveth ;
Though here thou livest disgraced,
And she in heaven is placed,
Yet follow her whose light the world reviveth !

Follow those pure beams whose beauty burneth,
That so have scorched thee,
As thou still black must be,
Till her kind beams thy black to brightness turneth.

Follow her ! while yet her glory shineth :
There comes a luckless night,
That will dim all her light ;
And this the black unhappy shade divineth.

Follow still ! since so thy fates ordained ;
The sun must have his shade,
Till both at once do fade ;
The sun still proved, the shadow still disdained.

MY love hath vowed he will forsake me,
    And I am already sped ;
Far other promise he did make me
    When he had my maidenhead.
If such danger be in playing
    And sport must to earnest turn,
I will go no more a-maying.

Had I foreseen what is ensued,
    And what now with pain I prove,
Unhappy then I had eschewed
    This unkind event of love :
Maids foreknow their own undoing,
    But fear naught till all is done,
When a man alone is wooing.

Dissembling wretch, to gain thy pleasure,
    What didst thou not vow and swear ?
So didst thou rob me of the treasure
    Which so long I held so dear.

Now thou provest to me a stranger :
  Such is the vile guise of men
When a woman is in danger.

That heart is nearest to misfortune
  That will trust a feigned tongue ;
When flatt'ring men our loves importune
  They intend us deepest wrong.
If this shame of love's betraying
  But this once I cleanly shun,
I will go no more a-maying.

WHEN to her lute Corinna sings,
    Her voice revives the leaden strings,
And doth in highest notes appear,
As any challenged Echo clear ;
But when she doth of mourning speak,
E'en with her sighs the strings do break.

And as her lute doth live or die,
Led by her passion, so must I !
For when of pleasure, she doth sing,
My thoughts enjoy a sudden spring ;
But if she doth of sorrow speak,
E'en from my heart the strings do break.

TURN back, you wanton flyer,
    And answer my desire,
With mutual greeting :
Yet bend a little nearer,

True beauty still shines clearer,
In closer meeting.
Hearts, with hearts delighted,
Should strive to be united ;
Either other's arms with arms enchaining :
Hearts with a thought,
Rosy lips with a kiss still entertaining.
What harvest half so sweet is
As still to reap the kisses
Grown ripe in sowing?
And straight to be receiver
Of that, which thou art giver,
Rich in bestowing?
There's no strict observing
Of times' or seasons' swerving ;[1]
There is ever one fresh spring abiding.
Then what we sow with our lips,
Let us reap, love's gains dividing !

IT fell on a summer's day,
    While sweet Bessy sleeping lay,
In her bower, on her bed,
Light with curtains shadowed,
Jamy came : she him spies,
Opening half her heavy eyes.

Jamy stole in through the door,
She lay slumb'ring as before ;

[1] Old ed. "changing."

Softly to her he drew near,
She heard him, yet would not hear :
Bessy vowed not to speak,
He resolved that dump to break.

First a soft kiss he doth take,
She lay still and would not wake ;
Then his hands learned to woo,
She dreamt not what he would do,
But still slept, while he smiled
To see love by sleep beguiled.

Jamy then began to play,
Bessy as one buried lay,
Gladly still through this sleight
Deceived in her own deceit ;
And since this trance begoon,
She sleeps every afternoon.

THE cypress curtain of the night is spread,
   And over all a silent dew is cast.
The weaker cares, by sleep are conquered :
But I alone, with hideous grief aghast,
In spite of Morpheus' charms, a watch do keep
Over mine eyes, to banish careless sleep.

Yet oft my trembling eyes through faintness close,
And then the Map of Hell before me stands ;
Which ghosts do see, and I am one of those
Ordained to pine in sorrow's endless bands,

Since from my wretched soul all hopes are reft
And now no cause of life to me is left.

Grief, seize my soul ! for that will still endure
When my crazed body is consumed and gone ;
Bear it to thy black den ! there keep it sure
Where thou ten thousand souls dost tire upon !
Yet all do not afford such food to thee
As this poor one, the worser part of me.

FOLLOW your saint, follow with accents sweet !
    Haste you, sad notes, fall at her flying fleet !
There, wrapped in cloud of sorrow, pity move,
And tell the ravisher of my soul I perish for her love :
But if she scorns my never-ceasing pain,
Then burst with sighing in her sight and ne'er return
        again !

All that I sung still to her praise did tend ;
Still she was first ; still she my songs did end :
Yet she my love and music both doth fly,
The music that her Echo is and beauty's sympathy.
Then let my notes pursue her scornful flight !
It shall suffice that they were breathed and died for
        her delight.

FAIR, if you expect admiring ;
    Sweet, if you['d] provoke desiring ;
Grace dear love with kind requiting !
Fond, but if thy light be blindness ;
False, if thou affect unkindness ;
Fly both love and love's delighting !
Then when hope is lost and love is scorned,
I'll bury my desires, and quench the fires that ever yet
      in vain have burned.

Fates, if you rule lovers' fortune ;
Stars, if men your powers importune ;
Yield relief by your relenting !
Time, if sorrow be not endless,
Hope made vain, and pity friendless,
Help to ease my long lamenting !
But if griefs remain still unredressed,
I'll fly to her again, and sue for pity to renew my hopes
      distressed.

THOU¹ art not fair, for all thy red and white,
    For all those rosy ornaments in thee ;

¹ There are two other versions of this poem (which has been
erroneously attributed to Dr. Donne and to Joshua Sylvester) in
Harl. MS. 6910, fol. 150.

    " Thou shalt not love me, neither shall these eyes
    Shine on my soul shrouded in deadly night ;
    Thou shalt not breathe on me thy spiceries,
    Nor rock me in thy quavers of delight

Thou art not sweet, though made of mere delight,
Nor fair nor sweet, unless thou pity me.
I will not soothe thy fancies : Thou shalt prove
That beauty is no beauty without love.

Yet love not me, nor seek thou to allure
My thoughts with beauty, were it more divine :

> Hold off thy hands ; for I had rather die
> Than have my life by thy coy touch reprieved.
> Smile not on me, but frown thou bitterly :
> Slay me outright, no lovers are long lived.
> As for those lips reserved so much in store,
> Their rosy verdure shall not meet with mine.
> Withhold thy proud embracements evermore :
> I'll not be swaddled in those arms of thine.
>> Now show it if thou be a woman right,—
>> Embrace and kiss and love me in despight."
>> *Finis.   Tho: Camp:*

"BEAUTY WITHOUT LOVE DEFORMITY.

" Thou art not fair for all thy red and white,
For all those rosy temperatures in thee ;
Thou art not sweet, though made of mere delight,
Nor fair nor sweet unless thou pity me.
Thine eyes are black, and yet their glittering brightness
Can night enlumine in her darkest den ;
Thy hands are bloody, though [1] contrived of whiteness,
Both black and bloody, if they murder men ;
Thy brows, whereon my good hap doth depend,
Fairer than snow or lily in the spring ;
Thy tongue which saves (?) at every sweet word's end,
That hard as marble, this a mortal sting :
I will not soothe thy follies, thou shalt prove
That Beauty is no Beauty without Love."
>> *Finis.   Idem.*

---

[1] MS. "thoughts."

Thy smiles and kisses I cannot endure,
I'll not be wrapt up in those arms of thine :
Now show it, if thou be a woman right,—
Embrace, and kiss, and love me, in despite !

S EE where she flies enraged from me !
View her when she intends despite,
The wind is not more swift than she.
Her fury moved such terror makes
As to a fearful guilty sprite
The voice of heaven's huge thunder-cracks :
But when her appeased mind yields to delight,
All her thoughts are made of joys,
Millions of delights inventing ;
Other pleasures are but toys
To her beauty's sweet contenting.

My fortune hangs upon her brow ;
For as she smiles or frowns on me,
So must my blown affections bow ;
And her proud thoughts too well do find
With what unequal tyranny
Her beauties do command my mind.
Though, when her sad planet reigns,
Froward she be,
She alone can pleasure move,
And displeasing sorrow banish.
May I but still hold her love,
Let all other comforts vanish.

C

BLAME not my cheeks, though pale with love they
　　　be ;
The kindly heat unto my heart is flown,
To cherish it that is dismayed by thee,
Who art so cruel and unsteadfast grown :
For Nature, called for by distressed hearts,
Neglects and quite forsakes the outward parts.

But they whose cheeks with careless blood are stained,
Nurse not one spark of love within their hearts ;
And, when they woo, they speak with passion feigned,
For their fat love lies in their outward parts :
But in their breasts, where love his court should hold,
Poor Cupid sits and blows his nails for cold.

WHEN the god of merry love
　　　As yet in his cradle lay,
Thus his withered nurse did say :
" Thou a wanton boy wilt prove
To deceive the powers above ;
For by thy continual smiling
I see thy power of beguiling."

Therewith she the babe did kiss ;
When a sudden fire outcame
From those burning lips of his,
That did her with love inflame.
But none would regard the same :
So that, to her day of dying,
The old wretch lived ever crying.

MISTRESS,[1] since you so much desire
    To know the place of Cupid's fire,
In your fair shrine that flame doth rest,
Yet never harboured in your breast.
It 'bides not in your lips so sweet,
Nor where the rose and lilies meet ;
But a little higher, but a little higher ;
There, there, O there lies Cupid's fire.

Even in those starry piercing eyes,
There Cupid's sacred fire lies.
Those eyes I strive not to enjoy,
For they have power to destroy ;
Nor woo I for a smile or kiss,
So meanly triumphs not my bliss ;
But a little higher, but a little higher,
I climb to crown my chaste desire.

YOUR[2] fair looks inflame my desire :
    Quench it again with love !
Stay, O strive not still to retire :
    Do not inhuman prove !
If love may persuade,
    Love's pleasures, dear, deny not.
Here is a silent grovy shade ;
    O tarry then, and fly not !

[1] Cf. the song "Beauty, since you so much desire" in the *Fourth Book of Airs.*

[2] There is another version (far better) of this poem in the *Fourth Book of Airs,* " Your fair looks urge my desire."

Have I seized my heavenly delight
 In this unhaunted grove?
Time shall now her fury requite
 With the revenge of love.
Then come, sweetest, come,
 My lips with kisses gracing!
Here let us harbour all alone,
 Die, die in sweet embracing!

Will you now so timely depart,
 And not return again?
Your sight lends such life to my heart
 That to depart is pain.
Fear yields no delay,
 Secureness helpeth pleasure:
Then, till the time gives safer stay,
 O farewell, my life's treasure!

THE[1] man of life upright,
 Whose guiltless heart is free
From all dishonest deeds,
 Or thought of vanity;

The man whose silent days,
 In harmless joys are spent,
Whom hopes cannot delude
 Nor sorrow discontent;

---

[1] This poem (which was reprinted with some textual variations
in *Two Books of Airs*) has been wrongly attributed to Bacon.

That man needs neither towers
    Nor armour for defence,
Nor secret vauts [1] to fly
    From thunder's violence :

He only can behold
    With unaffrighted eyes
The horrors of the deep
    And terrors of the skies.

Thus, scorning all the cares
    That fate or fortune brings,
He makes the heaven his book,
    His wisdom heavenly things ;

Good thoughts his only friends,
    His wealth a well-spent age,
The earth his sober inn
    And quiet pilgrimage.

HARK, all you ladies that do sleep !
    The fairy-queen Proserpina
Bids you awake and pity them that weep .
    You may do in the dark
        What the day doth forbid ;
    Fear not the dogs that bark,
        Night will have all hid.

But if you let your lovers moan,
    The fairy-queen Proserpina

       [1] Old form of " vaults."

Will send abroad her fairies every one,
 That shall pinch black and blue
  Your white hands and fair arms
 That did not kindly rue
  Your paramours'[1] harms.

In myrtle arbours on the downs
 The fairy-queen Proserpina,
This night by moonshine leading merry rounds,
 Holds a watch with sweet love,
  Down the dale, up the hill ;
 No plaints or groans may move
  Their holy vigil.

All you that will hold watch with love,
 The fairy-queen Proserpina
Will make you fairer than Dione's dove ;
 Roses red, lilies white,
  And the clear damask hue,
 Shall on your cheeks alight :
  Love will adorn you.

All you that love or loved before,
 The fairy-queen Proserpina
Bids you increase that loving humour more :
 They that have not fed
  On delight amorous,
 She vows that they shall lead
  Apes in Avernus.

---

[1] " Paramour "=lover. (The word acquired its present offensive meaning at a later date.)

WHEN thou must home to shades of underground,
And there arrived, a new admired guest,
The beauteous spirits do engirt thee round,
White Iope,[1] blithe Helen, and the rest,
To hear the stories of thy finished love
From that smooth tongue whose music hell can move;

Then wilt thou speak of banqueting delights,
Of masques and revels which sweet youth did make,
Of tourneys and great challenges of knights,
And all these triumphs for thy beauty's sake :
When thou hast told these honours done to thee,
Then tell, O tell, how thou didst murder me.

COME, let us sound with melody, the praises
Of the King's King, th' omnipotent Creator,
Author of number, that hath all the world in
Harmony framed.

Heav'n is His throne perpetually shining,
His divine power and glory, thence He thunders,
One in All, and All still in One abiding,
Both Father and Son.

[1] Campion had in his mind a passage of Propertius, II. 28 :—
"Sunt apud infernos tot millia formosarum :
Pulchra sit in superis, si licet, una locis.
Vobiscum est Iope, vobiscum candida Tyro,
Vobiscum Europe, nec proba Pasiphae."

O sacred Sprite, invisible, eternal,
Ev'rywhere, yet unlimited, that all things
Can'st in one moment penetrate, revive me,
　　　　　　　O Holy Spirit !

Rescue, O rescue me from earthly darkness !
Banish hence all these elemental objects !
Guide my soul that thirsts to the lively fountain
　　　　　　　Of thy divineness !

Cleanse my soul, O God ! thy bespotted image,
Altered with sin so that heavenly pureness
Cannot acknowledge me, but in thy mercies,
　　　　　　　O Father of grace !

But when once Thy beams do remove my darkness ;
O then I'll shine forth as an angel of light,
And record, with more than an earthly voice, Thy
　　　　　　　Infinite honours.

FINIS.

A TABLE OF THE REST OF THE SONGS
CONTAINED IN THIS BOOK, MADE
BY PHILIP ROSSETER.

1. Sweet, come again.
2. And would you see.
3. No grave for woe.
4. If I urge my kind desires.
5. What heart's content.
6. Let him that will be free.
7. Reprove not love.
8. And would you fain.
9. When Laura smiles.
10. Long have mine eyes.
11. Though far from joy.
12. Shall I come if I swim.
13. Aye me! that love.
14. Shall then a traitorous.
15. If I hope I pine.
16. Unless there were consent.
17. If she forsake[1] me.
18. What is a day.
19. Kind in unkindness.
20. What then is love but.
21. Whether men do laugh.

[1] Old ed. "forsakes."

SWEET, come again !
  Your happy sight, so much desired,
 Since you from hence are now retired,
I seek in vain :
Still must I mourn
  And pine in longing pain,
  Till you, my life's delight, again
Vouchsafe your wished return.

If true desire,
  Or faithful vow of endless love,
  Thy heart inflamed may kindly move
With equal fire ;
O then my joys,
  So long distraught, shall rest,
  Reposed soft in thy chaste breast,
Exempt from all annoys.

You had the power
  My wand'ring thoughts first to restrain,
  You first did hear my love speak plain !
A child before,
Now it is grown
  Confirmed, do you it keep,
  And let it safe in your bosom sleep,
There ever made your own !

And till we meet,
   Teach absence inward art to find,
   Both to disturb and please the mind.
Such thoughts are sweet :
And such remain
   In hearts whose flames are true ;
   Then such will I retain, till you
To me return again.

A ND would you see my mistress' face ?
     It is a flowery garden place,
Where knots of beauties have such grace
That all is work and nowhere space.

It is a sweet delicious morn,
Where day is breeding, never born ;
It is a meadow, yet unshorn,
Which thousand flowers do adorn.

It is the heaven's bright reflex,
Weak eyes to dazzle and to vex :
It is th' Idea of her sex,
Envy of whom doth world perplex.

It is a face of Death that smiles,
Pleasing, though it kills the whiles :
Where Death and Love in pretty wiles
Each other mutually beguiles.

It is fair beauty's freshest youth,
It is the feigned Elizium's truth :
The spring, that wintered hearts reneweth ;
And this is that my soul pursueth.

NO grave for woe, yet earth my watery tears devours ;
Sighs want air, and burnt desires kind pity's showers :
Stars hold their fatal course, my joys preventing :
The earth, the sea, the air, the fire, the heavens vow my tormenting.

Yet still I live, and waste my weary days in groans,
And with woful tunes adorn despairing moans.
Night still prepares a more displeasing morrow ;
My day is night, my life my death, and all but sense of sorrow.

IF I urge my kind desires,
She unkind doth them reject ;
Women's hearts are painted fires
To deceive them that affect.
I alone love's fires include ;
She alone doth them delude.

She hath often vowed her love ;
But, alas ! no fruit I find.
That her fires are false I prove,
Yet in her no fault I find :
I was thus unhappy born,
And ordained to be her scorn.

Yet if human care or pain,
May the heavenly order change,
She will hate her own disdain,
And repent she was so strange :
For a truer heart than I,
Never lived or loved to die.

WHAT heart's content can he find,
    What happy sleeps can his eyes embrace,
That bears a guilty mind ?
  His taste sweet wines will abhor :
No music's sound can appease the thoughts
  That wicked deeds deplore.
The passion of a present fear
Still makes his restless motion there ;
And all the day he dreads the night,
And all the night, as one aghast, he fears the morning
    light.

But he that loves to be loved,
  And in his deeds doth adore heaven's power,
And is with pity moved ;
  The night gives rest to his heart,

The cheerful beams do awake his soul,
   Revived in every part.
He lives a comfort to his friends,
And heaven to him such blessing sends
That fear of hell cannot dismay
His steadfast heart that is [1] . . .

LET him that will be free and keep his heart from
       care,
  Retired alone, remain where no discomforts are.
For when the eye doth view his grief, or hapless ear
    his sorrow hears,
Th' impression still in him abides, and ever in one
    shape appears.

Forget thy griefs betimes ; long sorrow breeds long
    pain,
For joy far fled from men, will not return again ;
O happy is the soul which heaven ordained to live in
    endless peace !
His life is a pleasing dream, and every hour his joys
    increase.

You heavy sprites, that love in severed shades to dwell,
That nurse despair and dream of unrelenting hell,
Come sing this happy song, and learn of me the Art of
    True Content !
Load not your guilty souls with wrong, and heaven
    then will soon relent.

---

[1] In old ed. the type is broken away.

REPROVE not love, though fondly thou hast lost
   Greater hopes by loving :
Love calms ambitious spirits, from their breasts
  Danger oft removing :
Let lofty humours mount up on high,
  Down again like to the wind,
While private thoughts, vowed to love,
  More peace and pleasure find.

Love and sweet beauty makes the stubborn mild,
  And the coward fearless ;
The wretched miser's care to bounty turns,
  Cheering all things cheerless.
Love chains the earth and heaven,
  Turns the spheres, guides the years in endless peace :
The flowery earth through his power
  Receives her due increase.

AND would you fain the reason know
  Why my sad eyes so often flow ?
My heart ebbs joy, when they do so,
And loves the moon by whom they go.

And will you ask why pale I look ?
'Tis not with poring on my book :
My mistress' cheek, my blood hath took,
For her mine own hath me forsook.

Do not demand why I am mute :
Love's silence doth all speech confute.
They set the note, then tune the lute ;
Hearts frame their thoughts, then tongues their suit.

Do not admire why I admire :
My fever is no other's fire :
Each several heart hath his desire ;
Else proof is false, and truth a liar.

If why I love you should see cause :
Love should have form like other laws,
But Fancy pleads not by the clause :
'Tis as the sea, still vext with flaws.

No fault upon my love espy :
For you perceive not with my eye ;
My palate to your taste may lie,
Yet please itself deliciously.

Then let my sufferance be mine own :
Sufficeth it these reasons shown :
Reason and love are ever known
To fight till both be overthrown.

WHEN Laura smiles her sight revives both night
　　　　　and day ;
The earth and heaven views with delight her wanton
　　　　play :
And her speech with ever-flowing music doth repair
The cruel wounds of sorrow and untamed despair.

The sprites that remain in fleeting air
Affect for pastime to untwine her tressed hair :
And the birds think sweet Aurora, Morning's Queen,
    doth shine
From her bright sphere, when Laura shows her looks
    divine.

Diana's eyes are not adorned with greater power
Than Laura's, when she lists awhile for sport to lower :
But when she her eyes encloseth, blindness doth appear
The chiefest grace of beauty, sweetly seated there.

Love hath no power but what he steals from her bright
    eyes ;
Time hath no power but that which in her pleasure
    lies :
For she with her divine beauties all the world subdues,
And fills with heavenly spirits my humble Muse.

LONG have mine eyes gazed with delight,
    Conveying hopes unto my soul ;
In nothing happy, but in sight
    Of her, that doth my sight control :
But now mine eyes must lose their light.

My object now must be the air ;
    To write in water words of fire ;
And teach sad thoughts how to despair :
    Desert must quarrel with Desire.
All were appeased were she not fair.

D

For all my comfort, this I prove,
That Venus on the sea was born :
If seas be calm, then doth she love ;
If storms arise, I am forlorn ;
My doubtful hopes, like wind do move.

THOUGH far from joy, my sorrows are as far,
    And I both between ;
Not too low, nor yet too high
Above my reach, would I be seen.
Happy is he that so is placed,
Not to be envied nor to be disdained or disgraced.

The higher trees, the more storms they endure ;
Shrubs be trodden down :
But the Mean, the Golden Mean,
Doth only all our fortunes crown :
Like to a stream that sweetly slideth
Through the flowery banks, and still in the midst his
    course guideth.

SHALL I come, if I swim? wide are the waves, you
    see :
Shall I come, if I fly, my dear Love, to thee?
Streams Venus will appease ; Cupid gives me wings ;
All the powers assist my desire
Save you alone, that set my woful heart on fire !

You are fair, so was Hero that in Sestos dwelt ;
She a priest, yet the heat of love truly felt.
A greater stream than this, did her love divide ;
But she was his guide with a light :
So through the streams Leander did enjoy her sight.

A YE me ! that love should Nature's work accuse !
Where cruel Laura still her beauty views,
River, or cloudy jet, or crystal bright,
Are all but servants of herself, delight.

Yet her deformed thoughts, she cannot see ;
And that's the cause she is so stern to me.
Virtue and duty can no favour gain :
A grief, O death ! to live and love in vain.

S HALL then a traitorous kiss or a smile
All my delights unhappily beguile?
Shall the vow of feigned love receive so rich regard,
When true service dies neglected, and wants his due
        reward ?

Deeds meritorious soon be forgot,
But one offence no time can ever blot ;
Every day it is renewed, and every night it bleeds,
And with bloody streams of sorrow drowns all our
        better deeds.

Beauty is not by Desert to be won ;
Fortune hath all that is beneath the sun.
Fortune is the guide of Love, and both of them be
    blind :
All their ways are full of errors, which no true feet can
    find.

IF I hope, I pine ; if I fear, I faint and die ;
    So between hope and fear, I desperate lie,
Looking for joy to heaven, whence it should come :
But hope is blind ; joy, deaf ; and I am dumb.
Yet I speak and cry ; but, alas, with words of woe :
And joy conceives not them that murmur so.
He that the ears of joy will ever pierce,
Must sing glad notes, or speak in happier verse.

UNLESS there were consent 'twixt hell and heaven
    That grace and wickedness should be combined,
I cannot make thee and thy beauties even :
    Thy face is heaven, and torture in thy mind, '
For more than worldly bliss is in thy eye
And hellish torture in thy mind doth lie.

A thousand Cherubins fly in her looks,
    And hearts in legions melt upon their view :
But gorgeous covers wall up filthy books ;
    Be it sin to say, that so your eyes do you :
But sure your mind adheres not with your eyes,
For what they promise, that your heart denies.

But, O, lest I religion should misuse,
 Inspire me thou, that ought'st thyself to know
(Since skilless readers, reading do abuse),
 What inward meaning outward sense doth show :
For by thy eyes and heart, chose and contemned,
I waver, whether saved or condemned.

I F she forsake me, I must die :
 Shall I tell her so ?
Alas, then straight she will reply,
 " No, no, no, no, no !"
If I disclose my desperate state,
She will but make sport thereat,
 And more unrelenting grow.

What heart can long such pains abide ?
 Fie upon this love !
I would venture far and wide,
 If it would remove.
But Love will still my steps pursue,
I cannot his ways eschew :
 Thus still helpless hopes I prove.

I do my love in lines commend,
 But, alas, in vain ;
The costly gifts, that I do send,
 She returns again :
Thus still is my despair procured,
And her malice more assured :
 Then come, Death, and end my pain !

WHAT is a day, what is a year
　　Of vain delight and pleasure?
Like to a dream it endless dies,
　　And from us like a vapour flies:
And this is all the fruit that we find,
　　Which glory in worldly treasure.

He that will hope for true delight,
　　With virtue must be graced;
Sweet folly yields a bitter taste,
　　Which ever will appear at last:
But if we still in virtue delight,
　　Our souls are in heaven placed.

KIND in unkindness, when will you relent
　　And cease with faint love true love to torment?
Still entertained, excluded still I stand;
Her glove still hold, but cannot touch the hand.

In her fair hand my hopes and comforts rest:
O might my fortunes with that hand be blest!
No envious breaths then my deserts could shake,
For they are good whom such true love doth make.

O let not beauty so forget her birth,
That it should fruitless home return to earth!
Love is the fruit of beauty, then love one!
Not your sweet self, for such self-love is none.

Love one that only lives in loving you ;
Whose wronged deserts would you with pity view,
This strange distaste which your affections sways
Would relish love, and you find better days.

Thus till my happy sight your beauty views,
Whose sweet remembrance still my hope renews,
Let these poor lines solicit love for me,
And place my joys where my desires would be.

WHAT then is love but mourning ?
     What desire, but a self-burning ?
Till she, that hates, doth love return,
Thus will I mourn, thus will I sing,
" Come away ! come away, my darling ! "

Beauty is but a blooming,
Youth in his glory entombing ;
Time hath a while, which none can stay :
Then come away, while thus I sing,
" Come away ! come away, my darling ! "

Summer in winter fadeth ;
Gloomy night heavenly light shadeth :
Like to the morn, are Venus' flowers ;
Such are her hours : then will I sing,
" Come away ! come away, my darling ! "

WHETHER men do laugh or weep,
    Whether they do wake or sleep,
Whether they die young or old,
Whether they feel heat or cold ;
There is, underneath the sun,
Nothing in true earnest done.

All our pride is but a jest ;
None are worst, and none are best :
Grief and joy, and hope and fear,
Play their pageants everywhere :
Vain opinion all doth sway,
And the world is but a play.

Powers above in clouds do sit,
Mocking our poor apish wit ;
That so lamely, with such state,
Their high glory imitate :
No ill can be felt but pain,
And that happy men disdain.

FINIS.

Two Bookes of Ayres. The First Contayning Diuine and Morall Songs: The Second, Light Conceits of Louers. To be sung to the Lute and Viols, in two, three, and foure Parts: or by one Voyce to an Instrument. Composed by Thomas Campian. London: Printed by Tho. Snodham, for Mathew Lownes, and I. Browne cum Priuilegio. n.d. [circ. 1613]. fol.

TO THE RIGHT HONOURABLE, BOTH IN BIRTH AND VIRTUE, FRANCIS EARL OF CUMBERLAND.[1]

WHAT patron could I choose, great Lord, but you?
Grave words your years may challenge as their own :
And every note of music is your due,
   Whose house the Muses' Palace I have known.

To love and cherish them, though it descends
   With many honours more on you, in vain
Preceding fame herein with you contends,
   Who hath both fed the Muses and their train.

These leaves I offer you, Devotion might
   Herself lay open.　Read them, or else hear
How gravely, with their tunes, they yield delight
   To any virtuous and not curious ear :
Such as they are, accept them, noble Lord :
If better, better could my zeal afford.
                Your Honour's,
                  THOMAS CAMPION.[2]

[1] Francis Clifford, fourth Earl of Cumberland, succeeded, in 1605, his brother, George Clifford, third Earl, the well-known naval adventurer.　He died in 1641.

[2] Old ed. " Campian."

TO THE READER.

OUT of many songs which, partly at the request of friends, partly for my own recreation, were by me long since composed, I have now enfranchised a few; sending them forth divided, according to their different subjects, into several books.   The first are grave and pious : the second, amorous and light.   For he that in publishing any work hath a desire to content all palates, must cater for them accordingly.

> Non omnibus unum est
> Quod placet, hic spinas colligit, ille rosas.

These airs were for the most part framed at first for one voice with the lute or viol : but upon occasion they have since been filled with more parts, which whoso please may use, who like not may leave.   Yet do we daily observe that when any shall sing treble to an instrument, the standers by will be offering at an inward part out of their own nature; and, true or false, out it must, though to the perverting of the whole harmony.   Also, if we consider well, the treble tunes (which are with us, commonly called Airs) are but tenors mounted eight notes higher; and therefore an inward part must needs well become them, such as may take up the whole distance of the diapason, and fill up the gaping between the two extreme parts : whereby though they are not three parts in perfection, yet they yield a sweetness and content both to the ear and mind; which is the aim and perfection of Music.

Short airs, if they be skilfully framed, and naturally expressed, are like quick and good epigrams in poesy: many of them showing as much artifice, and breeding as great difficulty as a larger poem. Non omnia possumus omnes, *said the Roman epic poet.* But *some there are who admit only French or Italian airs; as if every country had not his proper air, which the people thereof naturally usurp in their music. Others taste nothing that comes forth in print; as if Catullus or Martial's* Epigrams *were the worse for being published.*

In these English airs, I have chiefly aimed to couple my words and notes lovingly together; which will be much for him to do that hath not power over both. The light of this, will best appear to him who hath paysed[1] our monosyllables and syllables combined: both of which, are so loaded with consonants, as that they will hardly keep company with swift notes, or give the vowel convenient liberty.

To conclude; my own opinion of these songs I deliver thus:

Omnia nec nostris bona sunt, sed nec mala libris;
Si placet hac cantes, hac quoque lege legas.

Farewell.

---

[1] Weighed.

A TABLE OF ALL THE SONGS CONTAINED
IN THESE BOOKS.

IN THE FIRST BOOK.

Songs of Four Parts.

1. Author of light.
2. The man of life upright.
3. Where are all thy beauties now?
4. Out of my soul's depth.
5. View me, Lord, a work of Thine.
6. Bravely decked come forth, bright day
7. To music bent is my retired mind.
8. Tune thy music to thy heart.
9. Most sweet and pleasing.
10. Wise men patience never want.
11. Never weather-beaten sail.
12. Lift up to heaven, sad wretch.
13. Lo, when back mine eye.
14. As by the streams of Babylon.
15. Sing a song of joy.
16. Awake, [awake,] thou heavy sprite.

Songs of Three Parts.

17. Come, cheerful day.
18. Seek the Lord.
19. Lighten, heavy heart, thy sprite.
20. Jack and Joan they think no ill.

Songs of Two Parts.

21. All looks be pale.

IN THE SECOND BOOK.

Songs of Three Parts.

1. Vain men whose follies.
2. How easily wert thou chained.
3. Harden now thy tired heart.
4. O what unhoped-for sweet supply.
5. Where she her sacred bower adorns.
6. Fain would I my love disclose.
7. Give Beauty all her right.
8. O, dear, that I with thee.
9. Good men, shew if you can tell.
10. What harvest half so sweet is.
11. Sweet, exclude me not.
12. The peaceful western wind.
13. There is none, O none but you.
14. Pined I am and like to die.
15. So many loves have I neglected.
16. Though your strangeness.
17. Come away, armed with love's.
18. Come, you pretty false-eyed.
19. A secret love or two.
20. Her rosy cheeks.

Songs of Two Parts.

21. Where shall I refuge seek?

A UTHOR of light, revive my dying sprite !
  Redeem it from the snares of all-confounding
    night !
  Lord, light me to Thy blessed way !
For blind with worldly vain desires, I wander as a
    stray.[1]
Sun and moon, stars and under-lights I see ;
But all their glorious beams are mists and darkness,
    being compared to Thee.

Fountain of health, my soul's deep wounds recure ![2]
Sweet showers of pity rain, wash my uncleanness pure !
  One drop of Thy desired grace
The faint and fading heart can raise, and in joy's bosom
    place.
  Sin and death, hell and tempting fiends may rage,
But God His own will guard, and their sharp pains
    and grief in time assuage.

T HE[3] man of life upright,
    Whose cheerful mind is free
From weight of impious deeds
  And yoke of vanity ;

[1] Cf. Drayton's *The Crier* :—

> "If you my heart do see,
> Either impound it for a *stray*
> Or send it back to me."

[2] Cure.

[3] We have already had this poem with some textual variations
(pp. 20-1).

The man whose silent days
   In harmless joys are spent,
Whom hopes cannot delude
   Nor sorrows discontent ;

That man needs neither towers,
   Nor armour for defence,
Nor vaults his guilt to shroud
   From thunder's violence ;

He only can behold
   With unaffrighted eyes
The horrors of the deep
   And terrors of the skies.

Thus, scorning all the cares
   That fate or fortune brings,
His book the heavens he makes,
   His wisdom heavenly things ;

Good thoughts his surest friends,
   His wealth a well-spent age,
The earth his sober inn
   And quiet pilgrimage.

WHERE are all thy beauties now, all hearts
      enchaining?
Whither are thy flatterers gone with all their feigning ?
All fled ! and thou alone still here remaining !

Thy rich state of twisted gold to bays is turned !
Cold, as thou art, are thy loves, that so much burned !
Who die in flatterers' arms are seldom mourned.

Yet, in spite of envy, this be still proclaimed,
That none worthier than thyself thy worth hath blamed ;
When their poor names are lost, thou shalt live famed.

When thy story, long time hence, shall be perused,
Let the blemish of thy rule be thus excused,
" None ever lived more just, none more abused."

O UT of my soul's depth to Thee my cries have
      sounded :
Let Thine ears my plaints receive, on just fear grounded.
Lord, shouldst Thou weigh our faults, who's not con-
      founded ?

But with grace Thou censurest Thine when they have
      erred,
Therefore shall Thy blessed Name be loved and
      feared.
Even to Thy throne my thoughts and eyes are reared.

Thee alone my hopes attend, on Thee relying ;
In Thy sacred word I'll trust, to Thee fast flying,
Long ere the watch shall break, the morn descrying.

In the mercies of our God who live secured,
May of full redemption rest in Him assured :
Their sin-sick souls by Him shall be recured.

VIEW me, Lord, a work of Thine :
　　Shall I then lie drowned in night ?
Might Thy grace in me but shine,
I should seem made all of light.

But my soul still surfeits so
On the poisoned baits of sin,
That I strange and ugly grow,
All is dark and foul within.

Cleanse me, Lord, that I may kneel
At thine altar, pure and white :
They that once Thy mercies feel,
Gaze no more on earth's delight.

Worldly joys, like shadows, fade
When the heavenly light appears ;
But the covenants Thou hast made,
Endless, know nor days nor years.

In Thy Word, Lord, is my trust,
To Thy mercies fast I fly ;
Though I am but clay and dust,
Yet Thy grace can lift me high.

BRAVELY decked, come forth, bright day !
Thine hours with roses strew thy way,
    As they well remember.
Thou received shalt be with feasts :
Come, chiefest of the British guests,
    Thou Fifth of November !
Thou with triumph shalt exceed
    In the strictest Ember ;
For by thy return the Lord records His blessed deed.

Britons, frolic at your board !
But first sing praises to the Lord
    In your congregations.
He preserved your State alone,
His loving grace hath made you one
    Of his chosen nations.
But this light must hallowed be
    With your best oblations :
Praise the Lord ! for only great and merciful is He.

Death had entered in the gate,
And Ruin was crept near the State ;
    But Heaven all revealed.
Fiery powder hell did make
Which, ready long the flame to take,
    Lay in shade concealed.
God us helped, of His free grace :
    None to him appealed ;
For none was so bad to fear the treason or the place.

God His peaceful monarch chose,
To him the mist He did disclose,
      To him, and none other :
This He did, O King, for thee,
That thou thine own renown might'st see,
      Which no time can smother.
May blest Charles, thy comfort be,
      Firmer than his brother :
May his heart the love of peace and wisdom learn
   from thee !

TO music bent, is my retired mind,
   And fain would I some song of pleasure sing ;
But in vain joys no comfort now I find,
   From heavenly thoughts, all true delight doth spring :
Thy power, O God, Thy mercies, to record,
Will sweeten every note and every word.

All earthly pomp or beauty to express,
   Is but to carve in snow, on waves to write ;
Celestial things, though men conceive them less,
   Yet fullest are they in themselves of light :
Such beams they yield as know no means to die,
Such heat they cast as lifts the spirit high.

TUNE thy music to thy heart,
   Sing thy joy with thanks and so thy sorrow :
   Though Devotion needs not Art,
Sometimes of the poor the rich may borrow.

Strive not yet for curious ways :
Concord pleaseth more, the less 'tis strained ;
Zeal affects not outward praise,
Only strives to show a love unfeigned.

Love can wondrous things effect,
Sweetest sacrifice all wrath appeasing ;
Love the Highest doth respect ;
Love alone to Him is ever pleasing.

MOST sweet and pleasing are thy ways, O God,
Like meadows decked with crystal streams
and flowers :
Thy paths no foot profane hath ever trod,
Nor hath the proud man rested in Thy bowers :
There lives no vulture, no devouring bear,
But only doves and lambs are harboured there.

The wolf his young ones to their prey doth guide ;
The fox his cubs with false deceit endues ;
The lion's whelp sucks from his dam his pride ;
In hers the serpent malice doth infuse :
The darksome desert all such beasts contains,
Not one of them in Paradise remains.

WISE men patience never want ;
Good men pity cannot hide ;
Feeble spirits only vaunt
Of revenge, the poorest pride :
He alone, forgive that can,
Bears the true soul of a man.

Some there are, debate that seek,
　　Making trouble their content,
Happy if they wrong the meek,
　　Vex them that to peace are bent :
Such undo the common tie
Of mankind, Society.

Kindness grown is, lately, cold ;
　　Conscience hath forgot her part ;
Blessed times were known of old,
　　Long ere Law became an Art :
Shame deterred, not Statutes then,
Honest love was law to men.

Deeds from love, and words, that flow,
　　Foster like kind April showers ;
In the warm sun all things grow,
　　Wholesome fruits and pleasant flowers :
All so thrives his gentle rays,
Whereon human love displays.

NEVER weather-beaten sail more willing bent to
　　shore,
Never tired pilgrim's limbs affected slumber more,
Than my wearied sprite now longs to fly out of my
　　troubled breast.
O come quickly, sweetest Lord, and take my soul to
　　rest !

Ever blooming are the joys of heaven's high Paradise,
Cold age deafs not there our ears nor vapour dims our
    eyes :
Glory there the sun outshines; whose beams the
    Blessed only see.
O come quickly, glorious Lord, and raise my sprite to
    Thee !

L IFT up to heaven, sad wretch, thy heavy sprite !
   What though thy sins, thy due destruction threat?
The Lord exceeds in mercy as in might ;
His ruth is greater, though thy crimes be great.
Repentance needs not fear the heaven's just rod,
It stays even thunder in the hand of God.

With cheerful voice to Him then cry for grace !
Thy Faith and fainting Hope with Prayer revive ;
Remorse[1] for all that truly mourn hath place ;
Not God, but men of Him themselves deprive :
Strive then, and He will help ; call Him He'll hear :
The son needs not the father's fury fear.

L O, when back mine eye,
   Pilgrim-like, I cast,
What fearful ways I spy,
Which, blinded, I securely past !

---

[1] Pity.

But now heaven hath drawn
   From my brows that night ;
As when the day doth dawn,
So clears my long imprisoned sight.

Straight the caves of hell,
   Dressed with flowers I see :
Wherein false pleasures dwell,
That, winning most, most deadly be.

Throngs of masked fiends,
   Winged like angels, fly :
Even in the gates of friends
In fair disguise black dangers lie.

Straight to heaven I raised
   My restored sight,
And with loud voice I praised
The Lord of ever-during light.

And since I had strayed
   From His ways so wide,
His grace I humbly prayed
Henceforth to be my guard and guide.

AS by the streams of Babylon
   Far from our native soil we sat,
Sweet Sion, thee we thought upon,
And every thought a tear begat.

Aloft the trees, that spring up there,
Our silent harps we pensive hung :
Said they that captived us, " Let's hear
Some song, which you in Sion sung ! "

Is then the song of our God fit
To be profaned in foreign land ?
O Salem, thee when I forget,
Forget his skill may my right hand !

Fast to the roof cleave may my tongue,
If mindless I of thee be found !
Or if, when all my joys are sung,
Jerusalem be not the ground ! [1]

Remember, Lord, how Edom's race
Cried in Jerusalem's sad day,
" Hurl down her walls, her towers deface,
And, stone by stone, all level lay ! "

Curst Babel's seed ! for Salem's sake
Just ruin yet for thee remains !
Blest shall they be thy babes that take
And 'gainst the stones dash out their brains !

S ING a song of joy !
    Praise our God with mirth !
His flock who can destroy ?
Is He not Lord of heaven and earth ?

---

[1] A musical term,—the air on which variations were played.

Sing we then secure,
   Tuning well our strings !
With voice, as echo pure,
Let us renown the King of Kings !

First who taught the day
   From the East to rise?
Whom doth the sun obey
When in the seas his glory dies ?

He the stars directs
   That in order stand :
Who heaven and earth protects
But He that framed them with His hand ?

Angels round attend,
   Waiting on His will ;
Armed millions He doth send
To aid the good or plague the ill.

All that dread His name,
   And His 'hests observe,
His arm will shield from shame :
Their steps from truth shall never swerve.

Let us then rejoice,
   Sounding loud His praise :
So will He hear our voice
And bless on earth our peaceful days.

AWAKE, awake, thou heavy sprite,
   That sleep'st the deadly sleep of sin !
Rise now and walk the ways of light !
   'Tis not too late yet to begin.
Seek heaven early, seek it late :
True Faith still finds an open gate.

Get up, get up, thou leaden man !
   Thy track to endless joy or pain
Yields but the model of a span ;
   Yet burns out thy life's lamp in vain !
One minute bounds thy bane or bliss :
Then watch and labour, while time is !

COME, cheerful day, part of my life to me :
   For while thou view'st me with thy fading light,
Part of my life doth still depart with thee,
   And I still onward haste to my last night.
Time's fatal wings do ever forward fly :
So every day we live a day we die.

But, O ye nights, ordained for barren rest,
   How are my days deprived of life in you,
When heavy sleep my soul hath dispossest,
   By feigned death life sweetly to renew !
Part of my life in that, you life deny :
So every day we live a day we die.

SEEK the Lord, and in His ways persèver !
  O faint not, but as eagles fly,
  For His steep hill is high !
Then striving gain the top and triumph ever !

When with glory there thy brows are crowned,
  New joys so shall abound in thee,
  Such sights thy soul shall see,
That worldly thoughts shall by their beams be drowned.

Farewell, World, thou mass of mere confusion !
  False light, with many shadows dimmed !
  Old witch, with new foils trimmed !
Thou deadly sleep of soul, and charmed illusion !

I the King will seek, of Kings adored ;
  Spring of light ; tree of grace and bliss,
  Whose fruit so sovereign is
That all who taste it are from death restored.

LIGHTEN, heavy heart, thy sprite,
  The joys recall that thence are fled ;
Yield thy breast some living light ;
  The man that nothing doth is dead.
Tune thy temper to these sounds,
  And quicken so thy joyless mind ;
Sloth the worst and best confounds :
  It is the ruin of mankind.

From her cave rise all distastes,
  Which unresolved Despair pursues ;
Whom soon after Violence hastes,
  Herself, ungrateful, to abuse.
Skies are cleared with stirring winds,
  Th' unmoved water moorish grows ;
Every eye much pleasure finds
  To view a stream that brightly flows.

JACK and Joan they think no ill,
  But loving live, and merry still ;
Do their week-days' work, and pray
Devoutly on the holy day :
Skip and trip it on the green,
And help to choose the Summer Queen ;
Lash out, at a country feast,
Their silver penny with the best.

Well can they judge of nappy ale,
And tell at large a winter tale ;
Climb up to the apple loft,
And turn the crabs till they be soft.
Tib is all the father's joy,
And little Tom the mother's boy.
All their pleasure is Content ;
And care, to pay their yearly rent.

Joan can call by name her cows,
And deck her windows with green boughs ;

She can wreathes and tuttyes[1] make,
And trim with plums a bridal cake.
Jack knows what brings gain or loss ;
And his long flail can stoutly toss :
Makes the hedge, which others break ;
And ever thinks what he doth speak.

Now, you courtly dames and knights,
That study only strange delights ;
Though you scorn the homespun gray,
And revel in your rich array :
Though your tongues dissemble deep,
And can your heads from danger keep ;
Yet, for all your pomp and train,
Securer lives the silly swain.

ALL looks be pale, hearts cold as stone,
For Hally now is dead and gone !
        Hally, in whose sight,
              Most sweet sight,
        All the earth late took delight.
Every eye, weep with me !
Joys drowned in tears must be.

His ivory skin, his comely hair,
His rosy cheeks, so clear and fair,
        Eyes that once did grace
              His bright face,—
        Now in him all want their place.

                    [1] Nosegays.

Eyes and hearts weep with me !
For who so kind as he ?

His youth was like an April flower,
Adorned with beauty, love, and power.
    Glory strewed his way,
        Whose wreathes gay
    Now are all turned to decay.
Then again weep with me !
None feel more cause than we.

No more may his wished sight return,
His golden lamp no more can burn.
    Quenched is all his flame ;
        His hoped fame
    Now hath left him nought but name.
For him all weep with me !
Since more him none shall see.

THE SECOND BOOK OF AIRS, CONTAINING LIGHT CONCEITS OF LOVERS.

SUCH days as wear the badge of holy red
    Are for devotion marked and sage delight ;
The vulgar low-days, undistinguished,
    Are left for labour, games, and sportful sights.

This several and so differing use of time,
    Within th' enclosure of one week we find ;
Which I resemble in my Notes and Rhyme,
    Expressing both in their peculiar kind.

Pure Hymns, such as the Seventh Day loves, do lead ;
    Grave age did justly challenge those of me :
These weekday works, in order that succeed,
    Your youth best fits ; and yours, young Lord, they be,
As he is who to them their being gave :
If th' one, the other you of force must have.
            Your Honour's
                THOMAS CAMPION.[1]

TO THE READER.

THAT holy hymns with lovers' cares are knit
    Both in one quire here, thou mayest think't unfit.
Why dost not blame the Stationer as well,
Who in the same shop sets all sorts to sell ?
Divine with styles profane, grave shelved with vain,
And some matched worse. Yet none of him complain.

    [1] Old ed. " Campian."

VAIN men, whose follies make a god of Love,
　Whose blindness beauty doth immortal deem ;
Praise not what you desire but what you prove,
Count those things good that are, not those that seem :
I cannot call her true that's false to me,
Nor make of women more than women be.

How fair an entrance breaks the way to love !
How rich of golden hope and gay delight !
What heart cannot a modest beauty move?
Who, seeing clear day once, will dream of night ?
She seemed a saint, that brake her faith with me,
But proved a woman as all other be.

So bitter is their sweet that true content
Unhappy men in them may never find :
Ah ! but without them none.　Both must concent,
Else uncouth are the joys of either kind.
Let us then praise their good, forget their ill !
Men must be men, and women women still.

HOW eas'ly wert thou chained,
    Fond heart, by favours feigned !
Why lived thy hopes in grace,
Straight to die disdained ?
But since th' art now beguiled
By love that falsely smiled,
In some less happy place
Mourn alone exiled !
My love still here increaseth,
And with my love my grief,
While her sweet bounty ceaseth,
That gave my woes relief.
Yet 'tis no woman leaves me,
For such may prove unjust ;
A goddess thus deceives me,
Whose faith who could mistrust ?

A goddess so much graced,
That Paradise is placed
In her most heav'nly breast,
Once by love embraced :
But love, that so kind proved,
Is now from her removed,
Nor will he longer rest
Where no faith is loved.
If powers celestial wound us
And will not yield relief,
Woe then must needs confound us,
For none can cure our grief.

No wonder if I languish
Through burden of my smart :
It is no common anguish
From Paradise to part.

HARDEN now thy tired heart, with more than
flinty rage !
Ne'er let her false tears henceforth thy constant grief
assuage !
Once true happy days thou saw'st when she stood firm
and kind,
Both as one then lived and held one ear, one tongue,
one mind :
But now those bright hours be fled, and never may
return ;
What then remains but her untruths to mourn ?

Silly trait'ress, who shall now thy careless tresses place ?
Who thy pretty talk supply, whose ear thy music grace ?
Who shall thy bright eyes admire ? what lips triumph
with thine ?
Day by day who'll visit thee and say " Th'art only
mine " ?
Such a time there was, God wot, but such shall never
be :
Too oft, I fear, thou wilt remember me.

O WHAT unhoped for sweet supply !
　　O what joys exceeding !
What an affecting charm feel I,
　　From delight proceeding !
That which I long despaired to be,
To her I am, and she to me.

She that alone in cloudy grief
　　Long to me appeared :
She now alone with bright relief
　　All those clouds hath cleared.
Both are immortal and divine :
Since I am hers, and she is mine.

WHERE she her sacred bower adorns,
　　The rivers clearly flow ;
The groves and meadows swell with flowers,
　　The winds all gently blow.
Her sun-like beauty shines so fair,
　　Her spring can never fade :
Who then can blame the life that strives
　　To harbour in her shade ?

Her grace I sought, her love I wooed,
　　Her love thought to [1] obtain ;
No time, no toil, no vow, no faith,
　　Her wished grace can gain.

　　　　　[1] Old ed. " though I."

Yet truth can tell my heart is hers,
    And her will I adore ;
And from that love when I depart,
    Let heaven view me no more !

Her roses with my praye[r]s shall spring ;
    And when her trees I praise,
Their boughs shall blossom, mellow fruit
    Shall straw [1] her pleasant ways.
The words of hearty zeal have power
    High wonders to effect ;
O why should then her princely ear
    My words or zeal neglect?

If she my faith misdeems, or worth,
    Woe worth my hapless fate !
For though time can my truth reveal,
    That time will come too late.
And who can glory in the worth,
    That cannot yield him grace?
Content in everything is not,
    Nor joy in every place.

But from her bower of joy since I
    Must now excluded be,
And she will not relieve my cares,
    Which none can help but she ;
My comfort in her love shall dwell,
    Her love lodge in my breast,
And though not in her bower, yet I
    Shall in her temple rest.

    [1] Old form of "strew."

FAIN would I my love disclose,
　　Ask what honour might deny ;
But both love and her I lose,
From my motion if she fly.
Worse than pain is fear to me :
Then hold in fancy though it burn !
If not happy, safe I'll be,
And to my cloistered cares return.

Yet, O yet, in vain I strive
To repress my schooled desire ;
More and more the flames revive,
I consume in mine own fire.
She would pity, might she know
The harms that I for her endure :
Speak then, and get comfort so ;
A wound long hid grows past [1] recure.

Wise she is, and needs must know
All th' attempts that beauty moves :
Fair she is, and honoured so
That she, sure, hath tried some loves.
If with love I tempt her then,
'Tis but her due to be desired :
What would women think of men
If their deserts were not admired ?

[1] Old ed. "most."

Women, courted, have the hand
To discard what they distaste :
But those dames whom none demand
Want oft what their wills embraced.
Could their firmness iron excel,
As they are fair, they should be sought :
When true thieves use falsehood well,
As they are wise they will be caught.

G IVE beauty all her right,
  She's not to one form tied ;
Each shape yields fair delight,
  Where her perfections 'bide.
Helen, I grant, might pleasing be ;
And Ros'mond was as sweet as she.

Some the quick eye commends ;
Some swelling [1] lips and red ;
Pale looks have many friends,
  Through sacred sweetness bred.
Meadows have flowers that pleasure move,
Though roses are the flowers of love.

Free beauty is not bound
To one unmoved clime :
She visits every ground,
  And favours every time.
Let the old loves with mine compare,
My Sovereign is as sweet and fair.

[1] Old ed. "smelling."

O DEAR ! that I with thee might live,
　　From human trace removed !
Where jealous care might neither grieve,
　　Yet each dote on their loved.
While fond fear may colour find, love's seldom pleased ;
But much like a sick man's rest, it's soon diseased.

Why should our minds not mingle so,
　　When love and faith is plighted,
That either might the other's know,
　　Alike in all delighted ?
Why should frailty breed suspect, when hearts are
　　fixed ?
Must all human joys of force with grief be mixed ?

How oft have we ev'n smiled in tears,
　　Our fond mistrust repenting ?
As snow when heavenly fire appears,
　　So melts love's hate relenting.
Vexed kindness soon falls off and soon returneth :
Such a flame the more you quench the more it burneth.

GOOD men, show, if you can tell,
　　Where doth Human Pity dwell ?
Far and near her I would seek,
So vext with sorrow is my breast.
" She," they say, " to all, is meek ;
And only makes th' unhappy blest."

Oh ! if such a saint there be,
Some hope yet remains for me :
Prayer or sacrifice may gain
From her implored grace relief ;
To release me of my pain,
Or at the least to ease my grief.

Young am I, and far from guile,
The more is my woe the while :
Falsehood with a smooth disguise
My simple meaning hath abused :
Casting mists before mine eyes,
By which my senses are confused.

Fair he is, who vowed to me
That he only mine would be ;
But, alas, his mind is caught
With every gaudy bait he sees :
And too late my flame is taught
That too much kindness makes men freeze.

From me all my friends are gone,
While I pine for him alone ;
And not one will rue my case,
But rather my distress deride :
That I think there is no place
Where Pity ever yet did bide.

WHAT harvest half so sweet is
  As still to reap the kisses
 Grown ripe in sowing?
And straight to be receiver
Of that which thou art giver,
  Rich in bestowing?
Kiss then, my Harvest Queen,
  Full garners heaping!
Kisses, ripest when th' are green,
  Want only reaping.

The dove alone expresses
Her fervency in kisses,
  Of all most loving:
A creature as offenceless
As those things that are senseless
  And void of moving.
Let us so love and kiss,
  Though all envy us:
That which kind, and harmless is,
  None can deny us.

SWEET, exclude me not, nor be divided
  From him that ere long must bed thee:
All thy maiden doubts law hath decided;
  Sure [1] we are, and I must wed thee.

---

[1] Affianced.

Presume then yet a little more :
Here's the way, bar not the door.

Tenants, to fulfil their landlord's pleasure,
    Pay their rent before the quarter :
'Tis my case, if you it rightly measure ;
    Put me not then off with laughter.
Consider then a little more :
Here's the way to all my store.

Why were doors in love's despight devised ?
    Are not laws enough restraining ?
Women are most apt to be surprised
    Sleeping, or sleep wisely feigning.
Then grace me yet a little more :
Here's the way, bar not the door.

T HE peaceful western wind
    The winter storms hath tamed,
And Nature in each kind
The kind heat hath inflamed :
The forward buds so sweetly breathe
    Out of their earthy bowers,
That heaven, which views their pomp beneath,
    Would fain be decked with flowers.

See how the morning smiles
On her bright eastern hill,
And with soft steps beguiles
Them that lie slumbering still !

The music-loving birds are come
 From cliffs and rocks unknown,
To see the trees and briars bloom
 That late were overthrown.[1]

 What Saturn did destroy,
 Love's Queen revives again ;
 And now her naked boy
 Doth in the fields remain,
Where he such pleasing change doth view
 In every living thing,
As if the world were born anew
 To gratify the spring.

 If all things life present,
 Why die my comforts then ?
 Why suffers my content ?
 Am I the worst of men ?
O, Beauty, be not thou accused
 Too justly in this case !
Unkindly if true love be used,
 'Twill yield thee little grace.

THERE is none, O none but you,
 That from me estrange your sight,
Whom mine eyes affect to view
 Or chained ears hear with delight.

---

[1] Old ed. " ouer-flowne."

Other beauties others move,
   In you I all graces find ;
Such is the effect of love,
   To make them happy that are kind.

Women in frail beauty trust,
   Only seem you fair to me ;
Yet prove truly kind and just,
   For that may not dissembled be.

Sweet, afford me then your sight,
   That, surveying all your looks,
Endless volumes I may write
   And fill the world with envied books :

Which when after-ages view,
   All shall wonder and despair,
Woman to find man so true,
   Or man a woman half so fair.

PINED I am and like to die,
   And all for lack of that which I
   Do every day refuse.
If I musing sit or stand,
Some puts it daily in my hand,
   To interrupt my muse :
The same thing I seek and fly,
And want that which none would deny.

In my bed, when I should rest,
It breeds such trouble in my breast

That scarce mine eyes will close ;
If I sleep it seems to be
Oft playing in the bed with me,
　　But, waked, away it goes.
'Tis some spirit sure, I ween,
And yet it may be felt and seen.

Would I had the heart and wit
To make it stand and conjure it,
　　That haunts me thus with fear.
Doubtless 'tis some harmless sprite,
For it by day as well as night
　　Is ready to appear.
Be it friend, or be it foe,
Ere long I'll try what it will do.

SO many loves have I neglected
　　Whose good parts might move me,
That now I live of all rejected ;
　　There is none will love me.
Why is maiden heat so coy ?
　　It freezeth when it burneth,
Loseth what it might enjoy,
　　And, having lost it, mourneth.

Should I then woo, that have been wooed,
　　Seeking them that fly me ?
When I my faith with tears have vowed,
　　And when all deny me,

Who will pity my disgrace,
  Which love might have prevented?
There is no submission base
  Where error is repented.

O happy men, whose hopes are licensed
  To discourse their passion,
While women are confined to silence,
  Losing wished occasion !
Yet our tongues than theirs, men say,
  Are apter to be moving :
Women are more dumb than they,
  But in their thoughts more moving.

When I compare my former strangeness
  With my present doting,
I pity men that speak in plainness,
  Their true heart's devoting ;
While we (with repentance) jest
  At their submissive passion.
Maids, I see, are never blest
  That strange be but for fashion.

THOUGH[1] your strangeness frets my heart,
  Yet may not I complain :
You persuade me, 'tis but art,
  That secret love must feign.
If another you affect,
  'Tis but a show, t'avoid suspect.
Is this fair excusing? O, no ! all is abusing !

---

[1] This song is printed, with some textual variations, in Robert
Jones' *Musical Dream*, 1609. See *Lyrics from Elizabethan Song-
Books* (1887), pp. 134-5.

Your wished sight if I desire,
Suspicions you pretend :
Causeless you yourself retire,
While I in vain attend.
This a lover whets, you say,
Still made more eager by delay.
Is this fair excusing? O, no ! all is abusing !

When another holds your hand,
You swear I hold your heart :
When my rivals close do stand,
And I sit far apart,
I am nearer yet than they,
Hid in your bosom, as you say.
Is this fair excusing? O, no ! all is abusing !

Would my rival then I were,
Or [1] else your secret friend :
So much lesser should I fear,
And not so much attend.
They enjoy you, every one,
Yet I must seem your friend alone.
Is this fair excusing? O, no ! all is abusing !

COME away, armed with love's delights !
　　Thy spriteful graces bring with thee !
When love and longing fights,
　　They must the sticklers be.

[1] Old ed. "Some."

Come quickly, come ! the promised hour is well-nigh
    spent,
And pleasure being too much deferred, loseth her best
    content.

    Is she come ? O, how near is she !
        How far yet from this friendly place !
    How many steps from me !
        When shall I her embrace ?
These arms I'll spread, which only at her sight shall
    close,
Attending as the starry flower that the sun's noontide
    knows.

COME, you pretty false-eyed wanton,
    Leave your crafty smiling !
Think you to escape me now
    With slipp'ry words beguiling !
No ; you mocked me th'other day ;
    When you got loose, you fled away ;
But, since I have caught you now,
    I'll clip your wings for flying :
Smoth'ring kisses fast I'll heap,
    And keep you so from crying.

Sooner may you count the stars,
    And number hail down pouring,
Tell the osiers of the Thames,
    Or Goodwin sands devouring,

Than the thick-showered kisses here
  Which now thy tired lips must bear.
Such a harvest never was,
  So rich and full of pleasure,
But 'tis spent as soon as reaped,
  So trustless is love's treasure.

Would it were dumb midnight now,
  When all the world lies sleeping !
Would this place some desert were,
  Which no man hath in keeping !
My desires should then be safe,
  And when you cried then would I laugh :
But if aught might breed offence,
  Love only should be blamed :
I would live your servant still,
  And you my saint unnamed.

A SECRET love or two I must confess
    I kindly welcome for change in close playing,
Yet my dear husband I love ne'ertheless,
  His desires, whole or half, quickly allaying,
At all times ready to offer redress :
  His own he never wants but hath it duly,
  Yet twits me I keep not touch with him truly.

The more a spring is drawn the more it flows,
  No lamp less light retains by light'ning others :
Is he a loser his loss that ne'er knows ?
  Or is he wealthy that waste treasure smothers ?

My churl vows no man shall scent his sweet rose :
  His own enough and more I give him duly,
  Yet still he twits me I keep not touch truly.

Wise archers bear more than one shaft to field,
  The venturer loads not with one ware his shipping ;
Should warriors learn but one weapon to wield,
  Or thrive fair plants e'er the worse for the slipping ?
One dish cloys, many fresh appetite yield.
  Mine own I'll use, and his he shall have duly,
  Judge then what debtor can keep touch more truly.

H ER rosy cheeks, her ever-smiling eyes,
    Are spheres and beds where Love in triumph
      lies :
Her rubine lips, when they their pearl unlock,
Make them seem as they did rise
All out of one smooth coral rock.
O that of other creatures' store I knew
More worthy and more rare !
For these are old, and she so new,
That her to them none should compare.

O could she love ! would she but hear a friend !
Or that she only knew what sighs pretend !
Her looks inflame, yet cold as ice is she.
Do or speak, all's to one end,
For what she is that will she be.
Yet will I never cease her praise to sing,
Though she gives no regard :
For they that grace a worthless thing
Are only greedy of reward.

WHERE shall I refuge seek, if you refuse me?
In you my hope, in you my fortune lies,
In you my life ! though you unjust accuse me,
My service scorn, and merit underprize :
O bitter grief ! that exile is become
Reward for faith, and pity deaf and dumb !

Why should my firmness find a seat so wav'ring ?
My simple vows, my love you entertained ;
Without desert the same again disfav'ring ;
Yet I my word and passion hold unstained.
O wretched me ! that my chief joy should breed
My only grief and kindness pity need !

FINIS.

The Third and Fourth Booke of Ayres : Composed by Thomas Campian. So as they may be expressed by one Voyce, with a Violl, Lute, or Orpharion. London : Printed by Thomas Snodham. Cum Priuilegio. n. d. [circ. 1617.] fol.

A TABLE OF ALL THE SONGS CONTAINED IN THE TWO BOOKS FOLLOWING.

The Table of the First Book.

1. Oft have I sighed.
2. Now let her change.
3. Were my heart as.
4. Maids are simple, some men say.
5. So tired are all my thoughts.
6. Why presumes thy pride?
7. Kind are her answers.
8. O grief, O spite!
9. O never to be moved.
10. Break now, my heart and die.
11. If Love loves truth.
12. Now winter nights enlarge.
13. Awake, thou spring.
14. What is it [all] that men possess?
15. Fire that must flame.
16. If thou long'st so much.
17. Shall I come, sweet love?
18. Thrice toss these oaken.
19. Be thou then my Beauty.
20. Fire, fire, fire, fire I lo, here.
21. O sweet delight.
22. Thus I resolve.
23. Come, O come, my life's.
24. Could my heart more.
25. Sleep, angry beauty.
26. Silly boy, 'tis full moon yet.
27. Never love unless you can.
28. So quick, so hot.
29. Shall I then hope.

The Table of the Second Book.

1. Leave prolonging.
2. Respect my faith.
3. Thou joy'st, fond boy.
4. Veil, love, mine eyes.
5. Every dame affects good fame.
6. So sweet is thy discourse.
7. There is a garden in her face.
8. To his sweet lute.
9. Young and simple though I am.
10. Love me or not.
11. What means this folly?
12. Dear, if I with guile.
13. O Love, where are thy shafts?
14. Beauty is but a painted hell.
15. Are you what your?
16. Since she, even she.
17. I must complain.
18. Think'st thou to seduce.
19. Her fair inflaming eyes.
20. Turn all thy thoughts.
21. If any hath the heart to kill.
22. Beauty, since you.
23. Your fair looks.
24. Fain would I wed.

TO MY HONOURABLE FRIEND, SIR THOMAS MOUNSON, KNIGHT AND BARONET.

SINCE now these clouds, that lately over-cast
Your fame and fortune, are dispersed at last :
And now since all to you fair greetings make ;
Some out of love, and some for pity's sake :
Shall I but with a common style salute
Your new enlargement? or stand only mute?
I, to whose trust and care you durst commit
Your pined health, when art despaired of it?
I, that in your affliction often viewed
In you the fruits of manly fortitude,
Patience, and even constancy of mind
That rock-like stood, and scorned both wave and
      wind?
Should I, for all your ancient love to me,
Endowed with weighty favours, silent be?
Your merits and my gratitude forbid
That either should in Lethean gulf lie hid ;
But how shall I this work of fame express?
How can I better, after pensiveness,
Than with light strains of Music, made to move
Sweetly with the wide spreading plumes of Love?
These youth-born Airs, then, prisoned in this book,
Which in your bowers much of their being took,
Accept as a kind offering from that hand
Which, joined with heart, your virtue may command !

Who love a sure friend, as all good men do,
Since such you are, let those affect you too.
And may the joys of that Crown never end,
That innocence doth pity and defend.

Yours devoted,

THOMAS CAMPION.[1]

OFT have I sighed for him that hears me not ;
Who absent hath both love and me forgot.
O yet I languish still through his delay :
Days seem as years when wished friends break their
day.

Had he but loved as common lovers use,
His faithless stay some kindness would excuse :
O yet I languish still, still constant mourn
For him that can break vows but not return.

NOW let her change and spare not !
Since she proves strange I care not :
Feigned love charmed so my delight
That still I doted on her sight.
But she is gone, new joys embracing
And my desires disgracing.

[1] Old ed. "Campian."

When did I err in blindness,
Or vex her with unkindness ?
If my cares served her alone,
Why is she thus untimely gone ?
True love abides to th' hour of dying :
False love is ever flying.

False ! then, farewell for ever !
Once false proves faithful never :
He that boasts now of thy love,
Shall soon my present fortunes prove.
Were he as fair as bright Adonis,
Faith is not had, where none is.

WERE my heart as some men's are, thy errors
would not move me ;
But thy faults I curious find and speak because I love
thee :
Patience is a thing divine and far, I grant, above me.

Foes sometimes befriend us more, our blacker deeds
objecting,
Than th' obsequious bosom guest, with false respect
affecting.
Friendship is the Glass of Truth, our hidden stains
detecting.

While I use of eyes enjoy and inward light of reason,
Thy observer will I be and censor, but in season :
Hidden mischief to conceal in State and Love is
treason.

" MAIDS are simple," some men say,
    "They, forsooth, will trust no men."
But should they men's wills obey,
Maids were very simple then.

Truth, a rare flower now is grown,
Few men wear it in their hearts ;
Lovers are more easily known
By their follies than deserts.

Safer may we credit give
To a faithless wandering Jew
Than a young man's vows believe
When he swears his love is true.

Love they make a poor blind child,
But let none trust such as he :
Rather than to be beguiled,
Ever let me simple be.

SO tired are all my thoughts, that sense and spirits
        fail :
Mourning I pine, and know not what I ail.
O what can yield ease to a mind
            Joy in nothing that can find ?

How are my powers fore-spoke? What strange dis-
    taste is this?
Hence, cruel hate of that which sweetest is!
Come, come delight! make my dull brain
        Feel once heat of joy again.

The lover's tears are sweet, their mover makes them
    so;
Proud of a wound the bleeding soldiers grow.
Poor I alone, dreaming, endure
        Grief that knows nor cause nor cure.

And whence can all this grow? even from an idle mind,
That no delight in any good can find.
Action alone makes the soul blest:
        Virtue dies with too much rest.

WHY presumes thy pride on that that must so
        private be,
Scarce that it can good be called, though it seems best
    to thee,
Best of all that Nature framed or curious eye can see?

'Tis thy beauty, foolish Maid, that like a blossom,
    grows;
Which who views no more enjoys than on a bush a
    rose,
That, by many's handling, fades: and thou art one of
    those.

If to one thou shalt prove true and all beside reject,
Then art thou but one man's good ; which yields a poor
    effect :
For the commonest good by far deserves the best
    respect.

But if for this goodness thou thyself wilt common
    make,
Thou art then not good at all : so thou canst no way
    take
But to prove the meanest good or else all good forsake.

Be not then of beauty proud, but so her colours bear
That they prove not stains to her, that them for grace
    should wear :
So shalt thou to all more fair than thou wert born
    appear.

KIND are her answers,
    But her performance keeps no day ;
Breaks time, as dancers
From their own music when they stray.
All her free favours and smooth words,
    Wing my hopes in vain.
O did ever voice so sweet but only feign ?
    Can true love yield such delay,
    Converting joy to pain ?

Lost is our freedom,
When we submit to women so :
Why do we need them
When, in their best they work our woe?
There is no wisdom
Can alter ends, by Fate prefixt.
O why is the good of man with evil mixt ?
Never were days yet called two,
But one night went betwixt.

O GRIEF, O spite, to see poor Virtue scorned,
     Truth far exiled, False Art loved, Vice adored,
Free Justice sold, worst causes best adorned,
     Right cast by Power, Pity in vain implored !
O who in such an age could wish to live,
When none can have or hold, but such as give?

O times, O men to Nature rebels grown,
     Poor in desert, in name rich, proud of shame,
Wise but in ill ! Your styles are not your own
     Though dearly bought ; Honour is honest fame.
Old stories, only, goodness now contain,
And the true wisdom that is just and plain.

O NEVER to be moved,
    O beauty unrelenting !
Hard heart, too dearly loved !
Fond love, too late repenting !

Why did I dream of too much bliss?
Deceitful hope was cause of this.
　　O hear me speak this, and no more,
　　"Live you in joy, while I my woes deplore!"

　　All comforts despaired
　　Distaste your bitter scorning;
Great sorrows unrepaired
　　Admit no mean in mourning:
Die, wretch, since hope from thee is fled.
He that must die, is better dead.
　　O dear delight yet, ere I die,
　　Some pity show, though you relief deny!

　　　　　　✦

BREAK now, my heart, and die! O no, she may
　　　relent.
Let my despair prevail! O stay, hope is not spent.
Should she now fix one smile on thee, where were
　　despair?
　　The loss is but easy, which smiles can repair.
　　A stranger would please thee, if she were as fair.

Her must I love or none, so sweet none breathes as
　　she;
The more is my despair, alas, she loves not me!
But cannot time make way for love through ribs of
　　steel?
　　The Grecian, enchanted all parts but the heel,
　　At last a shaft daunted, which his heart did feel.

IF love loves truth, then women do not love ;
    Their passions all are but dissembled shows ;
Now kind and free of favour if they prove,
    Their kindness straight a tempest overthrows.
Then as a seaman the poor lover fares ;
The storm drowns him ere he can drown his cares.

But why accuse I women that deceive ?
    Blame then the foxes for their subtle wile :
They first from Nature did their craft receive :
    It is a woman's nature to beguile.
Yet some, I grant, in loving steadfast grow ;
But such by use are made, not Nature, so.

O why had Nature power at once to frame
    Deceit and Beauty, traitors both to Love?
O would Deceit had died when Beauty came
    With her divineness every heart to move !
Yet do we rather wish, whate'er befall,
To have fair women false than none at all.

NOW winter nights enlarge
    The number of their hours ;
And clouds their storms discharge
Upon the airy towers.

Let now the chimneys blaze
And cups o'erflow with wine,
Let well-tuned words amaze
With harmony divine !
Now yellow waxen lights
Shall wait on honey love
While youthful revels, masques, and Courtly sights,
Sleep's leaden spells remove.

This time doth well dispense
With lovers' long discourse ;
Much speech hath some defence,
Though beauty no remorse.
All do not all things well ;
Some measures comely tread,
Some knotted riddles tell,
Some poems smoothly read.
The summer hath his joys,
And winter his delights ;
Though love and all his pleasures are but toys,
They shorten tedious nights.

AWAKE, thou spring of speaking grace ! mute rest
becomes not thee !
The fairest women, while they sleep, and pictures,
equal be.
O come and dwell in love's discourses !
Old renewing, new creating.
The words which thy rich tongue discourses,
Are not of the common rating !

Thy voice is as an Echo clear which Music doth beget,
Thy speech is as an Oracle which none can counterfeit :
  For thou alone, without offending,
   Hast obtained power of enchanting ;
  And I could hear thee without ending,
   Other comfort never wanting.

Some little reason brutish lives with human glory share ;
But language is our proper grace, from which they
  severed are.
  As brutes in reason man surpasses,
   Men in speech excel each other :
  If speech be then the best of graces,
   Do it not in slumber smother !

WHAT is it all that men possess, among themselves
   conversing ?
Wealth or fame, or some such boast, scarce worthy the
  rehearsing.
Women only are men's good, with them in love conversing.

If weary, they prepare us rest ; if sick, their hand attends
  us ;
When with grief our hearts are prest, their comfort best
  befriends us :
Sweet or sour, they willing go to share what fortune
  sends us.

What pretty babes with pain they bear, our name and
    form presenting !
What we get, how wise they keep ! by sparing, wants
    preventing ;
Sorting all their household cares to our observed con-
    tenting.

All this, of whose large use I sing, in two words is
    expressed :
Good Wife is the good I praise, if by good men
    possessed ;
Bad with bad in ill suit well ; but good with good live
    blessed.

FIRE that must flame is with apt fuel fed,
    Flowers that will thrive in sunny soil are bred.
How can a heart feel heat that no hope finds ?
Or can he love on whom no comfort shines ?

Fair ! I confess there's pleasure in your sight !
Sweet ! you have power, I grant, of all delight !
But what is all to me, if I have none ?
Churl, that you are, t'enjoy such wealth alone !

Prayers move the heavens but find no grace with you ;
Yet in your looks a heavenly form I view,
Then will I pray again, hoping to find,
As well as in your looks heaven in your mind !

Saint of my heart, Queen of my life and love,
O let my vows thy loving spirit move !
Let me no longer mourn through thy disdain ;
But with one touch of grace cure all my pain.

IF thou longest so much to learn, sweet boy, what
       'tis to love,
Do but fix thy thought on me and thou shalt quickly
       prove.
       Little suit, at first, shall win
           Way to thy abashed desire,
       But then will I hedge thee in
           Salamander-like with fire !

With thee dance I will, and sing, and thy fond
       dalliance bear ;
We the grovy hills will climb, and play the wantons
       there ;
       Other whiles we'll gather flowers,
           Lying dallying on the grass !
       And thus our delightful hours
           Full of waking dreams shall pass !

When thy joys were thus at height, my love should
       turn from thee ;
Old acquaintance then should grow as strange as
       strange might be ;
       Twenty rivals thou shouldst find,
           Breaking all their hearts for me,
       While to all I'll prove more kind
           And more forward than to thee.

Thus, thy silly youth, enraged, would soon my love
    defy ;
But, alas, poor soul too late ! clipt wings can never fly.
      Those sweet hours which we had past,
          Called to mind, thy heart would burn ;
      And couldst thou fly ne'er so fast,
          They would make thee straight return.

SHALL I come, sweet love, to thee,
    When the evening beams are set ?
Shall I not excluded be ?
    Will you find no feigned let ?
Let me not, for pity, more,
Tell the long hours at your door !

Who can tell what thief or foe,
    In the covert of the night,
For his prey will work my woe,
    Or through wicked foul despite ?
So may I die unredrest,
Ere my long love be possest.

But to let such dangers pass,
    Which a lover's thoughts disdain,
'Tis enough in such a place
    To attend love's joys in vain.
Do not mock me in thy bed,
While these cold nights freeze me dead.

THRICE [1] toss these oaken ashes in the air,
　Thrice sit thou mute in this enchanted chair ;
And thrice three times, tie up this true love's knot !
And murmur soft " She will, or she will not."

Go burn these poisonous weeds in yon blue fire,
These screech-owl's feathers and this prickling briar ;
This cypress gathered at a dead man's grave ;
That all thy fears and cares, an end may have.

Then come, you Fairies, dance with me a round !
Melt her hard heart with your melodious sound !
In vain are all the charms I can devise :
She hath an art to break them with her eyes.

[1] This poem was included in the 1633 edition of Joshua
Sylvester's works, among the "Remains never till now imprinted." Sylvester has not a shadow of claim to it. There is a
MS. copy of it in Harleian MS. 6910, fol. 150, where it is
correctly assigned to Campion. The MS. gives it in the form of
a sonnet :—

" Thrice toss those oaken ashes in the air,
And thrice three times tie up this true love's knot ;
Thrice sit you down in this enchanted chair,
And murmur soft " She will or she will not."
Go, burn those poisoned weeds in that blue fire,
This cypress gathered out a dead man's grave,
These screech-owl's feathers and the prickling briar,
That all thy thorny cares an end may have.
Then come, you fairies, dance with me a round !
Dance in a circle, let my love be centre !
Melodiously breathe an enchanted sound :
Melt her hard heart that some remorse may enter !
In vain are all the charms I can devise ;
She hath an art to break them with her eyes."

BE thou then my Beauty named,
    Since thy will is to be mine !
For by that I am enflamed,
  Which on all alike doth shine.
Others may the light admire,
I only truly feel the fire.

But if lofty titles move thee,
    Challenge then a Sovereign's place !
Say I honour when I love thee ;
    Let me call thy kindness Grace.
State and Love things diverse be,
Yet will we teach them to agree !

Or if this be not sufficing ;
    Be thou styled my Goddess then :
I will love thee, sacrificing ;
    In thine honour, hymns I'll pen.
To be thine what canst thou more ?
I'll love thee, serve thee, and adore.

FIRE, fire, fire, fire !
    Lo here I burn in such desire
That all the tears that I can strain
Out of mine idle empty brain
Cannot allay my scorching pain.

Come Trent, and Humber, and fair Thames !
Dread Ocean, haste with all thy streams !
    And if you cannot quench my fire,
    O drown both me and my desire !

    Fire, fire, fire, fire !
There is no hell to my desire.
See, all the rivers backward fly !
And th' Ocean doth his waves deny,
For fear my heat should drink them dry !
Come, heavenly showers, then, pouring down !
Come you, that once the world did drown !
Some then you spared, but now save all,
That else must burn, and with me fall !

O SWEET delight, O more than human bliss,
    With her to live that ever loving is ;
To hear her speak, whose words are so well placed,
That she by them, as they in her are graced :
Those looks to view, that feast the viewer's eye,
How blest is he that may so live and die !

Such love as this the golden times did know,
When all did reap, yet none took care to sow ;
Such love as this an endless summer makes,
And all distaste from frail affection takes.
So loved, so blessed, in my beloved am I ;
Which till their eyes ache, let iron men envy !

THUS I resolve, and time hath taught me so ;
　　Since she is fair and ever kind to me,
Though she be wild and wanton-like in show,
　　Those little stains in youth I will not see.
That she be constant, heaven I oft implore :
If prayers prevail not, I can do no more.

Palm tree the more you press, the more it grows ;
　　Leave it alone, it will not much exceed.
Free beauty if you strive to yoke, you lose :
　　And for affection, strange distaste you breed.
What Nature hath not taught, no Art can frame :
Wild born be wild still, though by force you tame.

COME, O come, my life's delight,
　　Let me not in languor pine !
Love loves no delay ; thy sight,
　　The more enjoyed, the more divine :
O come, and take from me
The pain of being deprived of thee !

Thou all sweetness dost enclose,
　　Like a little world of bliss.
Beauty guards thy looks : the rose
　　In them pure and eternal is.
Come, then, and make thy flight
As swift to me, as heavenly light.

COULD my heart more tongues employ
   Than it harbours thoughts of grief ;
It is now so far from joy,
   That it scarce could ask relief.
Truest hearts by deeds unkind
To despair are most inclined.

Happy minds, that can redeem
   Their engagements how they please !
That no joys or hopes esteem,
   Half so precious as their ease !
Wisdom should prepare men so
As if they did all foreknow.

Yet no art or caution can
   Grown affections easily change ;
Use is such a Lord of man
   That he brooks worst what is strange.
Better never to be blest
Than to lose all at the best.

SLEEP, angry beauty, sleep, and fear not me.
   For who a sleeping lion dares provoke ?
It shall suffice me here to sit and see
   Those lips shut up, that never kindly spoke.
What sight can more content a lover's mind
Than beauty seeming harmless, if not kind?

My words have charmed her, for secure she sleeps ;
  Though guilty much of wrong done to my love ;
And in her slumber, see ! she, close-eyed, weeps !
  Dreams often more than waking passions move.
Plead, Sleep, my cause, and make her soft like thee,
That she in peace may wake and pity me.

SILLY boy, 'tis full moon yet, thy night as day
      shines clearly ;
Had thy youth but wit to fear, thou couldst not love so
      dearly.
Shortly wilt thou mourn when all thy pleasures are
      bereaved ;
Little knows he how to love that never was deceived.

This is thy first maiden flame, that triumphs yet
      unstained ;
All is artless now you speak, not one word, yet, is
      feigned ;
All is heaven that you behold, and all your thoughts
      are blessed ;
But no spring can want his fall, each Troilus hath his
      Cressid.

Thy well-ordered locks ere long shall rudely hang
      neglected ;
And thy lively pleasant cheer read grief on earth
      dejected.
Much then wilt thou blame thy Saint, that made thy
      heart so holy,
And with sighs confess, in love that too much faith is
      folly.

Yet be just and constant still ! Love may beget a
    wonder,
Not unlike a summer's frost, or winter's fatal thunder.
He that holds his sweetheart true, unto his day of
    dying,
Lives, of all that ever breathed, most worthy the
    envỳing.

NEVER love unless you can
    Bear with all the faults of man :
Men sometimes will jealous be,
Though but little cause they see ;
And hang the head, as discontent,
And speak what straight they will repent.

Men that but one saint adore,
Make a show of love to more :
Beauty must be scorned in none,
Though but truly served in one :
For what is courtship, but disguise ?
True hearts may have dissembling eyes.

Men when their affairs require,
Must a while themselves retire :
Sometimes hunt, and sometimes hawk,
And not ever sit and talk.
If these, and such like you can bear,
Then like, and love, and never fear !

SO QUICK, so hot, so mad is thy fond suit,
 So rude, so tedious grown, in urging me,
That fain I would, with loss, make thy tongue mute,
 And yield some little grace to quiet thee :
An hour with thee I care not to converse,
For I would not be counted too perverse.

But roofs too hot would prove for me [1] all fire ;
 And hills too high for my unused pace ;
The grove is charged with thorns and the bold briar ;
 Grey snakes the meadows shroud in every place :
A yellow frog, alas, will fright me so,
As I should start and tremble as I go.

Since then I can on earth no fit room find,
 In heaven I am resolved with you to meet :
Till then, for hope's sweet sake, rest your tired mind
 And not so much as see me in the street :
A heavenly meeting one day we shall have,
But never, as you dream, in bed, or grave.

SHALL I then hope when faith is fled ?
 Can I seek love when hope is gone ?
 Or can I live when love is dead ?
Poorly he lives, that can love none.
  Her vows are broke and I am free ;
  She lost her faith in losing me.

---

[1] Old ed. " men."

When I compare mine own events,
When I weigh others' like annoy :
   All do but heap up discontents
That on a beauty build their joy.
       Thus I of all complain, since she
       All faith hath lost in losing me.

So my dear freedom have I gained,
Through her unkindness and disgrace :
   Yet could I ever live enchained,
As she my service did embrace.
       But she is changed, and I am free :
       Faith failing her, love died in me.

FOURTH BOOK OF AIRS.

TO MY WORTHY FRIEND MASTER JOHN MOUNSON, SON AND HEIR TO SIR THOMAS MOUNSON, KNIGHT AND BARONET.

ON you th' affections of your father's friends,
With his inheritance, by right descends :
But you your graceful youth so wisely guide
That his you hold, and purchase much beside.
Love is the fruit of Virtue ; for whose sake
Men only liking each to other take.
If sparks of virtue shined not in you then
So well, how could you win the hearts of men ?
And since that honour and well-suited praise
Is Virtue's golden spur, let me now raise
Unto an act mature your tender age ;
This half commending to your patronage,
Which from your noble father's, but one side,
Ordained to do you honour, doth divide.
And so my love betwixt you both I part,
On each side placing you as near my heart !

Yours ever,

THOMAS CAMPION.[1]

1 Old ed. "Campian."

TO THE READER.

THE Apothecaries have Books of Gold, whose leaves, being opened, are so light as that they are subject to be shaken with the least breath ; yet rightly handled, they serve both for ornament and use. Such are light Airs.

But if any squeamish stomachs shall check at two or three vain ditties in the end of this book, let them pour off the clearest and leave those as dregs in the bottom. Howsoever, if they be but conferred with the Canterbury Tales *of that venerable poet* Chaucer, *they will then appear toothsome enough.*

Some words are in these Books, which have been clothed in music by others, and I am content they then served their turn: yet give me now leave to make use of mine own. Likewise you may find here some three or four Songs that have been published before : but for them, I refer you to the Player's bill, that is styled, Newly revived, with Additions *; for you shall find all of them reformed, either in words or notes.*

To be brief. All these Songs are mine, if you express them well ; otherwise they are your own. Farewell.

Yours, as you are his,
THOMAS CAMPION.[1]

---

1 Old ed. " Campian."

L EAVE prolonging thy distress !
   All delays afflict the dying.
Many lost sighs long I spent, to her for mercy crying ;
   But now, vain mourning, cease !
   I'll die, and mine own griefs release.

Thus departing from this light
To those shades that end in sorrow,
Yet a small time of complaint a little breath I'll borrow,
   To tell my once delight
   I die alone through her despite.

R ESPECT my faith, regard my service past ;
   The hope you winged call home to you at last.
Great price it is that I in you shall gain,
So great for you hath been my loss and pain.
   My wits I spent and time for you alone,
   Observing you and losing all for one.

Some raised to rich estates in this time are,
That held their hopes to mine, inferior far :
Such, scoffing me, or pitying me, say thus,
" Had he not loved, he might have lived like us."
   O then, dear sweet, for love and pity's sake
   My faith reward and from me scandal take.

I

THOU joyest, fond boy, to be by many loved,
    To have thy beauty of most dames approved ;
For this dost thou thy native worth disguise
And playest the sycophant t' observe their eyes ;
Thy glass thou counsellest more to adorn thy skin,
That first should school thee to be fair within.

'Tis childish to be caught with pearl or amber,
And woman-like too much to cloy the chamber ;
Youths should the fields affect, heat their rough steeds,
Their hardened nerves to fit for better deeds.
Is 't not more joy strongholds to force with swords
Than women's weakness take with looks or words ?

Men that do noble things all purchase glory :
One man for one brave act hath proved a story :
But if that one ten thousand dames o'ercame,
Who would record it, if not to his shame ?
'Tis far more conquest with one to live true
Than every hour to triumph lord of new.

VEIL, Love, mine eyes ! O hide from me
    The plagues that charge the curious mind !
If beauty private will not be,
    Suffice it yet that she proves kind.
Who can usurp heaven's light alone ?
Stars were not made to shine on one !

Griefs past recure, fools try to heal,
   That greater harms on less inflict,
The pure offend by too much zeal ;
   Affection should not be too strict.
He that a true embrace will find,
To beauty's faults must still be blind.

E VERY dame affects good fame, whate'er her doings
    be,
But true praise is Virtue's bays which none may wear
   but she.
Borrowed guise fits not the wise, a simple look is best ;
Native grace becomes a face, though ne'er so rudely
   drest.
Now such new found toys are sold, these women to
   disguise,
That before the year grows old the newest fashion dies.

Dames of yore contended more in goodness to exceed
Than in pride to be envied, for that which least they
   need.
Little lawn then serve[d] the Pawn,[1] if Pawn at all
   there were ;
Homespun thread, and household bread, then held out
   all the year.

---

[1] The Pawn was a corridor serving as a bazaar in the Royal
Exchange (Gresham's).

But th'attires of women now wear out both house and
   land ;
That the wives in silks may flow, at ebb the good men
   stand.

Once again, Astrea, then, from heaven to earth descend,
And vouchsafe in their behalf these errors to amend !
Aid from heaven must make all even, things are so out
   of frame ;
For let man strive all he can, he needs must please his
   dame.
Happy man, content that gives and what he gives,
   enjoys !
Happy dame, content that lives and breaks no sleep
   for toys !

SO sweet is thy discourse to me,
   And so delightful is thy sight,
As I taste nothing right but thee.
O why invented Nature light ?
Was it alone for beauty's sake,
That her graced words might better take ?

No more can I old joys recall :
They now to me become unknown,
Not seeming to have been at all.
Alas ! how soon is this love grown
To such a spreading height in me
As with it all must shadowed be !

THERE[1] is a garden in her face,
  Where roses and white lilies grow ;
A heavenly paradise is that place,
Wherein all pleasant fruits do flow.
There cherries grow, which none may buy
Till " Cherry ripe" themselves do cry.

Those cherries fairly do enclose
Of orient pearl a double row ;
Which when her lovely laughter shows,
They look like rosebuds filled with snow.
Yet them nor peer nor prince can buy
Till " Cherry ripe" themselves do cry.

Her eyes like angels watch them still ;
Her brows like bended bows do stand,
Threatening with piercing frowns to kill
All that attempt, with eye or hand,
Those sacred cherries to come nigh
Till " Cherry ripe" themselves do cry.

[1] This poem is found in Alison's *Hour's Recreation*, 1606, and Robert Jones' *Ultimum Vale* (1608).

TO his sweet lute Apollo sung the motions of the
spheres ;
The wondrous order of the stars, whose course divides
the years ;
    And all the mysteries above :
    But none of this could Midas move,
Which purchased him, his ass's ears.

Then Pan with his rude pipe began the country wealth
t' advance,
To boast of cattle, flocks of sheep, and goats on hills
that dance ;
    With much more of this churlish kind,
    That quite transported Midas' mind,
And held him rapt as in a trance.

This wrong the God of Music scorned from such a
sottish judge,
And bent his angry bow at Pan, which made the piper
trudge :
    Then Midas' head he so did trim
    That every age yet talks of him
And Phœbus' right-revenged grudge.

YOUNG and simple though I am,
  I have heard of Cupid's name :
Guess I can what thing it is
Men desire when they do kiss.
Smoke can never burn, they say,
But the flames that follow may.

I am not so foul or fair
To be proud nor to despair ;
Yet [1] my lips have oft observed :
Men that kiss them press them hard,
As glad lovers use to do
When their new-met loves they woo.

Faith, 'tis but a foolish mind !
Yet, methinks, a heat I find,
Like thirst-longing, that doth bide
Ever on my weaker side,
Where they say my heart doth move.
Venus, grant it be not love !

If it be, alas, what then !
Were not women made for men ?
As good 'twere a thing were past,
That must needs be done at last.

---

1 "Yet my lips . . . new-met loves they woo" is the reading
given in Ferrabosco's *Airs*, 1609. In Campion's Song-book we
have a repetition of "Guess I can . . . follow may" from the
first stanza.

Roses that are overblown,
Grow less sweet ; then fall alone.

Yet not churl, nor silken gull,
Shall my maiden blossom pull ;
Who shall not I soon can tell ;
Who shall, would I could as well !
This I know, whoe'er he be,
Love he must or flatter me.

LOVE me or not, love her I must or die ;
Leave me or not, follow her, needs must I.
O that her grace would my wished comforts give !
How rich in her, how happy should I live !

All my desire, all my delight should be,
Her to enjoy, her to unite to me :
Envy should cease, her would I love alone :
Who loves by looks, is seldom true to one.

Could I enchant, and that it lawful were,
Her would I charm softly that none should hear.
But love enforced rarely yields firm content ;
So would I love that neither should repent.

WHAT means this folly, now to brave it so,
And then to use submission ?
Is that a friend that straight can play the foe ?
Who loves on such condition ?

Though briars breed roses, none the briar affect ;
    But with the flower are pleased.
Love only loves delight and soft respect :
    He must not be diseased.[1]

These thorny passions spring from barren breasts,
    Or such as need much weeding.
Love only loves delight and soft respect ;[2]
    But sends them not home bleeding.

Command thy humour, strive to give content,
    And shame not love's profession.
Of kindness never any could repent
    That made choice with discretion.

DEAR, if I with guile would gild a true intent,
    Heaping flatt'ries that in heart were never meant:
        Easily could I then obtain
            What now in vain I force ;
        Falsehood much doth gain,
            Truth yet holds the better course.

Love forbid that through dissembling I should thrive,
Or in praising you myself of truth deprive !
        Let not your high thoughts debase
           A simple truth in me :
        Great is Beauty's grace,
            Truth is yet as fair as she !

---

[1] Put to discomfort.
[2] This line has been repeated, by an error of the copyist or printer, from the previous stanza.

Praise is but the wind of pride, if it exceeds ;
Wealth, prized in itself, no outward value needs.
    Fair you are, and passing fair ;
      You know it, and 'tis true :
    Yet let none despair
      But to find as fair as you.

O LOVE, where are thy shafts, thy quiver, and thy
    bow ?
Shall my wounds only weep, and he ungaged go ?
Be just, and strike him, too, that dares contemn thee
    so !

No eyes are like to thine, though men suppose thee
    blind ;
So fair they level when the mark they list to find :
Then, strike, O strike the heart that bears the cruel
    mind !

Is my fond sight deceived ? or do I Cupid spy,
Close aiming at his breast by whom, despised, I die ?
Shoot home, sweet Love, and wound him, that he may
    not fly !

O then we both will sit in some unhaunted shade,
And heal each other's wound which Love hath justly
    made :
O hope, O thought too vain ! how quickly dost thou
    fade !

At large he wanders still : his heart is free from pain ;
While secret sighs I spend, and tears, but all in vain.
Yet, Love, thou knowest, by right, I should not thus
    complain.

BEAUTY is but a painted hell :
    Ay me, ay me !
She wounds them that admire it,
She kills them that desire it.
    Give her pride but fuel,
    No fire is more cruel.

Pity from every heart is fled :
    Ay me, ay me !
Since false desire could borrow
Tears of dissembled sorrow,
    Constant vows turn truthless,
    Love cruel, Beauty ruthless.

Sorrow can laugh, and Fury sing :
    Ay me, ay me !
My raving griefs discover
I lived too true a lover.
    The first step to madness
    Is the excess of sadness.

A RE you, what your fair looks express?
   O then be kind !
From law of nature they digress
   Whose form suits not their mind :
Fairness seen in th' outward shape,
Is but th' inward beauty's ape.

Eyes that of earth are mortal made,
   What can they view ?
All's but a colour or a shade,
   And neither always true :
Reason's sight, that is etern,
E'en the substance can discern.

Soul is the Man : for who will so
   The body name?
And to that power all grace we owe
   That decks our living frame.
What, or how had housen bin,
But for them that dwell therein?

Love in the bosom is begot,
   Not in the eyes ;
No beauty makes the eye more hot,
   Her flames the sprite surprise :
Let our loving minds then meet,
For pure meetings are most sweet.

S INCE she, even she, for whom I lived,
    Sweet she by fate from me is torn,
Why am not I of sense deprived,
    Forgetting I was ever born?
Why should I languish, hating light?
Better to sleep an endless night.

Be it either true, or aply feigned,
    That some of Lethe's water write,
'Tis their best medicine that are pained
    All thought to lose of past delight.
O would my anguish vanish so !
Happy are they that neither know.

I MUST[1] complain, yet do enjoy my love ;
    She is too fair, too rich in lovely parts :

[1] In Christ Church MS. 1, 5, 49, there is a copy of this song which differs considerably from the printed text. After the first stanza the MS. reads :—

    " Thus my complaints from her untruth arise,
    Accusing her and nature both in one ;
    For beauty stained is but a false disguise,
    A common wonder that is quickly gone,
    And false fair souls cannot, for all their feature,
    Without a true heart make a true fair creature.

    What need'[s]t thou plain if thou be still rejected?
    The fairest creature sometime may prove strange :
    Continual plaints will make thee still rejected,
    If that her wanton mind be given to range :
    And nothing better fits a man's true parts
    Than to disdain t'encounter fair false hearts."

The song is also found (with the same text as in Campion's Song-book) in Dowland's *Third Book of Songs or Airs*, 1603.

Thence is my grief, for Nature, while she strove
 With all her graces and divinest arts
To form her too too beautiful of hue,
She had no leisure left to make her true.

Should I, aggrieved, then wish she were less fair?
 That were repugnant to mine own desires.
She is admired, new lovers still repair,
 That kindles daily love's forgetful fires.
Rest, jealous thoughts, and thus resolve at last,—
She hath more beauty than becomes the chaste.

THINK'ST [1] thou to seduce me then with words
  that have no meaning?
Parrots so can learn to prate, our speech by pieces
  gleaning:
Nurses teach their children so about the time of
  weaning.

[1] The following version of this song is given in William
Corkine's *Airs,* 1610 :—

"Think you to seduce me so with words that have no meaning?
Parrots can learn so to speak, our voice by pieces gleaning :
Nurses teach their children so about the time of weaning.

"Learn to speak first, then to woo: to wooing much pertaineth,
He that hath not art to hide soon falters when he feigneth,
And as one that wants his wits he smiles when he complaineth.

"If with wit we be deceived, our falls may be excused :
Seeming good with flattery graced is but of few refused,
But of all accursed are they that are by fools abused."

Learn to speak first, then to woo : to wooing, much
    pertaineth :
He that courts us, wanting art, soon falters when he
    feigneth,
Looks asquint on his discourse, and smiles, when he
    complaineth.

Skilful anglers hide their hooks, fit baits for every
    season ;
But with crooked pins fish thou, as babes do, that want
    reason :
Gudgeons only can be caught with such poor tricks of
    treason.

Ruth forgive me, if I erred, from human heart's com-
    passion,
When I laughed sometimes too much to see thy foolish
    fashion :
But, alas, who less could do that found so good occa-
    sion !

HER fair inflaming eyes,
    Chief authors of my cares,
I prayed in humblest wise
    With grace to view my tears :
        They beheld me broad awake,
        But. alas, no ruth would take.

Her lips with kisses rich,
    And words of fair delight,

I fairly did beseech,
   To pity my sad plight :
      But a voice from them brake forth,
      As a whirlwind from the north.

Then to her hands I fled,
   That can give heart and all ;
To them I long did plead,
   And loud for pity call :
      But, alas, they put me off,
      With a touch worse than a scoff.

So back I straight returned,
   And at her breast I knocked ;
Where long in vain I mourned,
   Her heart, so fast was locked :
      Not a word could passage find,
      For a rock enclosed her mind.

Then down my prayers made way
   To those most comely parts,
That make her fly or stay,
   As they affect deserts :
      But her angry feet, thus moved,
      Fled with all the parts I loved.

Yet fled they not so fast,
   As her enraged mind :
Still did I after haste,
   Still was I left behind ;
      Till I found 'twas to no end,
      With a Spirit to contend.

TURN all thy thoughts to eyes,
   Turn all thy hairs to ears,
Change all thy friends to spies,
And all thy joys to fears :
     True love will yet be free,
     In spite of jealousy.

Turn darkness into day,
Conjectures into truth,
Believe what th' envious say,
Let age interpret youth :
     True love will yet be free,
     In spite of jealousy.

Wrest every word and look,
Rack every hidden thought,
Or fish with golden hook ;
True love cannot be caught.
     For that will still be free,
     In spite of jealousy !

IF any hath the heart to kill,
   Come rid me of this woeful pain !
For while I live I suffer still
  This cruel torment all in vain :
Yet none alive but one can guess
What is the cause of my distress.

Thanks be to heaven, no grievous smart,
  No maladies my limbs annoy ;
I bear a fond and sprightful heart,
  Yet live I quite deprived of joy :

K

Since what I had in vain I crave,
And what I had not now I have.

A love I had, so fair, so sweet,
  As ever wanton eye did see :
Once by appointment we did meet :
  She would, but ah, it would not be !
She gave her heart, her hand she gave ;
All did I give, she nought could have.

What hag did then my powers forespeak,
  That never yet such taint did feel !
Now she rejects me as one weak,
  Yet am I all composed of steel.
Ah, this is it my heart doth grieve :
Now though she sees, she'll not believe.

BEAUTY, since you so much desire
  To know the place of Cupid's fire,
About you somewhere doth it rest,
Yet never harbour'd in your breast,
Nor gout-like in your heel or toe,—
What fool would seek Love's flame so low ?
But a little higher, but a little higher,
There, there, O there lies Cupid's fire.

Think not, when Cupid most you scorn,
Men judge that you of ice were born ;
For though you cast love at your heel,
His fury yet sometimes you feel :
And whereabouts if you would know,
I tell you still not in your toe :
But a little higher, but a little higher,
There, there, O there lies Cupid's fire.

YOUR fair looks urge my desire :
   Calm it, sweet, with love !
Stay ; O why will you retire ?
   Can you churlish prove ?
If love may persuade,
   Love's pleasures, dear, deny not :
Here is a grove secured with shade :
   O then be wise, and fly not.

Hark, the birds delighted sing,
   Yet our pleasure sleeps :
Wealth to none can profit bring,
   Which the miser keeps.
O come, while we may,
   Let's chain love with embraces ;
We have not all times time to stay,
   Nor safety in all places.

What ill find you now in this,
   Or who can complain ?
There is nothing done amiss
   That breeds no man pain.
'Tis now flow'ry May ;
   But even in cold December,
When all these leaves are blown away,
   This place shall I remember.

FAIN would I wed a fair young man that day and
    night could please me,
When my mind or body grieved that had the power to
    ease me.
Maids are full of longing thoughts that breed a blood-
    less sickness,
And that, oft I hear men say, is only cured by quick-
    ness.
Oft I have been wooed and prayed, but never could be
    moved ;
Many for a day or so I have most dearly loved,
But this foolish mind of mine straight loathes the thing
    resolved ;
If to love be sin in me that sin is soon absolved.
Sure I think I shall at last fly to some holy order ;
When I once am settled there then can I fly no farther.
Yet I would not die a maid, because I had a mother :
As I was by one brought forth I would bring forth
    another.

Songs of Mourning: Bewailing the vntimely death of Prince Henry. Worded by Tho. Campion. And set forth to be sung with one voyce to the Lute, or Viol: By John Coprario. London: Printed for John Browne, and are to be sould in S. dunstons Churchyard. 1613. fol.

Prince Henry died 6 November, 1612, at the age of eighteen. His death was a national calamity, for he was a youth of high character and brilliant ability. By his patronage of letters he had endeared himself to the poets; and many were the elegies dedicated to his memory. Drayton, Chapman, Webster, Donne, Drummond and others passionately bewailed his loss. Campion's tribute was worthy of the occasion.

John Coprario, or Coperario, was an English composer. His real name was John Cooper; but he adopted the more sonorous name during his residence in Italy. There is an excellent account of him, by Mr. Barclay Squire, in the "Dictionary of National Biography."

ILLUSTRISSIMO POTENTISSIMOQUE PRINCIPI, FREDRICO QUINTO, RHENI COMITI PALATINO, DUCI BAVARIAE, ETC.

COGIMUR; invitis (Clarissime) parce querelis [1]
Te salvo; laetis non sinit esse Deus:
Nec speratus Hymen procedit lumine claro;
Principis extincti nubila fata vetant.
· *Illius inferias maesto jam Musica cantu*
Prosequitur, miseros hæc Dea sola juvat.
Illa suos tibi summittit (Dux inclite) quaestus,
Fraternus fleto quem sociavit amor:
Sed nova gaudia, sed tam dulcia foedera rupit
Fati infelicis livor, et hora nocens.
Quod superest, nimios nobis omni arte dolores
Est mollire animus, spes meliora dabit:
Cunctatosque olim cantabimus ipsi Hymenaeos, [2]
Laeta simul fas sit reddere vota Deo.

[1] Old ed. "*quærelis.*"
[2] Campion fulfilled his promise by writing a Masque (see p. 191) in celebration of the Marriage of the Count Palatine with the Princess Elizabeth.

AN ELEGY UPON THE UNTIMELY
DEATH OF PRINCE HENRY.

READ, you that have some tears left yet unspent,
  Now weep yourselves heart-sick, and ne'er repent:
For I will open to your free access
The sanctuary of all heaviness,
Where men their fill may mourn, and never sin :
And I their humble Priest thus first begin.

  Fly from the skies, ye blessed beams of light !
Rise up in horrid vapours, ugly night,
And fettered bring that ravenous monster Fate,
The felon and the traitor to our state !
Law-eloquence we need not to convince
His guilt ; all know it, 'tis he stole our Prince,
The Prince of men, the Prince of all that bore
Ever that princely name : O now no more
Shall his perfections, like the sunbeams, dare[1]
The purblind world ! in heav'n those glories are.
What could the greatest artist, Nature, add
T' increase his graces? divine form he had,
Striving in all his parts which should surpass ;
And like a well-tuned chime his carriage was,
Full of celestial witchcraft, winning all
To admiration and love personal.
His lance appeared to the beholders' eyes,
When his fair hand advanced it to the skies,
Larger than truth, for well could he it wield,
And make it promise honour in the field.

----

[1] I suppose "dare" has the meaning "amaze, stupefy."
There was a way of catching larks by *daring* them with a mirror.

When Court and Music called him, off fell arms,
And as he had been shaped for love's alarms,
In harmony he spake, and trod the ground
In more proportion than the measured sound.
How fit for peace was he, and rosy beds !
How fit to stand in troops of iron heads,
When time had with his circles made complete
His charmed rounds !   All things in time grow great.

This fear, even like a comet that hangs high,
And shoots his threat'ning flashes through the sky,
Held all the eyes of Christendom intent
Upon his youthful hopes, casting th' event
Of what was in his power, not in his will :
For that was close concealed, and must lie still,
As deeply hid as that design which late
With the French Lion died.   O earthly state,
How doth thy greatness in a moment fall,
And feasts in highest pomp turn funeral !

But our young Henry armed with all the arts
That suit with Empire, and the gain of hearts,
Bearing before him fortune, power, and love,
Appeared first in perfection, fit to move
Fixt admiration : though his years were green
Their fruit was yet mature : his care had been
Surveying India, and implanting there
The knowledge of that God which he did fear :
And ev'n now, though he breathless lies, his sails
Are struggling with the winds, for our avails
T' explore a passage [1] hid from human tract,

---

1 On 26 July, 1612, King James appointed Prince Henry
"supreme protector" of the expedition (fitted out by the Mus-
covy Company and East India Company) for the discovery of the
North-West Passage (*Cal. State Papers, Colon.*, 1513-1616, 616).

Will fame him in the enterprise or fact.
O Spirit full of hope, why art thou fled
From deeds of honour? why 's that virtue dead
Which dwelt so well in thee? a bower more sweet,
If Paradise were found, it could not meet.

    Curst then be Fate that stole our blessing so,
And had for us now nothing left but woe,
Had not th' All-seeing Providence yet kept
Another joy safe, that in silence slept:
And that same Royal workman, who could frame
A Prince so worthy of immortal fame,
Lives; and long may he live, to form the other
His expressed image, and grace of his brother,
To whose eternal peace we offer now
Gifts which he loved, and fed; musics that flow
Out of a sour and melancholic vein,
Which best sort with the sorrows we sustain.

TO THE MOST SACRED KING JAMES.

I.

O GRIEF, how divers are thy shapes wherein
        men languish!
  The face sometime with tears thou fill'st,
  Sometime the heart thou kill'st
    With unseen anguish.
Sometime thou smilest to view how Fate
      Plays with our human state:
So far from surety here
    Are all our earthly joys,
That what our strong hope builds, when least we fear,
    A stronger power destroys.

2.

O Fate, why shouldst thou take from Kings their joy
    and treasure ?
    Their image if men should deface
    'Twere death, which thou dost race
      Even at thy pleasure.
Wisdom of holy kings yet knows
      Both what it hath, and owes.
Heaven's hostage, which you bred
      And nursed with such choice care,
Is ravished now, great King, and from us fled
    When we were least aware.

TO THE MOST SACRED QUEEN ANNE.

1.

'TIS now dead night, and not a light on earth,
    Or star in heaven, doth shine :
Let now a mother mourn the noblest birth
    That ever was both mortal and divine.
  O sweetness peerless ! more than human grace !
  O flowery beauty !   O untimely death !
    Now, Music, fill this place
    With thy most doleful breath :
O singing wail a fate more truly funeral,
Than when with all his sons the sire of Troy did fall.

2.

Sleep, Joy ! die, Mirth ! and not a smile be seen,
  Or show of heart's content !
For never sorrow nearer touched a Queen,
    Nor were there ever tears more duly spent.
  O dear remembrance, full of rueful woe !
  O ceaseless passion ! O unhuman hour !
      No pleasure now can grow,
      For withered is her flower.
O anguish do thy worst and fury tragical,
Since fate in taking one hath thus disordered all.

TO THE MOST HIGH AND MIGHTY PRINCE CHARLES.

1.

FORTUNE and Glory may be lost and won,
    But when the work of Nature is undone
    That loss flies past returning ;
    No help is left but mourning.
What can to kind youth more despiteful prove
  Than to be robbed of one sole brother ?
            Father and Mother
Ask reverence, a brother only love.
Like age and birth like thoughts and pleasures move :
  What gain can he heap up, though showers of crowns
      descend,
  Who for that good must change a brother and a
      friend ?

2.

Follow, O follow yet thy brother's fame,
But not his fate : let's only change the name,
    And find his worth presented
    In thee, by him prevented.
O['e]r past example of the dead be great,
    Out of thyself begin thy story :
                Virtue and glory
Are eminent being placed in princely seat.
Oh, heaven, his age prolong with sacred heat,
    And on his honoured head let all the blessings light
    Which to his brother's life men wished, and wished
        them right.

TO THE MOST PRINCELY AND VIRTUOUS
THE LADY ELIZABETH.

1.

SO parted you as if the world for ever
    Had lost with him her light :
Now could your tears hard flint to ruth excite,
           Yet may you never
Your loves again partake in human sight :
O why should fate[1] such two kind hearts dissever
As nature never knit more fair or firm together?

2.

So loved you as sister should a brother
    Not in a common strain,

[1] Old ed. "love." The correction "fate" is written (in a hand-
writing of the early seventeenth century) in the margin of the British
Museum copy (G. 18).

For princely blood doeth vulgar fire disdain :
           But you each other
On earth embraced in a celestial chain.
Alas, for love ! that heav'nly-born affection
To change should subject be and suffer earth's infection !

TO THE MOST ILLUSTRIOUS AND MIGHTY FREDERICK THE FIFTH, COUNT PALATINE OF THE RHEIN.

I.

H OW like a golden dream you met[1] and parted,
     That pleasing straight doth vanish !
   O who can ever banish
The thought of one so princely and free-hearted !
But he was pulled up in his prime by fate,
And love for him must mourn though all too late.
     Tears to the dead are due, let none forbid
     Sad hearts to sigh : true grief cannot be hid.

II.

Yet the most bitter storm to height increased
     By heaven again is ceased :
     O time, that all things movest,
In grief and joy thou equal measure lovest :
Such the condition is of human life,
Care must with pleasure mix and peace with strife :
     Thoughts with the days must change ; as tapers
         waste,
     So must our griefs ; day breaks when night is past.

[1] The Count Palatine landed at Graves End on 16th October, 1612.

TO THE MOST DISCONSOLATE GREAT BRITAIN.

1.

WHEN pale famine fed on thee,
    With her unsatiate jaws ;
When civil broils set murder free
    Contemning all thy laws ;
When heav'n enraged consumed thee so
With plagues that none thy face could know,
      Yet in thy looks affliction then showed less
      Than [1] now for one's fate all thy parts express.

2.

Now thy highest states lament
    A son, and brother's loss ;
Thy nobles mourn in discontent,
    And rue this fatal cross ;
Thy commons are with passion sad
To think how brave a Prince they had :
      If all thy rocks from white to black should turn
      Yet could'st thou not in show more amply mourn.

TO THE WORLD.

1.

O POOR distracted world, partly a slave
    To pagans' sinful rage, partly obscured
With ignorance of all the means that save !
    And ev'n those parts of thee that live assured

[1] This is the reading in the music-text : the *repeat* gives "Thou now for one's fall," &c.

Of heav'nly grace, oh how they are divided
With doubts late by a kingly pen decided ! [1]
O happy world, if what the sire begun
Had been closed up by his religious son !

2.

Mourn all you souls oppressed under the yoke
Of Christian-hating Thrace ! never appeared
More likelihood to have that black league broke,
For such a heavenly Prince might well be feared
Of earthly fiends. Oh how is Zeal inflamed
With power, when Truth wanting defence is shamed !
O princely soul, rest thou in peace, while we
In thine expect the hopes were ripe in thee.

A TABLE OF ALL THE SONGS CONTAINED
IN THIS BOOK.

1. O Grief.
2. 'Tis now dead night.
3. Fortune and glory.
4. So parted you.
5. How like a golden dream.
6. When pale famine.
7. O poor distracted world.

FINIS.

[1] There may be a particular reference to King James's " Pre-
monition to all most mighty Monarchs, Kings, Free Princes, and
States of Christendom," 1609, written against Bellarmine.

The Discription of a Maske, Presented before the Kinges Maiestie at White-Hall, on Twelfth Night last, in honour of the Lord Hayes, and his Bride, Daughter and Heire to the Honourable the Lord Dennye, their Marriage hauing been the same Day at Court solemnized. To this by occasion other small Poemes are adioyned. Inuented and set forth by Thomas Campion Doctor of Phisicke. London Imprinted by Iohn Windet for Iohn Brown and are to be solde at his shop in S. Dunstones Churchycard in Fleetstreet. 1607. 4to.

Sir James Hay, created in 1615 Baron Hay of Sawley, and raised in 1622 to the dignity of Earl of Carlisle, was noted for his magnificent style of living (particularly during his embassy in France and Germany, 1619-1622), by which he greatly impoverished his estate. He married, in 1613, his second wife, Lucy, youngest daughter of Henry Earl of Northumberland, and died in 1636, leaving by his first wife a son James, second Earl of Carlisle. Clarendon has a character of him; and he is extolled in Lloyd's "State Worthies."

The present masque (which has been reprinted in the second volume of Nichols's "Progresses of King James") is of great rarity. On the back of the title-page is a copper-plate engraving (rudely coloured in the two copies that I have seen) of one of the masquers.

TO THE MOST PUISSANT AND GRACIOUS JAMES KING OF GREAT BRITAIN.

THE disunited Scythians when they sought
   To gather strength by parties, and combine
That perfect league of friends which once being
     wrought
No turn of time or fortune could untwine,
This rite they held : a massy bowl was brought,
And ev'ry right arm shot his several blood
Into the mazer till 'twas fully fraught.
Then having stirred it to an equal flood
They quaffed to th' union, which till death should last,
In spite of private foe, or foreign fear ;
And this blood-sacrament being known t' have past,
Their names grew dreadful to all far and near.
O then, great Monarch, with how wise a care
Do you these bloods divided mix in one,
And with like consanguinities prepare
The high, and everliving Union
    'Tween Scots and English ! who can wonder then
    If he that marries kingdoms, marries men?

AN EPIGRAM.

MERLIN, the great King Arthur being slain,
   Foretold that he should come to life again,
And long time after wield great Britain's state
More powerful ten-fold, and more fortunate.
Prophet, 'tis true, and well we find the same,
Save only that thou didst mistake the name.

AD INVICTISSIMUM SERENISSIMUMQUE
IACOBUM, MAGNAE BRITANNIAE
REGEM.

A NGLIAE, et unanimis Scotiae pater, anne maritus
Sis dubito, an neuter, (Rex) vel uterque simul.
Uxores pariter binas sibi jungat ut unus,
Credimus hoc, ipso te prohibente, nefas.
Atque, maritali natas violare parentem
Complexu, quis non cogitat esse scelus?
At tibi divinis successibus utraque nubit;
Una tamen conjux, conjugis unus amor.
Connubium O mirum, binas qui ducere et unam
Possis! tu solus sic, Iacobe, potes.
Divisas leviter terras componis in unam
Atque unam aeternum nomine reque facis:
Natisque, et nuptis, pater et vir factus utrisque es;
Unitis conjux vere, et amore parens.

TO THE RIGHT NOBLE AND VIRTUOUS
THEOPHILUS HOWARD,
Lord of Walden, son and heir to the
Right Honourable the Earl
of Suffolk.

IF to be sprung of high and princely blood,
If to inherit virtue, honour, grace,
If to be great in all things, and yet good,
If to be facile, yet t' have power and place,
If to be just, and bountiful, may get
The love of men, your right may challenge it.

The course of foreign manners far and wide,
The courts, the countries, cities, towns and state,
The blossom of your springing youth hath tried,
Honoured in ev'ry place and fortunate,
    Which now grown fairer doth adorn our Court
    With princely revelling and timely sport.

But if th' admired virtues of your youth
Breed such despairing to my daunted muse,
That it can scarcely utter naked truth,
How shall it mount as ravished spirits use
    Under the burden of your riper days,
    Or hope to reach the so far distant bays?

My slender Muse shall yet my love express,
And by the fair Thames' side of you she'll sing ;
The double streams shall bear her willing verse
Far hence with murmur of their ebb and spring.
    But if you favour her light tunes, ere long
    She'll strive to raise you with a loftier song.

TO THE RIGHT VIRTUOUS, AND HONOURABLE, THE LORD AND LADY HAYES.

SHOULD I presume to separate you now,
    That were so lately joined by holy vow,
For whom this golden dream which I report
Begot so many waking eyes at Court,

And for whose grace so many nobles changed,
Their names and habits, from themselves estranged?
Accept together, and together view
This little work which all belongs to you,
And live together many blessed days,
To propagate the honoured name of Hayes.

EPIGRAMMA.

*H*Æ*REDEM* (*ut spes est*) *pariet nova nupta Scot'*
   Anglum;
Quem gignet posthac ille, Britannus erit:
Sic nova posteritas, ex regnis orta duobus,
Utrinque egregios nobilitabit avos.

THE DESCRIPTION OF A MASQUE,

Presented before the King's Majesty at White Hall, on twelfth night last, in honour of the Lord Hayes and his bride, daughter and heir to the honourable the Lord Denny, their marriage having been the same day at Court solemnized.

AS in battles, so in all other actions that are to be reported, the first, and most necessary part is the description of the place, with his opportunities and properties, whether they be natural or artificial. The great hall (wherein the Masque was presented) received this division, and order. The upper part where the cloth and chair of state were placed, had scaffolds and seats on either side continued to the screen; right before it was made a partition for the dancing-place; on the right hand whereof were consorted ten musicians,

with bass and mean lutes, a bandora,[1] a double sack-
but,[2] and an harpsichord, with two treble violins ; on
the other side somewhat nearer the screen were placed
nine violins and three lutes, and to answer both the
consorts[3] (as it were in a triangle) six cornets, and
six chapel voices, were seated almost right against
them, in a place raised higher in respect of the piercing
sound of those instruments ; eighteen foot from the
screen, another stage was raised higher by a yard than
that which was prepared for dancing. This higher
stage was all enclosed with a double veil, so artificially
painted, that it seemed as if dark clouds had hung
before it : within that shroud was concealed a green
valley, with green trees round about it, and in the
midst of them nine golden trees of fifteen foot high,
with arms and branches very glorious to behold.
From the which grove toward the state[4] was made a
broad descent to the dancing place, just in the midst
of it ; on either hand were two ascents, like the sides
of two hills, drest with shrubs and trees ; that on the
right hand leading to the bower of Flora : the other
to the house of Night ; which bower and house were
placed opposite at either end of the screen, and
between them both was raised a hill, hanging like a
cliff over the grove below, and on the top of it a goodly
large tree was set, supposed to be the tree of Diana ;
behind the which toward the window was a small
descent, with another spreading hill that climbed up
to the top of the window, with many trees on the
height of it, whereby those that played on the hautboys

---

[1] A musical instrument resembling a guitar.
[2] Bass trumpet.   [3] Bands of musicians.
[4] Chair of state.

at the King's entrance into the hall were shadowed.
The bower of Flora was very spacious, garnished with
all kind of flowers, and flowery branches with lights
in them ; the house of Night ample and stately, with
black pillars, whereon many stars of gold were fixed :
within it, when it was empty, appeared nothing but
clouds and stars, and on the top of it stood three
turrets underpropt with small black starred pillars, the
middlemost being highest and greatest, the other two
of equal proportion : about it were placed on wire
artificial bats and owls, continually moving ; with
many other inventions, the which for brevity sake I
pass by with silence.

Thus much for the place, and now from thence let
us come to the persons.

The Masquers' names were these (whom both for
order and honour I mention in the first place).

1. *Lord Walden.*
2. *Sir Thomas Howard.*
3. *Sir Henry Carey, Master of the Jewel house.*
4. *Sir Richard Preston* ⎫ *Gent. of the K. Privy*
5. *Sir John Ashley* ⎭ *Chamber.*
6. *Sir Thomas Jarret, Pensioner.*
7. *Sir John Digby, one of the King's Carvers.*
8. *Sir Thomas Badger, Master of the King's Harriers.*
9. *Master Goringe.*

Their number nine, the best and amplest of numbers,
for as in music seven notes contain all variety, the
eight[h] being in nature the same with the first, so in
numbering after the ninth we begin again, the tenth
being as it were the diapason in arithmetic. The
number of *nine* is framed by the Muses and Worthies,

and it is of all the most apt for change and diversity
of proportion. The chief habit which the Masquers
did use is set forth to your view in the first leaf:[1]
they presented in their feigned persons the knights of
Apollo, who is the father of heat and youth, and con-
sequently of amorous affections.

The Speakers were in number four.

Flora, the queen of flowers, attired in a changeable taffeta gown, with a large veil embroidered with flowers, a
crown of flowers, and white buskins painted with flowers.

Zephyrus, in a white loose robe of sky-coloured
taffeta, with a mantle of white silk, propped with wire,
still waving behind him as he moved ; on his head he
wore a wreath of palm deckt with primroses and
violets, the hair of his head and beard were flaxen, and
his buskins white, and painted with flowers.

Night, in a close robe of black silk and gold, a black
mantle embroidered with stars, a crown of stars on her
head, her hair black and spangled with gold, her face
black, her buskins black, and painted with stars ; in
her hand she bore a black wand, wreathed with gold.

Hesperus, in a close robe of a deep crimson taffeta
mingled with sky-colour, and over that a large loose
robe of a lighter crimson taffeta ; on his head he wore
a wreathed band of gold, with a star in the front
thereof, his hair and beard red, and buskins yellow.

These are the principal persons that bear sway in
this invention, others that are but seconders to these,
I will describe in their proper places, discoursing the
Masque in order as it was performed.

[1] The engraving is reproduced in Nichols's " Progresses of
King James."

As soon as the King was entered the great Hall, the Hautboys (out of the wood on the top of the hill) entertained the time till his Majesty and his train were placed, and then after a little expectation the consort of ten began to play an air, at the sound whereof the veil on the right hand was withdrawn, and the ascent of the hill with the bower of Flora were discovered, where Flora and Zephyrus were busily plucking flowers from the bower, and throwing them into two baskets, which two Sylvans held, who were attired in changeable taffeta, with wreathes of flowers on their heads. As soon as the baskets were filled, they came down in this order ; first Zephyrus and Flora, then the two Sylvans with baskets after them ; four Sylvans in green taffeta and wreathes, two bearing mean lutes, the third, a bass lute, and the fourth a deep bandora.

As soon as they came to the descent toward the dancing place, the consort of ten ceased, and the four Sylvans played the same air, to which Zephyrus and the two other Sylvans did sing these words in a bass, tenor, and treble voice, and going up and down as they sung they strewed flowers all about the place.

SONG.

Now hath Flora robbed her bowers
To befriend this place with flowers :
Strow about, strow about !
The sky rained never kindlier showers.
Flowers with bridals well agree,
Fresh as brides and bridegrooms be :
Strow about, strow about !
And mix them with fit melody.
Earth hath no princelier flowers

Than roses white and roses red,
But they must still be mingled:
And as a rose new plucked from Venus' thorn,
So doth a bride her bridegroom's bed adorn.

Divers divers flowers affect
For some private dear respect:
　　Strow about, strow about!
Let every one his own protect;
But he's none of Flora's friend
That will not the rose commend.
　　Strow about, strow about!
Let princes princely flowers defend:
Roses, the garden's pride,
Are flowers for love and flowers for kings,
In courts desired and weddings:
And as a rose in Venus' bosom worn,
So doth a bridegroom his bride's bed adorn.

The music ceaseth and Flora speaks.

Flora. *Flowers and good wishes Flora doth present,*
　　Sweet flowers, the ceremonious ornament
　　Of maiden marriage, Beauty figuring,
　　And blooming youth; which though we careless
　　　　fling
　　About this sacred place, let none profane
　　Think that these fruits from common hills are
　　　　ta'en,
　　Or vulgar vallies which do subject lie
　　To winter's wrath and cold mortality.
　　But these are hallowed and immortal flowers
　　With Flora's hands gathered from Flora's bowers.
　　Such are her presents, endless as her love,
　　And such for ever may this night's joy prove.

Zephyrus, the western wind, of all the most mild and pleasant, who with Venus, the Queen of love, is said to bring in the spring, when natural heat and appetite reviveth, and the glad earth begins to be beautified with flowers.

Zeph. *For ever endless may this night's joy prove!*
So echoes Zephyrus the friend of Love,
Whose aid Venus implores when she doth bring
Into the naked world the green-leaved spring.
When of the sun's warm beams the nets we weave
That can the stubborn'st heart with love deceive.
That Queen of Beauty and Desire by me
Breathes gently forth this bridal prophecy :
Faithful and fruitful shall these bedmates prove,
Blest in their fortunes, honoured in their love.

Flor. *All grace this night, and, Sylvans, so must you,*
Off'ring your marriage song with changes new.

THE SONG IN FORM OF A DIALOGUE.

Can. *Who is the happier of the two,*
          A maid, or wife?
Ten. *Which is more to be desired*
          Peace or strife?
Can. *What strife can be where two are one,*
          Or what delight to pine alone?
Bas. *None such true friends, none so sweet life,*
          As that between the man and wife.
Ten. *A maid is free, a wife is tied.*
Can. *No maid but fain would be a bride.*
Ten. *Why live so many single then?*
          'Tis not I hope for want of men.
Can. *The bow and arrow both may fit,*
          And yet 'tis hard the mark to hit.
Bas. *He levels fair that by his side*
          Lays at night his lovely Bride.
Cho. *Sing Io, Hymen! Io, Io, Hymen!*

This song being ended the whole veil is suddenly

drawn, the grove and trees of gold, and the hill with
Diana's tree are at once discovered.

Night appears in her house with her Nine Hours,
appareled in large robes of black taffeta, painted
thick with stars, their hairs long, black, and spangled
with gold, on their heads coronets of stars, and their
faces black. Every Hour bore in his hand a black
torch, painted with stars, and lighted. Night presently
descending from her house spake as followeth.

Night. *Vanish, dark veils! let night in glory shine*
 As she doth burn in rage: come leave our shrine
 You black-haired Hours, and guide us with
 * your lights,*
 Flora hath wakened wide our drowsy sprites:
 See where she triumphs, see her flowers are
 * thrown,*
 And all about the seeds of malice sown!
 Despiteful Flora, is't not enough of grief
 That Cynthia's robbed, but thou must grace the
 * thief?*
 Or didst not hear Night's sovereign Queen
 * complain*
 Hymen had stolen a Nymph out of her train,
 And matched her here, plighted henceforth to be
 Love's friend, and stranger to virginity?
 And makest thou sport for this?
Flora. *Be mild, stern Night;*
 Flora doth honour Cynthia, and her right.
 Virginity is a voluntary power,
 Free from constraint, even like an untouched
 * flower*
 Meet to be gathered when 'tis throughly blown.

*Diana, the
Moon and
Queen of
Virginity, is
said to be
Regent and
Empress of
Night, and
is therefore
by Night de-
fended, as in
her quarrel
for the loss of
the Bride,
her virgin.*

The Nymph was Cynthia's while she was her
 own,
But now another claims in her a right,
By fate reserved thereto and wise foresight.

Zeph. *Can Cynthia one kind virgin's loss bemoan?*
How if perhaps she brings her ten for one?
Or can she miss one in so full a train?
Your Goddess doth of too much store complain.
If all her Nymphs would ask advice of me
There should be fewer virgins than there be.
Nature ordained not men to live alone,
Where there are two a woman should be one.

Night. *Thou breath'st sweet poison, wanton Zephyrus,*
But Cynthia must not be deluded thus.
Her holy forests are by thieves profaned,
Her virgins frighted, and lo, where they stand
That late were Phœbus' knights, turned now
 to trees
By Cynthia's vengement for their injuries
In seeking to seduce her nymphs with love:
Here they are fixt, and never may remove
But by Diana's power that stuck them here.
Apollo's love to them doth yet appear,
In that his beams hath gilt them as they grow,
To make their misery yield the greater show.
But they shall tremble when sad Night doth
 speak,
And at her stormy words their boughs shall
 break.

Toward the end of this speech Hesperus begins to
descend by the house of Night, and by that time the
speech was finished he was ready to speak.

Hesp. *Hail reverend angry Night, hail Queen of*
  Flowers,
Mild spirited Zephyrus, hail, Sylvans and
  Hours.
Hesperus brings peace, cease then your needless
  jars
Here in this little firmament of stars.
Cynthia is now by Phœbus pacified,
And well content her nymph is made a bride.
Since the fair match was by that Phœbus graced
Which in this happy Western Isle is placed
As he in heaven, one lamp enlight'ning all
That under his benign aspect doth fall.
Deep oracles he speaks, and he alone
For arts and wisdom's¹ meet for Phœbus' throne.
The nymph is honoured, and Diana pleased:
Night, be you then, and your black Hours
    appeased:
And friendly listen what your queen by me
Farther commands: let this my credence be,
View it, and know it for the highest gem,
That hung on her imperial diadem.

Night. *I know, and honour it, lovely Hesperus,*
Speak then your message, both are welcome to us.

Hesp. *Your Sovereign from the virtuous gem she sends*
Bids you take power to retransform the friends
Of Phœbus, metamorphosed here to trees,
And give them straight the shapes which they
    did lese.²
    This is her pleasure.

Night. *Hesperus, I obey,*

Hesperus, the Evening star, fore-shews that the wished marriage-night is at hand, and for that cause is supposed to be the friend of bridegrooms and brides.

---

¹ Old ed. "wisedomes."   ² An old form of *lose.*

Night must needs yield when Phœbus gets the
  day.
Flora. *Honoured be Cynthia for this generous deed.*
Zeph. *Pity grows only from celestial seed.*
Night. *If all seem glad, why should we only lower?*
  Since t'express gladness we have now most
    power.
  Frolic, graced captives, we present you here
  This glass, wherein your liberties appear:
  Cynthia is pacified, and now blithe Night
  Begins to shake off melancholy quite.
Zeph. *Who should grace mirth and revels but the*
    Night?
  Next Love she should be goddess of delight.
Night. *'Tis now a time when (Zephyrus) all with*
    dancing
  Honour me, above Day my state advancing.
  I'll now be frolic, all is full of heart,
  And ev'n these trees for joy shall bear a part:
  Zephyrus, they shall dance.
Zeph. *Dance, Goddess? how?*
Night. *Seems that so full of strangeness to you now?*
  Did not the Thracian harp long since the same?
  And (if we rip the old records of fame)
  Did not Amphion's lyre the deaf stones call,
  When they came dancing to the Theban wall?
  Can music then joy? joy mountains moves
  And why not trees? joy's powerful when it
    loves.
  Could the religious Oak speak Oracle
  Like to the Gods? and the tree wounded tell
  T'Æneas his sad story? have trees therefore
  The instruments of speech and hearing more

Than th' have of pacing, and to whom but Night
Belong enchantments? who can more affright
The eye with magic wonders?   Night alone
Is fit for miracles, and this shall be one
Apt for this Nuptial dancing jollity.
Earth, then be soft and passable to free
These fettered roots: joy, trees! the time draws
    near
When in your better forms you shall appear.
Dancing and music must prepare the way,
There's little tedious time in such delay.

This spoken, the four Sylvans played on their instruments the first strain of this song following : and at the repetition thereof the voices fell in with the instruments which were thus divided : a treble and a bass were placed near his Majesty, and another treble and bass near the grove, that the words of the song might be heard of all, because the trees of gold instantly at the first sound of their voices began to move and dance according to the measure of the time which the musicians kept in singing, and the nature of the words which they delivered.

SONG.

Move now with measured sound,
You charmed grove of gold,
Trace forth the sacred ground
That shall your forms unfold.

Diana and the starry Night for your Apollo's sake
Endue your Sylvan shapes with power this strange
    delight to make.

M

Much joy must needs the place betide where trees for gladness move :
A fairer sight was ne'er beheld, or more expressing love.

Yet nearer Phœbus' throne
Meet on your winding ways,
Your bridal mirth make known
In your high-graced Hayes.

Let Hymen lead your sliding rounds, and guide them with his light,
While we do Io Hymen sing in honour of this night,
Join three by three, for so the night by triple spell decrees,
Now to release Apollo's knights from these enchanted trees.

This dancing-song being ended, the golden trees stood in ranks three by three, and Night ascended up to the grove, and spake thus, touching the first three severally with her wand.

Night. *By virtue of this wand, and touch divine,*
These Sylvan shadows back to earth resign :
Your native forms resume, with habit fair,
While solemn music shall enchant the air.

Either by the simplicity, negligence, or conspiracy of the painter, the passing away of the trees was somewhat hazarded ;

Presently the Sylvans with their four instruments, and five voices, began to play, and sing together the song following ; at the beginning whereof that part of the stage whereon the first three trees stood began to yield, and the three foremost trees gently to sink, and this was effected by an engine placed under the stage. When the trees had sunk a yard they cleft in three parts, and the Masquers appeared out of the tops of them, the trees were suddenly conveyed away, and the first three Masquers were raised again by the engine. They appeared then in a false habit, yet very fair, and in form not much unlike their principal and true robe. It was made of green taffeta cut into leaves, and laid upon cloth of silver, and their hats were suitable to the same.

the pattern of them the same day having been shown with much advantage and the nine trees being left unset together even to the same night.

SONG OF TRANSFORMATION.

Night and Diana charge,
  And th' Earth obeys,
Opening large
  Her secret ways,
While Apollo's charmed men
  Their forms receive again.
Give gracious Phœbus honour then,
And so fall down, and rest behind the train,
Give gracious Phœbus honour then
And so fall, &c.

When those words were sung, the three Masquers made an honour to the King, and so falling back the other six trees, three by three, came forward, and when they were in their appointed places, Night spake again thus :

Night. *Thus can celestials work in human fate,*
  Transform and form as they do love or hate ;
  Like touch and change receive.   The Gods
    agree :
  The best of numbers is contained in three.

THE SONG OF TRANSFORMATION AGAIN.
  Night and Diana, &c.

Then Night touched the second three trees and the stage sunk with them as before : and in brief the second three did in all points as the first. Then Night spake again.

Night. *The last, and third of nine, touch, magic wand,*
      And give them back their forms at Night's
            command.

Night touched the third three trees, and the same charm of Night and Diana was sung the third time ; the last three trees were transformed, and the Masquers raised, when presently the first Music began his full Chorus.

> *Again this song revive and sound it high :*
> *Long live Apollo, Britain's glorious eye !*

This chorus was in manner of an Echo, seconded by the cornets, then by the consort of ten, then by the consort of twelve, and by a double chorus of voices standing on either side, the one against the other, bearing five voices apiece, and sometime every chorus was heard severally, sometime mixed, but in the end all together : which kind of harmony so distinguished by the place, and by the several nature of instruments, and changeable conveyance of the song, and performed by so many excellent masters as were actors in that music, (their number in all amounting to forty two voices and instruments) could not but yield great satisfaction to the hearers.

While this chorus was repeated twice over, the nine masters in their green habits solemnly descended to the dancing place, in such order as they were to begin their dance, and as soon as the chorus ended, the violins, or consort of twelve began to play the second new dance, which was taken in form of an echo by the cornets, and then catched in like manner by the consort of ten, (sometime they mingled two musics together ; sometime played all at once ;) which kind of echoing music rarely became their sylvan attire, and was so truly mixed together, that no dance could ever be better graced than that, as (in such distraction of music) it was performed by the masquers. After this dance Night descended from the grove, and addressed her speech to the masquers, as followeth.

Night. *Phœbus is pleased, and all rejoice to see*
His servants from their golden prison free.
But yet since Cynthia hath so friendly smiled,
And to you tree-born knights is reconciled,
First ere you any more work undertake,
About her tree solemn procession make,
Diana's tree, the tree of Chastity,
That placed alone on yonder hill you see.
These green-leaved robes, wherein disguised you
            made
Stealths to her nymphs through the thick forest's
            shade,
There to the goddess offer thankfully,
That she may not in vain appeased be.
The Night shall guide you, and her Hours
            attend you
That no ill eyes, or spirits shall offend you.

At the end of this speech Night began to lead the way alone, and after her an Hour with his torch, and after the Hour a masquer ; and so in order one by one, a torch-bearer and a masquer, they march on towards Diana's tree. When the masquers came by the house of Night, every one by his Hour received his helmet, and had his false robe plucked off, and, bearing it in his hand, with a low honour offered it at the tree of Chastity, and so in his glorious habit, with his Hour before him, marched to the bower of Flora. The shape of their habit the picture before discovers, the stuff was of carnation satin laid thick with broad silver lace, their helmets being made of the same stuff. So through the bower of Flora they came, where they joined two torch-bearers, and two masquers, and when they past down to the grove, the Hours parted on either side, and made way between them for the masquers, who descended to the dancing-place in such order as they were to begin their third new dance. All this time of procession the six cornets, and six chapel voices sung a solemn motet of six parts made upon these words.

With spotless minds now mount we to the tree
Of single chastity.
The root is temperance grounded deep,
Which the cold-juiced earth doth steep :
Water it desires alone,
Other drink it thirsts for none :
Therewith the sober branches it doth feed,
Which though they fruitless be,
Yet comely leaves they breed,
To beautify the tree.

Cynthia protectress is, and for her sake
We this grave procession make.
Chaste eyes and ears, pure hearts and voices,
Are graces wherein Phœbe most rejoices.

The motet being ended, the violins began the third
new dance, which was lively performed by the masquers,
after which they took took forth the ladies, and danced
the measures with them ; which being finished, the
masquers brought the ladies back again to their places :
and Hesperus with the rest descended from the grove
into the dancing-place, and spake to the masquers as
followeth.

Hesperus. *Knights of Apollo, proud of your new*
          birth,
          Pursue your triumphs still with joy and
          mirth :
          Your changed fortunes, and redeemed estate,
          Hesperus to your Sovereign will relate.
          'Tis now high time he were far hence retired,
          Th' old bridal friend, that ushers Night
          desired
          Through the dim evening shades, then
          taking flight
          Gives place and honour to the nuptial Night.
          I, that wished evening star, must now make
          way
          To Hymen's rights much wronged by my
          delay.
          But on Night's princely state you ought
          t' attend,
          And t' honour your new reconciled friend.

Night. *Hesperus as you with concord came, ev'n so*
      'Tis meet that you with concord hence should
          go.
      Then join you, that in voice and art excel,
      To give this star a musical farewell.

A DIALOGUE OF FOUR VOICES, TWO BASSES AND TWO TREBLES.

1. *Of all the stars which is the kindest*
          To a loving Bride?
2. *Hesperus when in the west*
          He doth the day from night divide.
1. *What message can be more respected*
      Than that which tells wished joys shall be effected?
2. *Do not Brides watch the evening star?*
1. *O they can discern it far.*
2. *Love Bridegrooms revels?*
          1. *But for fashion.*
2. *And why?*   1. *They hinder wished occasion.*
2. *Longing hearts and new delights,*
   Love short days and long nights.
Chorus. *Hesperus, since you all stars excel*
          In bridal kindness, kindly farewell, farewell.

While these words of the Chorus (*kindly farewell,
farewell*) were in singing often repeated, Hesperus
took his leave severally of Night, Flora, and Zephyrus,
the Hours and Sylvans, and so while the chorus was
sung over the second time, he was got up to the grove,
where turning again to the singers, and they to him,
Hesperus took a second farewell of them, and so past
away by the house of Night. Then Night spake these

two lines, and therewith all retired to the grove where
they stood before.

Night. *Come, Flora, let us now withdraw our train*
That th' eclipsed revels may shine forth again.

Now the masquers began their lighter dances as
corantoes, levaltas and galliards, wherein when they
had spent as much time as they thought fit, Night
spake thus from the grove, and in her speech descended
a little into the dancing-place.

Night. *Here stay : Night leaden-eyed and sprited*
grows,
And her late Hours begin to hang their brows.
Hymen long since the bridal bed hath drest,
And longs to bring the turtles to their nest.
Then with one quick dance[1] sound up your
delight,
And with one song we'll bid you all good-night.

At the end of these words, the violins began the
4 new dance, which was excellently discharged by the
Masquers, and it ended with a light change of music
and measure. After the dance followed this dialogue of
2 voices, a bass and tenor sung by a Sylvan and an
Hour.

Ten. Sylvan. *Tell me, gentle Hour of Night,*
Wherein dost thou most delight ?
Bas. Ho. *Not in sleep.* Syl. *Wherein then ?*
Hour. *In the frolic view of men ?*
Syl. *Lovest thou music?* Hour. *O 'tis*
sweet.

----

[1] Old ed. " dence."

Syl. *What's dancing?* Hour. *Ev'n the mirth
          of feet.*
Syl. *Joy you in fairies and[1] in elves?*
Hour. *We are of that sort ourselves.*
          But, Sylvan, say why do you love
          Only to frequent the grove?
Syl. *Life is fullest of content,*
          Where delight is innocent.
Hour. *Pleasure must vary, not be long.*
          Come then let's close, and end our song.
Chorus. *Yet, ere we vanish from this princely sight,*
          *Let us bid Phœbus and his states good-
          night.*

This chorus was performed with several Echoes of
music, and voices, in manner as the great chorus
before. At the end whereof the Masquers, putting off
their vizards and helmets, made a low honour to the
King, and attended his Majesty to the banqueting
place.

To the Reader.

Neither buskin now, nor bays
Challenge I : a Lady's praise
Shall content my proudest hope.
Their applause was all my scope;
And to their shrines properly
Revels dedicated be :
Whose soft ears none ought to pierce
But with smooth and gentle verse.
Let the tragic Poem swell,
Raising raging fiends from hell;

---

[1] Old ed. "and id elues."

And let epic dactyls range
Swelling seas and countries strange :
Little room small things contains ;
Easy praise quites easy pains.
Suffer them whose brows do sweat
To gain honour by the great : [1]
It's enough if men me name
A retailer of such fame.

Epigramma.

Quid tu te numeris immisces ? anne medentem,
  Metra cathedratum ludicra scripta decent ?
Musicus et medicus, celebris quoque, Phœbe, poeta es,
  Et lepor aegrotos, arte rogante, juvat.
Crede mihi doctum qui carmen non sapit, idem
  Non habet ingenuum, nec geniuum medici.

FINIS.

[In the old edition follow five songs with the musical notes : "These songs were used in the Masque ; whereof the first two airs were made by M. Campion ; the third and last by M. Lupo ; the fourth by M. Tho. Giles : and though the last three airs were devised only for dancing, yet they are here set forth with words that they may be sung to the lute or viol." Song 1, "Now hath Flora" (p. 154); Song 2, "Move now with measured" (p. 161).

Song 3.

Shows and nightly revels, signs of joy and peace,
Fill royal Britain's Court while cruel war far off doth
  rage, for ever hence exiled.

[1] " By the great "—wholesale.

*Fair and princely branches with strong arms increase
From that deep-rooted tree whose sacred strength and
    glory foreign malice hath beguiled.
Our divided kingdoms now in friendly kindred meet
And old debate to love and kindness turns, our power
    with double force uniting;
Truly reconciled, grief appears at last more sweet
Both to ourselves and faithful friends, our undermining
    foes affrighting.*

Song 4.

*Triumph now with joy and mirth!
    The God of Peace hath blessed our land:
We enjoy the fruits of earth
    Through favour of His bounteous hand.*

*We through His most loving grace
    A king and kingly seed behold,
Like a sun with lesser stars
    Or careful shepherd to his fold:
Triumph then, and yield Him praise
That gives us blest and joyful days.*

Song 5.

*Time, that leads the fatal round,
Hath made his centre in our ground,
    With swelling seas embraced;
And there at one stay he rests,
And with the Fates keeps holy feasts,
    With pomp and pastime graced.
Light Cupids there do dance and Venus sweetly sings
With heavenly notes tuned to sound of silver strings:
Their songs are all of joy, no sign of sorrow there,
But all as starres¹ glist'ring fair and blithe appear."]*

¹ I keep the old spelling, as the word is here a dissyllable.

A Relation Of The Late Royall Entertainment Given By The Right Honorable The Lord Knowles, At Cawsome-House neere Redding: to our most Gracious Queene, Queene Anne, in her Progresse toward the Bathe, vpon the seuen and eight and twentie dayes of Aprill, 1613. Whereunto is annexed the Description, Speeches, and Songs of the Lords Maske, presented in the Banqueting-house on the Mariage night of the High and Mightie, Covnt Palatine, and the Royally descended the Ladie Elizabeth. Written by Thomas Campion.[1] *London, Printed for Iohn Budge, and are to be sold at his Shop at the South-doore of S. Pauls, and at Britaines Bursse. 1613. 4to.*

Sir William Knollys, second son of Sir Francis Knollys, was created Baron Knollys of Greys in Oxfordshire, by King James in the first year of his reign, Viscount Wallingford in 1616, and Earl of Banbury in 1526. He died 25 May, 1632, at the age of 88. It was his second wife, Elizabeth, daughter of the Earl of Suffolk, who received Queen Anne on her progress towards Bath. The *Relation* is reprinted in the second volume of Nichols's "Progresses of King James."

[1] In some copies the name is "Campian."

A Relation of the late Royal Entertainment given by the Right Honorable the Lord Knowles at Cawsome-House near Reading to our most gracious Queen, Queen Anne, in her Progress toward the Bath upon the seven and eight and twenty days of April, 1613.

Forasmuchas this late Entertainment hath been much desired in writing, both of such as were present at the performance thereof, as also of many which are yet strangers both to the business and place, it shall be convenient, in this general publication, a little to touch at the description and situation of Cawsome seat. The house is fairly built of brick,[1] mounted on the hillside of a park, within view of Reading, they being severed about the space of two miles. Before the park-gate, directly opposite to the house, a new passage was forced through earable[2] land, that was lately paled in, it being from the park about two flight-shots[3] in length; at the further end whereof, upon the Queen's approach, a Cynic appeared out of a bower, drest in a skin-coat, with bases,[4] of green calico, set thick with leaves and boughs: his nakedness being also artificially shadowed

---

[1] "This fair brick house was pulled down in the reign of George the First by the then possessor, Earl Cadogan, who erected the present elegant structure somewhat further from the Thames, and built a cedar room for the reception of the monarch. Capability Brown was employed in laying out the beautiful grounds. For a view and description of the modern house, see Neale's Seats, New Series, Vol. I."—*Nichols.*

[2] Corn-land. *Ear* = plough, till.

[3] *Flight* was a light far-flying arrow. *Flight-shot* was about a fifth of a mile.

[4] Skirts. The word was used in a variety of senses.

with leaves; on his head he wore a false hair, black and disordered, stuck carelessly with flowers.

The speech of the Cynic to the Queen and her Train.

Cynic. Stay; whether you human be or divine, here is no passage; see you not the earth furrowed? the region solitary? Cities and Courts fit tumultuous multitudes: this is a place of silence; here a kingdom I enjoy without people; myself commands, myself obeys; host, cook, and guest myself; I reap without sowing, owe all to Nature, to none other beholding: my skin is my coat, my ornaments these boughs and flowers, this bower my house, the earth my bed, herbs my food, water my drink; I want no sleep, nor health; I envy none, nor am envied, neither fear I nor hope, nor joy, nor grieve: if this be happiness, I have it; which you all that depend on others' service, or command, want: will you be happy? be private, turn palaces to hermitages, noises to silence, outward felicity to inward content.

A stranger on horse-back was purposely thrust into the troupe disguised, and wrapt in a cloak that he might pass unknown, who at the conclusion of this speech began to discover himself as a fantastic Traveller in a silken suit of strange checker-work, made up after the Italian cut, with an Italian hat, and a band of gold and silk, answering the colours of his suit, with a courtly feather, long gilt spurs, and all things answerable.

The Traveller's speech on horse-back.

Travell. Whither travels thy tongue, ill nurtured man? thy manners shew madness, thy nakedness

poverty, thy resolution folly. Since none will undertake thy presumption, let me descend, that I may
make thy ignorance know how much it hath injured
sacred ears.

*The Traveller then dismounts and gives his cloak
and horse to his foot-man: in the meantime the Cynic
speaks.*

Cyn. Naked I am, and so is truth ; plain, and so is
honesty ; I fear no man's encounter, since my cause
deserves neither excuse, nor blame.

Trav. Shall I now chide or pity thee? thou art
as miserable in life, as foolish in thy opinion. Answer
me? dost thou think that all happiness consists in
solitariness?

Cyn. I do.

Trav. And are they unhappy that abide in society?

Cyn. They are.

Trav. Dost thou esteem it a good thing to live?

Cyn. The best of things.

Trav. Hadst thou not a father and mother?

Cyn. Yes.

Trav. Did they not live in society?

Cyn. They did.

Trav. And wert not thou one of their society when
they bred thee, instructing thee to go and speak?

Cyn. True.

Trav. Thy birth then and speech in spite of thy spleen
make thee sociable ; go, thou art but a vain-glorious
counterfeit, and wanting that which should make thee
happy, contemnest the means. View but the heavens :
is there not above us a sun and moon, giving and
receiving light? are there not millions of stars that

N

participate their glorious beams? is there any element simple? is there not a mixture of all things? and wouldst thou only be singular? action is the end of life, virtue the crown of action, society the subject of virtue, friendship the band of society, solitariness the breach. Thou art yet young, and fair enough, wert thou not barbarous; thy soul, poor wretch, is far out of tune, make it musical; come, follow me, and learn to live.

Cyn. I am conquered by reason, and humbly ask pardon for my error, henceforth my heart shall honour greatness, and love society; lead now, and I will follow, as good a fellow as the best.

The Traveller and Cynic instantly mount on horseback, and hasten to the park-gate, where they are received by two Keepers, formally attired in green perpetuana,[1] with jerkins and long hose, all things else being in colour suitable, having either of them a horn hanging formally at their backs, and on their heads they had green Monmouth[2]-caps, with green feathers, the one of them in his hand bearing a hook-bill, and the other a long pike-staff, both painted green: with them stood two Robin-Hood men in suits of green striped with black, drest in doublets with great bellies and wide sleeves, shaped fardingale-wise at the shoulders, without wings;[3] their hose were round, with long green stockings; on their heads they wore broad flat caps with green feathers cross quite over them, carrying

---

1 Glossy cloth, of durable substance.

2 Old ed. "Mommoth-caps." (Monmouth-cap was a kind of flat cap.)

3 Appendages to the shoulders of a doublet.

green bows in their hands, and green arrows by their sides.

In this space cornets at sundry places entertain the time, till the Queen with her train is entered into the park: and then one of the Keepers presents her with this short speech.

Keeper. More than most welcome, renowned and gracious Queen, since your presence vouchsafes to beautify these woods, whereof I am keeper, be it your pleasure to accept such rude entertainment, as a rough wood-man can yield. This is to us a high holiday, and henceforth yearly shall be kept and celebrated with our country sports, in honour of so royal a guest; come, friends and fellows, now prepare your voices, and present your joys in a sylvan dance.

Here standing on a smooth green, and environed with the horse-men, they present a song of five parts, and withall a lively sylvan-dance of six persons: the Robin-Hood men feign two trebles; one of the Keepers with the Cynic sing two counter-tenors, the other Keeper the bass; but the Traveller being not able to sing, gapes in silence, and expresseth his humour in antic gestures.

A song and dance of six, two Keepers, two Robin-Hood men, the fantastic Traveller, and the Cynic.

I.

Dance now and sing; the joy and love we owe
Let cheerful voices and glad gestures show:
   The Queen of grace is she whom we receive:
   Honour and state are her guides,
   Her presence they can never leave.

Then in a stately sylvan form salute
  Her ever-flowing grace;
Fill all the woods with echoed welcomes,
  And strew with flowers this place;
Let ev'ry bough and plant fresh blossoms yield,
  And all the air refine:
Let pleasure strive to please our goddess,
  For she is all divine.

2.

Yet once again let us our measures move,
And with sweet notes record our joyful love.
  An object more divine none ever had:
  Beauty, and heav'n-born worth,
  Mixt in perfection never fade.
Then with a dance triumphant let us sing
  Her high advanced praise,
And ev'n to heav'n our gladsome welcomes
  With wings of music raise;
Welcome, O welcome, ever-honoured Queen,
  To this now-blessed place!
That grove, that bower, that house is happy
  Which you vouchsafe to grace.

This song being sung and danced twice over, they
fall instantly into a kind of coranto,[1] with these words
following :—

  No longer delay her,
  'Twere sin now to stay her
    From her ease with tedious sport;

---

[1] Old ed. "curranta." (A quick lively dance.)

> *Then welcome still crying*
> *And swiftly hence flying,*
> *Let us to our homes resort.*

In the end whereof the two Keepers carry away the Cynic; and the two Robin-Hood men the Traveller; when presently cornets begin again to sound in several places, and so continue with variety, while the Queen passeth through a long smooth green way, set on each side with trees in equal distance; all this while her Majesty being carried in her caroch.[1]

But because some wet had fallen that day in the forenoon (though the garden-walks were made artificially smooth and dry) yet all her foot-way was spread with broad-cloth, and so soon as her Majesty with her train were all entered into the lower garden, a Gardener, with his man and boy, issued out of an arbour to give her Highness entertainment. The Gardener was suited in gray with a jerkin double jagged all about the wings and skirts; he had a pair of great slops with a codpiece, and buttoned gamachios[2] *all of the same stuff: on his head he had a strawn hat, piebaldly drest with flowers, and in his hand a silvered spade. His man was also suited in gray with a great buttoned flap on his jerkin, having large wings and skirts, with a pair of great slops and gamachios of the same; on his head he had a strawn hat, and in his hand a silvered mattox. The Gardener's boy was in a pretty suit of flowery stuff, with a silvered rake in his hand. When they approached near the Queen, they all vailed bonnet; and*

---

[1] Coach.

[2] "*Gamashes.* The term was formerly applied to a kind of loose drawers or stockings worn outside the legs over the other clothing."—*Halliwell.*

lowting low, the Gardener began after his antic fashion this speech.

Gard. Most magnificent and peerless deity,[1] lo I, the surveyor of Lady Flora's works, welcome your grace with fragrant phrases into her bowers, beseeching your greatness to bear with the late wooden entertainment of the wood-men ; for woods are more full of weeds than wits, but gardens are weeded, and gardeners witty, as may appear by me. I have flowers for all fancies. Thyme for truth, rosemary for remembrance, roses for love, heartsease for joy, and thousands more, which all harmoniously rejoice at your presence ; but myself, with these my Paradisians here, will make you such music as the wild woodists shall be ashamed to hear the report of it. Come, sirs, prune your pipes, and tune your strings, and agree together like birds of a feather.

A song of a treble and bass, sung by the Gardener's boy and man, to music of instruments, that was ready to second them in the arbour.

1.

Welcome to this flowery place,
Fair Goddess and sole Queen of grace :
All eyes triumph in your sight,
Which through all this empty space
Casts such glorious beams of light.

2.

Paradise were meeter far
To entertain so bright a star :
But why errs my folly so ?

1 Here and elsewhere the old ed. reads " Diety "—which was an old form of " Deity."

Paradise is where you are :
Heav'n above, and heav'n below.

3.

Could our powers and wishes meet,
How well would they your graces greet !
Yet accept of our desire :
Roses, of all flowers most sweet,
Spring out of the silly briar.

After this song, the Gardener speaks again.

Gard. Wonder not (great goddess) at the sweetness
of our garden-air (though passing sweet it be). Flora
hath perfumed it for you (Flora our mistress, and your
servant) who invites you yet further into her Paradise ;
she invisibly will lead your grace the way, and we (as
our duty is) visibly stay behind.

*From thence the Queen ascends by a few steps into
the upper garden, at the end whereof, near the house,
this song was sung by an excellent counter-tenor voice,
with rare variety of division unto two unusual instruments, all being concealed within the arbour.*

1.

O joys exceeding,
From love, from power of your wished sight proceeding !
As a fair morn shines divinely,
Such is your view, appearing more divinely.

2.

Your steps ascending,
Raise high your thoughts for your content contending ;
All our hearts of this grace vaunting,
Now leap as they were moved by enchanting.

So ended the entertainment without the house for that time; and the Queen's pleasure being that night to sup privately, the King's violins attended her with their solemnest music, as an excellent consort in like manner did the next day at dinner.

Supper being ended, her Majesty, accompanied with many Lords and Ladies, came into the hall, and rested herself in her chair of state, the scaffolds of the hall being on all parts filled with beholders of worth. Suddenly forth came the Traveller, Gardener, Cynic, with the rest of their crew, and others furnished with their instruments, and in manner following entertain the time.

Traveller. A hall![1] a hall! for men of moment, rationals and irrationals, but yet not all of one breeding. For I an Academic am, refined by travel, that have learned what to courtship belongs, and so divine a presence as this; if we press past good manners, laugh at our follies, for you cannot shew us more favour than to laugh at us. If we prove ridiculous in your sights, we are gracious; and therefore we beseech you to laugh at us. For mine own part (I thank my stars for it) I have been laughed at in most parts of Christendom.

Gardener. I can neither brag of my travels, nor yet am ashamed of my profession; I make sweet walks for fair ladies; flowers I prepare to adorn them; close arbours I build wherein their loves unseen may court them; and who can do ladies better service, or more acceptable? When I was a child and lay in my cradle,

---

[1] "A hall!" *i.e.* make way! give room!

(a very pretty child) I remember well that Lady Venus appeared unto me, and setting a silver spade and rake by my pillow, bade me prove a gardener. I told my mother of it (as became the duty of a good child) whereupon she provided straight for me two great platters full of pap ; which having dutifully devoured, I grew to this portraiture you see, sprung suddenly out of my cabin, and fell to my profession.

Trav. Verily by thy discourse thou hast travelled much, and I am ashamed of myself that I come so far behind thee, as not once to have yet mentioned Venus or Cupid, or any other of the gods to have appeared to me. But I will henceforth boast truly, that I have now seen a deity as far beyond theirs, as the beauty of light is beyond darkness, or this feast, whereof we have had our share, is beyond thy sallets.

Cynic. Sure I am, it hath stirred up strange thoughts in me ; never knew I the difference between wine and water before. Bacchus hath opened mine eyes ; I now see bravery and admire it, beauty and adore it. I find my arms naked, my discourse rude, but my heart soft as wax, ready to melt with the least beam of a fair eye ; which (till this time) was as untractable as iron.

Gard. I much joy in thy conversion, thou hast long been a mad fellow, and now provest a good fellow ; let us all therefore join together sociably in a song, to the honour of good fellowship.

Cyn. A very musical motion, and I agree to it.

Trav. Sing that sing can, for my part I will only, while you sing, keep time with my gestures, à[1] *la mode de France.*

---

[1] Old ed. "*A la more du France.*"

A song of three voices with divers instruments.

Night as well as brightest day hath her delight,
Let us then with mirth and music deck the night.
Never did glad day such store
 Of joy to night bequeath :
Her stars then adore,
 Both in Heav'n, and here beneath.

2.

Love and beauty, mirth and music yield true joys,
Though the cynics in their folly count them toys.
Raise your spirits ne'er so high,
 They will be apt to fall :
None brave thoughts envỳ,
 Who had e'er brave thoughts at all.

3.

Joy is the sweet friend of life, the nurse of blood,
Patron of all health, and fountain of all good :
Never may joy hence depart,
 But all your thoughts attend ;
Nought can hurt the heart,
 That retains so sweet a friend.

At the end of this song enters Sylvanus, shaped after the description of the ancient writers ; his lower parts like a goat, and his upper parts in an antic habit of rich taffeta, cut into leaves, and on his head he had a false hair, with a wreath of long boughs and lilies, that hung dangling about his neck, and in his hand a cypress branch, in memory of his love Cyparissus. The Gardener, espying him, speaks thus.

Gard. Silence, sirs, here comes Sylvanus, god of
these woods, whose presence is rare, and imports
some novelty.

Trav. Let us give place, for this place is fitter for
deities than us.

*They all vanish and leave Sylvanus alone, who
coming nearer to the state, and making a low congee,
speaks.*

Sylvanus.

That health which harbours in the fresh-aired groves,
Those pleasures which green hill and valley moves,
Sylvanus, the commander of them all,
Here offers to this state imperial ;
Which as a homager he visits now,
And to a greater power his power doth bow.
Withal, thus much his duty signifies :
That there are certain semi-deities,
Belonging to his sylvan walks, who come
Led with the music of a sprightly drum,
To keep the night awake and honour you
(Great Queen) to whom all honours they hold due.
So rest you full of joy, and wished content,
Which though it be not given, 'tis fairly meant.

*At the end of this speech there is suddenly heard a
great noise of drums and fifes, and way being made,
eight pages first enter, with green torches in their
hands lighted; their suits were of green satin, with
cloaks and caps of the same, richly and strangely set
forth. Presently after them the eight Masquers came,
in rich embroidered suits of green satin, with high*

*hats of the same, and all their accoutrements answerable
to such noble and princely personages, as they concealed
under their vizards, and so they instantly fell into a new
dance : at the end whereof they took forth the Ladies,
and danced with them; and so well was the Queen
pleased with her entertainment, that she vouchsafed to
make herself the head of their revels, and graciously to
adorn the place with her personal dancing : much of
the night being thus spent with variety of dances, the
Masquers made a conclusion with a second new dance.*

*At the Queen's parting on Wednesday in the afternoon,
the Gardener with his man and boy and three handsome
country maids, the one bearing a rich bag with linen in
it, the second a rich apron, and a third a rich mantle,[1]
appear all out of an arbour in the lower garden, and
meeting the Queen, the Gardener presents this speech.*

Gardener.

Stay, goddess ! stay a little space,
Our poor country love to grace,
Since we dare not too long stay you,
Accept at our hands, we pray you,
These mean presents, to express
Greater love than we profess,
Or can utter now for woe
Of your parting hast'ned so.
Gifts these are, such as were wrought
By their hands that them have brought,

---

[1] "The presents are described in Mr. Chamberlain's letter as
'a dainty coverled or quilt, a rich carquenet, and a curious cabinet
to the value in all of £1,500.'"—*Nichols.*

Home-bred things, which they presumed,
After I had them perfumed
With my flowery incantation,
To give you in presentation
At your parting.   Come, feat lasses,
With fine curtsies, and smooth faces,
Offer up your simple toys
To the mistress of our joys ;
While we the sad time prolong
With a mournful parting song.

*A song of three voices continuing while the presents
are delivered and received.*

I.

Can you, the author of our joy,
  So soon depart?
Will you revive, and straight destroy ?
  New mirth to tears convert?
O that ever cause of gladness
Should so swiftly turn to sadness !

2.

Now as we droop, so will these flowers,
  Barred of your sight :
Nothing avail them heav'nly showers
  Without your heav'nly light.
When the glorious sun forsakes us,
Winter quickly overtakes us.

3.

Yet shall our prayers your ways attend,
  When you are gone ;

And we the tedious time will spend,
Rememb'ring you alone.
Welcome here shall you hear ever,
But the word of parting never.

Thus ends this ample entertainment, which as it was most nobly performed by the right honourable the lord and lady of the house, and fortunately executed by all that any way were actors in it, so was it as graciously received of her Majesty, and celebrated with her most royal applause.

The Description, Speeches, and Songs, of The Lords' Masque, Presented in the Banqueting-House on the Marriage Night of the High and Mighty Count Palatine, and the Royally Descended the Lady Eliza-beth.[1]

I have now taken occasion to satisfy many, who long since were desirous that the Lords' masque should be published, which, but for some private lets, had in due time come forth. The Scene was divided into two parts. From the roof to the floor, the lower part being first discovered (upon the sound of a double consort, exprest by several instruments, placed on either side of the room) there appeared a wood in prospective, the

---

1 The marriage was celebrated on Shrove-Sunday, 14 February, 1612-13. "Of the Lords' Masque," writes Chamberlain, "I hear no great commendation save only for riches, their devices being long and tedious, and more like a play than a masque" (Winwood's "Memorials," iii. 435). But, as Nichols remarks, Chamberlain was not present. Those who were dissatisfied with Campion's masque must have been hard to please. It cost £400 (Nichols' "Progresses of King James," ii. 622),—a small sum compared with the lavish expenses frequently incurred on such occasions.

*innermost part being of relief, or whole round, the rest
painted. On the left hand from the seat was a cave,
and on the right a thicket, out of which came Orpheus,
who was attired after the old Greek manner, his hair
curled and long, a laurel wreath on his head, and in
his hand he bare a silver bird; about him tamely placed
several wild beasts: and upon the ceasing of the consort
Orpheus spake.*

Orpheus.

Again, again, fresh kindle Phœbus' sounds,
T'exhale Mania from her earthy den ;
Allay the fury that her sense confounds,
And call her gently forth ; sound, sound again.

*The consorts both sound again, and Mania, the
goddess of madness, appears wildly out of her cave.
Her habit was confused and strange, but yet graceful;
she as one amazed speaks.*

Mania.   What powerful noise is this importunes me,
T'abandon darkness which my humour fits ?
Jove's hand in it I feel, and ever he
Must be obeyed ev'n of the frantic'st wits.
Orpheus. Mania !
Mania. Hah !
Orpheus. Brain-sick, why start'st thou so ?
Approach yet nearer, and thou then shall
know
The will of Jove, which he will breathe from
me.

Mania. Who art thou ? if my dazzled eyes can see,
  Thou art the sweet enchanter heav'nly
    Orpheus.
Orpheus. The same, Mania, and Jove greets thee thus :
  Though several power to thee and charge
    he gave
  T'enclose in thy dominions such as rave
  Through blood's distemper, how durst thou
    attempt
  T'imprison Entheus whose rage is exempt
  From vulgar censure ? it is all divine,
  Full of celestial rapture, that can shine
  Through darkest shadows : therefore Jove
    by me
  Commands thy power straight to set Entheus
    free.
Mania. How can I ? Frantics with him many more
  In one cave are locked up; ope once the
    door,
  All will fly out, and through the world disturb
  The peace of Jove ; for what power then
    can curb
  Their reinless fury ?
Orpheus. Let not fear in vain
  Trouble thy crazed fancy ; all again,
  Save Entheus, to thy safeguard shall retire,
  For Jove into our music will inspire
  The power of passion, that their thoughts
    shall bend
  To any form or motion we intend.
  Obey Jove's will [1] then ; go, set Entheus free.

---

[1] Old ed. "willing."

O

Mania. I willing go, so Jove obeyed must be.

Orph. Let Music put on Protean changes now ;
  Wild beasts it once tamed, now let Frantics
  bow.

At the sound of a strange music twelve Frantics enter, six men and six women, all presented in sundry habits and humours. There was the lover, the self-lover, the melancholic-man full of fear, the school-man overcome with fantasy, the over-watched usurer, with others that made an absolute medley of madness; in midst of whom Entheus (or poetic fury) was hurried forth, and tost up and down, till by virtue of a new change in the music, the Lunatics fell into a mad measure, fitted to a loud fantastic tune; but in the end thereof the music changed into a very solemn air, which they softly played, while Orpheus spake.

Orph. Through these soft and calm sounds, Mania,
  pass
  With thy Fantastics hence ; here is no place
  Longer for them or thee ; Entheus alone
  Must do Jove's bidding now : all else be
  gone.

During this speech Mania with her Frantics depart, leaving Entheus behind them, who was attired in a close curace[1] of the antic fashion, bases with labels, a robe fastened to his shoulders, and hanging down behind; on his head a wreath of laurels, out of which grew a pair of wings; in the one hand he held a book, and in the other a pen.

[1] An old form of "cuirass."

Enth. Divinest Orpheus, O how all from thee
    Proceed with wondrous sweetness ! Am I free ?
    Is my affliction vanished ?

Orph. Too, too long,
    Alas, good Entheus, hast thou brooked this
        wrong.
    What ! number thee with madmen ! O mad age,
    Senseless of thee, and thy celestial rage !
    For thy excelling rapture, ev'n through things
    That seems most light, is borne with sacred
        wings :
    Nor are these musics, shows, or revels vain,
    When thou adorn'st them with thy Phœbean
        brain.
    Th'are palate-sick of much more vanity,
    That cannot taste them in their dignity.
    Jove therefore lets thy prisoned sprite obtain
    Her liberty and fiery scope again ;
    And here by me commands thee to create
    Inventions rare, this night to celebrate,
    Such as become a nuptial by his will
    Begun and ended.

Enth. Jove I honour still,
    And must obey. Orpheus, I feel the fires
    Are ready in my brain, which Jove inspires.
    Lo, through that veil I see Prometheus stand
    Before those glorious lights which his false hand
    Stole out of heav'n, the dull earth to inflame
    With the affects[1] of Love and honoured Fame.
    I view them plain in pomp and majesty,
    Such as being seen might hold rivality

Properties, qualities.

With the best triumphs.   Orpheus, give a call
With thy charmed music, and discover all.
Orph. Fly, cheerful voices, through the air, and clear
These clouds, that yon hid beauty may appear.

A Song.

1.

Come away ; bring thy golden theft,
   Bring, bright Prometheus, all thy lights ;
Thy fires from Heav'n bereft
   Show now to human sights.
Come [1] quickly, come ! thy stars to our stars straight
   present,
For pleasure being too much deferred loseth her best
   content.
What fair dames wish, should swift as their own
   thoughts appear ;
To loving and to longing hearts every hour seems a
   year.

2.

See how fair, O how fair, they shine !
   What yields more pomp beneath the skies ?
Their birth is yet divine,
   And such their form implies.
Large grow their beams, their near approach afford
   them so ;
By nature sights that pleasing are, cannot too amply
   show.
O might these flames in human shapes descend this
   place,
How lovely would their presence be, how full of grace !

---

[1] Cf. p. 81, " Come quickly, come ! the promised hour," &c.

In the end of the first part of this song, the upper part of the scene was discovered by the sudden fall of a curtain; then in clouds of several colours (the upper part of them being fiery, and the middle heightened with silver) appeared eight stars of extraordinary bigness, which so were placed, as that they seemed to be fixed between the firmament and the earth. In the front of the scene stood Prometheus, attired as one of the ancient heroes.

Enth. Patron of mankind, powerful and bounteous,
  Rich in thy flames, reverend Prometheus,
  In Hymen's place aid us to solemnise
  These royal nuptials ; fill the lookers' eyes
  With admiration of thy fire and light,
  And from thy hand let wonders flow to-night.

Prom. Entheus and Orpheus, names both dear to me,
  In equal balance I your third will be
  In this night's honour. View these heav'n-born
    stars,
  Who by my stealth are become sublunars ;
  How well their native beauties fit this place,
  Which with a choral dance they first shall
    grace ;
  Then shall their forms to human figures turn,
  And these bright fires within their bosoms
    burn.
  Orpheus, apply thy music, for it well
  Helps to induce a courtly miracle.

Orp. Sound, best of musics, raise yet higher our
    sprites,
  While we admire Prometheus' dancing lights.

A Song.

1.

Advance your choral motions now,
    You music-loving lights :
This night concludes the nuptial vow,
    Make this the best of nights :
So bravely crown it with your beams
    That it may live in fame
As long as Rhenus or the Thames.
    Are known by either name.

2.

Once more again, yet nearer move
    Your forms at willing view ;
Such fair effects of Joy and love
    None can express but you.
Then revel midst your airy bowers
    Till all the clouds do sweat,
That pleasure may be poured in showers
    On this triumphant seat.

3.

Long since hath lovely Flora thrown
    Her flowers and garlands here ;
Rich Ceres all her wealth hath shown,
    Proud of her dainty cheer.
Changed then to human shape, descend,
    Clad in familiar weed,
That every eye may here commend
    The kind delights you breed.

*According to the humour of this song, the stars
moved in an exceeding strange and delightful manner,
and I suppose few have ever seen more neat artifice*

*than Master Inigo Jones shewed in contriving their
motion, who in all the rest of the workmanship which
belonged to the whole invention shewed extraordinary
industry and skill, which if it be not as lively exprest
in writing as it appeared in view, rob not him of his
due, but lay the blame on my want of right apprehending his instructions for the adorning of his art. But
to return to our purpose; about the end of this song,
the stars suddenly vanished, as if they had been drowned
amongst the clouds, and the eight masquers appeared in
their habits, which were infinitely rich, befitting states[1]
(such as indeed they all were) as also a time so far
heightened the day before with all the richest show of
solemnity that could be invented. The ground of their
attires was massy cloth of silver, embossed with
flames of embroidery; on their heads, they had crowns,
flames made all of gold-plate enameled, and on the top
a feather of silk, representing a cloud of smoke. Upon
their new transformation, the whole scene being clouds
dispersed, and there appeared an element of artificial
fires, with several circles of lights, in continual motion,
representing the house of Prometheus, who then thus
applies his speech to the masquers.*

They are transformed.

Prometh. So pause awhile, and come, ye fiery sprites,[2]
    Break forth the earth like sparks t'attend
    these knights.

*Sixteen pages, like fiery spirits, all their attires being
alike composed of flames, with fiery wings and bases,
bearing in either hand a torch of virgin wax, come*

---

[1] Persons of rank.   [2] Old ed. "spirits."

forth below dancing a lively measure, and the dance being ended, Prometheus speaks to them from above.

The Torch-bearers' Dance.

Pro.   Wait, spirits, wait, while through the clouds
we pace,
And by descending gain a higher place.

The pages return toward the scene, to give their attendance to the masquers with their lights : from the side of the scene appeared a bright and transparent cloud, which reached from the top of the heavens to the earth : on this cloud the masquers, led by Prometheus, descended with the music of a full song; and at the end of their descent, the cloud brake in twain, and one part of it (as with a wind) was blown overthwart the scene.

While this cloud was vanishing, the wood being the under-part of the scene, was insensibly changed, and in place thereof appeared four noble women-statues of silver, standing in several niches, accompanied with ornaments of architecture, which filled all the end of the house, and seemed to be all of gold-smith's work. The first order consisted of pilasters all of gold, set with rubies, sapphires, emeralds, opals and such like. The capitals were composed, and of a new invention. Over this was a bastard order with cartouches reversed coming from the capitals of every pilaster, which made the upper part rich and full of ornament. Over every statue was placed a history in gold, which seemed to be of base relief; the conceits which were figured in them were these. In the first was Prometheus, embossing in clay the figure of a woman, in the second he was repre-

*sented stealing fire from the chariot-wheel of the sun;
in the third he is exprest putting life with this fire into
his figure of clay; and in the fourth square Jupiter,
enraged, turns these new-made women into statues.
Above all, for finishing, ran a cornice, which returned
over every pilaster, seeming all of gold and richly
carved.*

A full Song.

Supported now by clouds descend,
Divine Prometheus, Hymen's friend :
Lead down the new transformed fires
And fill their breasts with love's desires,
That they may revel with delight,
And celebrate this nuptial night.
So celebrate this nuptial night
   That all which see may say [1]
They never viewed so fair a sight
   Even on the clearest day.

*While this song is sung, and the masquers court the
four new transformed ladies, four other statues appear
in their places.*

Entheus. See, see, Prometheus, four of these first dames
   Which thou long since out of thy purchased [2]
     flames,
   Didst forge with heav'nly fire, as they were
     then
   By Jove transformed to statues, so again
   They suddenly appear by his command

---

[1] Old ed. "stay."   [2] Stolen.

At thy arrival.   Lo, how fixed thy stand ;
So did Jove's wrath too long, but now at last,
It by degrees relents, and he hath placed
These statues, that we might his aid implore,
First for the life of these, and then for more.

Prom.   Entheus, thy counsels are divine and just,
Let Orpheus deck thy hymn, since pray we
must.

The first invocation in a full song.

Powerful Jove, that of bright stars,
Now hast made men fit for wars,
Thy power in these statues prove
And make them women fit for love.

Orpheus. See, Jove is pleased ; statues have life and
move !
Go, new-born men, and entertain with love
The new-born women, though your number
yet
Exceeds their's double, they are armed with
wit
To bear your best encounters.   Court them
fair : ,
When words and music please, let none
despair.

The Song.

I.

Woo her, and win her, he that can !
Each woman hath two lovers,
So she must take and leave a man,
Till time more grace discovers.

This doth Jove to shew that want
　Makes beauty most respected ;
If fair women were more scant,
　They would be more affected.

2.

Courtship and music suit with love,
　They both are works of passion ;
Happy is he whose words can move,
　Yet sweet notes help persuasion.
Mix your words with music then,
　That they the more may enter ;
Bold assaults are fit for men,
　That on strange beauties venter.[1]

Promet.　Cease, cease your wooing strife ! see, Jove
　　　　intends
　　　To fill your number up, and make all friends.
　　　Orpheus and Entheus, join your skills once
　　　　more,
　　　And with a hymn the deity implore.

The second invocation to the tune of the first.
　　Powerful Jove, that hast given four,
　　Raise this number but once more,
　　That complete, their numerous[2] feet
　　May aptly in just measures meet.

*The other four statues are transformed into women,
in the time of this invocation.*

Enth.　The number's now complete, thanks be to
　　　Jove !
　　No man needs fear a rival in his love ;

1 Old ed. gives "venture ; " but "venter"—which is a
recognized old form of "venture "—is needed for the rhyme.
2 "Numerous "—keeping time.

For all are sped, and now begins delight
To fill with glory this triumphant night.

The masquers, having every one entertained his lady, begin their first new entering dance: after it, while they breathe, the time is entertained with a dialogue-song.

Breathe you now, while Io Hymen
  To the bride we sing :
O how many joys and honours,
  From this match will spring !
Ever firm the league will prove,
Where only goodness causeth love.
Some for profit seek
What their fancies most disleek [1] :
These love for virtue's sake alone :
Beauty and youth unite them both in one.

Chorus.
Live with thy bridegroom happy, sacred bride ;
How blest is he that is for love envied !

The masquers' second dance.

Breathe again, while we with music
  Fill the empty space :
O but do not in your dances
  Yourselves only grace.
Ev'ry one fetch out your fere,[2]
Whom chiefly you will honour here.
Sights most pleasure breed,
When their numbers most exceed.

---

[1] Old form of "dislike."   [2] Mate.

Choose then, for choice to all is free ;
Taken or left, none discontent must be.

Chorus.

Now in thy revels frolic-fair delight,
To heap joy on this ever-honoured night.

The masquers during this dialogue take out others to dance with them ; men women, and women men ; and first of all the princely bridegroom and bride were drawn into these solemn revels, which continued a long space, but in the end were broken off with this short song.

A Song.

Cease, cease you revels, rest a space ;
New pleasures press into this place,
Full of beauty and of grace.

The whole scene was now again changed, and became a prospective with porticoes on each side, which seemed to go in a great way ; in the middle was erected an obelisk, all of silver, and in it lights of several colours ; on the side of this obelisk, standing on pedestals, were the statues of the bridegroom and bride, all of gold in gracious postures. This obelisk was of that height, that the top thereof touched the highest clouds, and yet Sibylla did draw it forth with a thread of gold. The grave sage was in a robe of gold tuckt up before to her girdle, a kirtle gathered full and of silver ; with a veil on her head, being bare-necked, and bearing in her hands a scroll of parchment.

Entheus. Make clear the passage to Sibylla's sight,
    Who with her trophy comes to crown this
        night ;
    And, as herself with music shall be led,
    So shall she pull on with a golden thread
    A high vast obelisk, dedicate to Fame,
    Which immortality itself did frame.
    Raise high your voices now ; like trumpets
        fill
    The room with sounds of triumph, sweet and
        shrill.

A Song.

Come triumphing, come with state,
    Old Sibylla, reverend dame ;
Thou keep'st the secret key of fate,
    Preventing swiftest Fame.
This night breathe only words of joy,
And speak them plain, now be not coy.

Sibylla.

Debetur alto jure principium Jovi,
Votis det ipse vim meis, dictis fidem.
Utrinque decoris splendet egregium jubar ;
Medio triumphus mole stat dignus sua,
Cœlumque summo capite dilectum petit.
Quam pulchra pulchro sponsa respondet viro !
Quam plena numinis ! Patrem vultu exprimit,
Parens futura masculae prolis, parens
Regum, imperatorum. Additur Germaniae
Robur Britannicum : ecquid esse par potest ?
Utramque junget una mens gentem, fides,
Deique cultus unus, et simplex amor.

Idem erit utrique hostis, sodalis idem, idem
Votum periclitantium, atque eadem manus.
Favebit illis pax, favebit bellica
Fortuna, semper aderit adjutor Deus.
Sic, sic Sibylla; vocibus nec his deest
Pondus, nec hoc inane monumentum[1] trahit.
Et aureum est, et quale nec flammas timet,
Nec fulgura, ipsi quippe sacratur Jovi.

Pro. The good old sage is silenced, her free tongue
　　That made such melody, is now unstrung :
　　Then grace her trophy with a dance triumphant ;
　　Where Orpheus is none can fit music want.

A song and dance triumphant of the masquers.

1.

Dance, dance ! and visit now the shadows of our joy,
All in height, and pleasing state, your changed forms
　　employ.
And as the bird of Jove salutes with lofty wing the
　　morn,
So mount, so fly, these trophies to adorn.
Grace them with all the sounds and motions of delight,
Since all the earth cannot express a lovelier sight.
View them with triumph, and in shades the truth adore :
No pomp or sacrifice can please Jove's greatness more.

2.

Turn, turn ! and honour now the life these figures bear :
Lo, how heav'nly natures far above all art appear !

---

[1] Old ed. "momumentum."

Let their aspects revive in you the fire that shined so
    late,
Still mount and still retain your heavenly state.
Gods were with dance and with music served of old,
Those happy days derived their glorious style from gold :
This pair, by Hymen joined, grace you with measures
    then,
Since they are both divine and you are more than men.

Orph.   Let here Sibylla's trophy stand,
        Lead her now by either hand,
        That she may approach yet nearer,
        And the bride and bridegroom hear her
        Bless them in her native tongue,
        Wherein old prophecies she sung,
        Which time to light hath brought.
        She speaks that which Jove hath taught :
        Well may he inspire her now,
        To make a joyful and true vow.
Sib.   *Sponsam sponse toro tene pudicam,*
        Sponsum sponsa tene toro pudicum.
        Non haec unica nox datur beatis,
        At vos perpetuo haec beabit una
        Prole multiplici, parique amore.
        Laeta, ac vera refert Sibylla ; ab alto
        Ipse Juppiter annuit loquenti.
Pro.   So be it ever, joy and peace,
        And mutual love give you increase,
        That your posterity may grow
        In fame, as long as seas do flow.
Enth.   Live you long to see your joys,
        In fair nymphs and princely boys ;

Breeding like the garden flowers,
Which kind heav'n draws with her warm
    showers.

Orph.   Enough of blessing, though too much
Never can be said to such ;
But night doth waste, and Hymen chides,
Kind to bridegrooms and to brides.
Then, singing, the last dance induce,
So let good night present excuse.

The Song.

No longer wrong the night
Of her Hymenæan right ;
A thousand Cupids call away,
Fearing the approaching day;
The cocks already crow :
      Dance then and go !

*The last new dance of the masquers, which concludes
all with a lively strain at their going out.*

FINIS.

The description of a Maske: presented in the Banqueting roome at Whitehall, on Saint Stephens night last, At the Mariage of the Right Honourable the Earle of Somerset: And the right noble the Lady Frances Howard. Written by Thomas Campion. Whereunto are annexed diuers choice Ayres composed for this Maske that may be sung with a single voyce to the Lute or Base-Viall. London Printed by E. A. for Laurence Li'sle, dwelling in Paules Church-yard, at the signe of the Tygers head. 1614. 4to.

The ill-omened marriage of Robert Carr, Earl of Somerset, with the divorced wife of the Earl of Essex was celebrated at Whitehall, 26 December, 1613, in the presence of the King, Queen, Prince Charles, and many nobles and bishops. Campion's masque was worthy of a better occasion. Chamberlain's account of the reception of the masque is by no means flattering. In a letter to Mrs. Alice Carleton, sister to Sir Dudley Carleton, he writes: "I hear little or no commendation of the masque made by the Lords that night, either for device or dancing, only it was rich and costly" (Nichols's "Progresses of James I.," ii. 725). He had given the same unfavourable report about the masque that Campion prepared for the Princess Elizabeth's marriage.

Pulchro pulchra datur sociali fœdere ; amanti
Tandem nubit amans ; ecquid amabilius ?

Veræ [1] *ut supersint nuptiæ*
Præite duplici face :
Prætendat alteram necesse
Hymen, alteram par est Amor.

Uni ego mallem placuisse docto,
Candido, et fastu sine judicanti,
Millium quam millibus imperitorum
Inque videntûm.

---

[1] The same sentiment is more neatly and metrically expressed
in Campion's first book of Latin Epigrams (No. 68) :—

"*De Nuptiis.*
Rite ut celebres nuptias,
  Dupla tibi face est opus ;
Prætendat unum Hymen necesse,
  At alteram par est Amor."

The description of a Masque, presented in the Banqueting room at Whitehall, on St. Stephen's night last : At the Marriage of the right Honourable the Earl of Somerset, and the right noble the Lady Frances Howard.

IN ancient times, when any man sought to shadow or heighten his invention, he had store of feigned persons ready for his purpose, as satyrs, nymphs, and their like : such were then in request and belief among the vulgar. But in our days, although they have not utterly lost their use, yet find they so little credit, that our modern writers have rather transferred their fictions to the persons of enchanters and commanders of spirits, as that excellent poet Torquato Tasso hath done, and many others.

In imitation of them (having a presentation in hand for persons of high state) I grounded my whole invention upon enchantments and several transformations. The workmanship whereof was undertaken by M. Constantine,[1] an Italian, architect to our late Prince Henry : but he being too much of himself, and no way to be drawn to impart his intentions, failed so far in the assurance he gave that the main invention, even at the last cast, was of force drawn into a far narrower compass than was from the beginning intended : the description whereof, as it was performed, I will as briefly as I can deliver. The place wherein the masque was presented being the Banqueting house at Whitehall : the upper part, where the state[2] is placed, was theatred with pillars, scaffolds, and all

---

[1] "To Constantine de Servi Prince Henry assigned a yearly pension of £200 in July, 1612."—*Nichols.*

[2] Chair of state.

things answerable to the sides of the room. At the lower end of the hall, before the scene, was made an arch triumphal, passing beautiful, which enclosed the whole works. The scene itself (the curtain being drawn) was in this manner divided.

On the upper part there was formed a sky of clouds very artificially shadowed. On either side of the scene below was set a high promontory, and on either of them stood three large pillars of gold : the one promontory was bounded with a rock standing in the sea, the other with a wood. In the midst between them appeared a sea in perspective with ships, some cunningly painted, some artificially sailing. On the front of the scene, on either side, was a beautiful garden, with six seats apiece to receive the masquers : behind them the main land, and in the midst a pair of stairs made exceeding curiously in the form of a scallop shell. And in this manner was the eye first of all entertained. After the King, Queen, and Prince were placed, and preparation was made for the beginning of the masque, there entered four Squires, who as soon as they approached near the presence, humbly bowing themselves, spake as followeth.

The first Squire.

That fruit that neither dreads the Syrian heats,
Nor the sharp frosts which churlish Boreas threats,
The fruit of peace and joy our wishes bring
To this high state, in a perpetual spring.
Then pardon (sacred majesty) our grief
Unreasonably that presseth for relief.
The ground whereof (if your blest ears can spare

A short space of attention) we'll declare.
Great Honour's herald, Fame, having proclaimed
This nuptial feast, and with it all enflamed,
From every quarter of the earth twelve [1] knights
(In courtship seen, as well as martial fights)
Assembled in the continent, and there
Decreed this night a solemn service here.
For which, by six and six embarked they were
In several keels ; their sails for Britain bent.
But (they that never favoured good intent)
Deformed Error, that enchanting fiend,
And wing-tongued Rumour, his infernal friend,
With Curiosity and Credulity,
Both sorceresses, all in hate agree
Our purpose to divert ; in vain they strive,
For we in spite of them came near t'arrive,
When suddenly (as heaven and hell had met)
A storm confused against our tackle beat,
Severing the ships : but after what befel
Let these relate, my tongue's too weak to tell.

The second Squire.

A strange and sad ostent our knights distrest ;
For while the tempest's fiery rage increased,
About our decks and hatches, lo, appear
Serpents, as Lerna had been poured out there,
Crawling about us ; which fear to eschew,
The knights the tackle climbed, and hung in view,
When violently a flash of lightning came,
And from our sights did bear them in the flame :
Which past, no serpent there was to be seen,
And all was hushed, as storm had never been.

1 Old ed. "three."

The third Squire.

At sea their mischiefs grew, but ours at land,
For being by chance arrived, while our knights stand
To view their storm-tost friends on two cliffs near,
Thence, lo, they vanished, and six pillars were
Fixed in their footsteps ; pillars all of gold,
Fair to our eyes, but woeful to behold.

The fourth Squire.

Thus with prodigious hate and cruelty,
Our good knights for their love afflicted be ;
But, O, protect us now, majestic grace,
For see, those curst enchanters press in place
That our past sorrows wrought : these, these alone
Turn all the world into confusion.

Towards the end of this speech, two enchanters, and two enchantresses appear : Error first, in a skin coat scaled like a serpent, and an antic habit painted with snakes, a hair of curled snakes, and a deformed vizard. With him Rumour in a skin coat full of winged tongues, and over it an antic robe ; on his head a cap like a tongue, with a large pair of wings to it.

Curiosity in a skin coat full of eyes, and an antic habit over it, a fantastic cap full of eyes.

Credulity in the like habit painted with ears, and an antic cap full of ears.

When they had whispered awhile as if they had rejoiced at the wrongs which they had done to the knights, the music and their dance began : straight forth rushed the four Winds confusedly.

The Eastern Wind in a skin coat of the colour of the sun-rising, with a yellow hair, and wings both on his shoulders and feet.

The Western Wind in a skin coat of dark crimson, with crimson hair and wings.

The Southern Wind in a dark russet skin coat, hair and wings suitable.

The Northern Wind in a grisled skin coat, with hair and wings accordingly.

After them in confusion came the four Elements :

Earth, in a skin coat of grass green, a mantle painted full of trees, plants and flowers, and on his head an oak growing.

Water, in a skin coat waved, with a mantle full of fishes, on his head a dolphin.

Air, in a sky-coloured skin coat, with a mantle painted with fowl, and on his head an eagle.

Fire, in a skin coat, and a mantle painted with flames, on his head a cap of flames, with a salamander in the midst thereof.

Then entered the four parts of the earth in a confused measure.

Europe in the habit of an empress, with an imperial crown on her head.

Asia in a Persian lady's habit, with a crown on her head.

Africa like a queen of the Moors, with a crown.

America in a skin coat of the colour of the juice of mulberries, on her head large round brims of many-coloured feathers, and in the midst of it a small crown.

All these having danced together in a strange kind of confusion, passed away, by four and four.

At which time, Eternity appeared in a long blue taffeta robe, painted with stars, and on her head a crown.

Next, came the three Destinies, in long robes of

white taffeta like aged women, with garlands of Narcissus flowers on their heads ; and in their left hands they carried distaffs according to the descriptions of Plato[1] and Catullus, but in their right hands they carried altogether a tree of gold.

After them, came Harmony with nine musicians more, in long taffeta robes and caps of tinsel, with garlands gilt, playing and singing this song.

Chorus.

Vanish, vanish hence, confusion !
Dim not Hymen's golden light
 With false illusion.
The Fates shall do him right,
And fair Eternity,
 Who pass through all enchantments free.

Eternity sings alone.

Bring away this sacred tree,
The tree of grace and bounty,
 Set it in Bel-Anna's eye,
For she, she, only she
 Can all knotted spells untie.
Pulled from the stock, let her blest hands convey
 To any suppliant hand a bough,
 And let that hand advance it now
Against a charm, that charm shall fade away.

Toward the end of this song the three Destinies set the tree of gold before the Queen.

Chorus.

Since knightly valour rescues dames distressed,
By virtuous dames let charmed knights be released.

---

[1] See Plato *De Re Publica*, 617, d, and Catullus *De Nuptiis Pelei et Thetidos.*

After this Chorus, one of the Squires speaks.

Since knights by valour rescue dames distrest,
Let them be by the Queen of Dames released.
So sing the Destinies, who never err,
Fixing this tree of grace and bounty here,
From which for our enchanted knights we crave
A branch, pulled by your sacred hand, to have ;
That we may bear it as the Fates direct,
And manifest your glory in th' effect.
In virtue's favour then, and pity now,
(Great Queen) vouchsafe us a divine touched bough.

At the end of this speech, the Queen pulled a branch
from the tree and gave it to a nobleman, who delivered
it to one of the squires.

A song while the Squires descend with the bough
toward the scene.

Go, happy man, like th' evening star,
Whose beams to bridegrooms welcome are :
May neither hag, nor fiend withstand
The power of thy victorious hand.
The uncharmed knights surrender now,
By virtue of thy raised bough.

Away, enchantments ! vanish quite,
No more delay our longing sight :
'Tis fruitless to contend with Fate,
Who gives us power against your hate.
Brave knights, in courtly pomp appear,
For now are you long-looked-for here.

Then out of the air a cloud descends, discovering six of the knights alike, in strange and sumptuous attires, and withall on either side of the cloud, on the two promontories, the other six masquers are suddenly transformed out of the pillars of gold ; at which time, while they all come forward to the dancing place, this chorus is sung, and on the sudden the whole scene is changed : for whereas before all seemed to be done at the sea and sea coast, now the promontories are suddenly removed, and London with the Thames is very artificially presented in their place.

The Squire lifts up the bough.

Chorus.

Virtue and grace, in spite of charms,
Have now redeemed our men-at-arms,
There's no enchantment can withstand,
Where Fate directs the happy hand.

The masquers' first dance.
The third song of three parts, with a chorus of five parts, sung after the first dance.

While dancing rests, fit place to music granting,
Good spells the Fates shall breathe, all envy daunting,
Kind ears with joy enchanting, chanting.

Chorus.
Io, Io Hymen.

Like looks, like hearts, like loves are linked together :
So must the Fates be pleased, so come they hether,[1]
To make this joy persever, ever.

---

[1] An old form of "hither."

Chorus.
Io, Io Hymen!

Love decks the spring, her buds to th' air exposing,
Such fire here in these bridal breasts reposing,
We leave with charms enclosing, closing.

Chorus.
Io, Io Hymen!

The masquers' second dance.
The fourth song, a dialogue of three, with a chorus after the second dance.

1. *Let us now sing of Love's delight,*
   For he alone is lord to-night.
2. *Some friendship between man and man prefer,*
   But I th' affection between man and wife.
3. *What good can be in life,*
   Whereof no fruits appear?
1. *Set is that tree in ill hour,*
   That yields neither fruit nor flower.
2. *How can man perpetual be,*
   But in his own posterity?

Chorus.
That pleasure is of all most bountiful and kind,
That fades not straight, but leaves a living joy behind.

After this dialogue the masquers dance with the ladies, wherein spending as much time as they held fitting, they returned to the seats provided for them.

Straight in the Thames appeared four barges with skippers in them, and withall this song was sung.

Come ashore, come, merry mates,
With your nimble heels and pates:
Summon ev'ry man his knight,
Enough honoured is this night.
Now, let your sea-born goddess come,
Quench these lights, and make all dumb.
Some sleep; others let her call:
And so good-night to all, good-night to all.

At the conclusion of this song arrived twelve skippers
in red caps, with short cassocks and long flaps wide at
the knees, of white canvas striped with crimson, white
gloves and pumps, and red stockings : these twelve
danced a brave and lively dance, shouting and triumphing after their manner.

After this followed the masquers' last dance, where-
with they retired.

At the embarking of the Knights, the Squires
approach the state and speak.

The first Squire.

All that was ever asked, by vow of Jove,
To bless a state with, plenty, honour, love,
Power, triumph, private pleasure, public peace,
Sweet springs, and Autumns filled with due increase,
All these, and what good else thought can supply,
Ever attend your triple majesty.

The second Squire.

All blessings which the Fates prophetic sung
At Peleus' nuptials, and whatever tongue
Can figure more, this night, and aye betide,
The honoured bridegroom and the honoured bride.

All the Squires together.

Thus speaks in us th' affection of our knights,
Wishing your health, and myriads of good nights.

The squires' speeches being ended, this song is sung
while the boats pass away.

Haste aboard, haste now away!
Hymen frowns at your delay.
Hymen doth long nights affect;
Yield him then his due respect.
The sea-born goddess straight will come,
Quench these lights, and make all dumb.
Some sleep; others she will call :
And so good-night to all, good-night to all.

FINIS.

[The *Description* is followed by *Ayres, made by severall Authors,*
&c., which has a distinct title-page. The *Ayres* are the four
songs contained in the masque, with their musical notes.
"Bring away this sacred tree" (p. 218) was "made and exprest
by Mr. Nicholas Laneir," an Italian musician who had settled in
England. "Go, happy man" (p. 219), "While dancing rests"
(p. 220), and "Come ashore" (p. 222), were "composed by Mr.
Coprario and sung by Mr. John Allen, and Mr. Laneir." After
these songs a "song made by Th. Campion, and sung in the
Lords' Masque at the Count Palatine's Marriage, we have here
added, to fill up these empty pages." The song from the Lords'
Masque is "Woo her and win her he that can" (p. 202). Then
follows—
"The names of the masquers.

1. The Duke of Lenox.
2. The Earl of Pembroke.
3. The Earl of Dorset.
4. The Earl of Salisbury.
5. The Earl of Montgomery.
6. The Lord Walden.

7. The Lord Scroope.
8. The Lord North.
9. The Lord Hayes.
10. Sir Thomas Howard.
11. Sir Henry Howard.
12. Sir Charles Howard."]

Observations in the Art of English Poesie. By Thomas Campion. Wherein it is demonstratiuely prooued, and by example confirmed, that the English toong will receiue eight seuerall kinds of numbers, proper to it selfe, which are all in this booke set forth, and were neuer before this time by any man attempted. Printed at London by Richard Field for Andrew Wise. 1602. 8vo.

Q

TO THE RIGHT NOBLE AND WORTHILY HONOURED, THE LORD BUCKHURST,[1] LORD HIGH TREASURER OF ENGLAND.

IN two things (right honorable) it is generally agreed
that man excels all other creatures, in reason and
speech : and in them by how much one man sur-
passeth another, by so much the nearer he aspires to
a celestial essence.

Poesy in all kind of speaking is the chief beginner
and maintainer of eloquence, not only helping the ear
with the acquaintance of sweet numbers, but also
raising the mind to a more high and lofty conceit.
For this end have I studied to induce a true form of
versifying into our language : for the vulgar and unartificial custom of riming hath, I know, deterred
many excellent wits from the exercise of English
poesy. The observations which I have gathered for
this purpose, I humbly present to your Lordship, as
to the noblest judge of poesy, and the most honorable
protector of all industrious learning ; which if your
honour shall vouchsafe to receive, who both in your
public and private poems have so divinely crowned
your fame, what man will dare to repine or not strive
to imitate them ? Wherefore with all humility I subject

---

1 Thomas Sackville, 1st Baron Buckhurst, created Earl of
Dorset 13 March, 1603, d. 1608 ; author of the famous *Induction*
to the *Mirrour for Magistrates* and part-author of *Gorboduc*.
From the present dedication we learn that he had written other
things that were not published.

myself and them to your gracious favour, beseeching
you in the nobleness of your mind to take in worth [1]
so simple a present, which by some work drawn from
my more serious studies I will hereafter endeavour to
excuse.

Your Lordship's humbly devoted

THOMAS CAMPION.

[1] *Take in worth* = receive kindly.

THE WRITER TO HIS BOOK.

Whither thus hastes my little book so fast?
To Paul's Churchyard. What? in those cells to stand,
With one leaf like a rider's cloak put up
To catch a termer[1]? or lie musty there
With rimes a term set out, or two, before?
Some[2] will redeem me. Few. Yes, read me too.
Fewer. Nay love me. Now thou doat'st, I see.
Will not our English Athens art defend?
Perhaps. Will lofty courtly wits not aim
Still at perfection? If I grant? I fly.
Whither? To Paul's. Alas, poor book, I rue
Thy rash self-love. Go, spread thy pap'ry wings;
Thy lightness cannot help or hurt my fame.

[1] A name for those who visited London in term-time, the fashionable season.

[2] Here Campion is imitating Persius ("Quis leget haec? Min' tu istud ais?" &c.), who was a favourite with the Elizabethan poets.

Observations in the Art of English Poesy, by Thomas Campion.

The first Chapter, entreating of numbers in general.

THERE is no writing too brief that, without obscurity, comprehends the intent of the writer. These my late observations in English poesy I have thus briefly gathered, that they might prove the less troublesome in perusing, and the more apt to be retained in memory. And I will first generally handle the nature of numbers. Number is *discreta quantitas;* so that, when we speak simply of number, we intend only the dissevered quantity; but when we speak of a poem written in number, we consider not only the distinct number of the syllables, but also their value, which is contained in the length or shortness of their sound. As in music we do not say a strain of so many notes, but so many sem'briefs (though sometimes there are no more notes than sem'briefs), so in a verse the numeration of the syllables is not so much to be observed as their weight and due proportion. In joining of words to harmony there is nothing more offensive to the ear than to place a long syllable with a short note, or a short syllable with a long note, though in the last the vowel often bears it out. The world is made by symmetry and proportion, and is in that respect compared to music, and music to poetry: for Terence saith, speaking of poets, *artem qui tractant musicam*, confounding music and poesy together. What music can there be where there is no proportion observed? Learning first flourished in Greece, from thence it was derived unto the Romans, both diligent observers of the number, and quantity of syllables, not in their verses only, but likewise in their prose. Learning after the declining of the Roman Empire, and the pollution of their language through the conquest of the barbarians, lay most pitifully deformed, till the time of Erasmus, Rewcline, Sir Thomas More, and other learned men of that age, who brought the Latin tongue again to light, redeeming it with much labour out of the hands of the illiterate monks and friars : as a scoffing book, entituled *Epistolæ obscurorum virorum*, may sufficiently testify. In those lack-learning times, and in barbarized Italy, began that vulgar and easy kind of poesy which is now in use throughout most parts of Christendom, which we abusively call rime [1] and metre, of *rithmus* and *metrum*, of which I will now discourse.

The second Chapter, declaring the unaptness of rime in poesy.

I am not ignorant that whosoever shall by way of reprehension examine the imperfections of rime, must encounter with many glorious enemies, and those very expert, and ready at their weapon, that can, if need be, extempore (as they say) rime a man to death. Besides there is grown a kind of prescription in the use of rime, to forestall the right of true numbers, as also the consent of many nations, against all which it

---

[1] The old-fashioned notion that *rime* or *rhyme* was derived from *rhythmos* is, of course, erroneous.

may seem a thing almost impossible and vain to contend. All this and more can not yet deter me from a
lawful defence of perfection, or make me any whit the
sooner adhere to that which is lame and unbeseeming.
For custom, I allege that ill uses are to be abolished,
and that things naturally imperfect can not be perfected by use. Old customs, if they be better, why
should they not be recalled, as the ʃet flourishing
custom of numerous poesy used among the Romans
and Grecians : but the unaptness of our tongues, and
the difficulty of imitation disheartens us ; again the
facility and popularity of rime creates as many poets,
as a hot summer flies. But let me now examine the
nature of that which we call rime. By rime is understood that which ends in the like sound, so that verses
in such manner composed, yield but a continual
repetition of that rhetorical figure which we term
similiter desinentia, and that being but *figura verbi,*
ought (as Tully and all other rhetoricians have judicially observed) sparingly to be used, lest it should
offend the ear with tedious affectation. Such was that
absurd following of the letter amongst our English so
much of late affected, but now hissed out of Paul's
Churchyard : which foolish figurative repetition crept
also into the Latin tongue, as it is manifest in the book
of Pᵃ called *praelia porcorum,*[1] and another pamphlet
all of Fˢ, which I have seen imprinted ; but I will
leave these follies to their own ruin, and return to the
matter intended. The ear is a rational sense and a
chief judge of proportion, but in our kind of riming

[1] Campion is referring to the *Pugna Porcorum per P. Porcium
poetam* [Joan. Leonem], originally published in 1530. It begins—
"Plaudite, porcelli, porcorum pigra propago " &c.

what proportion is there kept, where there remains such a confused inequality of syllables? Iambic and trochaic feet which are opposed by nature, are by all rimers confounded, nay oftentimes they place instead of an iambic the foot Pyrrychius, consisting of two short syllables, curtailing their verse, which they supply in reading with a ridiculous, and unapt drawing of their speech. As for example :

Was it my destiny, or dismal chance ?

In this verse the two last syllables of the word *destiny*, being both short, and standing for a whole foot in the verse, cause the line to fall out shorter than it ought by nature. The like impure errors have in time of rudeness been used in the Latin tongue, as the *Carmina proverbialia* [1] can witness, and many other such reverend bables.[2] But the noble Grecians and Romans whose skilful monuments outlive barbarism, tied themselves to the strict observation of poetical numbers, so abandoning the childish titillation of riming, that it was imputed a great error to Ovid for setting forth this one riming verse,

Quot caelum stellas tot habet tua Roma puellas.

For the establishing of this argument, what better confirmation can be had, than that of Sir Thomas More in his book of Epigrams, where he makes two sundry epitaphs upon the death of a singing-man at Westminster,[3] the one in learned numbers and disliked,

---

[1] A volume of riming Latin proverbs entitled *Carminum Proverbialium . . . Loci Communes in gratiam juventutis selecti*, 8vo., published at London in 1577, passed through many editions.

[2] Old form of *bawbles*.

[3] Here Campion seems to have made a slip. More's epitaphs

the other in rude rime and highly extolled : so that he concludes, *tales lactucas talia labra petunt*, like lips, like lettuce. But there is yet another fault in rime altogether intolerable, which is, that it enforceth a man oftentimes to abjure his matter, and extend a short conceit beyond all bounds of art ; for in quatorzains, methinks, the poet handles his subject as tyrannically as Procrustes the thief his prisoners,[1] whom when he had taken, he used to cast upon a bed, which if they were to short to fill, he would stretch them longer, if too long, he would cut them shorter. Bring before me now any the most self-loved rimer, and let me see if without blushing he be able to read his lame halting rimes. Is there not a curse of nature laid upon such rude poesy, when the writer is himself ashamed of it, and the hearers in contempt call it riming and ballating? What divine in his sermon, or grave counsellor in his oration, will allege the testimony of a rime? But the divinity of the Romans and Grecians was all written in verse ; and Aristotle, Galen, and the books of all the excellent philosophers are full of the testimonies of the old poets. By them was laid the foundation of all human wisdom, and from them the knowledge of all antiquity is derived. I will propound but one question, and so conclude this point. If the

were on a singing-man at Abingdon. The riming epitaph begins :—

" Hic jacet Henricus, semper pietatis amicus ;
Nomen Abyngdon erat, si quis sua nomina quaerat," &c.

[1] Ben Jonson remembered this passage when, in conversation with Drummond of Hawthornden, " He cursed Petrarch for reducting verses into sonnets, which, he said, was like that tyrant's bed where some who were too short were racked, others too long cut short."

Italians, Frenchmen and Spaniards, that with commendation have written in rime, were demanded
whether they had rather the books they have published
(if their tongue would bear it) should remain as they
are in rime, or be translated into the ancient numbers
of the Greeks and Romans, would they not answer into
numbers? What honour were it then for our English
language to be the first that after so many years of
barbarism could second the perfection of the industrious Greeks and Romans? which how it may be
effected I will now proceed to demonstrate.

The third Chapter, of our English numbers in general.

There are but three feet which generally distinguish
the Greek and Latin verses: the dactyl, consisting of
one long syllable and two short, as *vĭvĕrĕ*; the
trochee, of one long and one short, as *vītă*; and the
iambic of one short and one long, as *ămōr*.[1] The
spondee of two long, the tribrach of three short, the
anapæstic of two short and a long, are but as servants
to the first. Divers other feet, I know, are by the
grammarians cited, but to little purpose. The heroical
verse that is distinguished by the dactyl hath been
oftentimes attempted in our English tongue, but with
passing pitiful success; and no wonder, seeing it is an
attempt altogether against the nature of our language.
For both the concourse of our monosyllables make our
verses unapt to slide; and also, if we examine our
polysyllables, we shall find few of them, by reason of
their heaviness, willing to serve in place of a dactyl.
Thence it is, that the writers of English heroics do so

---

[1] An unlucky example this; for the second syllable of *amor* is
short.

often repeat *Amyntas, Olympus, Avernus, Erinnis,* and such-like borrowed words, to supply the defect of our hardly entreated dactyl. I could in this place set down many ridiculous kinds of dactyls which they use, but that it is not my purpose here to incite men to laughter. If we therefore reject the dactyl as unfit for our use (which of necessity we are enforced to do) there remain only the iambic foot, of which the iambic verse is framed, and the trochee from which the trochaic numbers have their original. Let us now then examine the property of these two feet, and try if they consent with the nature of our English syllables. And first for the iambics, they fall out so naturally in our tongue, that if we examine our own writers, we shall find they unawares hit oftentimes upon the true iambic numbers, but always aim at them as far as their ear without the guidance of art can attain unto, as it shall hereafter more evidently appear. The trochaic foot, which is but an iambic turned over and over, must of force in like manner accord in proportion with our British syllables, and so produce an English trochaical verse. Then having these two principal kinds of verses, we may easily out of them derive other forms, as the Latins and Greeks before us have done : whereof I will make plain demonstration, beginning at the iambic verse.

The fourth Chapter, of the iambic verse.

I have observed, and so may any one that is either practised in singing, or hath a natural ear able to time a song, that the Latin verses of six feet, as the heroic and iambic, or of five feet as the trochaic, are in nature all of the same length of sound with our English

verses of five feet ; for either of them, being timed with
the hand, *quinque perficiunt tempora*, they fill up the
quantity (as it were) of five sem'briefs; as for example,
if any man will prove to time these verses with his
hand.

A pure iambic.
Suis et ipsa Roma viribus ruit.

A licentiate iambic.
Ducunt volentes fata, nolentes trahunt.

An heroic verse.
Tityre, tu patulæ recubans sub tegmine fagi.

A trochaic verse.
Nox est perpetua una dormienda.

English iambics pure.
*The more secure, the more the stroke we feel
Of unprevented harms; so gloomy storms
Appear the sterner if the day be clear.*

The English iambic licentiate.
Hark how these winds do murmur at thy flight.

The English trochee.
Still where envy leaves, remorse doth enter.

The cause why these verses differing in feet yield the
same length of sound, is by reason of some rests which
either the necessity of the numbers, or the heaviness
of the syllables, do beget.   For we find in music that
oftentimes the strains of a song cannot be reduced to
true number without some rests prefixed in the beginning and middle, as also at the close if need requires.
Besides, our English monosyllables enforce many
breathings which no doubt greatly lengthen a verse, so

that it is no wonder if for these reasons our English verses of five feet hold pace with the Latins of six. The pure iambic in English needs small demonstration, because it consists simply of iambic feet, but our iambic licentiate offers itself to a farther consideration ; for in the third and fifth place we must of force hold the iambic foot ; in the first, second, and fourth place we may use a spondee or iambic and sometime a tribrach or dactyl, but rarely an anapæstic foot, and that in the second or fourth place. But why an iambic in the third place ? I answer, that the forepart of the verse may the gentlier slide into his dimetre, as for example sake divide this verse :

Hark how these winds do murmur at thy flight.

Hark how these winds, there the voice naturally affects a rest ; then *murmur at thy flight,* that is of itself a perfect number, as I will declare in the next chapter ; and therefore the other odd syllable between them ought to be short, lest the verse should hang too much between the natural pause of the verse, and the dimetre following ; the which dimetre, though it be naturally trochaical, yet it seems to have his original out of the iambic verse. But the better to confirm and express these rules, I will set down a short poem in licentiate iambics, which may give more light to them that shall hereafter imitate these numbers.

Go, numbers, boldly pass, stay not for aid
Of shifting rime, that easy flatterer,
Whose witchcraft can the ruder ears beguile;
Let your smooth feet, inured to purer art,
True measures tread. What if your pace be slow,

And hops not like the Grecian elegies?
It is yet graceful, and well fits the state
Of words ill-breathed and not shaped to run.
Go then, but slowly, till your steps be firm;
Tell them that pity, or perversely scorn,
Poor English poesy as the slave to rime,
You are those lofty numbers that revive
Triumphs of princes, and stern tragedies:
And learn henceforth t'attend those happy sprites
Whose bounding fury height and weight affects.
Assist their labour, and sit close to them,
Never to part away till for desert
Their brows with great Apollo's bays are hid.
He first taught number and true harmony,
Nor is the laurel his for rime bequeathed;
Call him with numerous accents paised [1] by art,
He'll turn his glory from the sunny climes
The North-bred wits alone to patronise:
Let France their Bartas, Italy Tasso praise;
Phœbus shuns none but in their flight from him.

Though, as I said before, the natural breathing-place
of our English iambic verse is in the last syllable of
the second foot, as our trochee after the manner of
the Latin heroic and iambic rests naturally in the
first of the third foot; yet no man is tied altogether to
observe this rule, but he may alter it, after the judgment of his ear, which poets, orators, and musicians
of all men ought to have most excellent. Again,
though I said peremptorily before, that the third, and
fifth place of our licentiate iambic must always hold an

------

[1] Weighed.

iambic foot, yet I will shew you example in both places where a tribrach may be very formally taken, and first in the third place :

Some trade in Barbary, some in Turkey trade.

Another example :

Men that do fall to misery, quickly fall.

If you doubt whether the first of *misery* be naturally short or no, you may judge it by the easy sliding of these two verses following.

The first :

Whom misery cannot alter, time devours.

The second :

What more unhappy life, what misery more ?

Example of the tribrach in the fifth place, as you may perceive in the last foot of the fourth [1] verse :

Some from the starry throne his fame derives,
Some from the mines beneath, from trees or herbs :
Each hath his glory, each his sundry gift,
Renowned in every art there lives not any.

To proceed farther, I see no reason why the English iambic in his first place may not as well borrow a foot of the trochee as our trochee, or the Latin hendeca-syllable, may in the like case make bold with the iambic : but it must be done ever with this caveat, which is, that a spondee, dactyl, or tribrach do supply the next place : for an iambic beginning with a single

---

[1] Old ed. "fift."

R

short syllable, and the other ending before with the like, would too much drink up the verse if they came immediately together.

The example of the spondee after the trochee :

As the fair sun the lightsome heav'n adorns.

The example of the dactyl.

Noble, ingenious, and discreetly wise.

The example of the tribrach.

Beauty to jealousy brings joy, sorrow, fear.

Though I have set down these second licenses as good and airable enough, yet for the most part my first rules are general.

These are those numbers which nature in our English destinates to the tragic and heroic poem : for the subject of them both being all one, I see no impediment why one verse may not serve for them both, as it appears more plainly in the old comparison of the two Greek writers, when they say, *Homerus est Sophocles heroicus*, and again, *Sophocles est Homerus tragicus*, intimating that both Sophocles and Homer are the same in height and subject, and differ only in the kind of their numbers.

The iambic verse in like manner being yet made a little more licentiate, that it may thereby the nearer serve for comedies, and then may we use a spondee in the fifth place, and in the third place any foot except a trochee, which never enters into our iambic verse but in the first place, and then with his caveat of the other feet which must of necessity follow.

The fifth Chapter, of the iambic dimetre, or English march.

The dimetre (so called in the former chapter) I intend next of all to handle, because it seems to be a part of the iambic, which is our most natural and ancient English verse. We may term this our English march, because the verse answers our warlike form of march in similitude of number. But call it what you please, for I will not wrangle about names, only intending to set down the nature of it and true structure. It consists of two feet and one odd syllable. The first foot may be made either a trochee, or a spondee, or an iambic at the pleasure of the composer, though most naturally that place affects a trochee or spondee ; yet by the example of Catullus in his hendecasyllables, I add in the first place sometimes an iambic foot. In the second place we must ever insert a trochee or tribrach, and so leave the last syllable (as in the end of a verse it is always held) common. Of this kind I will subscribe three examples, the first being a piece of chorus in a tragedy.

Raving war, begot
In the thirsty sands
Of the Libyan Isles,
Wastes our empty fields;
What the greedy rage
Of fell wintry storms
Could not turn to spoil,
Fierce Bellona now
Hath laid desolate,

Void of fruit, or hope.
Th' eager thrifty hind,
Whose rude toil revived
Our sky-blasted earth,
Himself is but earth,
Left a scorn to fate
Through seditious arms :
And that soil, alive
Which he duly nurst,
Which him duly fed,
Dead his body feeds :
Yet not all the globe
His tough hands manured
Now one turf affords
His poor funeral.
Thus still needy lives,
Thus still needy dies
Th' unknown multitude.

An example lyrical.

Greatest in thy wars,
Greater in thy peace,
Dread Elizabeth ;
Our muse only truth,
Figments cannot use,
Thy rich name to deck
That itself adorns :
But should now this age
Let all poesy feign,
Feigning poesy could
Nothing feign at all
Worthy half thy fame.

An example epigrammical.

Kind in every kind
This, dear Ned, resolve.
Never of thy praise
Be too prodigal;
He that praiseth all
Can praise truly none.

The sixth Chapter, of the English trochaic verse.

Next in course to be entreated of is the English trochaic, being a verse simple, and of itself depending. It consists, as the Latin trochaic of five feet, the first whereof may be a trochee, a spondee, or an iambic, the other four of necessity all trochees, still holding this rule authentical, that the last syllable of a verse is always common. The spirit of this verse most of all delights in epigrams, but it may be diversely used, as shall hereafter be declared. I have written divers light poems in this kind, which for the better satisfaction of the reader, I thought convenient here in way of example to publish. In which though sometimes under a known name I have shadowed a feigned conceit, yet is it done without reference, or offence to any person, and only to make the style appear the more English.

The first Epigram.

Lockly spits apace, the rheum he calls it,
But no drop (though often urged) he straineth
From his thirsty jaws, yet all the morning
And all day he spits, in ev'ry corner;

At his meals he spits, at ev'ry meeting;
At the bar he spits before the fathers;
In the court he spits before the graces;
In the church he spits, thus all profaning
With that rude disease, that empty spitting:
Yet no cost he spares, he sees the doctors,
Keeps a strict diet, precisely useth
Drinks and baths drying, yet all prevails not.
'Tis not China (Lockly), Salsa Guacum,
Nor dry Sassafras can help, or ease thee;
'Tis no humour hurts, it is thy humour.

The second Epigram.

Cease, fond wretch, to love, so oft deluded,
Still made rich with hopes, still unrelieved.
Now fly her delays; she that debateth
Feels not true desire; he that, deferred,
Others' times attends, his own betrayeth:
Learn t'affect thyself, thy cheeks deformed
With pale care revive by timely pleasure,
Or with scarlet heat them, or by paintings
Make thee lovely; for such art she useth
Whom in vain so long thy folly loved.

The third Epigram.

Kate can fancy only beardless husbands,
That's the cause she shakes off ev'ry suitor,
That's the cause she lives so stale a virgin,
For before her heart can heat her answer,
Her smooth youths she finds all hugely bearded.

The fourth Epigram.

All in satin Oteny will be suited,
Beaten¹ satin (as by chance he calls it);
Oteny sure will have the bastinado.

The fifth Epigram.

Toasts as snakes or as the mortal henbane
Hunks detests when huffcap² ale he tipples,
Yet the bread he grants the fumes abateth:
Therefore apt in ale: true, and he grants it:
But it drinks up ale: that Hunks detesteth.

The sixth Epigram.

What though Harry brags, let him be noble;
Noble Harry hath not half a noble.

The seventh Epigram.

Phœbe, all the rights Elisa claimeth,
Mighty rival, in this only diff'ring
That she's only true, thou only feigned.

The eighth Epigram.

Barnzy³ stiffly vows that he's no cuckold,
Yet the vulgar ev'rywhere salutes him

---

¹ I have often met the expression "beaten satin" or "beaten silk," but I am not sure that I understand what it means. In the absence of any authoritative explanation I suggest that "beaten" may mean "embroidered." Cf. Guilpin's "Skialetheia," epigram 53—
     "He wears a jerkin *cudgelled* with gold lace."

² A term for strong ale.

³ In spite of Campion's assertion that "though sometimes under a known name I have shadowed a feigned conceit, yet is it done without reference or offence to any person," this epigram seems to refer to Barnabe Barnes and Gabriel Harvey.

With strange signs of horns, from ev'ry corner;
Wheresoe'er he comes a sundry cuckoo
Still frequents his ears, yet he's no cuckold.
But this Barnzy knows that his Matilda
Scorning him with Harvy plays the wanton;
Knows it? nay desires it, and by prayers
Daily begs of heav'n, that it for ever
May stand firm for him, yet he's no cuckold:
And 'tis true, for Harvy keeps Matilda,
Fosters Barnzy, and relieves his household,
Buys the cradle, and begets the children,
Pays the nurses, ev'ry charge defraying,
And thus truly plays Matilda's husband:
So that Barnzy now becomes a cipher
And himself th' adult'rer of Matilda.
Mock not him with horns, the case is altered;
Harvy bears the wrong, he proves the cuckold.

The ninth Epigram.

Buffe loves fat viands, fat ale, fat all things.
Keeps fat whores, fat offices, yet all men
Him fat only wish to feast the gallows.

The tenth Epigram.

Smith, by suit divorced, the known adult'ress
Freshly weds again; what ails the mad-cap
By this fury? ev'n so thieves by frailty
Of their hemp reserved, again the dismal
Tree embrace, again the fatal halter.

The eleventh Epigram.

His late loss the wiveless Higs in order
Ev'rywhere bewails to friends, to strangers;

Tells them how by night a youngster armed
Sought his wife (as hand in hand he held her)
With drawn sword to force; she cried, he mainly
Roaring ran for aid, but (ah), returning,
Fled was with the prize the beauty-forcer,
Whom in vain he seeks, he threats, he follows.
Changed is Helen, Helen hugs the stranger
Safe as Paris in the Greek triumphing.
Therewith his reports to tears he turneth,
Pierced through with the lovely dame's remembrance;
Straight he sighs, he raves, his hair he teareth,
Forcing pity still by fresh lamenting.
Cease, unworthy, worthy of thy fortunes.
Thou that couldst so fair a prize deliver,
For fear unregarded, undefended,
Hadst no heart I think, I know no liver.[1]

The twelfth Epigram.

Why droopst thou, Trefeild? will Hurst the banker
Make dice of thy bones? by heav'n he cannot.
Cannot? What's the reason? I'll declare it,
They're all grown so pocky and so rotten.

The seventh Chapter, of the English elegiac verse.

The elegiac verses challenge the next place, as being of all compound verses the simplest. They are derived out of our own natural numbers as near the imitation of the Greeks and Latins as our heavy syllables will permit. The first verse is a mere licentiate iambic; the second is framed of two united

---

[1] The liver was supposed to be the seat of love.

dimetres. In the first dimetre we are tied to make the first foot either a trochee or a spondee, the second a trochee and the odd syllable of it always long. The second dimetre consists of two trochees (because it requires more swiftness than the first) and an odd syllable, which being last, is ever common. I will give you example both of elegy and epigram, in this kind.

An Elegy.

Constant to none, but ever false to me,
  Traitor still to love through thy faint desires,
Not hope of pity now nor vain redress
  Turns my griefs to tears and renewed laments.
Too well thy empty vows and hollow thoughts
  Witness both thy wrongs and remorseless heart.
Rue not my sorrow, but blush at my name,
  Let thy bloody cheeks guilty thoughts betray.
My flames did truly burn, thine made a show,
  As fires painted are which no heat retain,
Or as the glossy pyrop feigns to blaze,
  But, touched, cold appears, and an earthy stone.
True colours deck thy cheeks, false foils thy breast,
  Frailer than thy light beauty is thy mind.
None canst thou long refuse, nor long affect,
  But turn'st fear with hopes, sorrow with delight,
Delaying, and deluding ev'ry way
  Those whose eyes are once with thy beauty chained.
Thrice happy man that ent'ring first thy love,
  Can so guide the straight reins of his desires,
That both he can regard thee, and refrain :
  If graced firm he stands, if not, eas'ly falls.

Example of Epigrams, in elegiac verse.

The first Epigram.

Arthur brooks only those that brook not him,
  Those he most regards, and devoutly serves :
But them that grace him his great brav'ry scorns,
  Counting kindness all duty, not desert :
Arthur wants forty pounds, tries [1] *ev'ry friend,*
  But finds none that holds twenty due for him.

The second Epigram.

If fancy cannot err which virtue guides,
  In thee, Laura, then fancy cannot err.

The third Epigram.

Drue feasts no Puritans; the churls, he saith,
  Thank no men, but eat, praise God, and depart.

The fourth Epigram.

A wise man wary lives, yet most secure,
  Sorrows move not him greatly, nor delights.
Fortune and death he scorning, only makes
  Th' earth his sober inn, [2] *but still heav'n his home.*

The fifth Epigram.

Thou tell'st me, Barnzy, [3] *Dawson hath a wife :*
  Thine he hath, I grant ; Dawson hath a wife.

---

1 Old ed. " tyres."

2 Cf. the last two stanzas of " The man of life upright " (p. 21).

3 Again the reference is to Barnabe Barnes ; and the same remark applies to the seventh Epigram.

The sixth Epigram.

Drue gives thee money, yet thou thank'st not him,
But thank'st God for him, like a godly man.
Suppose, rude Puritan, thou begst of him,
And he saith " God help !" who's the godly man ?

The seventh Epigram.

All wonders Barnzy speaks, all grossly feigned:
Speak some wonder once, Barnzy; speak the truth.

The eighth Epigram.

None then should through thy beauty, Laura, pine,
Might sweet words alone ease a love-sick heart :
But your sweet words alone, that quit so well
Hope of friendly deeds, kill the love-sick heart.

The ninth Epigram.

At all thou frankly throw'st, while Frank, thy wife,
Bars not Luke the main; Oteny bar the bye.

The eighth Chapter, of ditties and odes.

To descend orderly from the more simple numbers
to them that are more compounded, it is now time to
handle such verses as are fit for ditties or odes;
which we may call lyrical, because they are apt to be
sung to an instrument, if they were adorned with
convenient notes. Of that kind I will demonstrate
three in this chapter, and in the first we will proceed
after the manner of the Sapphic, which is a trochaical
verse as well as the hendecasyllable in Latin. The
first three verses therefore in our English Sapphic are

merely those trochaics which I handled in the sixth
chapter, excepting only that the first foot of either of
them must ever of necessity be a spondee to make the
number more grave. The fourth and last closing
verse is compounded of three trochees together, to
give a more smooth farewell, as you may easily observe
in this poem made upon a triumph at Whitehall,
whose glory was dashed with an unwelcome shower,
hindering the people from the desired sight of her
Majesty.

The English Sapphic.

Faith's pure shield, the Christian Diana,
England's glory crowned with all divineness,
Live long with triumphs to bless thy people
  At thy sight triumphing.
Lo, they sound; the knights, in order armed,
Ent'ring threat the list, addressed to combat
For their courtly loves; he, he's the wonder
  Whom Eliza graceth.
Their plumed pomp the vulgar heaps detaineth,
And rough steeds: let us the still devices
Close observe, the speeches and the musics
  Peaceful arms adorning.
But whence show'rs so fast this angry tempest,
Clouding dim the place? behold, Eliza
This day shines not here! this heard, the lances
  And thick heads do vanish.

The second kind consists of dimetre, whose first foot
may either be a spondee or a trochee. The two verses
following are both of them trochaical, and consist of
four feet, the first of either of them being a spondee or

trochee, the other three only trochees. The fourth
and last verse is made of two trochees. The number
is voluble and fit to express any amorous conceit.

The example.

Rose-cheeked Laura, come;
Sing thou smoothly with thy beauty's
Silent music, either other
        Sweetly gracing.
Lovely forms do flow
From concent divinely framed;
Heav'n is music, and thy beauty's
        Birth is heavenly.
These dull notes we sing
Discords need for helps to grace them,
Only beauty purely loving
        Knows no discord,
But still moves delight,
Like clear springs renewed by flowing,
Ever perfect, ever in them-
        selves eternal.

The third kind begins as the second kind ended,
with a verse consisting of two trochee feet; and then,
as the second kind had in the middle two trochaic
verses of four feet, so this hath three of the same nature,
and ends in a dimetre as the second begun. The
dimetre may allow in the first place a trochee or a
spondee, but no iambic.

The example.

Just beguiler,
Kindest love, yet only chastest,

Royal in thy smooth denials,
Frowning or demurely smiling,
    Still my pure delight.

    Let me view thee
With thoughts and with eyes affected,
And if then the flames do murmur,
Quench them with thy virtue, charm them
    With thy stormy brows.

    Heav'n so cheerful
Laughs not ever, hoary winter
Knows his season; even the freshest
Summer morns from angry thunder
    Jet [1] *not still secure.*

The ninth Chapter, of the Anacreontic verse.

If any shall demand the reason why this number being in itself simple, is placed after so many compounded numbers, I answer, because I hold it a number too licentiate for a higher place, and in respect of the rest imperfect, yet is it passing graceful in our English tongue, and will excellently fit the subject of a madrigal, or any other lofty or tragical matter. It consists of two feet, the first may be either a spondee or trochee, the other must ever represent the nature of a trochee, as for example :

    Follow, follow,
    Though with mischief
    Armed, like whirlwind
    Now she flies thee ;
    Time can conquer
    Love's unkindness ;

---

[1] " Jet   walk proudly.

Love can alter
Time's disgraces :
Till death faint not
Then, but follow.
Could I catch that
Nimble traitor
Scornful Laura,
Swift-foot Laura,
Soon then would I
Seek avengement.
What's th' avengement ?
Ev'n submissly
Prostrate then to
Beg for mercy.

Thus have I briefly described eight several kinds of
English numbers simple or compound. The first was
our iambic pure and licentiate. The second, that
which I call our dimetre, being derived either from
the end of our iambic, or from the beginning of our
trochaic. The third which I delivered was our English
trochaic verse. The fourth our English elegiac. The
fifth, sixth, and seventh, were our English Sapphic and
two other lyrical numbers, the one beginning with that
verse which I call our dimetre, the other ending with
the same. The eighth and last was a kind of Anacreontic verse, handled in this chapter. These numbers which by my long observation I have found agree-
able with the nature of our syllables, I have set forth
for the benefit of our language, which I presume the
learned will not only initiate, but also polish and
amplify with their own inventions. Some ears accus-
tomed altogether to the fatness of rime, may perhaps

except against the cadences of these numbers, but let
any man judicially examine them, and he shall find
they close of themselves so perfectly, that the help of
rime were not only in them superfluous, but also absurd.
Moreover, that they agree with the nature of our
English it is manifest, because they entertain so
willingly our own British names, which the writers in
English heroics could never aspire unto, and even our
rimers themselves have rather delighted in borrowed
names than in their own, though much more apt and
necessary. But it is now time that I proceed to the
censure of our syllables, and that I set such laws upon
them as by imitation, reason, or experience, I can confirm. Yet before I enter into that discourse, I will
briefly recite and dispose in order all such feet as are
necessary for composition of the verses before described. They are six in number, three whereof consist of two syllables, and as many of three.

Feet of two syllables.

Iambic : ⎫   ⎧ *rĕvēnge*
Trochaic : ⎬ as ⎨ *bēautў*
Spondee : ⎭   ⎩ *cōnstānt*

Feet of three syllables.

Tribrach : ⎫   ⎧ *mĭsĕrў*
Anapaestic : ⎬ as ⎨ *mĭsĕrīes*
Dactyl : ⎭   ⎩ *dēstĭnў.*

The tenth Chapter, of the quantity of English syllables.

The Greeks in the quantity of their syllables were
far more licentious than the Latins, as Martial in his
epigram of Earinon witnesseth, saying, *Musas qui*

S

colimus severiores. But the English may very well challenge much more license than either of them, by reason it stands chiefly upon monosyllables, which in expressing with the voice, are of a heavy carriage, and for that cause the dactyl, tribrach, and anapæstic are not greatly missed in our verses. But above all the accent of our words is diligently to be observed, for chiefly by the accent in any language the true value of the syllables is to be measured. Neither can I remember any impediment except position that can alter the accent of any syllable in our English verse. For though we accent the second of *Trumpington* short, yet is it naturally long, and so of necessity must be held of every composer. Wherefore the first rule that is to be observed is the nature of the accent, which we must ever follow.

The next rule is position, which makes every syllable long, whether the position happens in one or in two words, according to the manner of the Latins, wherein is to be noted that *h* is no letter.

Position is when a vowel comes before two consonants, either in one or two words. In one, as in *best, e* before *st,* makes the word *best* long by position. In two words, as in *settled love : e* before *d* in the last syllable of the first word, and *l* in the beginning of the second makes *led* in *settlēd* long by position.

A vowel before a vowel is always short, as *flīing,*[1] *dīing, gŏïng,* unless the accent alter it, as in *dĕnīing.*

The diphthong in the midst of a word is always long, as *plaïing, decēïving.*

The synalæphas or elisions in our tongue are either necessary to avoid the hollowness and gaping

---

[1] I have kept the old spelling in *fliing, diing,* &c.

in our verse as *to*, and *the*, *t'enchant*, *th' enchanter*, or
may be used at pleasure, as for *let us* to say *let's;* for
we will, *we'll;* for *every*, *ev'ry;* for *they are*, *th' are;*
for *he is*, *he's;* for *admired*, *admir'd;* and such
like.

Also, because our English orthography (as the
French) differs from our common pronunciation, we
must esteem our syllables as we speak, not as we
write ; for the sound of them in a verse is to be valued,
and not their letters ; as for *follow*, we pronounce
follo; for *perfect*, *perfet;* for *little*, *littel;* for *love-sick*,
love-sik; for *honour*, *honor;* for *money*, *mony;* for
dangerous, *dangerus;* for *raunsome*, *raunsum;* for
though, *tho;* and their like.

Derivatives hold the quantities of their primitives,
as *dĕvōut*, *dĕvōutlў*, *prŏfāne*, *prŏfānelў;* and so do the
compositives, as *dĕsērv'd*, *ūndĕsērv'd*.

In words of two syllables, if the last have a full and
rising accent that sticks long upon the voice, the first
syllable is always short, unless position, or the diphthong doth make it long, as *dĕsīre*, *prĕsērve*, *dĕfīne*,
prŏfāne, *rĕgārd*, *mănūre*, and such like.

If the like dissyllables at the beginning have double
consonants of the same kind, we may use the first
syllable as common, but more naturally short, because
in their pronunciation we touch but one of those
double letters, as *ăllēnd*, *ăpcăr*, *ŏpōse*. The like
we may say when silent and melting consonants meet
together, as *ăddrēst*, *rĕdrēst*, *ŏprēst*, *rĕprēst*, *rĕtrīv'd*,
and such like.

Words of two syllables that in their last syllable
maintain a flat or falling accent, ought to hold their
first syllable long, as *rīgŏr*, *glōrў*, *spīrīt*, *fūrў*, *lābōŭr*,

and the like : ăny, măny, prĕty, hŏly, and their like,
are excepted.

One observation which leads me to judge of the
difference of these dissyllables whereof 1 last spake, I
take from the original monosyllable; which if it be
grave, as shāde, I hold that the first of shādy must be
long ; so trūe, trūlў; hāve, hāvĭng; tīre, tīrĭng.

Words of three syllables for the most part are
derived from words of two syllables, and from them
take the quantity of their first syllable, as flōurĭsh,
flōurĭshĭng, long ; hŏlў, hŏlĭness, short; but mĭ in
mĭser being long, hinders not the first of mĭsery to
be short, because the sound of the i is a little
altered.

De, dĭ, and pro, in trisyllable (the second being
short) are long, as dēsŏlāte, dĭlĭgĕnt, prōdĭgal. Re is
ever short, as rĕmĕdў, rĕfĕrēnce, rĕdŏlĕnt, rĕvĕrĕnd.

Likewise the first of these trisyllables is short, as
the first of bĕnĕfit, gĕnĕral, hĭdĕous, mĕmŏrў, nŭmĕrous,
pĕnĕtrāte, sĕpărate, tĭmŏrous, vărĭant, vărĭous, and so
may we esteem of all that yield the like quickness of
sound.

In words of three syllables the quantity of the middle
syllable is lightly taken from the last syllable of the
original dissyllable, as the last of dĕvīne, ending in a
grave or long accent, make the second of dĕvīnĭng
also long, and so ĕspīe, ĕspīĭng, dĕnīe, dĕnīĭng: con-
trarywise it falls out if the last of the dissyllable bears
a flat or falling accent, as glŏrĭe, glŏrĭĭng, ĕnvĭe,
ĕnvĭĭng, and so forth.

Words of more syllables are either borrowed and
hold their own nature, or are likewise derived and so
follow the quantity of their primitives, or are known

by their proper accents, or may be easily censured by
a judicial ear.

All words of two or more syllables ending with a
falling accent in *y* or *ye*, as *fairlie, demurelle, beawtie,
pittie;* or in *ue*, as *virtuĕ, rēscuĕ;* or in *ow*, as *follŏw,
hŏllŏw;* or in *e*, as *parlĕ, Daphnĕ;* or in *a*, as *mannă;*
are naturally short in their last syllables. Neither let
any man cavil at this licentiate abbreviating of syllables,
contrary to the custom of the Latins, which made all
their last syllables that ended in *u* long, but let him
consider that our verse of five feet, and for the most
part but of ten syllables, must equal theirs of six feet
and of many syllables, and therefore may with suffi-
cient reason adventure upon this allowance. Besides,
every man may observe what an infinite number of
syllables both among the Greeks and Romans are
held as common. But words of two syllables ending
with a rising accent in *y* or *ye*, as *denye, descrye*, or in
ue, as *ensue*, or in *ee*, as *forsee*, or in *oe*, as *foregoe*, are
long in their last syllables, unless a vowel begins the
next word.

All monosyllables that end in a grave accent are
ever long, as *wrath, hăth, thēse, thōse, tōoth, sōoth,
thrōugh, dāy, plāy, featē, speedē, strīfe, flōw, grōw, shōw.*

The like rule is to be observed in the last of dissyllables, bearing a grave rising sound, as *devine,
delaie, retire, refuse, manure*, or a grave falling sound,
as *fortune, pleasure, rampire.*

All such as have a double consonant lengthening
them, as *wārre, bārre, stārre, fūrre, mūrre*, appear to
me rather long than any way short.

There are of these kinds other, but of a lighter sound,
that if the word following do begin with a vowel are

short, as *doth, though, thou, now, they, two, too, flye, dye, true, due, see, are, far, you, thee*, and the like.

These monosyllables are always short, as *ă, thĕ, thĭ, shĕ, wĕ, bĕ, hĕ, nŏ, tŏ, gŏ, sŏ, dŏ*, and the like.

But if *i* or *y* are joined at the beginning of a word with any vowel, it is not then held as a vowel, but as a consonant, as *jealousy, juice, jade, joy, Judas, ye, yet, yel, youth, yoke.* The like is to be observed in *w*, as *winde, wide, wood :* and in all words that begin with *va, ve, vi, vo,* or *vu,* as *vacant, vew, vine, voide,* and *vulture.*

All monosyllables or polysyllables that end in single consonants, either written, or sounded with single consonants, having a sharp lively accent, and standing without position of the word following, are short in their last syllable, as *scăb, flĕd, pārtĕd, Gŏd, ŏf, ĭf, bāndŏg, ānguĭsh, sĭck, quĭck, rīvăl, wĭll, pēoplĕ, sīmplĕ, comĕ, somĕ, hĭm, thĕm, frŏm, sūmmŏn, thĕn, prŏp, prŏspĕr, hōnoŭr, lāboŭr, thĭs, hĭs, spēechĕs, gŏddŭsse, pĕrfĕct, bŭt, whăt, thăt,* and their like.

The last syllable of all words in the plural number that have two or more vowels before *s,* are long, as *virtūes, dutīes, miserīes, fellowēs.*

These rules concerning the quantity of our English syllables I have disposed as they came next into my memory ; others, more methodical, time and practice may produce. In the mean season, as the grammarians leave many syllables to the authority of poets, so do I likewise leave many to their judgments ; and withal thus conclude, that there is no art begun and perfected at one enterprise.

FINIS.

Tho. Campiani Epigrammatum libri II. Vmbra. Elegiarum liber vnus. Londini Excudebat E. Griffin, Anno Domini. 1619. 8vo.

Tho: Campiani

Epigrammatum

Liber primus.

1. AD EXCELSISSIMUM FLORENTISSIMUMQUE CAROLUM, MAGNAE BRITANNIAE PRINCIPEM.

L UDICRA qui tibi nunc dicat, olim (amplissime
  Princeps),
Grandior ut fueris, grandia forte canet,
Quaeque genus celebrare tuum et tua lucida possunt
  Facta, domi crescunt, sive patrata foris.
At tenues ne tu nimis (optime) despice musas ;
  Pondere magna valent, parva lepore juvant.
Regibus athletae spatiis grati esse solebant
  Apricis ; nani ridiculique domi.
Magnus Alexander magno plaudebat Homero,
  Suspiciens inter praelia ficta deos :
Caesar, major eo, Romana epigrammata legit ;
  Sceptrigera quaedam fecit et ipse manu.
Talia sed recitent alii tibi (maxime Princeps) ;
  Tu facias semper maxima, parva lege.
Enecat activam quia contemplatio vitam
  Longa, brevis, necnon ingeniosa, fovet.

2. *De libris suis.*

Nuper cur natum libro praepono priori?
Principis est aequum principe stare loco.

3. *Ad Lectorem.*

Nec sua barbaricis Galeno scribere visum est,
   In mensa nullum qui didicere modum ;
Nec mea commendo nimium lectoribus illis
   Qui sine delectu vilia quaeque legunt.

4. *In Nervam.*

Ad coenam immunis propter joca salsa vocatur
   Nerva ; suum fas est lingere quemque salem.

5. *In Tabaccam.*

Aurum nauta suis Hispanus vectat ab Indis,
   Et longas queritur se subiisse vias.
Majus iter portus ad eosdem suscipit Anglus,
   Ut referat fumos, nuda Tabacca, tuos,
Copia detonsis quos vendit Ibera Britannis,
   Per fumos ad se vellera cal'da trahens.
Nec mirum est stupidos vitiatis naribus Anglos
   Olfacere Hesperios non potuisse dolos.

6. *Dec auro potabili.*

Pomponi, tantum vendis medicabilis auri,
   Quantum dat fidei credula turba tibi :
Evadunt aliqui, sed non vi futilis auri ;
   Servantur sola certius ergo fide.

7. *Ad Berinum.*

Nomen traxit Amor suum, Berine,
A fervente mari, unde diva mater

Est e fluctibus orta sals-amaris
(Verum vivida si refert vetustas),
Credo non sine maxima procella.
Nec dici temere hoc putes, Berine ;
Quippe instar maris aestuant amantes,
Saepe et naufragium rei queruntur,
Plusque illa fidei ; vorax Charybdis
Maecha est, et furia acrior marina.

8. *In Villum.*

Discursus cur te bibulum jam musaque fallit ?
Humectas mentis lampada, Ville, nimis.

9. *In Nervam.*

Fratres, cognatos, natos, et utrunque parentem [1]
  Composuit constans Nervaque rectus adhuc ;
Solus stirpe manens e tanta, sanguinis omne
  Jam decus in venis comprimit ille suis.
Ergo beatorum mensas vir providus ambit,
  Inde sibi sanguis crescat ut usque novus.
Jamque pater, mater, jam fratres, atque nepotes,
  Spreto est externo sanguine, Nerva, tibi.

10. *In Mathonem.*

Ebrius uxorem duxit Matho, sobrius horret,
  Cui nunc in sola est ebrietate salus.

11. *De bona Fama.*

Qui sapit in multis, vix desipuisse videri
  Ulla in re poterit ; tam bona Fama bona est.

---

[1] Old ed. "querentem." The correction is made in the *Errata*
at the end of the book.

12. *Ad Calvum.*

Cantor saltatorque priori de ordine certant
   Calve ; sed ante choros musica nata fuit :
Dignior et motus animi quae temperat ars quam
   Corporis est, quanto corpore mens melior.

13. *Ad Cosmum.*

Plena boni est mulier bona, res pretiosaque, Cosme :
   Rara sed esse nimis res pretiosa solet.

14. *In Lycum.*

Non ex officiis quae mutua gratia debet
   Ferre per alternas atque referre vices,
Sed Lycus ex usu privato pendit amicos ;
   Nec tacet ; et solus quod sapit, inde putat.
Pectore vir bonus et sapiens cernetur aperto ;
   Non itidem malus ; is, quod sapit, omne tegit :
Sis licet ex fructu nummorum jam, Lyce, dives,
   Fictae ne speres fenus amicitiae.

15. *Ad Eurum.*

Multum qui loquitur, si non sapit, idque vetustum est ;
   Caccula causidicus si sapit, Eure, novum est.

16. *Ad Haedum.*

In multis bene cum feci tibi, non bene nosti ;
   Si malefecissem, notior (Haede) forem.

17. *In Barnum.*[1]

In vinum solvi cupis Aufilena quod haurit,
   Basia sic felix, dum bibit illa, dabis ;

---

[1] Campion is here ridiculing the sixty-third sonnet of Barnabe
Barnes. Marston in the "Scourge of Villainy," and Nashe in
"Have with you to Saffron Walden," had taken Barnes to task
for his unfortunate conceit.

Forsitan attinges quoque cor ; sed (Barne) matella
Exceptus tandem, qualis amator eris ?

18. *In Cacculam.*

Caccula causidicus quid nî ditissimus esset ?
Et loquitur nemo magis, et verba omnia vendit.

19. *In Sabellum.*

Nummos si repeto (Sabelle) rides ;
Coenam si nego, perfuris (Sabelle).
Utrumvis pariter mihi molestum est :
In re non fero seria jocosum ;
In re non fero serium jocosa.

20. *In Sectorem Zonarium.*

Artifices inter Sector Zonarius omnes
Lucrum non fallax solus ubique facit ;
Namque opera expleta, cuncta sine lite morave,
Mercedem propria continet ille manu.

21. *In Nervam.*

Temperiem laudare tuam vis Nervaque tangi ;
Ex tactu tepidus, Nerva, fatebor, eras.
Sed quid homo tepidus sonat Anglis ipse docebo ;
Scilicet haud multum qui bonus, aut malus est.

22. *In Tuccam.*

Non "salve," sed "solve" tibi Lycus obvius infit ;
Urbanus sed tu nil nisi, Tucca, "vale."

23. *In Calum.*

Colligit, et scriptos Calus in se ridet iambos :
Vix credas homini quam maledicta placent.

Invidiamque viro ceu quid probat utile magno ;
Quem "metui potius quam placuisse" juvat ;
Haec Calus : at Genius quandoque susurrat in aure,
" Est gravis Invidiae saepe ruina comes."

24. *In Marinam.*

Docta minus, moechis ut erat contenta duobus,
     Sic etiam bigis vecta Marina fuit :
Nunc eadem solis agitur fastosa quadrigis,
     Nunc igitur moechos bis capit illa duos.

25. *In Tatium.*

Haud melior Tatio vir erat, nec amicior alter ;
     Hoc tolerabilior jam Calus ; aula docet.
Nam faciles nondum gustata potentia reddit,
     Et prima prohibet plurima fronte pudor.
Simplicitate sua sic virgo educta pudice
     Lusus declinat, verbaque nuda nimis :
Aptior haec tandem licet obtrectante labello
     Basiolum discit reddere, parque pari ;
Inde manum tangi patitur, tectasque mamillas,
     Nec refugit quamvis arctior instat amans.
Ast Venerem simul illa sapit, tacitosque Hymenaeos,
     Impune et fieri perdita quaeque videt ;
Perfricta quid non audebit denique fronte,
     Aut quem nequitiae ponet aperta modum ?
Pessimus ex pravo sic nascitur aulicus usu ;
     Nec mirum, cui non imperat una Venus.

26. *In Acerrum.*

Cautus homo est, et Acerrus habet quot lumina quondam
     Argus, at haec dubie cuncta, nihilve vident.

27. *In Calum.*

Ne quem nunc metuas in te atros scribere versus ;
  Nigrorem Aethiopi qui paret, ecquis erit ?
Perfosso quid opus nova figere spicula corde?
  Quis dabit in misera pocula dira phthisi ?
Omnis cura tibi, Cale, sit de funere, tanquam
  Mortuus, et speres jam bona verba licet.

28. *Ad Licinium.*

Vir bonus esse potest, Licini, cui femina nulla
  Imperat ; at contra vir malus esse potest.

29. *In Gaurum.*

Causidicos in lite paras tibi, Gaure, peritos,
  Quorum tu meritis munera nulla negas :
In morbo medicos contra conducis inertes,
  Quamque potes minimo ; sic tibi, Gaure, sapis ?
Haeredi siquidem rem, vitam nemo relinquet ;
  Haeredi potius vivitur, anne tibi ?

30. *In Pardalum.*

Ex quibus existunt animalia spagyrus isdem [1]
  Dicet ali ; verum est, id ratioque docet.
Ex sale, mercurioque, et sulphure corpora constant,
  Ut Paracelsiacae perstrepit aura scholae.
Pardalus idcirco chymicus tumidusque professor,
  Pro modico modium jam solet esse salis ;
Idque agit assidue magis ut se nutriat, inquit :
  Sulphur sic utinam mercuriumque voret.

31. *In Corvinum.*

Bassano multum debet Corvinus ; honorem
  Jure suo, gratum munificoque animum :

[1] Old ed. " iisdem.

Bassanus ne hilum Corvino ; qui male gratus
Cunctorum amisit mutua jura hominum.

32. *In Histricum.*

Tritas rogo cur habeat Histricus vestes ;
An deficit res, aut fides ? negat : Quaero
Novis quid obstet. Vestiarium non fert,
Ait, qui adaptet sibi : timet titillari.

33. *In Albium.*

An te quod pueri in via salutent
    Ignoti, gravis intumescis, Albi,
Incedens veluti novus Senator,
    Fixis vultibus, et gradu severo?
Erras ; non honor hic, metus profecto est ;
    Nam, tristis ferulae memor, puellus
Quid nî cogitet ex ineptiente
    Ista te gravitate paedagogum?

34. *De Epigrammate.*

Sicut et acre piper mordax epigramma palato
Non omni gratum est : utile nemo negat.

35. *In Corvinum.*

Quis non te, Corvine, omni jam munere dignum
    Et gratum exemplo te celebrante feret ?
Nam Venerem tibi dat Galla, idque palam omnibus
    effers,
    Tanti ne meriti non videare memor.

36. *De Utilitate.*

Utilis est nulli semet qui negligit ; omni
    Vix usquam spreta est utilitate bonus.

37. *In Nervam.*

Vinum amat, horret aquam ; qua visa Nerva recurrit,
Ut solet a rabido morsus, Amate, cane.
Porrecto vini cyatho fugitat canis ; illi
Ostendas lympham quando fugare velis.

38. *Ad Ponticum.*

Argus habet natos sex, nullam, Pontice, natam ;
Vulgo si credis, sobrius Argus homo est.

39. *Ad Cosmum.*

Versum qui semel ut generat nullum necat, idem
Non numeris gaudet, Cosme, sed innumeris.

40. *De Henrico 4. Francorum Rege.*

Henricum gladio qui non occidere posset,
Cultello potuit : parva timere bonum est.

41. *Ad Serenissimam Annam Reginam.*

Anna, tuum nomen si derivetur ab anno,
Nominibus quadrant annua quaeque tuis :
Annua dona tibi debentur, et annua sacra ;
Atque renascendi per nova saecla vices.

42. *Ad eandem.*

Quattuor Anna elementa refert, venerabile nomen ;
Divisus partes, Anna, tot annus habet.
Anna retro est eadem, sed non reflectitur annus ;
Hic in se moriens, salva sed illa redit.

43. *Ad Sereniss. Carolum Principem.*

Scotia te genuit, cepit mox Anglia parvum ;
Sed tu, quod spero, Carole, neuter eris.

T

Unica te faciet nam magna Britannia magnum ;
Nomina conveniunt factaque magna tibi.

44. *Ad Augustiss. Jacobum Regem.*

Curta tuum cur haec metuunt epigrammata nomen ?
Debetur famae maxima musa tuae.

45. *Ad Castricum.*

Acceptum pro me perhibes te, Castrice, ludis
Admissum ; pro te captus at ejicior :
Esse mei similem non est tibi causa dolendi,
Sed me tam similem poenitet esse tui.

46. *Ad Rob. Caraeum* [1] *Equitem Auratum nobilissimum.*

Olim te duro cernebam tempore Martis,
In se cum fureret Gallia, qualis eras.
Teque, Caraee, diu florentem vidimus aula,
Dux, idem et princeps, dum tua cura fuit.
Unus erat vitae tenor, et prudentia juncta
Cum gravitate tibi sic quasi nata foret :
Nec mutavit honor, nec te variabilis aetas ;
Qui novit juvenem, noscet itemque senem.

47. *In Tuccam.*

Consuluit medicum de cordis Tucca tremore ;
Morbum (proh) talem miles habere potest !

48. *In Cacculam.*

Vulgares medici tussi, febrique medentur,
Et vitiis quorum causa cuique patet.
Morbi sed cerebri convulso corpore, vel cum
Non movet, exposcunt haud levis artis opem.

---

[1] Sir Robert Carey, first Earl of Monmouth.

Aemulus hinc causam defendit Caccula nullam
Quae justa, aut bona sit ; pessima sola placet.
Hanc agit intrepide semper, victorque triumphat,
Tanquam is [1] cujus ope est Attica pulsa lues.

49. *De Terminis forensibus.*

Anglorum Jurisconsulti quatuor uno
Exposcunt anno, termini at îs [2] duo sunt :
Terminus a quo res trudunt, et terminus ad quem ;
Mutua qui sumunt nomina saepe sua.

50. *Ad Ponticum.*

Convivas alios quaeras tibi, Pontice ; coeno
Lautius atque hodie tutius ipse domi :
Nam me qui monuit vester modo rufus olebat
Ac si esset totus caseus, isque vetus,
Et tostus decies ; atqui hunc meus horret utervis
Suffitum genius ; Pontice, coeno domi.

51. *In Tabaccam.*

Cum cerebro inducat fumo hausta Tabacca stuporem,
Nonne putem stupidos quos vapor iste capit?

52. *Ad Sabellum.*

Filia, sive uxor peccat, tua culpa, Sabelle, est ;
Per se nulla bona est ; nulla puella mala ;
Soli debetur custodi femina quicquid
In vita spurce, sive decenter agit.

53. *De Gauro.*

Nil dum facit temere, nihil facit Gaurus.

[1] Hippocrates.   [2] Old ed. "ijs."

54. *In Acmen.*

Est dives Titus, id fateris, Acme ;
Et te conjugio expetit misellam ;
Illum tu fugis, attamen beatum :
Quare? non sapit, inquis ; et quid inde?
An si quis prior est Ulysse coelebs,
Non reddes, simul hunc sinu maritum
Complexa es, stolidum magis Batillo ?

55. *In Glaucum.*

Debilis eunuchus sit, sit castratus oportet ;
Tam Glauco invisum'est omne virile genus.

56. *In Laurentiam.*

Imberbi, si cui, Laurentia nubere vovit,
Invenit multos haec sibi fama procos ;
Impubes omnes, mora quos in amore pilosos
Reddidit ; ignoto sic perit illa viro.

57. *In Lalum.*

Aedes Lalo amplae sat sunt, sed aranea telis
Immunis totas inficit, ille sinit.
Quoque magis numero crescunt, gaudet magis, unus
Tetras bestiolas has amat, atque fovet ;
Non tamen ut bellas ; nec quod medicina pusillis
Vulneribus tela est ; toxica nulla facit.
Verum est cum muscis lis non medicabilis ; illas
Insequitur demens, omnimodeque necat ;
Idque opus imposuit misero festiva puella,
Ala cui muscae laesus ocellus erat.

58. *In Nervam.*

Dissecto Nervae capite, haud (chirurge) cerebrum
Conspicis ; eia, alibi quaere ; ubi? ventriculo.

59. *Ad Aprum.*

Causidicus qui rure habitat, vicina per arva
Si cui non nocuit, jam benefecit, Aper.

60. *Ad Pontilianum.*

Qua celebrata Lyco fuerant sponsalia luce,
　Captus homo tota mente repente fuit :
Idque velut monstri quid demiraris? at illo
　Quis non insanit (Pontiliane) die?

61. *Ad Berinum.*

Vidisti cacodaemonem, Berine ;
Qua tandem specie? canis nigri, inquis.
Vah ; dicam melius, canem figura
Vidisti cacodaemonis, Berine.

62. *Ad Aulum.*

Cum scribat nunquam Corvinus non satur, Aule,
Tantum jejuni carminis unde facit?

63. *Ad Lauram.*

Egregie canis, in solis sed, Laura, tenebris ;
　Nil bene fortassis non facis in tenebris.

64. *Ad Ponticum.*

Re nulla genio cum pigro (Pontice) noster
　Consentit genius ; sed velut ignis aquae
Miscetur, pariter suscepta negotia reptant
　Invite, pariter somnus utrumque premit.
Mens hebet, herba velut, vicino infecta veneno,
　Tota mihi ; vel ceu flamma repressa furit.
Tale mihi tuus est solanum, Pontice, summus
　Patronus Decius, nescio quale tibi.

65. *De Honore.*

Qui plus quam vires tolerant subit amplior aequo,
Is merito dici possit honoris ἵνς.

66. *Ad Salustium.*

Hesterna tibi gratulor, Salusti,
De coena magis ob jocos inermes,
Et suaves animo calente risus,
Hausto non timide novo rubello ;
Quam de istis avibus quater sepultis,
Selectis dapibus tuo palato ;
Quae mensa positae, sed expianda,
Efflavere stygem, suoque nostrum
Tetro nunc feriunt odore nasum.
Sed me reprimo quamlibet gravatum,
Nam res candida fama mortuorum est.

67. *In Cossum.*

Condidit immenso puerilia membra sepulchro
   Filioli, multo marmore claustra tegens,
Cossus, quanta duos caperent satis ampla Typhaeos,
   Solus consilii conscius ipse sui.
Ergo impar spectator opus miratur ; at illud
   Ingenium authoris ceu levis umbra refert :
Aedes qui tantas habitat miser, ut bene possent
   Cum turba proceres sustinuisse duos.

68. *De Nuptiis.*

Rite ut celebres nuptias,
   Dupla tibi face est opus ;
Praetendat unam Hymen necesse,
   At alteram par est amor.

69. *Ad Guil. Camdenum.*

Legi operosum jamdudum, Camdene, volumen,
  Quo gens descripta, et terra Britanna tibi est,
Ingenii felicis opus, solidique laboris ;
  Verborum, et rerum, splendor utrinque nitet.
Lectorem utque pium decet, hoc tibi reddo merenti,
  Per te quod patriam tam bene nosco meam.

70. *De suis.*

Rerum quae nova nunc Britannicarum
Exorta est facies ? Vetus recessit
Prorsus sobrietas ; gula, insolensque
Cultu insania, futilisque pompa
Pessundant populum manu potentem ;
Sic pauci ut bene de suoque vivant ;
Vixque ex omnibus invenire quenquam est
Qui non accipit ipse foenus, aut dat.

71. *Ad Glaucum.*

Exemplo quicquid fit, justum creditur esse ;
  Exemplis fiunt sed mala, Glauce, malis.

72. *De Medicis.*

Gnarus judicat aurifex metalla,
Dat gemmis pretium, et suum valorem :
Doctos sed medicos, bene et merentes,
Tantum ponderat imperita turba.

73. *In Ligonem.*

Invideat quamvis sua verba Latina Britannis
  Causidicis, docto nunc Ligo fertur equo.
Et medici partes agit undique notus ; Alenum [1]
  Scenarum melius vix puto posse decus.

  [1] Edward Allen, the famous actor.

74. *De Senectute.*

Est instar vini generosi docta senectus ;
Quo magis annosa est, acrior esse solet.

75. *Ad Calvum.*

Insanos olim prior aetas dixit amantes ;
Non sanos hodie dicere, Calve, licet.

76. *Ad Maurum.*

Perpulchre calamo tua, Maure, epigrammata pingis ;
Apparet chartis nulla litura tuis.
Pes seu claudus erit, seu vox incongrua, nunquam
Expungis quidquam ; tam tibi pulchra placent.
Pulchra sed haec oculis ut sint, tamem auribus horrent ;
* Horrida vox omnis, lusce, litura fuit.

77. *In Cinnam.*

Notos, ignotos, celsos, humilesque salutat
Cinna ; joco populi dicitur ergo Salus.

78. *In Tuccam.*

Sit licet oppressus, licet obrutus aere alieno
Tucca, nihil sentit : quam sapit iste stupor !

79. *In Nervam.*

Coctos Nerva cibos crate aut sartagine torret
Usque in carbonem ; deliciasque vocat.
Quid potius cuperet quam carbonarius esse
Helluo inops, cui plus quam caro carbo placet ?

80. *Ad Eurum.*

Solus pauper amat Macer beatas,
Lautas sed nimis ; atque fastuosas ;
Laudari cupit, Eure, non amari.

81. *Ad Ponticum.*

Propria si sedes jecur est, et fomes, amoris,
    Haud tuus esse potest, Pontice, sanus amor.

82. *In Ligonem.*

Ligo Latine vulnerarium potum
Dicere volebat ; vulverarium dixit.

83. *In Daedalum.*

Parva te mare navigasse cymba
Magnum, Daedale, praedicas ; quid ad me
Cymba si Styga transmees eadem ?

84. *Ad Justinianum.*

Vir bonus et minime vis litigiosus haberi,
    " Et lites," coram judice, mitis ais,
" Non amo, nec temere cuiquam struo ;" gratia causae
    Major ut accedat (Justiniane) tuae.
Invidiam, ah, nescis quantam tua candida verba,
    Quas inimicitias, quae tibi bella parant,
Quosve illic risus astantibus ipse moveres,
    Damnans juridicis utile litis onus,
Quamque patet turbis bonitas tua : tres tibi scribent
    Mane dicas aliqui ; mox alii atque alii ;
Nec succrescenti posthac a lite quiesces,
    Idque alieno etiam judice : jamne tremis ?

85. *In Cacculam.*

Legis cum sensum pervertis ; forsitan illud
Jure facis, sed non, Caccula, jure bono.

86. *Ad Papilum.*

Papile, non amo te, nec tecum coeno libenter,
    Nec tamen hoc merito fit, fateorque, tuo :

Sed nimis ore refers miscentem tristia Picum
  Toxica, suspectum te tua forma facit :
Anguillam quisquis timet, esse hanc autumat anguem,
  Et non esse sciat, cogitat esse tamen.

87. *In Lycum.*

Conjugio est junctos qui separat execrandus ;
  Pugnantes dirimi non sinit ergo Lycus.

88. *In Bostillum.*

Magna Bostillus magnum se venditat aula ;
  Aulae magna tamen plus bovis olla capit.

89. *Ad Eurum.*

Non laute vivis, sed laete ; negligis urbem ;
  Attamen urbani plenus es, Eure, joci ;
Tam lepido tibi fit rus ipsa urbanius urbe,
  Rusque tuum in se nil rusticitatis habet.

90. *In Mathonem.*

Martis ut affirmat, Veneris sed vulnere claudus
  It Matho, scit morbum dissimulare suum ;
Et fictum narrat, medico indulgente, duellum ;
  Prostrato inflictum sed sibi vulnus, ait.

91. *In Myrtillam.*

O dira pestis utriusque Myrtilla
Sexus, liquescens dulcium ore Sirenum :
Parumne ducis credulos amatores
Si perdis omnes, artibus animos îsdem [1]
Quin optumarum polluas puellarum,
Ut nulla propter te indole ex sua vivat
Simul aure putrida hauserit tuos cantus ?

---

[1] Old ed. "ijsdem."

O pestis omni pestilentior peste !
Haud saeviit adeo Atticis senex Cous [1]
A moenibus quam [2] depulit sacram tabem :
Madore [3] nec quae languido Britannorum
Terrebat animos omnium nova strage ;
Crebrave [4] sternutatione quae lues longe
Grassata miseram solitudinem vidit ;
Nec enim parem poeticis inaudire est
Scriptis, sed omnes una pestis haec pestes
Superat, sit illa vera, sit licet ficta.

92. *In Pseudomedicum.*

Invento ex libro Medicus qui creditur esse ;
Fortunae, non is filius artis erat.

93. *Ad Mantalum.*

Non satis est supra vulgus quod, Mantale, sentis,
Consilium si non exprimis ore gravi.
Distinguit ratio a brutis, oratio sed nos
Inter nos, animae lux et imago loquens.

94. *De Francisci Draci nave.*

En Draci sicco tabescit littore navis, [5]
Aemula sed sphaerae, pulcher Apollo, tuae.
Illa nam vectus vir clarus circuit orbem,
Thymbraeo et vidit vix loca nota deo.

---

[1] " Senex Cous "—Hippocrates, who is stated (on doubtful authority) to have stopped the plague at Athens by burning fires throughout the city, and by other devices.

[2] *Quum* in the old ed. ; corrected in the *Errata*.

[3] In 1563 the Sweating Sickness raged violently ; but the reference may be to a more recent visitation.

[4] In 1580 an influenza of a virulent type passed over Europe.

[5] Drake's ship, the " Golden Hind," was long preserved at Deptford.

Cujus fama recens tantum te praeterit, Argo,
Quantum mortalem Delia sphaera ratem.

95. *In Morachum.*

Mors nox perpetua est ; mori proinde
Non suadet sibi nyctalops Morachus,
In solis titubans ne eat tenebris.

96. *In obitum Hen: Mag: Brit: Principis.*

Grandior, et primis fatis post terga relictis,
Concipiens animo jam nova regna suo,
Princeps corripitur vulgari febre Britannus ;
Hinc lapso ut coepit vivere flore perit.
Sic moriemur ? ad haec ludibria nascimur ? et spes,
Fortunaeque hominum tam cito corruerint ?

97. *De Fran: Draco.*

Nomine Dracus erat signatus ut incolat undas ;
Dracum namque anatem lingua Britanna vocat.

98. *In obitum Jacobi Huissii.*

Heu non maturo mihi fato, dulcis Huissi,
Occidis, heu, annis digne Methusaliis ;
Occidis ex morbo quem fraus et avara Synerti
Saevitia ingenuit ; cui mala multa viro
Det Deus ; et, lachrymis quotquot tua funera flerunt
In diras versis, ira odioque necent.

99. *In Bostillum.*

Audiit ut cuculos comedi Bostillus in aula
Moechus, abit metuens, prospiciensque sibi.

100. *In Fannium.*

Hispani bibit indies lagenam
Vini Fannius, usque cruditatem
Causatur stomachi ; novem decemve
Ante annis cucumem unicum quod edit

Maturum minus ; isthic, isthic usque
Haerens ventriculum gravat, nec esse
Hispani immemorem sinit Lyaei.

101. *In Aprum.*

Impurus, sexu nec Aper scortator in uno,
  Cum lotii clausus forte meatus erat,
Sic periit ; misero sua facta urina ruina est,
  Et poenae causa in pene nocente fuit.

102. *Ad Calvum.*

Non Anglos carnis defectu, Calve, bovinae
  Caletum Galli deseruisse ferunt,
Sed condimenti quod profert acre sinapi ;
  Hoc joculoque sibi Gallia tota placet.
Coccineo hanc hosti nuper cum dederet urbem,
  Neutrius Gallo copia, crede, fuit.

103. *In Corvinum.*

Effodiat sibi, Calve, oculos Corvinus, Homero,
  Ut sperat, similis non tamen esse potest.

104. *In Cinnam.*

Daemonis effigie compressit Cinna puellam ;
  Deinde sacerdotem se facit ; atque fugat
Daemonium ut voluit ; gravida sed virgine, nescit
  Anne pater Daemon vel sacer hospes erat.

105. *Ad Naevolam.*

Ebrius occurrit quoties tibi Naevola, vinum
  Non nimium, dicis, sed bibit ille malum.

106. *In Calvum.*

. Divinas bona, Calve, tibi, sed sola futura
  Semper ; et haec semper sola futura puto.

107. *Ad Eurum.*

Vocem Lyctus habet parem cicadis ;
Aut qualem tenues feruntur umbrae
Ad ripas Stygis edere ejulantes.
Hunc si quis novus audiat loquentem,
Exhaustum poterit phthisi putare ;
Ipsum sin oculis metit, Cyclopum
Ceu spectans aliquem timebit auctis
Membris horribilem, atque ventricosum.
Vox tam disparilis fit unde, dicam ?
Sic, Eure, expediam : creâsse mutum
Naturam voluisse credo Lyctum ;
Errantemque dedisse semimutum.

108. *Ad eundem.*

Mentem pervertit gravis ut jactura Metello,
Sic inopinatum Lysitelique lucrum.
Harum quae major fuerit dementia quaeris?
Damna ferens ; curas nam petit, Eure, duas.

109. *Ad Ponticum.*

Qualiscunque suam contemnit femina famam,
Nullum, etsi decies, Pontice, jurat, amat.

110. *In Lychen.*

Graecia praeclare pulchras vocat ἀλφεσιβοίας ;
Quippe proci prestant munera, forma procos ;
Sed formosa Lyche vivit neglecta ; quot alma
Nam Cytherea trahit, fusca Minerva fugat.

111. *In Floram.*[1]

Omnia consciolis, bona tantum narrat amanti
Flora ; ita flaccescit fama, virescit amor.

[1] Old ed. " Florum."

112. *Ad Arcanam.*

Quod sis casta (Arcana) nego, deciesque negabo,
  Credaris tota talis in urbe licet.
Nam tuus insequitur dum putida scorta maritus,
  Dum turpi, et vario ruptus amore perit :
Crede mihi quotquot noti meretricibus illis
  Sunt homines, noti sunt, Arcana, tibi :
Sive equites, seu magnatum de stemmate creti ;
  Ruris an urbis erit ; pomifer, anne cocus ;
Omnes, mille licet, te sunt, O casta, potiti ;
  Omnium et in morbos sic vitiata ruis.

113. *Ad Ponticum.*

Suspecto quid fure canes cum, Pontice, latrent
  Dixissent melius, si potuere loqui ?

114. *Ad Labienum.*

Nonnullis medicina placet nova, notaque sordet ;
  Sed tutas praefer tu, Labiene, novis.

115. *In Album.*

Quem vitae cursum, quam spem, sortemve sequaris,
  Quaerendo tremulus factus es, Albe, senex,
Sic tumulo mox ut nequeas inscribere " Vixi ;"
  Embrioque, aut minus hoc, cum morieris, eris.

116. *De Lycori et Berino.*

Gratis non amat, et sapit Lycoris :
  Moechae dat nihil, et sapit Berinus.

117. *Ad Gallam.*

Cum loqueris resoni prodit se putrida nasi
  Pernicies : si vis, Galla, placere, tace.

118. *In Nervam.*

Et miser atque vorax optat sibi Nerva podagram,
Solis divitibus qualis adesse solet.
Errat si putat id voti prodesse gulosis ;
Nam quid lauta juvat mensa, jacente fame ?

119. *Ad Ponticum.*

Femina vindicta citiusne ardescit amore ?
Phoebo, si dicis, Pontice, major eris.

120. *Ad Labienum.*

Vinum theriacam magnam dixere vetusti
Auctores ; gratum est hoc, Labiene, tibi.
Hinc te secure Baccho sine fine modoque
Imples ; visceribus sanus an aeger idem est.
Sed ne delires ; dirum namque ipsa venenum
Theriaca est, sumas si, Labiene, nimis.

121. *In Lausum.*

Lausus ut aeterna degit sub nube tabaccae,
Conjux ardenti sic sua gaudet aqua :
Vir fumum, haec flammam bibit ; infumata maritus
Tanquam perna olim, frixa sed uxor erit.

122. *Ad Ponticum.*

Poenituisse Midam voti sat constat avari,
Cumque cibus potusque aureus omnis erat.
Nunc aurum sed eum potare Chymista doceret,
Iratosque sibi ludere posse deos.
Quid mirum tales auri si nectare lactet ?
Immunes morbis, dîs [1] similesque facit.
Sed non dîs [1] similes sunt quos spes aurea fallit ;
Quales sint igitur (Pontice)? dissimiles.

---

[1] Old ed. "dijs."

123. *In Aulum.*

Ex speculo pictor se pinxit ut Aulus, amicae
Dat tabulam ; speculo mallet amica frui.

124. *De Henrico Principe.*

Occubuit primis Henricus clarus in annis ;
Nec [1] spolium mortis, sed pudor ille fuit.

125. *Ad Paridem.*

Ut vetus adscivit sibi magna Britannia nomen,
  Pingere se sexus caepit uterque, Pari ;
Haud sine vulneribus veteres tinxere Britanni
  Corpora, divelli nec timuere cutem :
Parcere sed Pictos sibi praecipit aula novellos,
  Et tenera leves arte polire genas.
Barbariem antiqui mores sapuere ; recentes
  Mollitiem ; neutrum mî placet ergo, Pari.

126. *In Vacerram.*

Damnatis quoties Vacerra turpe
Immiscet joculis, id esse dictum
Non (ut velle videtur ore blaeso)
Imprudenter ait, sed impudenter.

127. *Ad Furium.*

Sub medium culpae, Furi, cum conjuge moechum
Prendit Aper ; taurum jam vitulumne vocas?

128. *Ad Berinum.*

Uxor quod nimium tua sit fecunda, Berine,
  Conquereris ; castae sic tamen esse solent :

---

[1] Old ed. "Non." In the list of *Errata* we are told to read
"Nec."

U

Addis ut implacido sit et ore, et more molesta,
Et pugnax ; castae sic tamen esse solent :
Quin aliis lepidam dicis magis atque benignam
Quam tibi : sic castae non tamen esse solent.

129. *Ad Eurum.*

Mortuus Hermus abhinc tribus est aut quattuor annis ;
Immo vivit, ais ; mortuus, Eure, mihi est.

130. *Ad Crispum.*

Mutua multa licet sestertia poscat amicus,
    Maxima religio est, Crispe, negare tibi.
Sic numeras tamen ut lachrimis credaris obortis
    Quod facis officii poenituisse tui.
Nil tibi, Crispe, deest nisi digni vultus amici ;
    Nam, non ut decet, at quod decet usque facis.

131. *Ad Chloen.*

Mortales tua forma quod misellos
Multos illaqueet, Chloe, superbis :
Hoc sed nomine carnifex triumphet.

132. *In Labienum.*

Pedere cum voluit potuit Labienus ; Hibernum[1]
Virtute hac potuit perdere cum voluit.

133. *In Brussilium.*

Ardet Brussilii uxor histrionem ;
Is funambulam ; utrinque flamma saevit,
Nullo extinguibilis liquore, nullo.
Primum grande nemus voravit, inde

---

[1] Many of our old writers have remarked on the sensitiveness of Irishmen.

Villas tres, ovium greges, boumque
Circum pascua tosta mugientum,
Vix aula furor abstinet paterna ;
Et si fas miseris malum ominari,
Tandem cum domino domum cremabit.

134. *In Cacculam.*

Caccula cum tu sis vetus accusator, adaugens
Crimina, quam causas daemonis instar agis !

135. *In Cinnam.*

Dic sapere, et sapiet ; stupidum dic, Cinna stupescet ;
Si furere, insanus ; si premis, aeger erit ;
Dic modo, fiet idem quod dicis ; nec simulare
Novit, habent vires verba veneficii.

136. *Ad Calvum.*

Ne tibi, Calve, petas socios in amore fideles,
Si quod amas metuis perdere, solus ama.
Nocte suo fidum domino domuique molossum
Una salax[1] cogit prodere cuncta canis :
Nocturni id fures norunt, quantumque libido
Tentabit firmam dejicietque fidem.

137. *Ad Harpalum.*

Nec bene, nec belle, semper tamen, Harpale, cantas ;
Artem disce, canes sic minus, at melius.

138. *In Porcum et Nervam.*

Desinit auditis campanis meiere Porcus,
Sit vesica licet mole molesta gravi.
Haud lotium contra, sonuit si fistula, fraenat
Nerva ; sed invito sic ruit omne, miser

1 Old ed. "salix."

Ut penitus madeat ; nec ei prodesse matella
Possit, ita audaces evocat imber aquas.
Motus tam discors illis qua vi fit, Aquinus
Quaerat ; nos risu res satis ipsa juvat.

139. *In Poetastros.*

Sulphure vincenda est prurigo poetica nullo ;
Sed neque Mercurio, quem fugat illa deum.

140. *De Germanis.*

Germanus minime quod sit malus, efficit aequum
Tota quod explosis gens amat effugiis.
Nam diverticulis cum lex laetabitur, ansam
Dat fraudi, multos nec sinit esse bonos.

141. *In Glaucum.*

Alas amisit Glaucus, draco nam fuit olim ;
Nunc serpens factus nec leve virus habet.

142. *In Aprum.*

Septem civis Aper degit, tot et aulicus, annos ;
Vivere scit melius quam, Labiene, morti.

143. *In Crispinum.*

Uxorem Crispinus habet, tamen indigus unum
Vix alit, extremam sensit uterque famem.
Ipsam dives amat Florus, fremit ergo maritus,
Quanquam rivali nunc opus esse videt.
Moechum saepe vocat, sed cum, qui sustinet, ipse
Qua fruitur, victu, vestibus, aere domum,
Dispeream nisi sit vere Crispinus adulter ;
Sponsus, qui sponsi munia Florus obit.

144. *De sudore Britannico.*

Quidni pestis sit sudor malus Anglica? cives
Hibernis gaudent sole vigente togis.

145. *Ad Thespilem.*

Inferius labrum cur mordes, Thespilis? illi
Ne noceas, si vis basia laeta tibi.
Alterum iners cupido quamvis famuletur amanti,
At magis hoc docta mobilitate placet.

146. *Ad Ponticum.*

Quanto causidicum magis arguo, si malus idem est,
Tanto plus laudo, Pontice, si bonus est.

147. *Ad Gallam.*

An tua plus sitiat lingua, an plus, Galla, loquatur,
Ardua res dictu plenaque litis erit.
Nam quoties sitit illa bibis; bene potaque garris;
Procreat unde novam multa loquela sitim.
Dum bibis ergo invita taces, mora nec datur illis;
Indefessa anima sed bibis, aut loqueris.

148. *De Londinensibus.*

Sunt Londinenses Coritani, sive Brigantes,
Seu Cambri; raros urbs alit ampla suos.
Sic Londinates producit mixta propago,
Plurimus inter quos semicolonus erit,
Aegre mutandus; partis nam fenore nummis
Quantum quisque potest praedia civis emit,
In rus festinans, aetas nî praepedit, ipse:
Haeredi saltem dant nova rura locum,
Qui, sem-urbanus, velut hermaphroditus habetur
Indigenis, nam nil rus nisi rure placet.

Quippe canes, vel equos semper, vel aratra loquuntur ;
Illis caetera sunt maxima barbaries.
O utinam civis tantum civilia tractet ;
Rustica qui ruri non alienus erit.

149. *Ad Arethusam.*

Cernitur in nivea cito, si fit, sindone labes :
Formosis eadem lex, Arethusa, datur.

150. *Ad Justinianum.*

Causidicos ditat, res perdit et una clientes,
Uno quae verbo est, Justiniane, mora.

151. *De horologio portabili.*

Temporis interpres, parvum congestus in orbem,
Qui memores repetis nocte dieque sonos :
Ut semel instructus jucunde sex quater horas
Mobilibus rotulis irrequietus agis !
Nec mecum quocunque feror comes ire gravaris,
Annumerans vitae damna, levansque, meae.

152. *Ad Eurum.*

Nec turpe lucrum, nec decus, nec in plebem
Invida potestas, pulchra sed poetarum
Votum pudicum est fama ; bonis meta
Omnibus, at illis unica, et mera, et sola ;
Auferre quam merentibus furens nescit
Vis vulnerata divitum : Aulus hinc vivit ;
Liberque Junius ; et amabilis Flaccus ;
Et vile quisquis vulgus, Eure, fastidit.

153. *Ad Labienum.*

Mentiri pro te servo si sis bonus author ;
Pro se mentiri, cur, Labiene, vetas ?

154. *Ad Haemum*

Difficile est reperire fidem, si quaeris in aula,
    Paene ubi delator tertius, Haeme, vir est.
Talem pone novis nimium qui partibus haeret ;
    Officiosus homo est ? insidiosus erit.

155. *Ad Justinianum.*

Quatuor et viginti Arthuri regia mensa
    Convivas aluit ; quaeque rotunda fuit.
Mensis jam reges longis utuntur, at uni
    Vix est convivae, Justiniane, locus :
Augustus toto cum maximus esset in orbe,
    Illi convictor sat Maro gratus erat.
Sed sine compare sit Maro, sic sine compare rex est
    Delicias populus quem vocat ipse suas.

156. *Ad Faustinum.*

Curvam habeat tua cervicem, Faustine, puella :
    Sic, tanquam cupiat basia, semper erit.

157. *Ad Justinianum.*

Si quaeruntur opes, vel honores, sive voluptas,
    Vix est qui fruitur, Justiniane, satis.
Nam satis est quicquid naturae sufficit ; ultra
    Quod poscit mens, est, Justiniane, nimis.

158. *In Haedum.*

Causidicus bene dotatam cum duxerat Haedus,
    Nulla viro vigilis cura clientis erat.
Vere sed expleto, cum dote extinguitur uxor,
    Desertoque animi detumuere novi.

Hinc parat omnimodis pulsos revocare clientes ;
Nam nunc si causas non agit Haedus, egct.

159. *Ad Eurum.*

Qui compotorem sibimet proponit amicum,
Compos propositi non erit, Eure, sui.

160. *Ad Glubum.*

Haeres avari, Glube, feneratoris
Viperca qui nunc flagra flet tua causa ;
Praedia, age, vende, pasce scorta, scurrasque ;
Disperde maleparta alea, gula, luxu,
Egensque quaeras fenore at triplo nummos ;
Instesque, licet irrideant trapezitae ;
Nec desine usque dum infimus rogatorum
Te filium fateare feneratoris.

161. *Ad Amatum.*

Multas cum visit regiones Pactus et urbcs,
In patriam laete deinde receptus erat.
Ut mos est, rogat hunc civis de mercibus, armis
Miles ; de ruris rustica cura bonis ;
Aulicus ad vestes quod pertinet ; aulica fucos,
Atque oleum ¹ talci ; singula quisque sua :
Solus qui solo nutritur jure Britanno,
Externa de re quaerit, Amate, nihil.

162. *In Tuccam.*

Plus aequo gladio pacis qui tempore credit,
Tucca, suo, gladio sed sine, saepe perit.

163. *Ad Luciam.*

Lucia, vir nihili est qui quanti virgo sit acris
Curat : venalem sic sibi quaerat equum.

¹ *Oil of talc*—an esteemed cosmetic when these epigrams were
written.

Nequicquam magna certant de dote puellae,
  Plus auro innuptas vita pudica beat.

164. *In Cacculam.*

Acturus causas amisit Caccula vocem,
  Inter praecones illico quaerit eam,
Causidicosque illos qui vociferare solebant
  Ingenti strepitu ; deserit inde forum,
Femellasque rogat sua quae venalia clamant,
  Urbanis servis deinde molestus erat ;
Turrim mox adiit, cunctos rogitansque, locosque
  Omnes vestigans : vox tamen usque latet.
Bombarda tandem, quae turrim evertere posset,
  Explosa, inventa Caccula voce redit.

165. *De servo suo.*

Servo iter ingressus gladium committo ferendum ;
  Mox soli atque omni cum sine teste sumus,
"Aurum," noster ait, "gestas, here ; nec latet ; id jam
  Auferre armati vis ab inerme potest ;
Factum quis prodet? dominum spoliare sed absit ;
  Sed facilis res est, si volo ; nolo tamen."
"Credo," aio, et laudo pro tempore ; pergit ineptus
  Dicere qualis hero quamque fidelis erit.
Inde domum laetus redeo, gladioque recepto
  Ejicio vacuum, despicioque fidem ;
Parque pari referens, "fidum te sensimus," inquam,
  "Et retinere licet, si volo ; nolo tamen.
Nam neque credendus, nec habendus, talia servus
  Aut qui concipere, aut non reticere, potest."

166. *Ad Haedum.*

Ignarum juvenem nudum cur trudis in urbem ?
  Neglecto caecum quis duce tentat iter ?

Gnossia non totidem domus est erroribus, Haeme,
Fallax, his filo quamlibet esset opus,
Aetati crudae quot vita urbana tenebras
Objicit, impuras et sine luce vias.
Ne duce destituas titubantem nocte dieque
Filiolum, salvum si cupis, Haeme, tibi.

167. *Ad Labienum.*

Tres novit, Labiene, Phoebus artes ;
Ut narrant veteres sophi ; peraeque
Quas omnes colui, colamque semper :
Nunc omnes quoque musicum, et poetam
Agnoscunt, medicumque Campianum.

168. *Ad Calathen.*

Graecas, Latinas, litterasque Gallicas
Laudo : puellae lingua sed si sit bona,
Cur uteretur, Calathe, alia quam sua ?

169. *In Naevolam.*

Tres est pollicitus rationes Naevola Cinnae,
Nummos quî nollet reddere : reddit eas :
Nil quod debetur prima ; altera nil quod haberet ;
Tertia non presto est : Naevola debet eam.

170. *Ad Eurum.*

Pro patria si quis dulci se dixerit, Eure,
Velle mori, ridens "ut sibi vivat," ais,
"Civis avarus ; et ut servetur Caccula rostris ;
Splendeat ut picta veste rotaque Calus."
Sic tu ; pro patria fortis cadet attamen omnis ;
Si bona sit, merita est ; sin mala, dulce mori.

171. *In Crassum.*

Crassus ab urbe profecturus, quam firmiter haerens,
  Ludorum causa, desidiosus amat :
Tres licet haud ultra noctes sit rure futurus,
  Idque absolvat iter dimidiata dies :
Solemnem ad caenam primos invitat amicos,
  Ceu natalitiam quam celebrare parat ;
Magna cum pompa, curva resonante sedetur
  Buccina, et in vitrum plena refusa salus,
Convivas aequo quae jure perambulat omnes ;
  Auspicium felix hinc sibi sumit iter.
Crassus, at extremis tanquam rediturus ab Indis,
  Mox testamentum perficit ; inde nova
Nata salus, reditum faustum quae spondet amico ;
  Postremo edictum tempus euntis erat ;
Maiae nimirum (coelo suadente) calendis
  Exibit ; nonae jamque Decembris erant.

172. *Ad Lollium.*

Ut locupleti addat pauper, praepostera res est :
  Divitis est, Lolli, gloria sola, dare.

173. *Ad Lauram.*

Singula dum miror tua labra, oculosque, genasque ;
  Quicquid id est verbis, Laura, modesta premis.
Crines sin laudo, perfusa rubore silescis ;
  Quam misere non hos esse fatere tuos !

174. *Ad Ponticum.*

Hic, illic, et ubique, et nullibi, Pontice, lex est ;
  Cumque tenes vinctam, te latebrosa fugit.
Pauciloqua antiquis constabat certa Britannis ;
  At nunc ambigua est lex sine lege loquens.

175. *Ad Afram.*

Calcat sublimis vulgaria verba poesis,
  Nec narrat, sed res ambitiosa creat.
Ludere si libet, aetatis tibi reddere florem,
  Par Hecubae quanquam sis, prius, Afra, valet,
Quadrupedis [1] pigrae quam ros, cerussave inuncta,
  Vel minium Venetum, fulva vel empta coma ;
Dentes seu vere quos inserit Argus eburnos,
  Totaque mangonis pharmacopoea Lami.
Suaviter illa tibi canet optatos Hymenaeos,
  Et gratis faciet ; quod tamen, Afra, veta :
Oscula det juvenis, sed anus ferat aurea dona, ·
  Carminibus celebris quae cupit esse bonis.

176. *Ad Albericum.*

Res est quemlibet una quae benignum
Et gratis facere (Alberice) possit ;
Nullum laedere, quamlibet merentem.

177. *In Largum.*

Vendit Largus oves, laudatque emptoribus illas
Ut teneras ; teneras sed sibi laudat aves.

178. *Ad Carolum Fitzgeofridum.*[2]

Jamdudum celebris scriptorum fama tuorum,
  In me autem ingenue non reticendus amor.
Frustra obnitentem si non fortuna vetasset,
  In veteres dederat, Carole, delicias :

---

1 *Quadrupedis pigrae ros* is, I suppose, asses' milk, which was formerly used for blanching the skin.

2 The author of a spirited poem, "Sir Francis Drake, His honorable Life's Commendation," &c., 1596; a volume of Latin epigrams and epitaphs, entitled "Affaniae," published in 1601 ; and several sermons. He has two epigrams to Campion in "Affaniae."

Haec tibi qualiacunque tamen nova lusimus, ut nos
Usque amplecteris non alieno animo.

179. *Ad Stellam.*

Vis, Stella, nomen inseri nostris tuum
   Compendiosis versibus?
An sat tibi est, O delicata, sidera
   Inter minora si mices?

180. *Ad Ed. Mychelburnum.*[1]

Immemor O nostri quid agit? nec enim tibi magnus
Natalis frustra rediit, monitorque vetustae
Semper amicitiae novus, et jam debitor annus;
Accipe nostra prior, tenui sed carmina cultu,
Qualia sunt domini longo de funere rapta;
Posterior tua si compti quid musa resolvet,
Festinans lepido quod portet epistola versu,
Unicus antidotos facile exuperaveris omnes.
Haec pauca interea, leve tanquam munus, habeto,
Quae novus ex usu merito tibi destinat annus,
Jusque sodalitii officio quocunque tuetur.
Quanta sit horrifici Jovis inclementia cernis;
Ut valeas lignis opus est; et si sapis, ipsi
Cum falce, et tento nolles parsisse Priapo.

181. *In Glaucum.*

Tempore mitescit quantumvis fructus acerbus;
   Fitque sapor gratus, qui modo crudus erat.
At Glaucus quanto evadit maturior annis,
   Austerus tanto fit magis atque magis.
Conjugis exemplo jam desinat esse malignus;
   Nam suavis, lepida est, nec gravis illa viris.

---

[1] The brothers Edward, Laurence, and Thomas Mychelburn seem to have been intimate friends of Campion. Charles Fitz-Geffrey in "Affaniae" addressed several epigrams to them.

182. *Ad Rutham.*

Non satis hoc caute dixti modo, Rutha, sorori,
　"Te tam formosam, non pudet esse levem?"
Illud nam dictum subito sic laesa retorsit,
　"Te non formosam non juvat esse levem."

183. *In Gaurum.*

Perpetuo loqueris, nec desinis; idque molestum
　Omnibus est; et scis; sed tibi, Gaure, places.

184. *In Auricium.*

Haud quenquam sinis, Aurici, te adire,
　Quantumvis humili allocutione;
At nos alloquimur poli utriusque
Rectorem, et rutila manu tonantem:
An non tu nimium tumes, sacerdos?

185. *Ad Herennium.*

Alcinoo mortem toties minitatus (Herenni),
　Cur occurrenti postea mitis eras?
Effraenem quamvis nequeas compescere linguam,
　At te jam video posse tenere manum.

186. *Ad Augustiss: Carolum magnae Britanniae Principem, Walliae principatum pro veteri ritu auspicaturum, die 4. No:*[1]

Laetus Britannis, ecce, festinat dies,
　Quintumque nunc praeoccupat
Sacrum Novembris; perge, ter beata lux,
　Quam festa signabit nota.
Maturus annis, mente nec princeps minor
　Britanniarum Carolus,
Ornandus hodie regiis insigniis,
　Exibit ut sponsus novus,

1 4th November, 1616.

Puris ephebis cinctus, et procerum choro,
  Ceu gemma pompa in aurea ;
Exceptus hilari confluentum murmure,
  Clarisque vulgi plausibus.
Prodi, O beate, rem capesse publicam,
  Umbra nimis torpes diu :
Vestigiis jam assuesce majorum inclitis,
  Praestantioris aemulus.
Pulchram tibi hic sit primus ad famam dies ;
  At nemo norit ultimum.

187. *Ad magnam Britanniam.*

Reddidit antiquum tibi, magna Britannia, nomen
  Rex magnus, magnos dum facit ille suos.

188. *De Regis reditu e Scotia.*[1]

Nil Ptolomaeus agit, caelique volumina nescit,
  Nam nunc a gelido cardine (Phoebe) redis,
Et veris formosa rosis Aurora refulget :
  Hunc, precor, aeternum reddat Apollo diem.

189. *Ad ampliss. totius Angliae Cancellarium, Fr. Ba.*

Debet multa tibi veneranda (Bacone) poësis
  Illo de docto perlepidoque libro,
Qui manet inscriptus *Veterum Sapientia ;* famae
  Et per cuncta tuae saecla manebit opus ;
Multaque te celebrent quanquam tua scripta, fatebor
  Ingenue, hoc laute tu mihi, docte, sapis.

190. *Ad eundem.*

Patre, nec immerito, quamvis amplissimus esset,
  Amplior, ut virtus, sic tibi crescit honor.
Quantus ades, seu te spinosa volumina juris,
  Seu schola, seu dulcis Musa (Bacone) vocat !

[1] In 1617.

Quam super ingenti tua re Prudentia regnat,
　Et tota aethereo nectare lingua madens !
Quam bene cum tacita nectis gravitate lepores !
　Quam semel admissis stat tuus almus amor !
Haud stupet aggesti mens in fulgore metalli ;
　Nunquam visa tibi est res peregrina, dare.
O factum egregie, tua (Rex clarissime) tali
　Gratia cum splendet suspicienda viro !

191. *Ad Hymettum.*

Sis probus usque licet, timidus tamen ipse teipsum
　Deseris, obsequio debet inesse modus,
Vilis erit cunctis sibi qui vilescit, Hymette :
　Non omnis pudor aut utilis aut bonus est.

192. *Ad Ed: Mychelburnum.*

Nostrarum quoties prendit me nausea rerum,
　Accipio librum mox, Edoarde, tuum,
Suavem qui spirat plenus velut hortus odorem,
　Et verni radios aetheris intus habet.
Illo defessam recreo mentemque animumque,
　Ad joca corridens deliciasque tuas ;
Haud contemnendo vel seria tecta lepore,
　Cuncta argumentis splendidiora suis.
Haec quorsum premis ?[1] ut pereant quis talia condit ?
　Edere si non vis omnibus, ede tibi.

---

[1] Charles Fitz-Geffrey, in the second book of " Affaniae," 1601,
makes a similar appeal to Edward Mychelburn :
　　" Ergone, dure parens, pluteo sepelire profundo
　　　　Ingenii poteris pignora dia tui ? " &c.
I am curious to see Mychelburn's writings ; perhaps they may
turn up some day in MS.

193. *Ad Sitim.*

Sitis malorum pessimum,
Aegris molestum sobriis,
Sanis inutile ebriis,
Si sanus ullo sit modo
Qui non nisi ut bibat bibit,
Semper paludc plus madens,
Sitiens tamen tosta magis
Multis arena solibus.
Nunc est benigna ut sis, Sitis,
Bustis avari Castoris
Diesque noctesque asside,
Qui te volens vivens tulit ;
Consors amicum protege,
Picto sedens in marmorc ;
Qui nubilo caelo cave
Ne sic madescat, Castoris
Ut ossa sicca perluat ;
Sed unicum te sentiat
Qui te colebat unicus,
Sorore cum tua Fame :
At non amantem me tui
Cum febre pariter desere,
Sitis, malorum pessimum.

194. *Ad Lupum.*

Nemo virtutem non laudat, saevit et idem
  In vitium, hoc hominum sed, Lupe, more facit.
Nam quis ob hoc drachmam virtuti praebet egenti ?
  Aut in se vitium non amat, atque fovet ?

195. *Ad Eurum.*

Insanum cupidis labris ne tange Lyaeum ;
  Sic minus audentem te trahet, Eure, Venus.

Nec Veneri indulge, quamvis bona forma vocabit ;
　　Nam minus in votis sic tibi Bacchus erit.

196. *Ad Gallum.*

Quod nemo fecit sanus, neque fecerit unquam,
　　Tu facis, invideas cum mala, Galle, Fabro ;
Sollicitus domini quod nunc terit atria magni ;
　　At nescis hac quam conditione perit ;
Qui soli parat usque adeo servire patrono,
　　Ut non prospiciat libera tecta sibi.
Idque cavet dominus, modice dum plurima donat ;
　　Perpetuo, at parco fomite spemque levat.
Vixque solubilibus vinctum tenet usque catenis,
　　Exercens variis nocte dieque modis,
De libertatis nequando cogitet usu.
　　Jam vice vis fungi, livide Galle, Fabri ?

197. *Ad Lecesterlandium.*

Amplis grandisonisque, Lecesterlandie, verbis
　　Implacabiliter vociferare soles,
Uxor dum queritur quod fit tibi curta supellex ;
　　Fibula sed verbis aequiparanda tuis.

198. *Ad Hippum.*

Quanquam non simplex votum, facis attamen unum ;
　　Nam praeter vinum nil petis, Hippe, bonum.

199. *Ad Faustinum.*

Da mihi, da semper, nam quod, Faustine, dedisti
　　Esse datum nollem ; res cito parva perit.
Sin taedet, dandoque velis imponere finem ;
　　Da semel, ut nunquam cogar egere datis.

200. *Ad Phloen.*

Quid custodita de virginitate superbis,
  Jam licet annumeres ter tria lustra, Phloe?
Intactam nam te cum vix tria lustra videbas,
  Haud potuit cassa vendere lena nuce.
Gloria virginitas formosis, dedecus aeque
  Turpibus est, aetas si sit utrique gravis.

201. *Ad Volumnium.*

Rident rusticulam, anseremque multi;
Ignavos asinos, oves, bovesque;
At non est homine imperitiore
Irridendum animal magis, Volumni;
Tanto ridiculus magis, Volumni, est,
Quanto plus sapere obtinet videri.
Nam quis non medicum excipit Ligonem,
Vectum quadrupede,[1] intimis cachinnis,
Coum[2] qui colit atque Pergamenum?[3]
Multis sed sapit, imperatque multis
Ut vitae dominus, tremorque mortis;
Tanto ridiculus magis, Volumni, est.

202. *Ad Mycillum.*

Nullos non laudas, Suffenos, sive Cherillos,
  Seu quos in circo cruda juventa legit;
Candidus hinc censor dici contendis, at omnes
  Qui laudat, nullum laude, Mycille, beat.

203. *Ad Furium.*

Semper ad arma soles, Furi, clamare; cubili
  Sive lates, seu te compita plena vident.
Sed nunquam profers Veneris sint, Martis an arma;
  Utcunque infelix, te duce, miles erit.

---

[1] At this time doctors usually rode on mules when they went to visit their patients.
[2] Hippocrates.   [3] Aesculapius.

204. *In Helyn.*

Captat amatores quoties se dicit amare ;
Fallax obsequium est ; non amat, hamat Helys.

205. *Ad Vincentium.*

Dum placeo tibi, Vincenti, mea plurima poscis
Mutua, te simul at ceperit ira levis,
Mox eadem quamvis male custodita remittis :
Lucrum est, Vincenti, displicuisse tibi.

206. *In Hebram.*

Difficilis non est, nec amantem respuit unum ;
Unum vero unum vix amat Hebra diem.

207. *Ad Cacculam.*

Dicere te invitum cuiquam male, Caccula, juras ;
Invitus tune es (Caccula) causidicus?

208. *Ad Calvum.*

Lingua proterva, rapax manus, et gula, Calve, profunda ;
Haec tria sunt Davi commoda sola tui.
Illo praetereunte fremunt quacunque molossi ;
Sentit et in primo limine nostra canis.
Adveniente coci removent patinasque cibosque,
Arctius et retinet pallia quisque sua.
Audito fugitant femellae ; Caccula quamquam
Natus litigiis, illius ora timet.
Saepe domi ne te nunc visam terret imago
Orci, nam servat Cerberus ipse fores.
Dis genitos quaeras, hunc nî dimittis, amicos,
Clavisque accinctos Amphitryoniades.

209. *Ad Philochermum.*

Quaeris tu quare tibi musica nulla placeret ;
Quaero ego, cur nulli tu, Philocherme, places ?

210. *Ad doctos Poëtas.*

Nullus Maecenas dabit hac aetate Poëtis
Ut vivant ; melius sed bona fama dabit.

211. *Ad Rusticum.*

Rustice, sta, paucis dum te moror, auribus adsis ;
   Dic age, cujas es ? Salsburiensis, ais ?
Pembrochi viduam [1] num tu Sidneida nosti ?
   Non : saltem natos ? [2] cum sit uterque potens ;
A thalamis alter [3] regis celeberrimus heros ;
   Alter [4] at in thalamis ? proh tenebrose, negas ?
Inclitus ergo senex Hertfordius [5] an tibi notus ?
   Tantumdem : conjux quid speciosa senis ?
Non : non ? anne tuum scis nomen ? si id quoque
     nescis,
Caetera condono hac conditione tibi.

212. *Ad Cacculam.*

Causidicus tota cum sis notissimus urbe,
   Atque alienas res irrequietus agas,
Ducere cur cessas uxorem, Caccula ? lites
   Non est ut fugias, litigiosus homo es.

[1] Mary, daughter of Sir Henry Sidney ; widow of Henry Herbert, second Earl of Pembroke ; "Sidney's sister, Pembroke's mother."

[2] William Herbert, third Earl of Pembroke, and Philip Herbert, created in 1605 Earl of Montgomery.

[3] The Earl of Montgomery, who was Gentleman of the King's Bedchamber.

[4] The Earl of Pembroke, who had married the daughter and heiress of the Earl of Shrewsbury.

[5] Edward Seymour, Lord Hertford, b. 1547, d. 1621 ; eldest son (by the second marriage) of the Protector Somerset. The "conjux speciosa" was his third wife, Frances, daughter of Thomas, Viscount Howard of Bindon.

213. *Ad Calvum.*

Atroniam ut pulchram laudas, ut denique bellam,
  At minor hac Rhodius forte colossus erat.
Et capite, ac humeris superaret Amazonas omnes ;
  Ad quam, si confers, Penthesilea foret
Qualis cum vetula pappat nutrice puella ;
  Sola gigantei est germinis illa fides.
Cum video, spectrum videor mihi (Calve) videre,
  Et vix luminibus cernere vera meis.
Cujus ne temere attentes tu basia, totum
  Ejus in os poterit nam caput ire tuum.

214. *De sacra dote.*

Verba sacerdotem duo constituunt, sacer et dos ;
  Saepe sed occurrit vir sine dote sacer.

215. *Ad Rufum.*

Quos toties nummos oras, tibi, Rufe, negare
  Relligio est ; gravius, sed dare, forsan erit.
Nam meus infaustus cunctis solet aureus esse,
  Et semper damni plus mea dona ferunt.
Conciet hinc Bacchus, vel fallax alea bellum ;
  Labe vel asperget non bene parta Venus ;
Omnia sponte sua mala quae vitabit egestas :
  Nescis quas turbas plena crumena dabit.
Damnosos juveni currus invitus Apollo
  Concessit, nummos sic tibi, Rufe, nego.
Nec promissa Deus potuit revocare nociva, .
  Sed tibi promitto, sed tibi dono nihil.
Tu fortunatos qui prosint, quaere patronos ;
  Ast ego, ne noceant nostra, cavebo tibi.

216. *Ad Gallum.*

Perdidit ebrietas multos, tibi proficit uni,
  Galle, licet valide membra caputque gravet.

Hinc morbum simulas et acuta pericula lecto
  Postridie stratus vix animamque [1] trahens ;
Tunc inimicitias componis et eximis iris
  Expositum pectus sollicitumque metu :
Et pacem accitis evincis ab hostibus, omnes
  Expiraturis nam decet esse pios ;
Deinde reviviscis cuncto securus ab hoste,
  Et Martem Bacchum fallere, Galle, doces.

217. *Ad Cacculam.*

Quae speciem instaurant partes has, Caccula, verum est
Ad speciem quod habes ; nec tamen ad speciem.

218. *Ad Stellam.*

Pictor formosam quod finxit, Stella, Minervam
Carpis ; at hoc similis fit magis illa tibi.

219. *Ad Ponticum.*

Uxorem nosti Camerini, Pontice, quam sit
  Toto deformis corpore et ore tetro :
Casta tibi visa, et merito ; sed moecha reperta est ;
  Hanc vir in hesterno prendit adulterio.
Proh ! quantum saevisse putas ? Nil, Pontice, laetus
  Ipsam sed laudans coepit amare magis ;
Nam credebat, ait, turpem prius ; atque adeo ut, se
  Praeter, qui ferret tangero nemo foret.

220. *Ad Blandinum.*

Immemor esse tui dicor, Blandine, mearum
  Nulla tuum siquidem pagina nomen habet.
Sed Blandine, iterum atque iterum, Blandine legaris
  Ne, Blandine, ferar non memor esse tui.

----

[1] "Animumq ;" in old ed. ; corrected in the *Errata.*

221. *Ad Marianum.*

Prudens pharmacopola saepe vendit
Quid pro quo, Mariane, quod reprendis,
Hoc tu sed facis, oenopola, semper.

222. *Ad Tho: Munsonium,*[1] *Equitem auratum et Baronetum.*

Quicquid in adversis potuit constantia rebus,
Munsoni, meritis accumulare tuis
Addidit et merito victrix Dea, jamque sat ipse
Fama et fortunis integer amplus eris.

223. *Ad Eundem.*

Ne te spes revocet nec splendor vitreus aulae,
In te, Munsoni, spes tua major erit.

224. *Ad Gulielmum Strachacum.*

Paucos jam veteri meo sodali
Versus ludere, musa, ne graveris
Te nec taedeat his adesse nugis,
Semper nam mihi carus ille comptis
Gaudet versiculis facitque multos,
Summus Pieridum unicusque cultor.
Hoc ergo breve, musa, solve carmen
Strachaeo veteri meo sodali.

225. *Ad Lectorem.*

Fit sine lege liber, salvo cui demere toto
Particulas licet, aut apposuisse novas.
Sat, Lector, numeri ; numeris si sat tibi factum est ;
Cui numeri potius, quam numerosa placent.

[1] See *Introduction.*

1. *Ad Sereniss. Carolum Principem.*

NON veterem tibi dono librum, clarissime Princeps,
    Tanquam donatum ; si tamen ire jubes,
Splendorem fortasse novum trahet, et melior jam
Prodibit cum se noverit esse tuum.

2. *Ad Lectorem.*

Lusus si mollis, jocus aut levis, hic tibi, Lector,
    Occurrit, vitae prodita vere scias,
Dum regnat Cytheraea : ex illo musa quievit
    Nostra diu, Cereris curaque major erat :
In medicos ubi me campos deduxit Apollo,
    Aptare et docuit verba Britanna sonis :
Namque in honore mihi semper fuit unicus ille,
    Cujus ego monitis obsequor usque lubens.
Quid facerem ? quamvis alieno tempore, Phoebus,
    En, vocat, et recitat pulveris ore scelus,
Respondente cheli, metuendaque dulce sonanti,
    Quo sic perfudit mentem animumque meum,

Cogerer ut chartis, male sed memor, illa referre
 Quae cecinit mira dexteritate deus.
Hinc rediit mihi musa vetus, sed grandior, et quae
 Nunc aliqua didicit cum gravitate loqui ;
Et nova non invita mihi, diversaque dictat,
 Omnia quae, Lector candide, reddo tibi.

3. *Ad Librum.*

I nunc quicquid habes ineptiarum
Damnatum tenebris diu, libelle,
In lucem sine candidam venire
Excusoris ope eruditioris :
Exinde ut fueris satis polite
Impressus, nec egens novi nitoris,
Mychelburnum adeas utrumque nostrum,
Quos aetas, studiumque par amorque,
Mi connexuit optume merentes :
Illis vindicibus nihil timebis
Celsas per maris aestuantis undas
Rhenum visere, Sequanum, vel altum
Tibrim,[1] sive Tagi aureum fluentum.

4. *Ad Pacem de augustiss : Reg.*
Elizabetha.

O pax beatis, unicum decus terris,
Quam te lubens osculor, amabilis mater,
Rerumque custos, et benigna servatrix !
Quae sola te tuetur integram nobis,
Non illam amem, illam venerer omnibus dictis,
Factisque ? pro illa unquam mori reformidem ?
Illam quis amens proditam exteris optet,
Domi suis quae pacem et exteris donat ?

---

[1] Old ed. " Tibrem."

5. *In Calvum.*

Risi, Calve, hodie satis superque,
Notorum quia quemque ut attigisti,
Currentem licet et negotiosum,
Sistebas, retinens, toga prehendens ;
Tum demum rogitas equumne grandem
Empturus sit, et optimum, et valentem ;
Nec cessas odiosus abnuentem
Unumquemque trecenties rogare.
Quin me jam decies eras de eodem
Aggressus ; memini, fuit molestum.
Si quisquam interea tuum caballum
Posset ridicule satis tabella
Pro re pingere, squalidum, vietum,
Morbosus timide pedes levantem,
Pictor vendiderit prius tabellam
Quam tu vendideris tuum caballum.

6. *Ad Clonium.*

Fitne id quod petimus ? mihi si persuaseris, inquis :
  Siccine nos semper ludis, inepte Cloni ?
Unum nunc utinam tibi persuadere liceret :
  Ut cito suspendas te, miser, illud erit.

7. *In Crispum.*

Crispus amat socios, ut avara Lycoris amantes ;
  Ut libros Casinus bibliopola suos ;
Civis ut emptores Vincentius ; utque clientes
  Caccula causidicus ; sacra sacrator Helix ;
Non laudem, non quod verum mercantur amorem,
  Sed prodesse magis quod sua cuique solent.

8. *In Calvum.*

In circo modo Calve te prementem
Ut vidi nitidae latus puellae,
Sermonique avide viam astruentem ;
Mox divam Venerem, Leporem, Amoremque
Orabam tibi, ne inficetus illam
De grandi quid equo tuo rogares.

9. *In obitum Gual. Devoreux*[1] *fratris clariss.* *Comitis Essexiae.*

Pilas volare qui jubebat impius
Forata primus igne ferra suscitans,
Ei manus cruenta, cor ferum fuit.
Fenestra quanta mobili hinc deae patet
Ferire possit ut malos, bonos simul.
Quid alta fortitudo mentis efferae,
Torive corporis valent ? ruunt globi,
Praeitque caecitas, et atra nubila,
Sonique terror aethera et solum quatit.
Maligna fata, Devoreux, et unice,
Et alme frater incliti ducis, sacro
Tibi igne perdidere saucium caput,
Equo labansque funebri, heu, acerbum onus
Tuis, revectus arduum ad jugum redis ;
Rotaque subgemente curribus jaces
Molesta pompa fratri, et omnibus bonis.
Peribit ergo Rhona, pulsa corruet
Fero canente classicum tuba sono,
Et ulta stabis inter umbra caelites.

---

[1] Walter Deveureux, brother of the Earl of Essex, was killed by a musket-shot under the walls of Rouen in September, 1591 ("Lives and Letters of the Deveureux," i. 231, 233).

10. *Ad Melleam.*

O nimis semper mea vere amata
Mellea, O nostri pia cura cordis,
Quanta de te perpetuo subit mi
        Causa timoris !

Eminus quanquam jaculetur altus
Aureos in te radios Apollo,
Torqueor ne fictus amans in illis
        Forte lateret.

Et procul caelo pluvias cadentes
In sinus pulchros agitante vento,
Horreo, insanum placidus tonantem
        Ne vehat imber.

Somnians, et res vigilans ad omnes,
Excitor ; noctuque pavens dieque ;
Saepe si vestra potuit quis esse
        Quaero sub umbra.

11. *De obitu Phil : Sydnaei equitis aurati generosissimi.*

Matris pennigêrum alites Amorum,
Quid suaves violas per et venustas
Nequicquam petitis rosas Philippum,
Dumis usque " Philip, Philip," sonantes.
Confossum modo nam recepit Orcus,
Omnes dum superare bellicosa
Fama audet juvenis.   Renunciate
Funestum Veneri exitum Philippi,
Vatem defleat ut suorum Amorum.

12. *In Melleam.*

Mellea[1] mi si abeam promittit basia septem ;
  Basia dat septem, nec minus inde moror :
Euge, licet vafras fugit haec fraus una puellas,
  Basia majores ingerere usque moras.

13. *In Cultellum.*

Cultelle, Veneri te quis iratus faber
Tam triste dira contudit ferrum manu ?
Labella bellae caesa funesto scatent
Per te cruore : ah nectaris quantum perit !
Heu, heu, puellae personat planctu domus ;
Furit, dolori tantus accessit timor ;
Nec acquiescit uspiam ; impotens loqui,
Et basiare jam, quod est miserrimum :
At tu sceleste frustulatim diffluens
Poenas Amori, sed nimis seras, dabis.

14. *Ad Caspiam.*

Virgo compressa est, invitaque, Mellea jurat ;
  Furem cur nollet prodere voce, rogo.
Se mala respondit clamare cupisse, prehendi
  Solam cum solo sed metuisse viro.
O pudor insignis, facilisque modestia, qualem
  Optarem soli, Caspia dura, tibi !

---

[1] Compare a song in Robert Jones' *Second Book of Songs and Airs*, "My love bound me with a kiss," &c. I suspect that Campion wrote that song. At the end of each stanza are the lines—

> "Alas, that women doth not know
> Kisses make men loath to go,"

which bear a very close resemblance to lines 3-4 of the present epigram.

15. *Ad eandem.*

Phoenicem simulas, Caspia, Persicam,
Quae nunquam sociis ardet amoribus,
Flamma sed moriens nascitur e sua.
Exors tu pariter, solaque amantium
Congressus fugis, et contiguas faces ;
Verum insana diem ne reparabilis
Expectes volucris, fataque vivida ;
Formae flamma etenim nulla tuae parem
Quibit reddere, non si Venus aurea
Aut pulchrum in cinerem se Charites dabunt.·

16. *Ad Labienum.*

Quae celare cupit non peccat femina, dicis,
    Quae celat, peccat ; sed, Labiene, minus.

17. *In Carinum.*

Cogito saepe, Carine, sed infeliciter, unde
    Signarit vultus tanta rubedo tuos :
Nam sumptus ne sis vinosus terret, avaro
    Conditur gelida nec nisi coena fame.
Porro incoenatus nonnumquam, sordide, dormis,
    Aridulusque siti somnia vana vides.
Esurientis at ora magis pallore notantur,
    Et macilenta creat livida signa fames.
Quaero igitur tanti quae sit tibi causa ruboris ;
    Forsitan hanc speciem pictus ab arte petis :
Sed reliqua ut pingas quare vis pingere nasum
    Non video ; totusque haereo et excrucior.

18. *In Melleam.*

Anxia dum natura nimis tibi, Mellea, formam
Finxit, fidem oblita est dare.[1]

19. *Ad Calvum.*

Italico vultu donas mihi Calve, machaeram ;
More Britannorum protinus accipio.
Id mi succenses ; nunc ergo remittere conor ;
Quo more id faciam non tamen invenio.

20. *Ad Naevolam.*

Desine, nam scelus est, neu perdere, Naevola, tentes
Quod mihi suspirat Mellea basiolum.
Qui ferro necat, aut rigido cor transigit ense,
Terrenam molem dividit ille animae.
Dulcia sed temere qui basia solvit amantum,
Caelitus unitas dividit ille animas.

21. *Ad Calvum.*

Femina cum pallet ne dicas pallida quod sit,
Si, Calve, ingenui munus obire velis :
Languentem reficit mulier laudata colorem,
Totum quem formae credita culpa premit.

22. *In Lycum.*

Cum, Lyce, vovisti serum tibi funus, opinor
Te latuit lapidem rene latere tuo.

---

1 So in the *Fourth Book of Airs* ("I must complain yet do enjoy my love ")—

> "for Nature while she strove
> With all her graces and divinest arts
> To make her too too beautiful of hue,
> She had no leisure left to make her true."

23. *Ad Lucium.*

Crassis invideo tenuis nimis ipse, videtur
Satque mihi felix qui sat obesus erit.
Nam vacat assidue mens illi, corpore gaudet,
Et risu curas tristitiamque fugat.
Praecipuum venit haec etiam inter commoda, Luci,
Quod moriens minimo saepe labore perit.

24. *Ad Marinum.*

Parvi tu facis optimos poetas ;
Laudas historicos, amasque laxum
Sermonem, pedibus gravis Marine ;
Sparsas nec sale fabulas moraris.
Cur mirabilis omnibus, Marine,
Scriptor fit Plato? quippe fabulosus.

25. *In Maurum.*

Tres elegos Maurus totidemque epigrammata scripsit,
Supplicat et Musis esse poeta novem.

26. *In Cottam.*

Cotta per aestates ut in hortis dormiat urgent
Uxor obesa, Canis, torrida Zona, torus.

27. *De Catullo et Martiale.*

Cantabat Veneres meras Catullus ;
Quasvis sed, quasi silva, Martialis
Miscet materias suis libellis,   .
Laudes, stigmata, gratulationes,
Contemptus, joca, seria, ima, summa ;
Multis magnus hic est, bene ille cultis.

V

28. *Ad Meroen.*

Scortatorem optes, Meroe nasuta, maritum ;
Diminui nasum sic puto posse tuum.

29. *Ad Lupum.*

Adversus sortem [1] poterit vis nulla valere,
Et fateor ; sed quis tum, Lupe, fortis erit?

30. *Ad Haemum.*

Notorum mandas morientum nomina libro,
Atrum quem merito funereumque vocas :
Sin cupis, Haeme, pius laetusque notarius esse,
Inscribas vivos ; sic liber albus erit.

31. *In Ottuellum.*

Promissis quoties videt capillis
Blanditur mihi tonsor Ottuellus,
Cum vix curticomo feret salutem.
An tonsoribus, ut suis puellis,
Cari sunt et amabiles comati,
His formae studio, lucelli utrisque?

32. *Ad Philochermum.*

Quae potuit rivos retinere et saxa movere
Musica, te nulla parte, vel arte, movet ;
Quod facit ergo cave, Philocherme, tarantula [2] vulnus,
Ictus enim, ni fit musica grata, peris.

[1] Old ed. "fortem."
[2] "After being bitten by the Tarantula, there was, according to popular opinion, no way of saving life except by music. . . . It was customary, therefore, so early as the commencement of the seventeenth century, for whole bands of musicians to traverse

33. *Ad Janum.*

Cur tibi displiceat tua, Jane, quod uxor ametur?
An tibi quam nemo possit amare placet?

34. *Ad Laur: Mychelburnum.*

Quis votis tibi, Somne, supplicabit
Tam surdo atque hebeti deo, clientem
Qui sex continuas jacere noctes
Molli me vigilem toro sinebas,
Disperdique vaga cor inquietum
Fessa et lumina cogitatione?
Sed postquam salibus cubilibusque,
Laurenti, excipior tuis, solutos
Cepit grata simul quies ocellos.
Quod sane ob meritum puella si quae,
Laurenti, vigiles queretur horas
Dum pulchra speculo intuetur ora,
Mittam ad te, lepidum deum soporis.

35. *Ad Justinianum.*

Tu tanquam violas, laurum, et thyma dicis olere
Os consobrinae, Justiniane, tuae;
Ac veluti minio buccas, et labra notari:
Ipso quin minio picta labella rubent,
Atque genae; floresque remansos spiritus halat:
Ex vero omnia habet; sed nihil ex proprio.

36. *In Cottam.*

Non ego ne dicas vereor si quid tibi dico;
Sed ne non dicas, Cotta, sed adjicias.

Italy during the summer months, and what is quite unexampled either in ancient or modern times, the cure of the *Tarantati* in the different towns and villages was undertaken on a grand scale."—Hecker's "Epidemics of the Middle Ages," pp. 121-2.

37. *Ad Caspiam.*

Asperas tristis minitetur iras
Spemve promittat facies serenam,
Semper horresco, quoniam satis te,
            Caspia, novi :

Cum furis pulso retrahis capillos,
Evocas morsu rigido cruorem,
Quicquid occurrit, nimis ah perite
            Dextera torquet :

Fulmen hoc te terribilem, cruentam
Sed manus reddit furibunda, et hinc te
Sive ridentem metuo, benigne
            Sive loquentem.

Forte sopitum haud aliter leonem
Conspicit silvis tremulus viator,
Et pedem flectens, cavet excitari
            Ne fera possit.

38. *In Galbam.*

Natum Galba suum, domesticumque,
Extremus quasi Persa sit, vel Indus
Tractat, quod nothus est ; nec alloquendum
Censet, more nisi et stilo insolenti,
Et nudo capite, hospes ut videri
Omnino novus exterusque [1] possit.
Annon Galba satis superque ineptit ?

---

[1] Old ed. "extetusque."

39. *In Nervam.*

Abstrahis a domini coena te, Nerva, sacrati,
    Nec tamen ut caecus numinis hostis abes ;
Nec tibi quod panis vel vinum displicet : immo
    Invitamenti vim levioris habent.
Causa duplex prohibet ; quia ventri nil emis una ;
    Altera quod nimis haec sit sibi coena brevis.

40. *Ad nobiliss : virum Gul : Percium.*[1]

Gulelme gente Perciorum ab inclita,
Senilis ecce projicit nives hiems,
Tegitque summa montium cacumina :
Et aestuosus urget hinc Notus, gelu
Coactus inde Thracius, rapit diem
Palustris umbra, noxque nubibus madet.
Tibi perennis ergo splendeat focus,
Trucemque plectra pulsa mulceant Jovem :
Refusus intumescat Evius sciphis,
Novumque ver amoenus inferat jocus ;
Novas minister ingerat faces, ruit
Glocestriensium[2] in te amica vis, simul
Furorem ut hauriant levem, faceciis
Simulque molle lusitent per otium.

41. *Ad Bassum.*

Indiget innumeris vir magnus ; major at illo est
    Omnibus his quisquis, Basse, carere potest.

42. *In Hyrcamum et Sabinum.*

Hyrcamum graviter Sabinus odit,
Hyrcamusque male invicem Sabinum ;

---

[1] The author of "Sonnets to the Fairest Caelia," 1594, and of other pieces. He was the third son of Henry Percy, Earl of Northumberland.

[2] Percy belonged to Glocester Hall, now Worcester College, Oxford.

Hyrcami cilia atque caecitatem
Rides, ille tuam, Sabine, barbam
Hirsutam, indomitam, et quasi cacatam.
Alternis odiis peritis ambo,
Incondite itidem superbientes
Ambo, tum tetrici, atque curiosi,
Exortes comitum, tenebrici ambo ;
Vos sic unanimes, fere iidem et ambo,
Quare tam male convenitis ambo ?

43. *In Rufum.*

Nupsit anus, sed amans dentes non Isba malignos
    Sustinet ut possit, Rufe, nocere tibi.
Nam quem tritum habuit felix modo despuit unum,
    Jamque tuus passer, jamque columba tua est.
Et tenero faciet lepidissima murmura rostro,
    Basia per morsus nec metuenda dabit.
Femineo placeant mala immatura palato,
    Sed rugosa viros canaque poma juvent.
Rufe, novo fas sit tantum vovisse marito,
    Ne reparet dentes vivida nupta suos.

44. *Ad Accam.*

Partem das animae, sed quae tibi tota fruenda est ;
    Tu, mihi da partem qua licet, Acca, frui.

45. *In Carinum.*

Pulvilli totidem colore, vultu,
Textura, imparilique [1] sectione
Distincti, in tenebras tuas, Carine,
Mirabar quibus artibus venirent.
Perspexi modo ; scilicet tabernas

---

[1] Old ed. "imparitique."

Omnes despolias, trahens ab illis
Ornamenta tuum in cubilulillum : [1]
Quae postquam subigis tuis rapinis
Ignotos penitus lares subire,
More istic faciunt, nec est stupendum,
Pulvilli siquidem tui, Carine,
Jam spectent varie se, et insolenter.

46. *De morte canis.*

Desinite, O pueri, jentacula vestra timere,
  Non eritis nostrae postea praeda cani :
Quod lacera scit plebs errans per compita veste,
  Cur manet ex hujus parta quiete quies.

47. *In credulos cives.*

Bis sex Londinum vita concedit in una,
  Bis sex juratos urbs speciosa vocat.
Dispeream praeter speciem vocemque virorum
  Bis sex istorum millia si quid habent.
Nam sensus, animosque suos in judice ponunt ;
  Ex se non norunt ore favere reis :
Servatum quis enim, cui judex defuit, unum
  Secula per bis sex vidit in urbe reum ?

48. *Ad Melleam.*

Scelesta, quid me ? mitte, jam certum est, vale :
Longe repostas persequar terrae plagas,
Tuis vel umbras Tartari fucis procul.
Nec me retentare oris albicans [2] rubor,
Nec exeuntem lucidum hinc et hinc jubar
Lenire speret : Circe, in aeternum vale.

---

[1] Old ed. "cubilutillum"—corrected in the *Errata.*
[2] Old ed. "albicanus."

Rides inepta? siccine irati stupes
Minas amantis? sic genas guttis lavas?
Magisne rides? tam meus suavis tibi est
Discessus? at nunc non eo, ut fleas magis.

49. *In Turbonem.*

Turbo, deos manes celsi tu pondere gressus
Tota in se terres ne sua tecta ruant.

50. *Ad Caspiam.*

Si quid amas, inquis, mea Caspia, desine amare ;
Flammas ne calcant sic prohibere potes.
Ecquando coelum frondescit? terra movebit
Astra? vel auditis non tremet agna lupis?
Omnia naturae jam se contraria vertant ;
Aspera sic tandem Caspia mitis erit.

51. *In Lycum.*

Quod pulcher puer est potes videre ;
Quod te blandus amat, potes videre ;
Quod tecum bibit, et potes videre ;
Sed quae Lesbius impudenter audet
A tergo, Lyce, non potes videre.

52. *Ad Afram.*

Purgandae praefectum urbis notat, Afra, lutosa
Frons tua neglecti muneris esse reum.

53. *Ad Caspiam.*

Ne[1] tu me crudelis ames, nec basia labris
Imprime, nec collo brachia necte meo.
Supplex orabam satis haec, satis ipsa negabas,
Quae nunc te patiar vix cupiente dari.

---

[1] Cf. pp. 15-17 : " Thou art not fair," &c.

Eia age jam vici, nam tu si femina vere es,
Haec dabis invito terque quaterque mihi.

54. *Ad Amorem.*

Cogis ut insipidus sapiat, damnose Cupido,
Mollis at insipidos qui sapuere facis.
Qui sapit ex damno misere sapit ; O ego semper
Desipuisse velim, sis modo mollis, Amor.

55. *Ad Paulam.*

Grates, Paula, tuis ago libenter
Magnis pro meritis, anus jocosa ;
Languenti mihi quae diem diemque
Assidens, strepitu et levi cachinno
Sustentare animum obrutum solebas.
Nec certe ingenium moror retusum,
Absurdumque satis ; valere apud me
Debet plus animi tui voluntas ;
Hausta non pharetra facetiarum,
Ridendam quoque te dabas amico.

56. *Ad Caspiam.*

Cur istoc duro lacrimae de marmore manent
Quaeris, naturae, Caspia, sacra docens.
Docta sed in causas nimium descendis inanes,
Nam lacrimas haec flent saxa miserta meas.

57. *In Berinum.*

Demonstres rogo mî tuos amores,
Non ut surripiam tibi, Berine,
Sed tanta ut scabie abstinere possim.

58. In Erricum.

Tene Lycus faecem dicit? tene, Errice, faecem?
 Ah nimis indigne dicit, et improprie,
Faex a materia siquidem meliore creatur,
 At tua stirps tecum sordida tota fuit.

59. In Aemiliam.

Cum sibi multa dari cupiat, multisque placere,
 Quo probior tanto est nequior Aemilia.
Namque operam accepto Thais pro munere reddit;
 Illa nihil, sed lucrum ex probitate facit.
Ora, manus, oculosque gerat matrona pudicos;
 Unius haud partis sola pudicitia est.
Omnibus arridere, omnesque inducere amantes,
 Quanquam intacta potest, nulla pudica potest.

60. In Lycium et Clytham.[1]

Somno compositam jacere Clytham
Advertens Lycius puer puellam,
Hanc furtim petit, et genas prehendens
Molli basiolum dedit labello.
Immotam ut videt, altera imprimebat
Sensim suavia, moxque duriora:
Istaec conticuit velut sepulta.
Subrisit puer, ultimumque tentat
Solamen, nec adhuc movetur illa
Sed cunctos patitur dolos dolosa.
Quis tandem stupor hic? cui nec anser
Olim, par nec erat vigil Sibylla;
Nunc correpta eadem novo veterno,
Ad notos redit indies sopores.

[1] Cf. p. 12: "It fell on a summer's day," &c.

61. *In eosdem.*

Assidue ridet Lycius Clytha ut sua dormit ;
Ridet et in somnis sed sua Clytha magis.

62. *In Ovellum.*

Dedecori cur sit multum quod debet Ovellus ?
Nam fidei quis non esse fatetur opus ?

63. *Ad Melleam.*

Insidias metuo quoties me, Mellea, pulchrum
Dicis, sic capitur non bene cautus amans ;
Formosusque sibi visus se credit amari,
Nequicquam ; specie luditur ipse sua.

64. *In gloriosum.*

In caput, Herme, tuum suggrundia nocte ruebant,
Haud istoc essent scilicet ausa die.

65. *In Pharnacem.*

Pharnax haud alii ut solent novellum
Si quando famulum sibi recepit
In tectum, faciem viri, torosque
Inspectat ; studia ingenîve dotes ;
Sed quantum esuriens edat bibatque.

66. *Ad Caspiam.*

Per nemus Elisium Dido comitata Sichaeum
Pallida perpetuis fletibus ora rigat ;
Et memor antiqui semper, Narcisse, furoris
Umbram sollicitas per vada nigra tuam.
Debet ab adverso quisquis tabescit amore
Supplicium Stygia ferre receptus aqua.
Caspia, si pro te morientem poena moratur,
Esto tuis semper jungere labra labris.

67. *In Corvinum.*

Corvinus toties suis jocatur,
Nullum reddere suaviora posse,
Seu nymphas cecinit, trucesve pugnas,
Seu quicquid cecinit, bonum, malumve :
Hoc de se toties refert facetus,
Ut tandem fatuus sibi ipse credat.

68. *Ad Melburniam.*

Olim inter silvas, et per loca sola, Dianam
  Cum nymphis perhibent abstinuisse viris ;
Votivasque sacris seclusas aedibus, atram
  Fama quibus pepulit relligiosa notam.
Tu sed pulchra, diserta, frequens, Melburnia, vivis ;
  Virgo et anus nullis nota cupidinibus.

69. *Ad Tho : Mychelburnum.*[1]

Tu quod politis ludere versibus
Fratrum elegantum tertius incipis,
Thoma, nec omnes occiduas sinis
Horas relabi prorsus inutiles ;
Dis sic beatis me similem facis,
Ut laeter una jam numero impari.
Ergo peraeque dividuum tribus
Me dono vobis, quilibet integrum
Ut Campianum possideat sibi,
Primus, secundus, tertius invicem :
De parte ne sis sollicitus tua.

70. *Ad Carolum Fitz Geofridum.*[2]

Carole, si quid habes longo quod tempore coctum
  Dulce fit, ut radiis fructus Apollineis,

---

[1] See note, p. 301.   [2] See note, p. 300.

Ede, nec egregios conatus desere, quales
   Nescibit vulgus, scit bona fama tamen.
Ecce virescentes tibi ramos porrigit ultro
   Laurus ; et in Lauro est vivere suave decus.

71. *Ad Menum.*

Te quod amet, quantumque, palam solet omnibus
    Hermus
   Dicere, sic fratres, sic quoque, Mene, patrem,
Et quoscunque tuos ; tacet is de conjuge tantum,
   Horum quam vestrum plus tamen extat amor.
Exemplo quis enim cari livescit amici ?
   Multorum invidiam sed trahit omnis amans.
Ergo leves populi contemnas, Mene, susurros :
   Vero vis testi credere ? crede tibi.
Livida vix unquam propriis innititur alis
   Fama, sed Icariis ; dum volat illa, perit.

72. *Ad Papilum.*

Cum tibi barba foret quam Zeno, quamque Cleanthes
   Optaret, totam deputat Hanno tibi,
Ingentem in te vindictam meditatus ut hostis ;
   Quod damnum ut repares, Papile, jure paras :
Causidicosque gravi turgescens consulis ira,
   Quam spe lucrifici laetitiaque fovent :
Ex notis fore juratos, quod perditur oris
   Qui decus agnoscent, rem graviterque ferent ;
Et mulctam statuent inimici nomine grandem :
   Hoc suadent illi, Papile, tuque voras.
Sed mihi, quantumvis in neutro jure perito,
   Auscultato parum : sint, age, dicta prius
Omnia vera, tamen, citius quam causa adolescet,
   Tota renascetur, Papile, barba tibi.

73. *Ad Philomusum.*

Ridiculum plane quiddam facis atque jocosum,
   Et surdo et stupido dum, Philomuse, canis.
Omnia nam surdus miratur, sed nihil audit ;
   Contra audit stupidus cuncta, probatque nihil.

74. *In Milvium.*

Quam multa veluti somnia accidunt vivis,
Quae cum palam vident libenter haud credunt !
Quis sat stupescit ? torvus et senex ille,
Profectus ima ex sorde, Milvius terram
Ut nauseet, equesque urbe nobilis tota,
Matronam et hanc, et illam, et alteram stupret ?
Est nostra tanquam turpe somnium vita ;
Id comprobat mors ipsa, cujus adventu
Expergefacta mens suum petit coelum,
Terrestriumque infra superbias ridet.

75. *Ad Crispum.*

Crispe mones ut amem, sed caute, ne mihi probro
   Sit quod amem ; caute nunquis amare potest ?
Est velut ignis amor, nihil est detectius illo,
   Protinus indicio proditur ipse suo.

76. *Ad Calvum.*

Nunquam perficies, testeris ut omnia, Calve,
   Numina, quin minus assentiar atque minus.
Credita quae primo res est, repetita rubescit,
   Labitur et nimium sollicitata fides.
Tam multis homini nemo se purgat amico :
   Invidiam toties deposuisse parit.

77. *Ad Ed: Mychelburnum.*

Ibit fraternis elegis ornata sub umbras,
  Munia si ad manes perveniunt superûm ;
Et multum veneranda leves, Edoarde, tenebit
  Aspectuque animas exequiisque soror.
O felix si non fata importuna fuissent,
  Si non immature optima deficerent !
Quid nunc perpetuum fas est sperare beatis ?
  Quid connubia ? quid floridae amicitiae ?
Aetas quid ? nondum sex luna impleverat orbes
  Deseruit juvenem cum malefidus Hymen :
Cum desiderio sed enim decedere vita,
  Non mors, longa mora est ; non obit aeger, abit.

78. *In obitum Fran : Manbaei.*

Quid tu ? quid ultra, Phoebe, languenti diem
Aperis ? beatos ista lux magis decet ;
Sordes et umbras semper infelix amat
Aerumna, misero nulla nox atra est satis.
Heu, heu, sequar quocunque me rapiet dolor,
Et te per atra Ditis inferni loca,
Manbaee, lachrimis ora perfusus, petam ;
Flectamque manes planctu et infimos deos,
Liminaque dira molliam, ac usque horridas
Acherontis undas ; cuncta nam pietas potest :
Quaqua redibis moeror inveniet viam.
Tum rursus alma luce candebit polus,
Ultroque flores terra purpureos dabit ;
Omnia virebunt ; sentiet mundus suum
Decus renasci, sentiet tremulum mare,
Suumque flebit ipse Neptunus nefas.
Ah, siste vanos impetus, demens furor,

Ostiaque mente ficta Ditis excute,
Occlusa vivis, nec reclusa mortuis :
Fac jure tu quod quilibet miser potest,
Luge ; supersit hic tibi semper labor.

79. *De homine.*

Est homo tanquam flos, subito succrescit et aret ;
    Vis hominem floremque una eademque rapit.
Ceu flos est? minus est : nam mors ut utrumque
    coaequat,
    Quam bene flos, hominis tam male funus olet.

80. *In Barnum.*[1]

Mortales decem tela inter Gallica caesos,
    Marte tuo perhibes, in numero vitium est :
Mortales nullos si dicere, Barne, volebas,
    Servasset numerum versus, itemque fidem.

81. *In Lupum.*

Cum tacite numeras annos patris improbus haeres,
    Sic, Lupe, succlamas, "Omnia tempus habent ;"
Sumptus sive gravet, seu te mulctaverit uxor,
    Concludis vehemens, "Omnia tempus habent."

---

[1] Campion is again girding at Barnabe Barnes. This epigram
was in the lost edition of 1595; for Nashe refers to it in *Have
with you to Saffron Walden*, 1596 :—"One of the best articles
against Barnes I have overslipt, which is that he is in print for a
braggart in that universal applauded Latin poem of Master
Campion's; where in an epigram entituled *In Barnum*, beginning thus,

    Mortales decem tela inter Gallica cæsos

he shows how he bragged, when he was in France, he slew ten
men, when (fearful cowbaby) he never heard piece shot off but he
fell flat on his face. To this effect it is, though the words somewhat vary."—Works, ed. Grosart, iii. 162-3.

Sic semper ; chymico nunc te committis Orello,
  Mox vere ut dicas, " Omnia tempus habent."

82. *Ad Caspiam.*

Nescio quid aure dum susurras, Caspia,
Latus sinistrum intabuit totum mihi.

83. *Ad Turanium et Nepheium.*

Mî Turanule, tuque, mî Nephêi,
Quin effunditis intimos cachinnos?
Hem, murum prope dirutum videte
Coram qui peragit domi latenter
Quod debent saturi ; ecce servus autem
Caute praemonitus, caputque nudus
Stat praefixus hero, ne obambulantes
Spectent luminibus parum benignis ;
Dextra composite tenet galerum
A tergo dominum lubens adorans ;
Nasum sed graviter premit sinistra
A tergo dominum haud lubens odorans.
O servum lepidum, probum, pudicum,
Vultu qui superat tacente mimos,
Tarltonum et streperi decus theatri ?

84. *In Janum.*

Sabbato opus nullum nisi per scelus igne piandum
  Posse exerceri, fervide Jane, putas :
Jane, voras medice pilulas, at non operantur,
  Has puto te sacro sumere posse die.

85. *In Samnium.*

Quae ratio, aut quis te furor impulit, improbe Sanni,
  Femineum ut sexum mente carere putes :
Cum mea diffusas felix per pectus amantum
  Unica possideat Caspia centum animas.

Z

86. *Ad Arnoldum.*

Non si displiceat tibi vita, Arnolde, graveris ;
Hac ut displiceat conditione data est.

87. *Ad Genium suum.*

Quid retines? quo suadet Amor, Jocus atque Lyaeus,
Ibo ; sed sapiam ; jam sine, care Geni.

88. *Ad Nassum.*

Commendo tibi, Nasse, paedagogum
Sextillum et Taciti canem Potitum,
Teque oro tua per cruenta verba,
Et per vulnificos sales, tuosque
Natos non sine dentibus lepores,
Istudque ingenii tui per acre
Fulmen, ridiculis et inficetis,
Irati ut tonitru Jovis, timendum ;
Per te denique Pierum serenum,
Parnassumque, Heliconaque, Hippocrenenque,
Et quicunque vacat locus Camaenis,
Nunc oro, rogoque, improbos ut istos
Mactes continuis decem libellis ;
Nam sunt putiduli atque inelegantes,
Mireque exagitant sacros poetas,
Nasonemque tuum et tuum Maronem,
Quos ut te decet aestimas, tegisque
Ne possint per ineptias perire.
Quare si sapis, undique hos latrones
Incursabis et erues latentes ;
Conceptoque semel furore nunquam
Desistes ; at eos palam notatos
Saxis contuderit profana turba.

89. *Ad Caspiam.*

En miser exclusus jaceo, ceu montibus altis,
    Caspia, nix nullo respiciente cadit :
Meque tuus liquefecit amor violentius absens,
    Sol teneram injecto quam solet igne nivem.

90. *Ad Calvum.*

Est quasi jejunum viscus tua, Calve, crumena ;
    Id bile, hanc vacuam servat amore jecur.

91. *In Byrseum.*

Multis ad socerum queritur de conjuge Byrseus,
    Nupta quod externos suescit amare viros :
At breviter socer, "Et talis mi," ait, "illius olim
    Mater erat ; credo, femina et omnis erit.
Commune et juvenile malum est, quod serior aetas
    Sanabit, spero, sanctaque canities."
"De me nec socero verum est hoc," Byrsee, clamas :
    Sed potuit, sed habet fabula ficta salem.

92. *Ad Caspiam.*

Ecquando vere promissam, Caspia, noctem,
    Praestabis, cupido facta benigna mihi ?
Nox ea, si moriar, sat erit mihi sola beato ;
    Si vivo, non sunt millia mille satis.

93. *In Bretonem.*[1]

Carmine defunctum, Breto, caute inducis Amorem ;
    Nam numeris nunquam viveret ille tuis.

94. *Ad Corvinum.*

Sextum perfidiae haud satis prudenter,
Corvine, insimulas, redarguisque
Nequaquam meminisse quod spospondit

---

[1] Nicholas Breton, who deserved better treatment at Campion's hands.

Aequali, vel enim potentiori ;
Quin eludere, si sit usus, ipsum
Audere intrepide suos parentes.
Laesam dic age vi 'n fidem experiri?
Hunc ad coenam hodie vocato, vel cras,
Vel tu postridie, perendieve,
Sin mavis vel ad ultimas calendas ;
Ni praesto fuerit, per et tabernas
Omnes undique quaeritans volarit,
Quas te nec meminisse jam, nec unquam
Usurpasse oculis in hunc diem usque
Audacter mihi deierare fas sit :
Postremo nisi praebeat vocanti
Convivam memorem se, et impigellum,
Coenam coxeris hanc meo periclo.
Nullumne hoc specimen fidelitatis?

95. *Ad Hyspalum.*

Sanum lena tibi promittat ut, Hyspale, scortum,
Puram sentina quis sibi quaeret aquam?

96. *Ad Licinium.*

Non quod legitimum id bonum necesse
Censetur, Licini ; bonum sed ipsum
Semper legitimum putare par est :
Fenus nam licitum fatemur omnes,
Nemo non malus at bonum vocabit.

97. *In avarum.*

Omnia dum nimium servas, miser, omnia perdis,
Nec tua sunt toties quae tua, Paule, vocas.

98. *In Lupercum.*

Uxorem Lycii senex Lupercus
Strato admoverat, imminens puellae ;
Absentis domini exilit molossus

Subventurus herae, vagasque morsu
Partes mollis adulteri revulsit.
Stat moechus lachrimans sine ejulatu,
Testes nequitiae suae recusans,
Testes nequitiae suae requirens.
O rem ridiculam ! magisne dicam
Hanc plane miseram ? canem viro esse
Plus quam femina, quam uxor est, fidelem !

99. *In Erricum.*

Cum Stygio terrere umbras vultu, Errice, possis,
Dic per Plutonem quid tibi cum speculo ?

100. *Ad Tuccam.*

Nil aeris, magnam sed habes tu, Tucca, crumenam ;
Atque animum, quantum nulla crumena capit.

101. *Ad Pontilianum.*

Quod juvenis, locuplesque sibi conscisceret ipse
Eutrapilus mortem, Pontiliane, stupes ;
Nam neque spretus amor, nec dedecus impulit atrum,
Non jactura gravis, nec sine mente furor ;
Haud dolor excrucians, tetri aut fastidia morbi ;
Cunctos causa fugit, sed mihi vera patet :
Hanc voco desidiam, quam res accendere nulla
Cum potuit, vitae nausea summa fuit.

102. *De Puella ignota.*

Regalem si quis cathedram prope percutit hostem,
Exigitur sonti vindice lege manus.
Impune ergo feret quae cor mihi figit amicum,
Virgo, oculis feriens quo stetit illa loco?
Parce tamen rigidumque nimis summitte vigorem,
Sacrosanctum jus : arbiter assit Amor,
Ille Amor aethereos qui non violarit ocellos ;
Non ego, non tanti funera mille forent.

103. *Ad Chloen.*

Mittebas vetulam, Chloe, ministram,
Lippam, tarpidedem, et febriculosam
Ad me luce nova aureos rogatum ;
Si tu cur rediit rogas inanis,
Mane istuc mihi non placebat omen.

104. *In Philonem.*

Dulcis cum tibi Bassiana nupsit,
Nemo non male clamitans ferebat
Tam pulchram illepido dari puellam,
Torvus quique adeo et nigellus esses.
Caedis te, Philo, post reum malignae
Suspensum populus frequens Tyburni
Spectans, et querulam expiationem,
Occasumque tuum pie gemiscens,
Turmatim redit ; obviisque narrat
Exemplum juvenis viri, et torosi,
Perdigna facie artubusque pulchris :
Sic praebet miseris nimis popellus,
Detrectatque male imprecans beatis.
At vobiscum agitur satis benigne
Os durum quibus, horridique vultus,
Aut distorti oculi, patensve nasus,
Pulchri nam fieri, ut lubet, potestis ;
Si de quercu aliqua, per aut fenestram,
Vultis praetereuntibus parumper
Pendere horribili modo intuendi.
De vobis bona multa praedicabunt
Omnes, quique etiam solent in omnes
Quaevis dicere turpiora veris,
Vitae qui levibus bonis fruuntur.

105. *Ad Paulinum.*

Non agros, Pauline, tibi, non splendida tecta,
　Non aurum invideo, ferripedes nec equos :
Sed tam casta thoro, tam pulchra quod obtigit uxor,
　Tam lepida, alternoque obvia melle tibi ;
Moribus apta tuis et ficta per omnia votis :
　Invidiam faceret ni prohiberet amor.

106. *De se.*

Nos quibus unanimi cura est placuisse puellae,
　Quam multa insipide dicimus et facimus ?
Quae simul ad sese rediit mens, omnia ridet,
　Afficiturque videns ipsa pudore sui :
Sicut ego hesterna ; sed quid mea crimina stultus
　Profero ? non faciam, tuta silentia sunt.

107. *In matronam.*

Abscidit os Veneris famulae matrona, marito
　Ne mutuum rursus daret :
Quid fecit ? culpae cupiens occludere portam,
　Insulsa patefecit magis.

108. *Ad Cosmum.*

Cernit Aper vigilans annos post mille sepultos ;
　Talia sed caecus cernere, Cosme, potest.

109. *De Mellea et Caspia.*

Uror amat plures quod Mellea, Caspia nullos ;
　Non sine rivali est aut amor, aut odium.

110. *Ad Sabellum.*

Tuus, Sabelle, lippus iste cum furit
　Cunctis minatur clam venena Colchica,

Et atra quicquid ora Cerberi vomunt.
Ab India usque virus omne colligit,
Per uda stagna, perque murcidos lacus,
Emitque pluris aspidem, quam tu bovem :
Hiberniam odit, namque ibi nusquam nocens
Bestia timetur, pabulum quae toxicis
Praebere dirum possit, id Pico grave est.
Quin imprecari Tartarum deo solet
Lernae quod olim tabidam extinxit feram.
Hunc ego, Sabelle, rideo veneficum,
Tu vero ab istoc perdito retrahe pedem ;
Ulcisci amicum tutius, quam hostem potest.

111. *In Milvum.*

In putrem ut sensit se Milvus abire salivam
   Servatam testa condidit aureola ;
Et super inscripsit, " Milvi non ossa, cinisve,
   Sed Milvus, Milvi hîc sive saliva sita est."

112. *In Calpham.*

Ridicule semper quantum mihi, Calpha, videtur,
   A multis jactas te sine dote peti?
Nam quis quod nusquam est petat? aut captabit inani
   Siccum spe patrem, pumiceum vel avum?

113. *Ad Caspiam.*

Caspia, laudatur feritas in te, tua quicquid
   Atrum in candorem vertere forma potest.

114. *In amicum molestum.*

Non placet hostilem nimium propensus ad iram,
   Quive leves graviter fert inimicitias ;
Nec placet eructans odiose plurima quisquam,
   Fretus jam veteris nomine amicitiae

115. *In Hannonem.*

Divitias vocat Hanno suas sua carmina, tales
Morsus divitias Irus habere potest.

116. *Ad Cambricum.*

E multis aliquos si non despexit amantes,
  Si tua non fuerit rustica nata fremis?
Aut tam formosam tibi, Cambrice, non genuisses,
  Aut sineres nato munere posse frui.
Castae sint facies sua quas sinit esse pudicas,
  Pulchrior [1] huic forma est quam decet esse probis.

117. *Ad Leam.*

Privato commune bonum, Lea, cum melius fit,
  Obscurum plane est femina casta bonum.
Nam [2] nulli nota, aut ad summum permanet uni,
  Omnibus atque aliis est quasi nulla foret ;
Sin se divulget, mala fit ; quare illa bonarum
  Aut rerum minima est, aut, Lea, tota mala.

118. *De Amantibus.*

Olim si qua fidem violasset femina, quanquam
  Tunc extra legem viveret, inque nota ;
Una nocte novo si forte vacaret amanti,
  Materies elegis plena furoris erat.
Questus causa fides taceat jam lubrica, nostris
  Sat firma est, si sit sana puella satis.

[1] Cf. p. 126 :—
    " Rest, jealous thoughts, and thus resolve at last
    She hath more beauty than becomes the chaste."
[2] Cf. p. 93 :—" If to one thou shalt prove true," &c.

119. *De Venerea Lue.*

Aegram producit Venerem mundana Senectus,
    Contractamque nova perditione Luem ;
Suspectam quae nunc Helenam fecisset, et omnes
    Laidis arceret jure metuta procos.

120. *In Crassum.*

De sociis loquitur praeclare Crassus, et illis
    Quae non sunt tribuit praedia, rus, et agros ;
Ingenium, formam, genus, artes, omnia donat ;
    Tale sodalitium Tucca libenter amat.

121. *Ad Ed: Mychelburnum.*

Prudenter facis, ut mihi videtur,
Et sentis, Edoarde, qui optumum te
Longe pessima ab urbe sevocasti,
Vix anno ter eam, aut quater revisens ;
Tum Pauli simul ac vides cacumen,
Ad notos refugis cate recessus,
Urbis pestifera otia, et tenaces
Vitans illecebras, lubidinesque.
At nos interea hinc ineptiarum
Portenta undique mille defatigant ;
Conventus, joca, vina, bella, paces,
Ludi, damna, theatra, amica, sumptus ;
Inclusos itidem domi fabrorum
Aurigumque tonitrua, ejulatus,
Vagitusque graves agunt Averni
Usque in taedia ; rursus ambulantes
Occursu vario in via molestant
Curti causidici, resarcinatis
Qui gestant manibus sacros libellos ;
Horum te nihil impedit diserto

Quo minus celebres lepore musas
Sub jucunda silentia : O meorum
Cunctorum nimis, O nimis beate !

122. *In Gallam.*

Ilia cur tenue usque sonent tua nescio, Galla,
Te nisi quod cantor Tressilianus amet.

123. *In Fuscinum.*

Contrectare tuos nequeam, Fuscine, puellos
Non myrrham, non si thura, rosasque cacent.
Pro turpi est quicquid facilis natura negavit ;
Si faciem demas, nec placet ipsa Venus.

124. *Ad Caspiam.*

Admissum tarde, cito, Caspia, laesa repellis :
Constans ira, levis sed muliebris amor.

125. *Ad Candidum.*

Sis licet ingenuis nunc moribus, aequior ipso
Socrate, vel minima, Candide, labe carens,
Nescis qualis eris cum tu novus aleo fias,
Teque auctum lucrum qualibet arte trahat.
Victor ut evadas, nullum ut ferat alea damnum,
Attamen ingenium polluet illa tuum.

126. *In Gallam.*

Poscit amatorem fervens sibi Galla Priapum,
Frigida sed castum Thespilis Hippolitum :
Hinc ego Lampsacides fieri tibi, Thespilis, opto,
Gallae sed gelido purior Hippolito.

127. *In Berinum.*

Credita quae tibi sunt mutato nomine prodis,
    Nomine mutato cuncta licere putas ;
Cur tibi nil credam jam si vis, quaere, Berine ;
    Mutari nomen nolo, Berine, meum.

128. *Ad Sibyllam.*

Nil non a domino bonum creatum,
    Audacter satis hoc, Sibylla, dicis ;
Nec non ergo bonam creavit, Evam ;
    Illam sed tamen oscitante Adamo,
Ne[1] qua perciperet bonam creari.

129. *In Gallam.*

Tactam te, ad vivum sed nunquam, Galla, fateris ;
    Vah, quota pars carnis mortua, Galla, tuae est !

130. *Ad Eurum.*

Rerum nomina, resque mutat ipsas
    Usus multimoda vicissitate ;
Id si vis lepide aestimare dictum,
    Inspectes capita, Eure, feminarum ;
Nam pars illa novi satis dat una,
    Ne quid de mediis loquar, vel imis.

131. *Ad Paulinum.*

Quid, Pauline, meas amationes
    Inclamas ? quasi sit parum perire,
Ni tu hanc insuper aegritudinem addas.
    At si quid ratio ista promoveret,

---

[1] Old ed. " Ne quam perciperet "—corrected in the *Errat.*

Declamare aliquot dies polite,
Pulchre, et sobrius ipsemet potessim,
Depingens graphice protervi amoris
Mille incommoda, vel deinde mille,
Quae nusquam tibi dicta, scripta, picta
Occurrunt, neque visa somnianti
Unquam ; sed tamen usque me moleste
Castigas miserum, diu perorans ;
Obtundis, scio, perditum sinam me
Consulto fieri, lubet perire,
Suaves dum peream per ipse amores.

132. *In Cornutos.*

Uxoris culpa immeriti cur fronte mariti
  Cornua gestari ludicra fama refert ?
An quia terribilem furor irritus, atque malignum
  Efficit, armatis assimilemque feris ?
An quod ad hanc faciem satyros, umbrasque nocentes
  Fingimus, atque ipsum Daemona cornigerum ?
An quod apud populum tantum fortuna nocentes
  Reddit, nec verum crimina nomen habent ?

133. *Ad Hermum.*

In re si quacunque satisfacis, omnibus, Herme,
  Cur hoc uxori non facis, Herme, tuae ?

134. *Ad Aufilenam.*

En dat se locus arbitris remotis,
Aufilena, meo tuoque amori :
Quam nunc suave rubent repente malae,
Invitoque etiam rubore candent !
Quam mollis manus, et benigna colla !

Tam belli poterunt pedes latere ?
Vicina et genua, invidente palla ?
Quid me tam male pertinax repellis ?
Nempe est femineum parum efferari,
Sed tandem furor hic recedet ultro.
Aufugisti etiam ? vale, proterva,
Deformis, pede sordido et fugaci :
Vultus ergone tam feros probavi ?
Cervices rigidas ? manus rapaces ?
Non mi esset melius carere ocellis,
Quam sic omnia perperam videre ?

135. *Ad Battum.*

Qui tibi solus erat modo formidatus adulter,
　　Jam, Batte, excruciat prodigiosa Venus.
Quaevis Pasiphae est cogente libidine ; tu si
　　Rivalem admittas, denuo tutus eris.

136. *Ad Melleam.*

Quid macres, mea vita, quidve ploras ?
Nec fraudem paro, quod solent profani
Caros qui male deserunt amantes ;
Nec, praedator uti, arduum per aequor
Hispanas reveham Indicasque nugas :
Expers sed Veneris, Cupidinisque,
Silvae jam repeto virentis umbras,
Et dulcem placidamque ruris auram,
Ut memet reparem tibi, et reportem
Lucro millia mille basiorum.

137. *Ad Thelesinam.*

Expressos Helenae vultus Paridisque tabella
　　Foedârunt quaedam sicut ab ungue notae ;

Hoc, Thelesina, doles, sed et hoc bene convenit illis,
 Jurgia nam quovis esse in amore solent :
Quid cum te urgerem solam, quod amantis in ore
 Saeva impinxisti vulnera facta manu?

138. *In Fabrum.*

Heus, puer, haec centum defer sestertia Fabro !
 Quid stas, quid palles? quid lachrimas, asine?
Curre, inquam ! pueros quamvis praecidat inanes,
 De nummo poterit lenior esse tibi.

139. *In Afram.*

Cum tibi tot rugis veterascat nasus, ut illi
 Surgere Spartanus debeat, Afra, senex :
Cumque tuos dentes emat antiquarius Hammon,
 Prosint et tussi pharmaca nulla tuae ;
Nubere vis puero, primo moritura Decembri :
 Sic facere haeredem non potes, Afra, virum.

140. *Ad Cosmum.*

Ad vitam quid, Cosme, facit tua mortis imago?
 Esse ut te miserum, pulvereumque scias?
Cum sit certa tibi satis, obliviscere mortis ;
 Res vitae incertas has age ; vive, vale.

141. *Ad Aten.*

Reginae cum tres pomi de jure coirent,
 Te salebris, Ate, delituisse ferunt,
Et miseras risisse : quid hîc, dea, si licuisset
 Pro pomo rigidam supposuisse tibi?

142. *In Aprum.*

Crispo suasit Aper febricitanti
Pestem protinus hanc inebriatis

Tolli, sed penitus furente Baccho.
Assensum est ; bibitur simul ; valere
Crispus coepit, Aper febricitavit.

143. *In Fuscum.*

Quasvis te petere et sectari, Fusce, puellas
Credis, ridiculus nec reticere potes.
Haud aliter cymba vectus puer ire carinas
Ad se omnes dicit garrulus, atque putat.

144. *Ad Lucillum et Manbaeum.*

Carior, Lucille,[1] anima, vel illa
Esse si quidquam pote carius mî ;
Tuque, Manbaee, unanimi sodalis
    Delicium et mens.

Ecquid accepistis, eratne laetum,
Otia exegisse, Cupidinemque,
Et suos jam denique Campianum e
    Pectore amores?

Nam sat illuxisse dies videtur
Illa mî festiviter, et beate,
Quae brevi tantas penitus fugavit
    Luce tenebras?

I fuge hinc, abjecte Amor, exulatum!
Tam ferum haud par est hominum imperare
Mollibus curis, ad eas redi unde es
    Rupibus ortus.

---

1 Old ed. "Lucilli."

145. *In Mamurram.*

Pediculosos esse quis sanus negat
Versus Mamurrae Satyricos, si quis legit?
Mordent, timent ungues, pedes et sex habent.

146. *In Vincentium.*

Astrictus nunc est Vincentius aere alieno ;
In proprio nimium hic ante solutus erat.

147. *Ad Aemylium.*

Aegris imperat usque possitallam
Impostor Litus, Aemyli : quousque ?
Nummos ridicule usque dum dat aeger.

148. *In Parcos.*

Parcos ingenui non est laudare poetae,
Cui vetus horrendos antipathia facit.

149. *Ad Marcellum.*

Scilla verecunda est ; Scilla est, Marcelle, venusta ;
Si verum utrumque est, vix habet illa parem.

150. *Ad Mathonem.*

Arguo cur veram ficto sub nomine culpam
Quaeris, nec titulis te quoque signo tuis.
Nunquam si fingit non est epigramma poema ;
Vix est simpliciter cui, Matho, vera placent.

151. *Ad Cosmum.*

Laudatus melior fiet bonus, et bona laus est ;
Solis at quae sit debita, Cosme, bonis :
Re turgente mali quamvis et honore fruantur,
Laudem ne sperent ; non vacat illa malis.

A A

152. *In Olum.*

Sat linguae dedit, Ole, sator tibi ; parte sed ulla
   Hanc potuit melius figere quam capite :
Nam sentit tanquam lapis hoc ; tua voxque palati est,
   Faucis, pulmonis, denique mentis egens :
Si foret, Ole, tuam mihi fas disponere linguam,
   Haereret qua tu pedere parte soles.

153. *In eundem.*

Summo ut significet patrem sedisse Senatu,
   Hoc aliquando quod is pederat, Olus ait.

154. *In Hipponem.*

Lites dum premit Hippo fenerator,
Imam ad pauperiem redit, nec ullus
Ex omni magis est ei molestus
Sumptus, quam misero diu roganti
Assem quod dederat semel minutum,
Solum quem sibi nunc egenus optat ;
Laetus causidicis volensque cuncta
Praebebat siquidem, daturus et jam
Esset copia si secunda votis :
Invitus, genioque retrahente,
Solum sed tribuit gravatus assem.

155. *Ad Eurum.*

Eure, bonum non ordo facit, non res, locus, aetas :
   Fit licet his melior, nascitur ipse bonus.

156. *In Mycillum.*

Flagris morio caeditur, Mycillum
Pullum consiliarii Mycilli
Quod stultum vocitavit, at merentem ;
Dicat de patre jam, nihil pericli est.

157. *Ad Lalagen.*

Corpora mille utinam, Lalage, mea forma subiret ;
  Unum spes esset cedere posse mihi.

158. *Ad Haemum.*

Quasdam aedes narras ubi certis, Haeme, diebus
  Vilia de summo culmine saxa cadunt.
Daemonii hoc opera fieri contendis, at illud
  Vix credo ; credam si pretiosa cadent.

159. *Ad Argentinum.*

De gallinarum genere est tua fertilis uxor,
  Argentine, viro nam sine saepe parit.

160. *Ad Telesphorum.*

Nec tibi parca placet, nec plena, Telesphore, mensa ;
  Amplior haec avida est, ut minor illa, gula :
Quantus enim cibus est aliena in lance relictus
  Expleto quereris tu periisse tibi.

161. *Ad Cassilianam.*

Cur proba, cur cunctis perhibetur casta Nerine ?
  Assuevit nondum, Cassiliana, tibi.

162. *Ad Hermum.*

Ad latus, Herme, tuum spectans, siquando machaeram
  Laudo, tumes, dicens "illa paterna fuit."
Si vel equum celerem pede, sive armenta, vel aedes
  Miror, et haec fuerant omnia patris, ais.
Si vultum commendo tuum, fuit ille paternus ;
  Servumque et scortum, et singula patris habes.
Sed cum nulla sit, Herme, tuae constantia linguae,
  Hanc bene maternam, si fateare, licet.

163. *In Marcellinam.*

Virgo olim cinerem et lutum solebat
Marcellina avido ore devorare ;
Nunc moechos amat, at lutosiores
Ipso, Calve, luto ; quid esse credam ?
Annon pica animi quoque haec laborat ?

164. *Ad Eurum.*

Sacras somniat, Eure, conciones,
Et pronunciat ore sem' aperto
Pyrrhus ; dissimulat, nec est sacerdos.

165. *Ad Pontilianum.*

Nascitur in lucem primo caput, unde gubernat
Pars senior, coelo proxima, sphaera animae :
Huic decor oris inest, huic sermoque, mentis imago,
Et prope totus homo est, Pontiliane, caput.

166. *Ad Cosmum.*

Sub specie mala, Cosme, boni dominantur : honesti
Usus ut exoluit, sic decus omne perit.

167. *Ad Papilum.*

Non sapit in tenui qui re jus, Papile, sperat ;
Solis id magnis divitibusque datur.

168. *Ad Eurum.*

Dilutum judex vinum bibat, ut sonet ore
Jus quoque dilutum ; displicet, Eure, merum :
At nunc juridicus jus dicit, negligit aequum ;
Jus ita qui judex dicet iniquus erit.

169. *Ad Calvum.*

Et lare ridiculum est, aliena et quaerere terra
Pacem animi ; nusquam est, sit nisi, Calve, domi.

170. *In Melissam.*

Sex nupta et triginta annis, sterilisque, Melissa
Nata ex se tandem prole triumphat anus :
Cura dei, reges, vobis, proceresque, cavete,
Portentum statua parturiente fuit.

171. *Ad Daunum.*

Carmen, equestris homo, cur fingis, Daune? poeta
Si vis esse nimis forte pedester eris.

172. *Ad Cosmum.*

Cosme, licet media tua pangas carmina nocte,
Affulget schedae [1] dexter Apollo tuae.
Metrica scripturo sal vel sol adsit oportet
Perpetuo ; insulsa et frigida nemo sapit.

173. *Ad Eurum.*

Cui se, nec multis praeter se gaudet amicis,
Si nihil, Eure, vetat, noster amicus erit.

174. *Ad Labienum.*

Dum nimium multis ostendere quaeris amorem
In mensa, et positas extenuare dapes,
Obtundis ; nec coena gulae bene competit, in qua
Plus condimenti est quam, Labiene, cibi.

---

[1] Some corruption here ; for Campion must have known that
the first syllable of *schedae* is short. Qy. "schedulae" (a very
rare word)?

175. *In Pollionem.*

Magnificos laudat, misere sed Pollio vivit ;
Laudem fortassis rem putat esse malam.

176. *Ad Sibyllam.*

Omnes se cupiunt omni ratione valere ;
Attamen est verbum triste, Sibylla, vale.

177. *Ad Papilum.*[1]

Bellam dicebas Bellonam, Papile, sensi,
   Suavius hospitium castra inimica darent :
Inveniat quicum pugnet, mihi praefero pacem ;
   Ut tua sit soli Penthesilea tibi.

178. *Ad Gallam.*

Assurgunt quoties lachrimae tibi, si placet humor
Ut divertatur, mingere, Galla, potes.

179. *Ad Labienum.*

Quaeris completo quot sint epigrammata libro ;
   Sit licet incertum, sic numerare potes :
Plus minus, hebdomada quotquot nascuntur in una
   Londini, faciunt tot, Labiene, librum.
Nobiliumque minor numerus consetur utrinque,
   Turba sed obscurae plurima plebis erit.

180. *In Marcellinam.*

Larvas Marcellina horret, Lemuresque, sed illa
Nil timet in tenebris si comitata viro est.

181. *Ad Linum.*

Henrico, Line, septimo imperante,
Nondum pharmacopola quintus urbem

---

[1] Old ed. "Papiluum."

Infarsit numero, nec oenopola ;
Ingens nunc tribus utriusque crevit :
Primo sed praeit ordine oenopola,
Ac tanquam alterius parens videtur,
Morbos dum creat, inficitque nostra
Sensim corpora dulcibus venenis.
Quo tandem ruet haec vicissitudo ?
Quid dicam ? nisi Daemonas trecentos
Sementem facere hic superfluorum,
Omnes quos patimur licentiatos ?

182. *In Gallam.*

Galla melancholicam simulans, hilarare Lyaeo
Se solet, et fit non ficta melancholica.

183. *In Tabaccam.*

Haud vocat illepide meretricem Nerva Tabaccam,
Nam vendunt illam, prostituuntque lupae.

184. *Ad Mauriscum.*

Nullam Brunus habet manum sinistram,
Nec mancus tamen est ; sed est quod aiunt
Maurisce, ut caveas tibi, ambidexter.

185. *Ad Phillitim.*

Phillitis, tua cur discit saltare priusquam
  Firmiter in terra stare puella potest ?
Non metuis mox ne cadat immatura ? caducas
  Nae sua sic pupas membra rotare facit.

186. *Ad Lalagen.*

Lingua est Gallica lingua feminarum ;
Mollis, lubrica, blandiens labellis,

Affundens, Lalage, decus loquenti :
Terra est Anglica terra feminarum ;
Simplex, suavis, amans, locis honestans
Semper praecipuis genus tenellum.

187. *Ad Cyparissum.*

Ne nimis assuescas carni, Cyparisse, bovinae,
Cornua nam quis scit num generare potest ?

188. *Ad Hermum.*

Castae qui servit si sit miser, Herme, quid ille
Scortum qui metuit ? perditus, et nihili est.

189. *Ad Chloen.*

Pulchras Lausus amat ; Chloe, quid ad te ?
Pulchras non amat ergo Lausus omnes.

190. *Ad Pasiphylen.*

Qui te formosam negat haud oculos habet ; at te
Nauci qui pendit, Pasiphyle, cor habet.

191. *In Hermiam.*

Hermia cum ridet tetros hahahalat odores ;
Herme, ferenda magis si pepepedat erit.

192. *In Mycillum.*

Cantat nocte Mycillus ad fenestras
Formosae dominae, vigil, frequensque ;
Et cantat lepide, et patent fenestrae
Voci, at janua clausa sola surda est.

193. *Ad Calvum.*

Ex reditu lucrum facturus Naevola, praesens
Quod sperat recipit ; quam cito, Calve, redit ?

194. *Ad Haemum.*

Augeae stabulum, Haeme, non inique
Londinum vocitas ; scatet profecto
Multa impuritie ; haec ut eluatur
Jam plane Herculeo est opus labore :
Nam nunc undique foetidum est, at illic
Non fenum male olet, sed, Haeme, fenus.

195. *In Tuccam.*

Nil refert si nulla legas epigrammata, Tucca ;
De te scribuntur, non tibi ; Tucca, tace.

196. *Ad Nisam.*

Quod melius saltas insultas, Nisa, sorori,
Utraque at melior quae neque saltat erit.

197. *Ad Publium.*

Publi, sola mihi tacenda narras,
Sed quae si taceam, loquuntur omnes :
Dic tu tandem aliquid meri novelli,
Plane quod liceat loqui, aut tacere.

198. *Ad Cosmum.*

Qualis, Cosme, tuae est haec excusatio culpae ?
• Suasit Amor ! quasi non pessima dictet Amor !
Ille deus natos ferro violare parentes
Fecit, patronum quem tibi, inepte, paras.
Dic odio potius factum, dum mittis Amorem ;
Dic aliud, dic tu quicquid, amice, lubet.

199. *In Harpacem.*

Fenore[1] ditatus civis, nunc rusticus Harpax
Feno ditescit ; re minor, at melior.

---

[1] Old ed. '' Fauore ''—corrected in the *Errata.*

200. *Ad Olum.*

Nupsisse filiam, Ole, feneratori
Gestis ; quid ita? corrupta num datur? prorsus
Ut dicis, ais, et gravida : te, Ole, jam laudo
Qui fenus addis tale feneratori.

201. *Ad Daunum.*

Sponsam, ne metuas, castam tibi, Daune, remisi ;
Ipsam, ni credis tu mihi, Daune, roga.

202. *In Lagum.*

Cum vix grammatice sapiat tria verba ligare,
Dîs Lagus invitis versificator erit :
Evenit ebriolis vitium par, protinus omnes
Saltare incipiunt cum titubare timent.

203. *In Vergusium.*

Nil amat invectum Vergusius, extera damnat ;
Nec, vicina licet, Gallica vina placent :
Haud piper attinget crudus, procul aurea poma
Hesperidum calcat, nec pia thura probat.
Bombycis deridet opes, et patria laudat
Lanea, re vera non aliena sapit.
Sed tamen uxorem Rufini, jamque maritus,
Ardet : at haec trita et non peregina putat.

204. *In Hipponacem.*

Terget linteolis genas manusque,
Vix toto lavat Hipponax in anno,
Rugas dum metuens cutem puellis
Servat, sed bona perdidit paterna.
Non est lautus homo : quid ergo? tersus.

205. *Ad Calliodorum.*

Sollicitus ne sis signum fatale cometa
Ut quid portendat, Calliodore, scias ;
Expectes cladem (domini natale propinquat)
Non hominum, sed tu, Calliodore, boum.

206. *Ad Glaucum.*

Jus qui bonum vendit cocus
Melior eo est qui polluit
Jus omne fucis non bonis ;
Sit, Glauce, turgidus licet,
Raucisque saevior Notis.

207. *In Hannonem.*

Carmina multa satis pellucida, levia, tersa ;
Naturae vitreae sed nimis Hanno, creat.

208. *In Librarios.*

Impressionum plurium librum laudat
Librarius ; scortum nec hoc minus leno.

209. *Ad Gaurum.*

Pollio tam brevis est, tam crassus, ut esse Gigantis
Secti dimidium credere, Gaure, velis.

210. *Ad Ligonem.*

Cur non salutem te rogas equo vectum?
Ne equum tuum videar, Ligo, salutasse.

211. *Ad Albium.*

Dextre rem peragens, vel imperite ;
Vera an ficta loquens, jocosa vel tu,
Albi, seria, semper erubescis :

Hinc te ridiculum, levemque reddis.
At tandem vitium pudoris omne
Vis deponere? vis? adi lupanar.

212. *In Olynthum.*

Dum sedet in lasano dormescit praetor Olynthus,
Et facit in lecto quod facit in lasano.

213. *In Pandarum.*

Scrotum tumescit Pandaro ; tremat scortum.

214. *In Hannonem.*

Scorti trita sui vocat labella
Non mellita, sed Hanno saccarata ;
At nescit miser extrahi solere
Ex dulci quoque saccaro venenum.

215. *Ad Ligonem.*

Purgandus medici non est ope Caecilianus,
Purgandus tamen est ; num, Ligo, mira loquor?
Purgandus gravidae de suspitione puellae,
Ne te detineam, Caecilianus adest.

216. *In Mundum.*[1]

Mundo libellos nemo vendidit plures,
Novos, stiloque a plebe non abhorrenti ;
Quos nunc licet lectoribus minus gratos
Librarii emptitant, ea tamen lege
Ne Mundus affigat suis suum nomen.

217. *Ad Lausum.*

Non si quid juvenile habeant mea carmina, Lause ;
Sed vulgare nimis, sed puerile veto.

---

[1] Seemingly directed against that voluminous writer, Anthony Munday.

218. *Ad Bassum.*

Servum quando sequi cernit te, Basse, cinaedum
Uxori te vult Cinna preire tuae.

219. *Ad Lamianam.*

Nequidquam Lamiana cutem medicaris, et omni
Detersam tentas attenuare modo :
Innocua illa satis per se manet ; eripe luxum,
Eripe nocturnae furta nociva gulae.
Pucher ut in venis sanguis fluat atque benignus,
Cures ; curabis sic, Lamiana, cutem.

220. *In Ligonem.*

Funerea vix conspicimus sine veste Ligonem :
An quia tam crebri funeris author erat ?

221. *In Marsum et Martham.*

Marsus ut uxorem, sic optat Martha maritum :
Ambos quid prohibet quod voluere frui ?

222. *Ad Pontilianum.*

Iste Bromus quis sit qui se cupit esse facetum,
Plane vis dicam, Pontiliane ? planus.

223. *Ad Syram.*

Una re sapere omne feminarum
Se credit genus : illa res negare est.
Una re sapere ut magis studeret
Optandum foret : illa res tacere est.

224. *In Hermum.*

Omnibus officii ritu se consecrat Hermus,
Talia sed nunquam sacra litare solent.

Instituens natos frutices quo sideris ortu
Aërio credant capita inconstantia coelo.
Admonet immaturae hyemis, gelidaeque pruinae,
Imbriferumque Austrorum, horrendisonumque Aqui-
    lonum;
Grandine concussam Rhodopen, Taurumque nivalem,
Concretosque gelu prohibet transcendere montes ;
Tantum qui placido suspiras ore, Favoni,
Arboreos tibi commendat dea sedula fetus.
Fraga, rosas, violasque jubet latitare sub umbris ;
Forma rosis animos majores indidit, ausis
Tollere purpureos vultus, et despicere infra
Pallentes odio violas, tectasque pudore.
Diva rosas leviter castigat, et admonet aevi
Labilis ; aspiceres foliis prodire ruborem,
Et suspendentes ora annutantia flores.
    Accelerant Nymphae properata ex ordine matri
Pensa ostentantes, quarum pulcherrima Iole
Asportat gremio texturas millecolores.[1]
Hanc olim ambierat furtim speciosus Apollo ;
Muneribus tentans, et qua suasisse loquela
Posset ; saepe adhibet placidam vim, saepe et amantum
Blanditias cupidus, sed non cupiente puella.
Brachia circumdat collo, simul illa repellit ;
Instat hic, illa fugit ; duplicant fastidia flammas ;
Ardet non minus ac rutilo Semeleia proles
Cum curru exciderat, totumque incenderat orbem.
Spes sed ut illusas vidit deus, et nihil horum
Virginis aversam potuisse inflectere mentem,
Dira subinde vovet, pervertens fasque nefasque ;
Illicitumque parat spreto medicamen amori,

---

[1] Old ed. gives " mille colores " as separate words.

Lactucas humectantes gelidumque papaver,
Cyrceiaeque simul stringit terrestria mala
Mandragorae, condens sudatos pixide rores.
  Nox erat, incedit nullo cum murmure Phoebus,
Nulli conspiciendus adit spelaea puellae;
Illa toro leviter roseo suffulta jacebat,
Sola struens flores varia quos finxerat arte.
Candida lucebat fax, hanc primum inficit atra
Nube, deinde linit medicati aspergine succi
Pulvillosque leves et picti strata cubilis;
Terque soporiferas demulcet pollice chordas
Plectripotens, nectitque Hecateio carmine somnos.
Virgineos oculos vapor implicat, excipit artus
Alta quies, et membra toro collapsa recumbunt.
Vidit et obstupuit deus; inter spemque metumque
Accedit, refugitque iterum; suspirat ab imo
Pectore; nec pietas, nec siderea ora puellae
Plura sinunt: sed amor, sed ineffraenata libido
Quid castum in terris intentatumve relinquit?
Oscula non referenda serit, tangitque, premitque;
Illa (quod in somnis solet) ambigua edidit ore
Murmura, ploranti similis nec digna ferenti;
Saepe manu urgentem quamvis sopita repellit,
Nequidquam, raptor crebris amplexibus haeret,
Vimque per insidias fert, indulgetque furori.
Nec satis est spectare oculis, tetigisse, fruique,
Ingratum est quicquid sceleris latet; illaque turpe
Quod patitur vitium quia non sensisse videtur,
Maestus abit (revocante die) spoliumque pudoris
Tanquam invitus habet; semper sibi quod petat ultra
Invenit ingeniosus amor, crescitque favendo.   ·
  Tandem discusso nova nupta sopore resurgit,
Illam sed neque turba vocat, neque clari Hymenaei

Illius ante fores iuvenum non inclita pompa
Conspicitur, placide caris commista puellis.
Omnia muta tacent, pariter tacuisset Iole,
Verum nescio quae morborum insignia terrent ;
Nec valet a stomacho, nec non tremulum omnia frigus
Membra quatit : cubito incumbens sic anxia secum :
" Numquid et hoc morbi est ? nam quae mutatio sanas
Attentat vires ? nec enim satis illa placebant,
l'ostrema quae nocte timens insomnia vidi.
Quos ego praeterii fluctus ! quae praelia sensi
In somnis ! quantis, O di, transfixa sub hastis
Occubui ! vereor diros ne iratus Apollo
In me condiderit parientia spicula morbos.
Sed nec Apollineas pestes, nec respicit iras
Hic in corde pudor meus ; hoc solamen, Iole,
Semper habes, moriare licet, moriere pudica."
Assurgit, cingitque operi se, candida fecit
Lilia, quae gustare cupit, quia candida fecit :
Quidque oculi cernunt animus desiderat ; aegrum
Pectus ferre moras nescit, votisve carere.
Singula quae gravidae possunt ignara ferebat ;
Torpores lassata graves, fastidia, bilem ;
Luminaque in morbum veniunt, putat illa fuisse
Obtutu nimio ; causas ita nectit inanes.
Sed simul atque impleri uterum, sensitque moveri
Vivum aliquid, potuitque manu deprendere [1] motus ;
Exanimata metu nemorum petit avia tecta
Tristis, ut expleret miserando pectora planctu.
      " Crudeles," ait, " et genus implacabile, Divi,
Quas tandem aerumnas animique et corporis hausi
Immerita ? assurgunt etiam nova monstra ; tumere

_____
[1] Old ed. " dependere "—corrected in the *Errata.*

Coepit uter nobis ; jam virgo puerpera fiam ;
Nec dubitat natura suas pervertere leges
Quo magis excrucier possimque horrenda videri,
Demque pudicitiae, sceleris sed nomine, poenas.
Quo fugiam? quae nunc umbrae? quae nubila frontem,
Vel tumulum hunc defuncti animi tectura cupressus?
Quam bene cum tenebris mihi convenit! horreo Solem ;
Jam culpa possum, sed non caruisse timore ;
Frangitur ingenuus pudor, et succumbit in ipsa
Suspicione mali, scelerisque ab imagine currit,
Ceu visis fugiunt procul a pallentibus umbris.
Infelix partus, nisi quid monstrosius illo est,
Absque tuo genitore venis, nomenque paternum
Si quis quaerat habes nullum ; patrem assere primum,
Post tibi succedam gravis atque miserrima mater."
    Talia jactantem ventis laeva arbitra risit
Invida populea latitans sub cortice Nais ;
Laetaque per sentes repit, tenuesque myricas ;
Sed simul explicuit se, proditione superba,
Praecipitique gradu loca nota perambulat, omnes
Suscipiens nymphas, referensque audita, nec illa
Per se magna satis, reddit majora loquendo ;
Et partes miserantis agit, vultusque stupentes
Effingit, monstrumque horret, crimenque veretur.
Inde per alternos rumores fama vagatur,
Flebiliorque deae tandem florentia tecta
Pervenit, illa novo temere conterrita monstro
Exiliit, natamque animo indignata requirit.
Sed procul ut matrem approperantem vidit Iole
Concidit exanimis, gemitus timor exprimit altos,
Exortosque utero creat ingeminatque dolores.
Continuo silva effulsit velut aurea, et omne
Per nemus auditur suave et mirabile murmur.

Diva pedem, perculsa soni novitate, repressit,
Interea sine ploratu parit, ipsaque tellus
Effudit molles puero incunabula flores.
Occurrit natae Berecynthia, prima nepotem
Suscipit, ille niger totus, ni candida solis
Haeserat effigies sub pectore, patris imago.
 Sed non ambiguo jam personat omnia cantu
Phoebus, et ardentes incendit lumine silvas,
Dum sua furta canens miseram solatur Iolen ;
Obstupuit dea, nunc lucos, nunc humida natae
Lumina suspiciens, vultusque pudore solutos.
" Proditor," exclamat, "non haec, si Iupiter aequus,
Probra mihi vel tecta diu, vel inulta relinquam.
Quo fugis ? infestum caput inter nubila, Phoebe,
Nequicquam involvis ; scelus et tua facta patebunt,
Nec mihi surripiet fuga te, sequar ocior Euris,
Maternusque dolor vires dabit, iraque justa."
Nec mora, per nubes summi ad fastigia coeli
Contendit ; nymphae tristi exanimaeque sorori
Circumfusae acres tentant lenire dolores,
Et placidis dictis tristes subducere curas.
Illa immota sedet, tacitoque incensa furore
Ardet, et ingenti curarum fluctuat aestu.
 "Felices quibus est concessum," ait, "intemerata
Virginitate frui ! mea jam defloruit aetas
Immature ; heu maternos sensisse dolores,
Gaudia non potui ; sed me nec gaudia tangunt ;
Nec duri, si non infamia juncta, dolores.
Nox et somne, meo pars insidiata pudori,
Hos mihi pro meritis partus, haec pulchra dedistis
Pignora, formosique patris referentia vultus ?
Nempe ego, Phoebe, tuos amplexus dura refugi,
Et simplex, tali quam posses prole beare.

Atque utinam caruisse tuo, speciose, liceret
Munere ! quantumvis indocta et stulta putarer,
Non tamen infamis, turpique cupidine laesa,
Cogerer ad nigros animam demittere manes."
Sic effata, aliquid vultu letale minanti,
Deficit, excipiunt Nymphae, manibusque levatam
Celsa ferunt in tecta deae stratisque reponunt.

    Cuncta Jovi interea narraverat ordine Phoebus,
Factaque lascivis praetexuit impia verbis ;
Addiderat cycnumque, et terga natantia tauri,
Furtivumque aurum, et duplicatae praemia noctis.
Jupiter officii tanti memor, irrita risit
Vota deae, justumque odium in ludibria vertit.
Illa sed ingenti luctu confusa recedit,
Conqueriturque fidem divum, saevoque ululatu
Indefessa diu languentes suscitat iras ;
At nulla in terris tanti vis nata doloris
Quam non longa dies per amica oblivia solvat.

    Jamque puer, tacite praeterlabentibus annis,
Paulatim induerat juveniles corpore vultus ;
Cui quamvis nullo variantur membra colore,
Multus inest tamen ore lepos, tinctosque per artus
Splendescit mira novitate illecta venustas.
Si niger esset Amor, vel si modo candidus ille,
Jurares in utroque deum ; non dulcior illo
Ipsa Venus, Charitesque, et florida turba sororum.
Huic olim nymphae nomen fecere Melampo,
Lucentesque comis gemmas, laterique pharetram
Aptarunt, qualem cuperet gestare Cupido.
Ille levem tenera sectatur arundine praedam
Aurorae ut primo rarescit lumine coelum ;
Mox fervente aestu viridantes occupat umbras,
Aut ab euntis aquae traducit murmure somnum.

Tempus erat placidis quo cuncta animalia terris
Solverat alta quies, solita cum Morpheus arte
(Somnia vera illi nullo mandante deorum)
Florigeram penetrat vallem, sopitaque ludit
Pectora nympharum, portentaque inania fingit,
Horribilesque metus; mox laetis tristia mutat,
Inducitque leves choreas, convivia, lusus,
Secretosque toros, simulataque gaudia amoris;
Saepe alias Satyro informi per devia turpes
Tradit in amplexus, alias tibi, pulcher Adoni,
Aut, Hyacynthe, tibi per dulcia vincula nectit.
Sic deus effigies varias imitatus, opaca
Dum loca percurrit, sopitum forte Melampum
Cernit odorato densoque in flore jacentem :
Accedit prope, spectanti dat Cynthia lumen.
" Et quid," ait, " mira nostram dulcedine mentem
Percellit? meve illudis, formose Cupido?
Sideream nigra frontem cur inficis umbra?
Jam placet iste color? vilescunt lilia? sordent
Materni flores? sed ubi nunc arcus et auro
Picta pharetra tibi? cui tu, lascive, sororum
Hac struis arte malum? tua quem nova captat imago?
At si non amor es, quis es? an furtiva propago
Atrigenae noctis? num crescit gratia tanta
E tenebris, jucunde, tibi? tam vividus unde
Ridet in ore lepos? tale et sine lumine lumen?
Ut decet atra manus, somno quoque mollior ipso,
Qui te sed leviter tangi sinit, aptus amori!
O utinam quae forma tuos succenderet ignes
Cognôrim ! puer illa foret, seu femina, seu vir,
Quam cupide species pro te mutarer in omnes !
Utcunque experiar, spes nulla sequetur inertes.
Induit ex illo facies sibi mille decoras,

Versat et aetates sexumque, cüilibet aptans
Ornatus varios ; nequicquam, immobilis haeret
Spiritus, et placido pueri mens dedita somno est.
Jamque fatigatus frustratum deflet amorem
Morpheus, indulgens animo pronoque furori.
  Luce sub obscura procul hinc telluris in imo
Persephones patet atra domus, sed pervia nulli ;
Quam prope secretus, muro circundatus aereo,
Est hortus, cujus summum provecta cacumen
Haud superare die potuit Jovis ales in uno.
Immensis intus spatiis se extendit ab omni
Parte, nec Elisiis dignatur cedere campis,
Finibus haud minor, at laetarum errore viarum
Deliciisque loco longe jucundior omni.
Et merito, his umbrae nam diversantur in hortis
Quot nunc pulcharum sunt, saeclo quotve fuere
Primo, quotve aliis posthac visentur in annis.
Vallem vulgus amat, quarum peragendaque sylvis
Fabula sit, liquidis spectant in fontibus ora,
Aut varias nectunt vivo de flore corollas ;
At quibus urbanae debetur turgida vitae
Mollities, studiis aliis, alioque nitori
Assuescunt animos, nil simplicitatis habentes.
Altior, et longe secretior heroinis
Contingit sedes, Parnasso suavior ipso ;
Gemmarum locus, atque oculorum lumine lucet.
Non huc fas cuiquam magnûm penetrare deorum ;
Soli sed Morpheo, cui nil sua fata negarunt,
Concessum est, pedibus quamvis incedere lotis :
Illum durus amor, sibi nil spondente salutis
Arte sua, tandem his languentem compulit hortis,
Tot puero ex formis ut fingat amabile spectrum.
  Primo fons aditu stat molli fultus arena,

Intranti gradibus variisque sedilibus aptus.
Hic se cum redeunt, labem si traxerat ullam
Vita, lavant, purae remeantque penatibus umbrae.
Morpheus hac utrumque pedem ter mersit in unda,
Et toties mistis siccat cum floribus herbis ;
Inde vias licitas terit, et velatus opaca
Nube, lubens saturat jucundis lumina formis.
Aspicit has tacita sua mutua fata sub umbra
Narrantes, choreis certantes mollibus illas
Quas olim didicere, vel ignes voce canentes
Quales senserunt dum lubrica vita manebat.
Sed deus obliquo species sibi lumine notas
Praeterit, Antiopam Nycteida, Deiphilemque,
Tyndaridemque Helenam, desponsatamque priori
Hermionem, calido dotatam sanguine nuptam ;
Argiam, et Rhodopen, victoris et Hippodamiam
Expositam thalamis, pomis captasque puellas,
Roxanamque, Hieramque, ut cognita sidera spectans
Negligit, innumerasque pari candore micantes.
Hinc dorsum sublime petit per amoena roseta
Evectus, picta et multo viridaria flore.
Undanti circum locus est velut insula valle
Inclusus, formis aptus privusque Britannis,
Densis effulgens tanquam via lactea stellis.
Prima suo celerem tenuit Rosamunda decore
Ingenti, cui Shora comes rutilantibus ibat
Admiranda oculis, gravis utraque conscia sortis.
Inde Geraldinam [1] coelesti suspicit ore
Fulgentem, Aliciamque [2] caput diademate cinctam,

---

[1] Lady Elizabeth Fitzgerald, the "Geraldine" of Surrey's sonnets.

[2] Alice, daughter of Sir John Spencer of Althorpe. She mar-

Casti constantisque animi lucente trophaeo.
Nec tamen his contentus abit deus, altius ardet
Accelerare pedem, fulgor procul advocat ingens
Apparens oculis, majoraque sidera spondet.
Emicat e viridi myrteto stella Britanna,
Penelope,[1] Astrophili quae vultu incendet amores
Olim, et voce ducem dulci incantabit Hibernum.
Constitit eximiae captus dulcedine formae
Morpheus, atque uno miratur corpore nasci
Tot veneres, memori quas omnes mente recondit.
Proxima Franciscae[2] divina occurrit imago,
Ejaculans oculis radios, roseisque labellis
Suave rubens, magni senis excipienda cubili.
Mollis odoriferis prope Catherina[3] sedebat
Fulta rosis, tacitam minitantur lumina fraudem,
Cara futura viro, toto spectabilis orbe.[4]
Conjugibus laetae minus huic speciosa Brigetta[5]
Succedit, radiis et pulchris Lucia[6] fervens.
Formam forma parit, nova spectantemque voluptas

ried (1) Ferdinando, fifth Earl of Derby, (2) Thomas Egerton, Baron Ellesmere, Lord Chancellor.

[1] Lady Penelope Rich, the "Stella" of Sidney's sonnets. The next line refers to her marriage (if marriage it was) with Charles Blount, eighth Lord Mountjoy, Lord Lieutenant of Ireland.

[2] Frances, daughter of Thomas, Viscount Howard of Bindon. "Magni senis excipienda cubili" refers to her marriage with the old Lord Hertford. See p. 309, note 5.

[3] "Catherina . . . toto spectabilis orbe."—Doubtless Catherine Parr, whose third husband was Henry VIII. She had four husbands ("conjugibus laetae minus").

[4] Old ed. "ore."

[5] "Brigetta" may be Bridget Fitzgerald, daughter of the twelfth Earl of Kildare; she married (1) Earl of Tyrconnel, (2) Viscount Kingsland.

[6] The famous Lucy, Countess of Bedford.

Decipit oblitum veteris, placidaeque figurae.
Utque satur conviva deus rediturus, apricam
Planitiem duo forte inter nemora aurea septam
Cernit, et in medio spatiantem, corpore celso,
Egregiam speciem, magnae similemque Dianae.
Nube sed admota propius dum singula spectat ;
Digna sorore Jovis visa est, aut conjuge ; sola
Majestate levis superans decora omnia formae,
Haec comitata suis loca jam secreta pererrat,
Conscia fatorum, dicetur et Anna Britanna
Olim, fortunae summa ad fastigia surgens.
Altera subsequitur felix, et amabilis umbra,
Cui Rheni imperium, et nomen debetur Elizae.
Morpheus hic haeret, capiunt hae denique formae
Formarum artificem, nec se jam proripit ultra.
Gratia, nec venus ulla fugit, congesta sed unam
Aptat in effigiem, Policleto doctior ipso.
Sic redit ornatus, tenero metuendus amico,
Cujus in amplexus ruit, haud renuente puello.
Quo non insignis trahis exuperantia formae
Humanum genus ? hac fruitur, Junonis ut umbra
Ixion, falso delusus amore Melampus.
Sed patris adventu, somno jam luce fugato,
Gaudia vanescunt, atque experrectus amata
Spectra puer quaerit nequicquam, brachia nudum
Aëra circumdant, nil praeter lumina cernunt.
Saepe repercussis coelo connivet ocellis,
Amissi cupidus visi, dulcisque soporis ;
Et caput inclinat, sed acutas undique spinas
Curae supponunt tristes, arcentque quietem.
Nusquam quod petit apparet, nec praemia noctis
Permittit constare dies, ut inania tollit.
Saevit at introrsum furor, et sub pectore flammas

Exacuit, subditque novas ; inimica dolori
Lux est, oblectat nox, et loca lumine cassa.
Silvarum deserta subit, clausosque recessus
Insanus puer, et dubio marcescit amore ;
Sperat et in tenebris aliquid, terraque soporem
Porrectus varie captat ; tum murmure leni
" Somne, veni," spirat ; "prodi, O lepidissime divum ;
Et mihi redde meam," prope sponsam dixerat amens ;
" Redde mihi quaecunque fuit, vel virgo, vel umbra,
Qualiscunque meo placuit, semperque placebit
Infelici animo ; veri, vel ficti Hymenaei
Quid refert ? vitae domina est mens unica nostrae,
Sed non talis erat quem vidi vultus inanis,
Quod sensi corpus certe fuit, oscula labris
Fixa meis haerent ; si quid discriminis hoc est,
Nunc frigent, eadem cum praebuit illa calebant.
Illa, quid illa ? miser quod amo jam nescio quid sit ›
Hoc tantum scio, conceptu formosius omni est.
Terra sive lates, suspensa vel aëre pendes,
Vel coelum, quod credo magis, speciosa petisti ;
Pulchra redi, et rursus te amplexibus insere nostris.
Pollicita es longum, nec me mens fallit, amorem.
Dic ubi pacta fides nunc ? nondum oblita recentis
Esse potes voti cum me fugis, et revocari
A caro non laetaris, quem spernis, amante."
Sic varias longo perdit sermone querelas,
Atque eadem repetit, nec desinit ; igne liquescit
Totus, et ardenti cedit vis victa dolori.
Mente sed ereptam vigili dum quaeritat umbram,
Umbrae fit similis ; tenui de corpore sanguis
Effluit, et paulatim excussus spiritus omnis
Deserit exanimum pectus, motusque recedit ;
Optatumque diu fert mors, sed sera, soporem.

Corpus at inventum terrae mandare parabant
Lugentes nymphae, flores herbasque ferentes
Funereas plenis calathis ; quae vidit Apollo
Omnia, et iratus puero hunc invidit honorem :
Utque erat in manibus nympharum non grave pondus,
Labitur, obscuram sensim resolutus in umbram ;
Et fugit aspectum solis, fugietque per omne
Tempus, perpetuo damnatus luminis exul.

ELEGIA I.

VER anni lunaeque fuit ; pars verna diei ;
  Verque erat aetatis dulce, Sibylla, tuae.
Carpentem vernos niveo te pollice flores
  Ut vidi, dixi " tu dea Veris eris."
Et vocalis " eris" blanditaque reddidit Eccho ;
  Allusit votis mimica nympha meis.
Vixdum nata mihi simulat suspiria, formam
  Quae dum specto tuam plurima cudit Amor.
Si taceo, tacet illa ; tacentem spiritus urit :
  Si loquor, offendor garrulitate deae.
Veris amica Venus fetas quoque sanguine venas
  Incendit flammis insidiosa suis.
Nec minus hac immitis Amor sua spicula nostro
  Pectore crudeli fixit acuta manu.
" Heu miser," exclamo, " causa non laedor ab una ;"
  " Una," Eccho resonat ; " Quam," rogo, " diva,
    refers?
Anne Sibyllam ?" " illam," respondit : sentio vatem
  Mox ego veridicam, fatidicamque nimis :
Nam perii, et verno quae coepit tempore flamma,
  Jam mihi non ullo frigore ponet hyems.

2.

Cum speciosa mihi mellitaque verba dedisti,
　　Despectisque aliis primus et unus eram :
Mene tuos posuisse sinu refovente calores
　　Vana putas? an sic femina nota mihi ?
Errabas, fateor, veros non sensimus ignes,
　　Nec mihi mutandus tam cito crescit amor.
Nos elephantinos nutrimus pectore fetus,
　　Qui bene robusti secula multa vident ;
Dum tua diversis varie mens rapta procellis
　　Nescit in assueto littore stare diu ;
Qui mihi te pactam vidit per foedera sacra,
　　Cum rediit, vidit foedera nulla dies.
Ottale, successor meus, haud invisa tenere
　　Per me regna potes, non diuturna tamen.
Si promissa semel constaret semper amanti,
　　Non cuperet tua nunc esse, sed esse mea :
Pacta prius nostris penitus complexibus haesit,
　　Illius illecebrans gratia nota mihi est ;
Nota sed ante aliis, mecum quos expulit omnes ;
　　Teque eadem quae nos, Ottale, damna manent.
Nec tibi proficiet quod sis formosus habendi,
　　Femina non semper pendet ab ore viri.
Carbones aliquae, vel si quid tetrius illis,
　　Deliciis spretis, saepe vorare solent.
Vidi ego quae cinerem lingua glutiret avara,
　　Jamque " In amaritie quam mihi suavis !" ait.
Multa suis mulier sentit contraria votis,
　　Prendere quae nemo prae levitate potest.
Ottale, nullus eris si tu sincerus amator,
　　Ni malus et fallax, Ottale, nullus eris.
Nam quis eam teneat, cujus levis ante recurrit
　　Sidere quam firmo pectore possit amor ?

3.

Ni bene cognosses, melius me nemo meorum,
    Hoc condonassem nunc ego, Calve, tibi.
Nec mihi dum constat satis hoc quo nomine signem ;
    Erroremne tuum, stultitiamne vocem.
Irascor veteri, quod me magis urit, amico ;
    Nec nos vulgari foedere junxit amor.
Ira loqui cogit quam vellem durius in te ;
    Es nimis incautus ; nec tibi, Calve, sapis ;
Formosam qui cum dominam sine teste teneres,
    Raro qua, fateor, pulcrior esse solet ;
Quaeque tuis multo tibi carior esset ocellis,
    Pro qua vovisses forsan, amice, mori :
Hanc mihi, quemque adeo nosti, tu credere bardus
    Ut velles ? talem siccine, crude, mihi ?
Quid facerem ? quis vel potuit minus ? illico captus
    Ostendo ingenium, nec bene sanus amo.
Muneribus tento, cunctaque Cupidinis arte,
    Qua non est, et scis, notior ulla mihi.
Vici, et jam (testis mihi sit chorus omnis Amantum)
    Osculor invitus, quod tua sola foret.
Iste voluptatem mihi scrupulus abstulit omnem,
    Et summe iratus tunc tibi, Calve, fui,
Quod tua culpa minus fidum te fecit amico ;
    Qua nisi te purges, non cadet ira mihi.

4.

Ille miser faciles cui nemo invidit amores,
    Felle metuque nimis qui sine tutus amat ;
Noctes atque dies cui prona inservit amica,
    Officio, regno, et nomine pulsa suis.
Nam quis te dominam post tot servilia dicet ?
    Ora quis ignavae victa stupebit iners ?

Imperet, et jubeat quae se constanter amari
    Expetit ; utcunque est, obsequium omne nocet.
Qua (bene quod sperabat) amantes reppulit arte
    Penelope, docta scilicet usa mora,
Hac magis incendit, cupidosque potentius ussit ;
    Deceptamque sua risit ab arte Deus.
Nec minus ipsa dolos persensit callida, vinci
    Fraude sua voluit, dissimulare tamen :
Discite, formosae, non indulgere beatis,
    Fletibus assuescat siquis amare velit.
Nec tristes lachrimae, cita nec suspiria desint,
    Audiat et dominae dicta superba tremens :
Sit tamen irarum modus, haud illaeta labori
    Nox fessum reparet, pacificusque torus ;
Quaeque minas misero jactarunt pulchra labella
    Mordeat, et victor pectora dura premat ;
Tum leviter niveis incumbens ore mamillis
    Sanguineam exugat dente labroque notam :
Sic velut acer eques per pascua laeta triumphet,
    Femina jam partes sola ferentis agat.
Sed simul orta dies perverterit otia noctis,
    Cum veste antiquos induat illa animos :
Jamque assurgenti speculumque togamque ministret,
    Praestet aquam manibus, calceolumque pedi.
Postilla assideat, fessus si forte videtur ;
    Sin minus, actutum projiciendus erit.
Custos regni amor est ; dominantes servat amores
    Saevitia, et nullo jure inhibente metus.
Odi quod nimium possim, truculenta sit opto,
    Dum mea formosa est, dummodo grata mihi.
Turbato quot apes furem sectantur ab alveo,
    Tot mihi rivales displicuisse velim.
Dulce nec invitam foret eripuisse puellam

E medio juvenum triste minante choro,
  Multorumque oculis pariter votisque placentem
Posse per amplexus applicuisse mihi.
Spartanae nomen tantum famamque secutus
  Primus apud Graios ausus amare Paris ;
Quodque vir ille palam, timide petiere Pelasgi,
  Crimine utrique pares, unus adulter erat.
Quove animo Trojae portas subiisse putatis
  Cum rapta insignem conjuge Priamidem ?
Aurato curru rex, et regina volentes
  Accurrunt ; fratres, ecce, vehuntur equis ;
Et populus circum, juvenesque patresque, globantur,
  Aemula spectatum multa puella venit.
Unam omnes Helenam spectant, gratantur ovantes
  Omnes uni Helenae ; sed Paris ipse sibi.
Illi vel fratres talem invidere, sed illi
  Suave fuit, quod res invidiosa fuit.
O felix cui per tantos nupsisse tumultus
  Contigit, et dignum bello habuisse torum !
Ut tam pulcra meis cedant quoque praemia coeptis,
  Optarem pugnas et tua fata, Pari.

5.

Prima suis, Fanni, formosis profuit aetas,
  Solaque de facie rustica pugna fuit ;
Donec vis formae succrevit, viribus aurum,
  Quo sine nunc vires, et bona forma jacet.
Ergo sapis triplici nummos qui congeris arca ;
  Semper quod dones, quodque supersit habes.
Ultro te juvenes, ultro petiere puellae,
  Rivales de te diraque bella movent.
At non arenti color est tibi laetior arvo,
  Labra sed incultis asperiora rubis.

Vel nulli, vel sunt atri rubigine dentes,
    Jamque anima ipsa Stygem et busta senilis olet.
Forsitan ingenium quod amabile ducis amantes ;
    Hei mihi, quod nimium est haec quoque causa levis !
Sit tamen ampla satis per se ; tibi nulla fuisset,
    Qui nihilo plus quam magna crumena sapis.
Ceu lepidus coleris tamen et formosus Adonis,
    Nec fugit amplexus lauta puella tuos.
Nonnullae accedunt quas tu, furiose, repellis ;
    Pulsisque, ut par est, lachrima crebra cadit.
O felix, si non odiosa podagra gravaret !
    Nervus et effctus, membraque inepta senis !
Si non ingratae Veneris funesta puellae
    Supplicia afflictus pesque manusque daret !
Te tamen haud ulli possunt arcere dolores
    Cum petit amplexus femina cara tuos.
Plurima possit amor ; verum si olfecerit aurum
    Mulcebit barbam Mellia nostra tuam.

6.

Caspia, tot poenas meruit patientia nostra ?
    Culpa erat insistens primo in amore fides ?
Mene fugis quod jussa feram ? quod fortis amator
    Non succumbo malis quae dare multa potes ?
Troile, non illud nocuit tibi, Cressis acerbas
    Eripuit tandem commiserata moras.
Non illud solis in terris questa puella est,
    Dum rapit infidum mobilis aura virum.
Saepe alios levitas, sed nos constantia laedit ;
    Supplicium pietas et benefacta timent.
Forsan erit miserorum aliquis gravis ultor amantum,
    Cui longa poenas pro feritate dabis.
Ah memini ignoto languentia membra dolore,

Et speciem ereptam pene fuisse tibi ;
More meo lachrimans aderam, fidusque minister,
   Tum mihi facta malis lenior ipsa tuis :
Protinus insensum tibi supplex invoco numen,
   Et subita ex votis est revocata salus.
Tanti erit in nostro semel ingemuisse furore,
   Tanta erat in propriis pax aliena malis.
Quid precibus valeam tua pectora ferrea norunt,
   Et nossent melius, sed mea fata vetant.
Multa tamen cupiam pro te discrimina inire,
   Multa jube, dulcis nam labor omnis erit.
Dulcis erit, sed erit labor ; heu miserere laboris ;
   Noster ab hac nimium parte laborat amor.
Saevitiam natura feris, sed moribus apta
   Corpora, et arma manu, fronte, vel ore dedit :
Humana includi formoso pectore corda
   Jussit, in hac specie quaeritur unus amor.
Quo speciosa magis tanto tu mitior esses :
   Me miserum ! tanto saevior ira tua est.
Ingentesque animos assumis conscia formae,
   Virtutes novit femina quaeque suas.
Si lubet accedat reliquis clementia, palmam
   Ut sine rivali me tribuente feras.
Dotibus ingenii superas et corporis omnes,
   Hoc uno vinci nomine turpe puta.

7.

Tene ego desererem ? mater velit anxia natum,
   Unanimem aut fratrem prodere cara soror ?
Delerem ex animo tam suaves immemor horas ?
   Delicias, lusus, basia docta, jocos ?
Desine jam teneros fletu corrumpere ocellos :
   Ante calor flammis excidet, unda mari,

Et prius a domina discedent sidera luna,
    Quam te destituat, me violante, fides.
Ista manus nobis aequalia foedera sanxit,
    Quam tu nunc lachrimis suspiciosa lavas.
Semper habes aliquid querulo sub corde timoris,
    Femineo multi sunt in amore metus.
Saepe mihi Thesei memoras fugientia vela,
    Utque erat indigno Dido cremata rogo.
Neglectis quaecunque solent miserisque nocere,
    Haec tua sed nondum pectora laesa dolent.
Quid feci? mea tu, cum non sint, crimina ploras;
    Hocne fides? mores hoc meruere mei?
Forte licet miseras fiducia fallat amantes,
    Plus illa insanus possit obesse metus.
Lugubri exemplo Cephali sat fabula nota est,
    Ne nimium ex Procri sit tibi, nostra, cave.

8.

Parce, puer Veneris, parce, imperiose Cupido,
    Jam nimis intentas vertis in ora faces:
Ah pudet, abjectus cecidi, miserere jacentis;
    Quem modo laesisti, nunc tueare, timor.
Rusticus ille prior fuit, ingratusque puellae,
    Hic tamen ingenue signa fatentis habet.
Vixdum prima diem reserarant lumina solis,
    Cum thalamum subii, pulchra Sibylla, tuum.
Horrida rura virum, sed non metuenda, tenebant;
    Tutum rivali fecit in urbe locum.
Ipsa etiam speciosa toro sed sola recumbens
    Adventum primo visa probare meum.
Dissimulans sic fata, "Quid hoc? absente marito
    Ad nuptae juvenem stare cubile decet?"
Ast ego, virgineum diffundens ore ruborem,

Respondi blandus quae mihi jussit Amor.
Longa dehinc variis teritur sermonibus hora
    Dum votis obstat sola ministra meis :
Optabam tacitus, licet haud inamabilis esset,
    Membra feris miserae diripienda dari.
Discedant famulae, quoties locus aptus amori,
    Nec domina sistant vel revocante gradus :
Adversatur herae si quae crudelis amanti est,
    Invidiamque sibi diraque bella parit.
Jamne vacat monstrare aliis praecepta pudoris
    Cum reus indoctae rusticitatis agar ?
Forte ministra moras, sed quas abitura, trahebat,
    Mansit et illa diu ut posset abesse diu.
Sed nec eat prorsus, justa illam causa morata est,
    Quae discedenti tum mihi nulla foret.
Verbis affari, nudos spectare lacertos ;
    Caetera ne liceant, haec quoque pondus habent.
Dum velut iratae cupio non esse molestus,
    In me odia incendi credulitate mea.
Tu tamen hanc veniam vati concede Cupido,
    Perque tuas juro, flammea tela, faces,
Nulla leves posthac conatus verba repellent ;
    Cassibus exibit femina nulla meis.
Candida seu nigra est, mollis seu dura, pudica
    Sive levis, juvenis sive adeo illa senex ;
Qualiscunque datur, modo sit formosa, rogare
    Non metuam, et longa sollicitare prece.
Quae nolit, poterit satis illa negare petenti ;
    Quae velit, illa tamen saepe petita, velit.
Nolit, sive velit, semper repetenda puella est ;
    Hoc ferri grate munus utrique solet.
Si perversa, tamen formam placuisse juvabit
    Si cupida, optato convenit apta viro.

Annuit, et vultu probat haec ridente Cupido,
  Jamque nova incedo mactus amator ope ;
Indico tamen hoc vobis, mala turba, puellae,
  Cum peto vos, culpam ne memorate meam.

9.

Ergo meam ducet? deducet ab urbe puellam
  Cui rutilo sordent ora perusta Cane ?
Mellea jamne meo valedicere possit amori,
  Urbeque posthabita vilia rura colet ?
Anne fides, sensusque simul periere ? sequetur
  Post tot formosos illa senile jugum ?
" Pauperis uxor sim potius quam regis amica,"
  Sic ais ; ah stulte relligiosa sapis !
Verum habeas ; quid enim tibi, perfida, tristius optem
  Quam tali dignam concubuisse viro ?
Utrique et similes parias ; patris exprimat ora
  Progenies ; mores ingeniumque tuum.
Vitam igitur nobis pingui de rure maritus
  Eripiet, miserae, perfugiumque animae ?
Tam tristes taedas poterit nox ulla videre ?
  Endimeoneis raptave Luna genis ?
Igneus horrentes inducat turbo procellas,
  Et rapiat flores aura profana sacros ;
Tartareique canes diros ululent Hymenaeos,
  Praedicat lites scissaque flamma facum.
Strataque cum lecti genialis sponsa recludit
  Per totum videat serpere monstra torum.
Vos parvique Lares, nocturni et ridiculi di,
  Terrea Pigmaeo gens oriunda Obera ;
Raso qui capitis, cilii, mentique capillo
  Luditis indignos, turba jocosa, viros :
Raptaque per somnum vehitis qui corpora, et altis

Fossis, aut udo ponitis illa lacu :
Confluite huc, vestro nimium res digna cachinno est,
   Eia agite, O lepidi, protinus ite, Lares,
Pulcramque informi positam cum conjuge sponsam
   Eripite, haud ullo conspiciente dolos ;
Amplexumque meos cum se sperabit amores,
   Stramineam pupam brachia dura ferant ;
Aut tritum teneat carioso pene Priapum,
   Praeclare ut miserum rideat omnis ager ;
Fabula nec toto crebrescat notior orbe,
   Huic cedant claudi probra venusta dei ;
Ipseque nescierim, quamvis dolor intus et ira
   Aestuet, in risus solvar an in lachrimas.

10.

Illa mihi merito nox est infausta notanda,
   Qua votum Veneri sprevit amica torum.
Sic promissa fides ? reditum sic ausa pacisci
   Improba deque meo vix revocanda sinu ?
Credideram, persuasit Amor, suasere tenenti
   Quae mihi discedens oscula longa dedit.
Ergo vigil, tacitusque tori de parte cubavi ;
   Esset ut infidae foedifragaeque locus.
Adjeci porro plumas et lintea struxi,
   Mollius ut tenerum poneret illa latus :
Nulla venit, quamvis visa est mihi saepe venire ;
   Quae cupidos oculos falleret umbra fuit.
Audito quoties dicebam murmure laetus
   " Jam venit ! " extendo brachia, nulla venit.
Me strepitu latebrosa attentum bestia lusit,
   Spemque avido ventis mota fenestra dedit.
Sic desiderio tandem languere medulla
   Coepit, inassuetis ignibus hausta fuit.

Jamque erat ut cuperem gelida de rupe, Prometheu,
   Expectare tuas, vulnere crudus, aves.
At quanto levior jam tum mihi poena fuisset
   Captasse impasti ludicra poma senis.
Ecquis erit miser? inveniat quam possit amare,
   Quam cupide indicta nocte manere velit.
Me videat quisquis sponsae perjuria nescit;
   En lachrimis oculi lividaque ora tument,
Insomnique horrent artus, dum forsitan illa
   Immemor, et dulci victa sopore, jacet.
Nec metuit promissa; fidem nam perdidit, et me;
   Nec timuit, quorum est numine abusa, deos.
Conventum in silvis statuit Babilonia Thisbe
   Cum juvene ardenti, sed prior ipsa venit:
Cumque viro periit, qui si potuisset abesse,
   Haud scio nox miserae tristior utra foret.
Non iter in silvas, nec erat tibi cura cavendi
   Custodes, potuit tota patere domus;
Si velles saltem, si non perjura fuisses,
   Basia si veri signa caloris erant.
Nam quid detinuit? famulis pax una: quid ergo?
   Sex septemve gradus? janua aperta? torus,
Et qui te misere remoratus quaerat in illo?
   Haeccine tam fuerat triste subire tibi?
Quam vellem causam vel inanem fingere posses,
   Invito ut faceres ista coacta metu:
Sed nihil occurrit, res est indigna, nefasque;
   Impia, fecisti dirum in amore scelus;
Quod nullis poterit precibus lachrimisve piari,
   Ni mihi sex noctes sacrificare velis.

11.

Qui sapit ignotas timeat spectare puellas ;
  Hinc juvenum atque senum maxima turba petit.
Incautos novitate rapit non optuma forma,
  Quemque semel prendit non cito solvit Amor.
Quod pulcrum varium est ; species non una probatur,
  Nec tabulis eadem conspicienda Venus.
Sive lepos oculis, in vultu seu rosa fulget,
  Compositis membris si decor aptus inest ;
Gratia sive pedes, leviter seu brachia motat ;
  Undique spectanti retia tendit Amor.
Distineat juvenem neque pompa, nec aurea vestis,
  Nec picti currus, marmoreaeve fores :
Raro urbem solus provecta nocte pererret,
  Nox tenebris fieri multa proterva sinit ;
Siqua die placita est, noctu pulcherrima fiet :
  Adde merum, Phaedram possit amare gener.
Haec ego : cum contra est telis facibusque minatus,
  Ni sileam, triplex pectore vulnus Amor.

12.

Qui gerit auspiciis res et, nisi consulat exta,
  Nil agit, hic subitos nescit abire dies.
Suspiciosa mora est, fortuna irridet inertes,
  Omnia praecipiti dans redimensque manu.
Dum Menelaus abest, Helenen Priameius urget,
  Urgentique aderant numina Fors et Amor.
Herus aeque omnes voluere cubilia, solus
  Leander Cypria sed duce victor amat.
Solus congreditur dubia sub luce puellam
  Defessam sacris ante ministeriis.

Saepe opportune cadit importuna voluntas,
    Insperataque sors ad cita vota venit.
Parva sed immemoris sponsi cunctatio Thisben
    Seque per umbrosum praecipitavit iter.
Una dies aufert quod secula nulla resolvent,
    Secula quod dederint nulla, dat una dies.
Mane rosas si non decerpis, vespere lapsas
    Aspicies spinis succubuisse suis.
Dum juvat, et fas est, praesentibus utere ; totum
    Incertum est quod erit ; quod fuit, invalidum.

13. *Ad Ed: Mychelburnum.*

Ergone perpetuos dabit umbra sororia fletus?
    Inque fugam molles ossea forma deas?
Sic, Edoarde, situ ferali horrenda Thalia
    Antiquosque sales deliciasque abiget?
Carmina nequaquam tangunt funebria manes,
    Impetrabilior saxa ad acuta canas.
Parce piam cruciare animam, si cara sorori
    Extinctae superest, ne sit iniqua tibi.
Aspice, distortis Elegeia lassa capillis
    Procubuit, lachrimis arida facta suis ;
Ecce, premit, frustraque oculos exsolvit inanes ;
    Prodiga quod sparsim fudit, egena sitit.
Sic projecta graves Istri glacialis ad undas
    Dicitur emeritum deposuisse caput.
Sic exhausta sacri vatis lugubre canendo
    Exilium, et tardos ad meliora [1] Deos.
Jam satis est, Edoarde, tui miserere, deaeque ;
    Fessa dea est nimium sollicitata diu.
Assueti redeant animi, solatia, lusus ;
    Exuat atratam vestra Thalia togam.

---

[1] Old ed. "meliore."

Nec te detineat formae pereuntis imago ;
 Ad manes abiit non reditura soror.
Neve recorderis quae verba novissima dixit ;
 Praesidio illa minus proficiente juvant.
Verba dolorem acuunt, solvunt oblivia curas ;
 Immemores animos cura dolorque fugit.
Sed tua si pietas monitis parere recusat,
 Aegraque mens constans in feritate sua est,
Nulla sit in terris regio, non ora, nec aetas
 Inscia ploratus, insatiate, tui.
Non Hyades tantum celebrent fulgentia coelo
 Sidera, fraternus quas reparavit amor ;
Quantum fama tuas lachrimas, obitusque sororis ;
 O bene defleto funere digna soror !
Et, tibi si placet hoc, indulge, Ed[o]arde, dolori ;
 Singultuque gravem pectore pasce animum.
Tristitiam levat ipsa dies ; gaudebit et ultro
 Ascitis tandem mens vegetare jocis.

FINIS.[1]

---

[1] A list of *Errata* follows in old ed. The corrections have been made in the text.

SCATTERED VERSES.

From *Davison's Poetical Rhapsody*, 1602.[1]

A Hymn in praise of Neptune.

OF Neptune's empire let us sing,
  At whose command the waves obey ;
To whom the rivers tribute pay,
Down the high mountains sliding :
To whom the scaly nation yields
Homage for the crystal fields
  Wherein they dwell :
And every sea-god pays a gem
Yearly out of his wat'ry cell
To deck great Neptune's diadem.

[1] The song was written in 1594 for the Gray's Inn Masque "Gesta Graiorum," which is printed in Nichols' "Progresses of Queen Elizabeth." Nichols' text differs slightly from Davison's. In l. 3 Nichols omits "the," and in l. 6 gives "their" for "the." For "echoes" (l. 13) Nichols reads "trumpets"; for "echoing rock" (l. 18), "echoing voice"; for "murmuring" (l. 19), "mourning"; and for "The praise" (l. 20), "In praise." Two absurd misreadings are given by Nichols,—"praise again" (l. 8) for "pays a gem," and "The waiters" (l. 13) for "The water."

Three other songs of Campion are given in the "Rhapsody,"—"And would you see my mistress' face," "Blame not my cheeks," and "When to her lute Corinna sings." They are from Campion and Rosseter's "Book of Airs."

The Tritons dancing in a ring
Before his palace gates do make
The water with their echoes quake,
Like the great thunder sounding :
The sea-nymphs chant their accents shrill,
And the sirens, taught to kill
 With their sweet voice,
Make ev'ry echoing rock reply
Unto their gentle murmuring noise
The praise of Neptune's empery.

Prefixed to JOHN DOWLAND'S
*The First Book of Songs or
Airs,* 1597.

*Thomæ Campiani Epigramma.
De instituto Authoris.*

FAMAM, posteritas quam dedit Orpheo,
 Dolandi, melius Musica dat tibi,
Fugaces reprimens Archetypis sonos ;
Quas et delicias praebuit auribus,
Ipsis conspicuas luminibus facit.

Prefixed to BARNABE BARNES'
Four Books of Offices, 1606.[1]

*In Honour of the Author by Tho: Campion, Doctor in
Physic.*
To the Reader.

THOUGH neither thou dost keep the keys of state
 Nor yet the counsels, reader, what of that ?

---

[1] In some copies Campion's verses are not found. Concerning
the relations between Campion and Barnes see *Introduction.*

Though th' art no law-pronouncer marked by fate,
Nor field-commander, reader, what of that?
Blanch not this book ; for if thou mind'st to be
Virtuous and honest it belongs to thee.
Here is the school of temperance and wit,
Of Justice and all forms that tend to it ;
Here Fortitude doth teach to live and die :
Then, Reader, love this book, or rather buy.

Ejusdem ad Authorem.

Personas propriis recte virtutibus ornas,
  Barnesi ; liber hic vivet, habet genium.
Personae virtus umbra est, hanc illa refulcit ;
  Nec scio splendescat corpus an umbra magis.

From RICHARD ALISON'S *An
Hour's Recreation in Music,*
1606.[1]

WHAT if a day, or a month, or a year
   Crown thy delights with a thousand sweet con-
      tentings?
Cannot a chance of a night or an hour
Cross thy desires with as many sad tormentings?
   Fortune, Honour, Beauty, Youth
   Are but blossoms dying ;
   Wanton Pleasure, doting Love,
   Are but shadows flying.

---

[1] Alison gives only two stanzas; and probably the three
bracketed stanzas—which are found in " The Golden Garland of

> All our joys are but toys,
> Idle thoughts deceiving ;
> None hath power of an hour
> In our lives' bereaving.

> Earth's but a point to the world, and a man
> Is but a point to the world's compared centre :
> Shall then a point of a point be so vain
> As to triumph in a silly point's adventure ?

Princely Delights" and in the " Roxburghe Ballads "—do not belong to Campion. In the " Golden Garland " and in the " Roxburghe Ballads " the third stanza, " What if a smile," follows the first stanza ; and Alison's second stanza, " Earth's but a point," is placed at the end of the song, altered as follows—

> " Then if all this have declared thine amiss,
> Take this from me for a gentle friendly warning ;
> If thou refuse and good counsel abuse,
> Thou mayst hereafter dearly buy thy warning.
> All is hazard that we have," &c.

In the " Roxburghe Ballads " a " Second Part " is appended. I have not reproduced it.

Chappell, in " Popular Music of the Olden Time," i. 310, has a long notice of the present song. " The music," he remarks, " is in a volume of transcripts of virginal music, by Sir John Hawkins ; in *Logonomia Anglica*, by Alexander Gil, 1619 ; in *Friesche Lust-Hof*, 1634 ; in D. R. Camphuysen's *Stichtelycke Rymen*, 4to, Amsterdam, 1647 ; in the Skene MS. ; in Forbes' *Cantus*, &c. The same words are differently set by Richard Allison." When Chappell stated that " neither the words nor music are found in Campion's printed collection," he overlooked the fact that " Thomas Campion, M.D." is printed below the song in Alison's song-book.

There was a fifteenth century song to which Campion was indebted ; for Mr. Halliwell-Phillipps pointed out (in 1840) " that one of the songs in Ryman's well-known collection of

All is hazard that we have,
There is nothing biding ;
Days of pleasure are like streams
Through fair meadows gliding.
Weal and woe, time doth go,
Time is never turning :
Secret fates guide our states,
Both in mirth and mourning.

the fifteenth century in the Cambridge Public Library com-
mences

'What yf a daye, or night, or howre,
Crowne my desyres wythe every delyghte ; '

and that in Sanderson's Diary in the British Museum, MSS.
Lansdowne 241, fol. 49, temp. Elizabeth, are the two first
stanzas of the song, more like the copy in Ryman, and differing
in its minor arrangements from the later version.   Moreover,
that the tune in Dowland's Musical Collection in the Public
Library, Cambridge, is entitled ' What if a day or a night or an
hour !' agreeing with Sanderson's copy."

The first two stanzas were anonymously printed as early as 1603,
at the end of "Ane verie excellent and delectabill Treatise intitulit
Philotvs.   Qvharin we may persave the greit inconveniences that
fallis out in the Mariage betwene age and zouth," Edinburgh, 4to.
A few textual variations occur.   " Philotus " gives :—

l. 2. "thy desire ;" " wisched contentings."
l. 3. " the chance."
l. 4. " thy delightes ;" " a thousand sad."
l. 7. " wanton plesoures."
l. 13. " of the world."
l. 14. " of the earths."
l. 15. " the point of."
l. 16. " As to delight."
l. 18. " Here is nothing."
l. 19. " are but streams."
ll. 21-22. " Well or wo tyme dois go, in tyme is no returning."
(In the " Golden Garland " and " Roxburghe Ballads " the
reading is " Wealth or woe. . . . There is no returning.")

[What [1] if a smile, or a beck, or a look,
Feed thy fond thoughts with many a sweet conceiving ;
May not that smile, or that beck, or that look,
Tell thee as well they are but vain deceiving ? [2]

> Why should beauty be so proud,
> In things of no surmounting ?
> All her wealth is but [a] shroud,
> Of [3] a rich accounting.
> Then in this repose no bliss,
> Which is vain and idle ;
> Beauty's flow'rs have their hours,
> Time doth hold the bridle.

What if the world, with allures of her wealth,
Raise thy degree to a place of high advancing ;
May not the world, by a check of that wealth,
Bring thee again to as low despised chancing ?

> Whilst the sun of wealth doth shine
> Thou shalt have friends plenty ;
> But, come want, then they repine,
> Not one abides of twenty.
> Wealth and friends holds and ends,
> As your fortunes rise and fall :
> Up and down, smile [4] and frown,
> Certain is no state at all.

What if a grief, or a strain, or a fit,
Pinch thee with pain of the feeling pangs of sickness :
May not that gripe, or that strain, or that fit
Shew thee the form of thine own true perfect likeness?

[1] In these bracketed stanzas I follow—with some slight corrections—the text of the "Golden Garland" and "Roxburghe Ballads." Chappell's text is somewhat different.

[2] "Golden Garland" and "Roxburghe Ballads" give "deceiuings."

[3] Chappell's reading "Nothing of accounting" is far better.

[4] So Chappell.—"Golden Garland" and "Roxburghe Ballads" give "rise" (caught from the preceding line).

Health is but a glimpse of joy,
Subject to all changes ;
Mirth is but a silly toy,
Which mishap estranges.
Tell me, then, silly man,
Why art thou so weak of wit,
As to be in jeopardy,
When thou mayst in quiet sit ?]

Prefixed to ALFONSO FERRA-
BOSCO'S *Airs*, 1609.

To the Worthy Author.

MUSIC'S rich master and the offspring
Of rich music's father,[1]
Old Alfonso's image living,
These fair flowers you gather
Scatter through the British soil ;
Give thy fame free wing,
And gain the merit of thy toil.
We whose loves affect to praise thee,
Beyond thine own deserts can never raise thee.

By T. Campion, Doctor in Physic.

---

[1] Alfonso Ferrabosco, the elder, was a famous musician ;
" inferior to none " (says Peacham in the " Compleat Gentleman ").

Prefixed to *Coryat's Cradities.*
1611.

*Incipit Thomas Campianus
Medicinae Doctor.*
In Peragrantissimi, Itinerosissimi,
*Montiscandentissimique Peditis Tho-
mae Coryati,* viginti hebdomadarium
Diarium, sex pedibus gradiens,
partim vero claudicans,
Encomiasticon.

*A*D *Venetos venit corio Coryatus ab uno
Vectus, et, ut vectus, paene revectus erat.
Nave una Dracus sic totum circuit orbem,
At rediens retulit te, Coryate, minus.
Illius undigenas tenet unica charta labores,
Tota tuos sed vix bibliotheca capit.
Explicit Thomas Campianus.*

Prefixed to THOMAS RAVENS-
CROFT'S *A Brief Discourse
of the true (but neglected) use
of Charact'ring the Degrees
by their Perfection, Imper-
fection, and Diminution
in Measurable Music,* &c.
1614. 4to.

M ARKS that did limit lands in former times
      None durst remove ; so much the common
         good
Prevailed with all men : 'twas the worst of crimes.
   The like in Music may be understood,
For that the treasure of the soul is next
   To the rich store-house of divinity :
Both comfort souls that are with care perplext,
   And set the spirit both from passions free.
The marks that limit Music here are taught,
   So fixed of old, which none by right can change,
Though Use much alteration hath wrought,
   To Music's fathers that would now seem strange.
The best embrace, which herein you may find,
And th' author praise for his good work and mind.

From a *MS. commonplace-book*
(of the middle of the seventeenth century) belonging to
his Grace the DUKE OF
BUCCLEUCH.

H IDE not,[1] sweetest Love, a sight so pleasing
  As those smalls [2] so light composed,
Those fair pillars your knees gently easing,
That tell wonders, being disclosed.
O show me yet a little more :
Here's the way, bar not the door.

How like sister's [3] twines these knees are joined
To resist my bold [4] approaching !
Why should beauty lurk, like [5] mines uncoined ?
Love is right and no encroaching.
O show me yet a little more :
Here's the way, bar not the door.

[1] I attribute these verses to Campion from internal evidence.
Compare " Sweet, exclude me not," pp. 74-5.

[2] MS. "smales." (*Small* was the term for the stock of a
pillar.)

[3] *Sister* was an old form of *sewster.* The expression *sister's
thread* is common : see Dyce's edition of Gifford's *Ford*, iii.
54.

[4] MS. "blood."

[5] MS. "like mine eyes vncoyned." (The amended text is
hardly satisfactory. Campion is comparing virgin beauty to the
uncoined metal in a mine.)

FINIS.